A NIGHT OF DRAGON WINGS

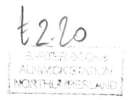

A Night of Dragon Wings

Dragonlore, Book Three

Daniel Arenson

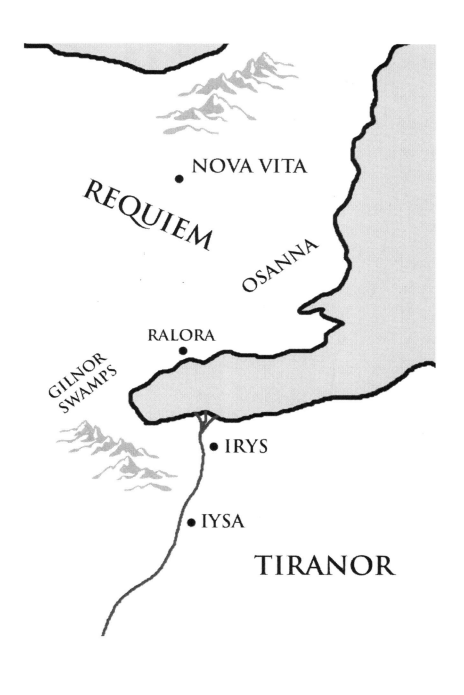

ZAR

The ropes chafed his wrists, and the blindfold squeezed his head like a vise, but Zar kept walking. He must have been walking for hours. A spearhead goaded his back, and he stumbled forward, breath rattling in his lungs. They had stabbed his back so many times, he imagined that it looked raw and red like minced meat. He could smell his own blood.

"Move it, scum!" said the guard behind him. Again the spearhead goaded him, a thrust too weak to puncture his flesh, but strong enough to shoot pain through him. "We haven't got all day!"

So it's still daytime, Zar thought. He would have thought night had fallen hours ago. The gravelly road stabbed his bare feet. His calves, his back, his head—they all throbbed. The wind blew hot and sandy against him. His throat was parched, his lips cracked; he wondered if thirst would kill him before the guards could.

Around him, he heard a hundred boots thumping, armor clanking, and scabbards clattering against greaves. A grunting sounded to his side, then a whip lashing flesh and a croak. Zar wanted to call out to his friends; even just speaking their names would comfort him.

They're taking us to die, he thought. *They will whip and stab and march us until we perish, and our bones will lie in the wilderness for crows to pick on.*

"Move, damn it!" cried the guard behind him, voice as gravelly as the road. "Faster!"

A whip cracked and pain exploded across Zar's back. He bit down on a scream. If he screamed, they would hurt him further. He had learned that lesson in the bowels of Solina's palace. *Never scream. Never make a sound. If you show pain, they will laugh, and they will crave more.*

He tried to remove his thoughts from this march, this thirst, this pain. He thought of his wife, a demure desert daughter, her hair so pale it was almost white, her skin deep gold, and her eyes blue like sky over dunes. He thought of his son, a suckling babe who would never know his father. He had done it for them. *All my crimes—for you.*

He had left his phalanx only for his family, only to be with them. He had abandoned his barracks to squeeze his wife's hand, to soothe her, to help the midwife guide his son into the desert. He had left for but a day, that was all—a dawn, an evening, a night of stars. That was all. The barracks guards had caught him holding his son, wrenched the babe from his arms, and dragged him back in chains.

But I saw my son. I saw him. I will die with a memory of his eyes.

He thought of those eyes as they walked the road, moving higher and higher, climbing a mountain that seemed to never end. As his feet bled and his back blazed, he thought of his son's eyes and his wife's smile, and Zar knew that no matter how much they hurt him, he had a pure memory. This memory they could not take away, not with all the blades and whips in the desert.

The wind lashed him. They marched. They marched endlessly.

Finally, after what seemed the ages of empires and the lifespan of mountains, he heard the guards inhale sharply.

"The tower," one man whispered.

Cold sweat washed Zar.

There was only one tower—*the* tower—which men spoke of with such reverence, such fear. The Ancients had called it *Tarath Gehena*—Tower of the Abyss—but few dared speak that tongue now. In his childhood, his grandmother would whisper that demons punished errant children in this tower. His friends would point at steeples in the city of Irys, trying to convince one another that here stood Tarath Gehena itself, the place of whispers and screams.

The tower. The place of the key. Sun God, the queen seeks to open the Iron Door.

Zar's knees shook and his breath rose to a pant. In the dungeon, he had prayed for death, comforted himself with the thought of thirst or injury sending him to eternal rest. In the shadow of Tarath Gehena, no such comfort could find him. No pure memory or hope could soothe him here.

Here there were only screams, terror, and undying agony.

They kept walking, quiet now. Zar could barely hear the clank of armor, the thud of boots, or the moans of his fellow prisoners. Until now every step had seemed an eternity; now Zar wished time would slow down. Too soon, far too soon, they stopped. Rough hands ripped the blindfold off his eyes.

Sun God save us, Zar thought, blinked in the sunset, and trembled.

They stood upon a mountain that rose from the desert: three haggard prisoners, bloodied and clad in rags; fifty soldiers in pale armor, golden suns upon their breastplates and their helms shaped as falcon heads; and a desert queen all in gold and platinum, twin sabres drawn in her hands. These soldiers of steel had tortured him, and this desert queen had ordered him broken, yet as night fell around them, Zar did not fear them. They were mere mortals. Before him it rose, a skeletal finger reaching into a crimson sky. The tower.

Zar had never before seen this place, not with his waking eyes. But he had dreamed of it countless times, then woke up in a cold sweat. He had seen it in his mind—when his grandmother whispered of its secrets, when his childhood friends bragged that they would climb it, and when Queen Solina's guards whipped him until the pain exploded into dreamscapes.

"The tower," he whispered, lips chapped and bleeding. "The place of the key."

Tarath Gehena rose knobby, black, and twisting like a melted candle of stone. The sun set behind it, spilling rivers of blood across the sky, the mountain, and the desert below. The tower's jagged crenellations rose like the crown of a demon king. At its base loomed a doorway, gaping and black like a cave. As the crimson clouds moved, the tower seemed to tilt. A shadow stirred between the battlements, and Zar's heart thrashed. He expected to see demons swarm toward him, but then the shadow vanished, leaving his heart racing and his clothes drenched with sweat.

Tarath Gehena, he thought. *A shattered bone of the Abyss risen into the world.*

Queen Solina walked forward, shoving her guards aside. Her eyes gleamed and a smile twitched across her lips, those lips twisted with an old scar. Despite the long march, she seemed unwearied, and little sand or dust clung to her breastplate and silken cloak. Her hair billowed, a pale banner.

"This is the place," she whispered, eyes alight and teeth bared in a grin. "This tower holds the key."

The sunset blazed against her, painting her blood-red, and madness shone in her eyes.

"You cannot open the door!" The words fled Zar's mouth, hoarse and shaking. "You will unleash something you cannot contai—"

A whip lashed his back, and a soldier kicked him, driving a steel-tipped boot into his side. Zar fell to his knees, gasping for breath. Tears budded in his eyes.

"Please," he whispered, trembling, remembering the stories his grandmother would tell: stories of demons peeling the skin off children, of reptiles writhing, of a horde of chaos with tarry wings and fangs to suck the souls of men. "Please, my queen, do not enter this tower. Do not take the key from within."

The soldiers raised whips and spears above him, and Zar winced, expecting the blows, but Solina held up her hand. The soldiers froze, weapons raised.

The Queen of Tiranor walked toward Zar, head tilted and lips still smiling, though no mirth filled her eyes, only cruelty like a scourge. She stood above him, a golden queen and him a wretched, bleeding shell of a man, wrists bound and body emaciated and broken. She spoke, voice soft and smooth like a morning breeze stirring the desert sands.

"You fear the tomb the key can unlock." She reached down and touched his forehead. Her hand was gloved in white moleskin, soft and warm. "You fear the creatures that dwell beyond the Iron Door."

Zar shivered on the ground. He feared this tower, this jagged sentinel; his stomach clenched and his skull seemed ready to crack. Yet this tower, for all its evil, merely contained a key.

But the door this key unlocks... The fortress it will allow her to enter...

He found himself weeping. "Please, my queen, please. Listen to the priests of the Sun God. Listen to the whispers of desert tribes, to the tales of grandmothers, to the horrors in old scrolls. Do not take this key."

Her face softened, the face of a woman seeing a wretched, kicked animal. She caressed his forehead, dirtying her gloves with his sweat and grime.

"Oh, dear miserable beast," she whispered. "*I* will not take the key from this tower. You and your friends will."

Sun God. Oh, Sun God, please no.

He flattened himself on the ground and kissed the dust at her feet. His body shook.

"Please, my queen, forgive me, I only... I only wanted to see my son, to—"

She spat on him. "Stand this wretch up," she said to her soldiers. Disgust now suffused her voice. "Let him enter last. I want him to watch his friends suffer first."

Guards grabbed Zar and yanked him to his feet. He writhed and kicked, heart thrashing, but could not free himself. After moons in Solina's dungeon, he was too weak, his arms thinned to the bone, his head always spinning, his heart always like a wild hare caught in his ribcage. To his right, he saw his fellow prisoners, two more souls who had languished in the queen's dungeons. They too were struggling in the grip of soldiers. They too were pale and emaciated, mere shells of humanity, their hair wispy and their eyes bulging.

"Send the first one in!" Solina shouted, voice echoing across the mountain. Zar thought that even the desert below, for leagues around, could hear her voice, the cry of a gilded goddess.

The soldiers dragged forward a prisoner—a cadaverous, bare-chested man named Rael, his back lashed and his left eye swollen shut. The man struggled, whimpered, and begged, but he could not free himself from the soldiers' grips. These were Queen Solina's personal guards, towering men—they stood near seven feet tall—bedecked in steel and platinum, automatons of metal, their faces hidden behind visors shaped as falcon beaks. Sometimes Zar wondered if any flesh lived beneath that metal, or if inside their armor they were nothing but godly flame.

"Please, my queen," Rael pleaded. As the soldiers dragged him toward the tower, he looked back, and his good eye met Zar's gaze.

Zar froze, his breath dying in his chest. He saw such horror, such grief in the man's one eye—a soul crumbling.

"Rael," he whispered.

"If you make it back, Zar, tell my wife I'm sorry," the haggard prisoner said. Blood flecked his lips. "Tell her I love her and I'm sorry."

Zar nodded, throat constricting. Rael had stabbed the man raping his wife; he had been caught, knife bloody in his hands.

"I'll look after her, Rael," he said, knowing that he was lying, knowing that he would never make it back home. "I promise. I—"

With a grunt, a soldier kicked Zar's back, sending him facedown into the dirt. His cheek hit a rock; he felt it pierce his skin. He coughed and spat blood, raised his head, and saw the soldiers shove Rael into the dark doorway of the tower.

"Find me the key and you will have freedom!" Solina shouted into the darkness, voice echoing. A grin played across her lips, twisting her scar, the old burn the weredragons had given her. "Find the key and the jewels of Tiranor will be yours!"

Zar lay on the ground, staring at the twisting pillar of stone. The red clouds swirled above it like pools of gods' blood. Was it possible? Could one of them—even Zar himself—find the key and receive freedom?

He clenched his jaw and winced when his shattered teeth touched.

"No," he whispered. "There will be no freedom if she unlocks the door this key can open. There will be no place to hide in the world."

He watched the tower.

Silence fell.

Solina stood before Tarath Gehena, hands opened at her sides, fingers twitching over the hilts of her sabres. Her soldiers stood like statues; not a piece of armor clinked. Zar pushed himself to his feet and watched. At his side, the second prisoner—a gaunt dusteater caught licking the forbidden spice in Irys's dregs—stood watching with sallow eyes; those eyes seemed dead, and her skin was already pale like a corpse. Even the wind stilled; the land itself seemed to be watching the tower with bated breath.

A deep, gravelly sound rose from the tower.

Again sweat drenched Zar.

Sun God, oh Sun God, save us.

His body trembled with new vigor. At first he thought that sound the creaking of stones, but then he realized: it was laughter—an inhuman, impossibly deep, demonic laughter.

A shrill scream pierced the air, cascaded down the mountainsides, and echoed across the desert.

"We must flee," Zar whispered. He turned to run, but soldiers grabbed him. Gloved fingers dug into his arms.

The deep laughter rolled, a sound of ancient evil, of pure malice, a sound like a parasite feasting as it bore through its host toward the heart. Wincing, Zar turned his head away from the tower; he could no longer look.

His gaze fell upon Queen Solina. He expected to see his queen shaken or remorseful, to see her skin pale and her eyes fearful, to hear her order them away from Tarath Gehena and back to their city. What he saw in his queen's eyes, however, terrified Zar as much as the laughter that rose from the tower.

Solina's eyes were wide, her grin toothy. Her chest rose and fell with excited breath. She seemed like a woman in ecstasy.

The deep laughter rose to a shriek, a sound so loud that Zar wept and even the soldiers cursed. Zar whipped his head back toward the tower and saw it shaking. The screams rose from it: the screams of demons and the anguished scream of a man.

Blood seeped from the doorway, so thick and dark it seemed almost black.

The human scream died, and the laughter of demons rolled across the mountain.

"Rael," Zar whispered. "I'm sorry, my friend."

A shadow stirred on the tower's top, moving between the crenellations. Zar froze and stared, heart hammering. He wanted to look away. He wanted to close his eyes. He wanted to do anything but stare at that shadow. And yet the darkness that stirred there held his gaze, as powerful as the soldiers who held his body. It seemed a human figure, Zar thought—a man cloaked in black, a hood hiding his face. The cloaked sentinel moved atop the tower, a thing of darkness; Zar saw no head within the shadows of that hood. The figure raised its hand. Zar's throat tightened and he winced; the hand was long and deathly gray, the fingers tapering into crimson claws.

A thing of darkness, Zar knew and wept. *A demon of the Abyss.*

The demon knelt and rose again. In its claws it held a bloody, lacerated corpse. The demon tossed the body from the parapet. It tumbled and thumped against the ground only feet away from Zar.

He couldn't help it. Zar screamed.

It was the corpse of Rael, gutted like a fish. They had cracked open the man's chest, scooped out his innards, and tossed aside this bloodied shell. Rael's dead eyes stared into his own.

Please, the eyes seemed to say. *Please, Zar, tell my wife I love her. Tell her that I'm sorry.*

Finally Zar could close his eyes. A tear streamed down to his lips.

"Goodbye, my friend," he whispered through chafed lips. "May your soul rise to the Sun God's courts of eternal light."

Solina walked toward the body, stood above it, and shook her head ruefully.

"Sad fool," she said. "He could have had his freedom; he was too weak." She turned toward her soldiers and raised her voice. "Send the next one in! Send the woman! Give her a sword; she can slay whatever evil lies inside or fall upon the blade."

The gaunt woman's eyes barely flicked as the guards untied her wrists, shoved her forward, and placed a sabre in her hands. After so many years crouched in alleys, licking the dust of the south, could she even feel pain and fear? Her eyes were sunken, already dead. She clutched the sabre before her; the blade reflected the red sunset as if already bloodied. Her only sign of life was sweat upon her brow and a tremble to her arms. Her lips, pale and dry, finally opened to speak.

"If I slay the evil inside," she rasped, "and if I find your key, I want the dust." She looked at Solina and her eyes reddened. A tear streamed down her cheek. "Please, my queen, if only a spoonful, if only a taste. I will find your key not for freedom, not for jewels, only for a sprinkling of the dust, my queen."

Solina sighed and shook her head. "Pathetic creature. You are a daughter of the desert! You are the stock of a noble breed, a warrior race of steel and sand and glory. And all you crave is that southern spice that twists you into a beast?" The queen spat. "But I will grant your wish. Bring me the key, and I will give you not a spoonful of dust, but great barrels of the stuff, so you may lick your desire for all your remaining days."

The dusteater's eyes widened, and she wept and trembled. "Thank you, my queen!" She could barely speak; her chest rose and fell as sobs racked her body. "I will find your key. I promise you, my queen."

With that, the dusteater turned, stepped toward the tower, and entered the darkness.

Zar stared, not daring to breathe. Queen Solina and her men stood frozen, eyes upon the tower. A single crow circled above, the only movement in the desert.

A scream rose.

Clashing steel rang.

Cruel, deep laughter bubbled.

Zar closed his eyes. *Sun God, oh Sun God.*

When a screech shattered the desert, Zar looked up to see the dark, cloaked figure reappear atop the tower. Once more, no light pierced its hood. Once more, its crimson claws rose. In its grip, it held a twisted corpse.

The creature tossed the body down, then disappeared back into the tower. When the body thumped against the ground, Zar stared for an instant, then doubled over and gagged. Whatever paltry scraps they had fed him—dry old bread and cheese—he now lost.

Please, Sun God, please, how can you let such horror exist under your light?

The dusteater had entered the tower a gaunt, nearly cadaverous woman. Now her body was bloated as if waterlogged. Her head bulged, twice its previous size. A twisted, parasitic creature melted into her body like a conjoined twin. Red eyes blinked upon her chest, and a shriveled hand thrust out from her belly, grasping at the air. A mewl rose from the wreck of a body; she was still alive.

Solina stared down in disgust. Even the queen finally seemed shaken, and her face paled. Her lips curled back in a snarl.

"Kill it!" she hissed to her soldiers. "Sun God, kill this thing."

The soldiers approached the twisting, gurgling creature. The parasite writhed across it, molded into the bloated body. The dusteaster's eyes twitched and shed tears, and her lips whispered. Zar could not hear her, but he could read her lips.

"Please," she begged. "Please kill me."

The soldiers thrust down their swords. Blood spurted. The creature convulsed, then lay still.

Solina shouted. "Send in the last one!"

Zar's knees trembled so badly, he'd have fallen had soldiers not grabbed him. When they began dragging him toward the tower, he kicked and struggled; it was like trying to break iron chains. As the tower grew closer, Zar saw shadows stir beyond its doorway, and he screamed and kicked and wept.

"Untie him!" Solina ordered. "Give him a sword!"

A soldier drew a dagger, pulled Zar's arms back, and sawed through the ropes binding his wrists. His arms blazed with pain as he raised them, and he found his wrists chafed raw and bloody. His fingers trembled and throbbed as the blood rushed back into them. Before Zar could even gasp with the pain, the soldiers shoved a sabre into his hands.

"Go on, you wretch," said one soldier, voice echoing inside his falcon helm—the man who had whipped and stabbed his back so many times. "Fetch us the key, maggot, and you'll have your sweet freedom, and you can return to your whore and miserable whelp."

Zar's eyes stung, the memories coursing through him: his son, his beautiful son with the blue eyes, fingers that clutched his, and soft hair like molten dawn. He could see him again.

All I must do is be strong, be brave, find the key... and I can go home.

Before him loomed the shadowy doorway. When he looked over his shoulder, he saw the queen there, her armor bright in the sunset, her eyes like sapphires. He saw her soldiers, fifty men clad in steel, swords in hand.

Or I can fight them, he thought. *I can swing my sword at them. I can try to cut them down. I can't kill them all, but maybe I can kill enough to run between them, to flee into the desert.*

He gritted his teeth, sending pain blazing down his jaw. Even if he did escape them, what then? They would hunt him. They would catch him. They would return him to the dungeon—to the whips, the pincers, the rats, the endless agony and screams. Here at least, in this tower, death could relieve him. It would be a gruesome death; the creatures inside could gut him, or mangle him, and he would scream... but at the end, they would kill him. That was more than Solina's dungeon offered.

And maybe... Zar swallowed a lump. *Maybe I can find the key. Maybe I can return home to my wife and son, a hero bearing jewels and glory.*

He squared his shoulders, swallowed again, and stepped into the tower.

Darkness swirled around him. Wind whispered like voices. He walked, step by step, sword trembling before him.

"Find the key!" Solina shouted behind him, but her voice was muffled and distant, an echo from a different lifetime. "Find the key for your freedom!"

He kept walking. His knees shook. The shadows engulfed him, then parted like a curtain, and Zar found himself standing in a round chamber.

His breath died on his lips.

The walls and floor were built of rough gray bricks. The room was empty but for a large, obsidian table engraved with a peering eye.

A creature sat at the table, fork and knife in hand. Zar nearly gagged; he had never seen a creature so grotesque. It looked like an obese, naked man, its folds of pale skin hiding its features—a creature like a great slab of melting butter. It seemed to have no eyes, only two slits. Two white folds opened to reveal a raw, red mouth and a wet tongue.

Zar wanted to stab the creature. He wanted to turn and flee. He wanted to close his eyes, curl up, and pray. Yet he stood frozen in disgust and terror as the creature raised its hand. Its fingers were fat as bread rolls, pale and glistening and ending with small claws. It pointed at a staircase behind the table; the stairs seemed to rise to a second story.

"Do I..." Zar's voice cracked, and he swallowed and tried again. "Do I climb? Is the key upstairs?"

The obese, pale creature said nothing, only kept pointing at the staircase. Its wrinkled slits stared at Zar like eyes. Its mouth opened again, revealing small sharp teeth.

Zar took a step toward the stairs, keeping one eye on the creature. Sword trembling in his thin hands, he began to climb. The stairs corkscrewed up, craggy under his bare feet, until they emerged into the second floor of the tower.

Zar felt himself blanch. He raised his shaking sword.

"Shine your light on me, Sun God," he whispered.

Fight it, he thought and clenched his jaw. *Kill it or your body too will fall from the tower.*

The second story looked much like the first, round and rough and empty. A creature lurked here too. At first Zar thought it a dog with two heads. But this canine creature was larger than a dog—closer in size to a horse—and its two heads were humanlike, bloated and staring with beady eyes. The two mouths opened and tongues unrolled, each a foot long and oozing.

"Stand back!" Zar said and sliced the air, blade whistling. He had been a soldier once. He had languished in Solina's dungeon for long moons, maybe for years, and his limbs were thin and shaking now, and his head spun. But the old soldier still whispered inside him, the soldier who had swung his blade in battle, fighting the weredragons in the tunnels of their northern lair. He could still wield a sword, and he could still kill.

As his blade swung, one of the creature's heads growled—a deep sound like thunder. The second head screeched—a sound like ripping skin. The dog bared sharp teeth, its muscles rippled, and it leaped toward him.

Zar screamed and swung his blade.

For the Sun God. For my wife. For my son.

His blade slammed into the creature's shoulder. Black blood spurted and clung to the steel, and Zar screamed again. The blood raced up the blade like a black, sticky demon. When it reached his hand, it drove into his flesh, and Zar realized: This was no black blood but a swarm of ants. The insects burrowed into his hand. He saw them crawling under the skin of his arm, racing to his chest.

His sword clanged against the floor.

The canine creature yowled. Its mouths opened wide. Its tongues reached out, red serpents, growing longer and longer. Zar stumbled back, and the tongues caught him, wrapped around him, and began to constrict him.

"Sun God!" he shouted. "Blessed be your light! Bless—"

A tongue twisted around his throat, squeezed him, and his voice died.

Blackness began spreading across his eyes. He fell to his knees, and the tongues pulled him closer, and teeth shone, and eyes blazed, and Zar wept.

The blackness overcame him, and he fell into a deep, endless void.

In the night, he walked through tunnels in a cold, northern land. His brothers walked behind him and fire roared ahead. The weredragons—shapeshifters of the north—filled the underground, and they *knew* these caves, they knew every tunnel and every bend, and they cut Zar's brothers down at every turn. Their blades thrust from shadows, and his brothers fell, and blood sluiced their feet, and everywhere he turned, he saw their pale skin and shining eyes. Zar wanted to flee, to find his way back into the light of the world, to let the heat of the Sun God warm him, yet more Tiran soldiers surged behind him, and his queen screamed for death and glory, and Zar kept moving deeper into darkness. Finally a weredragon all in armor, his beard fiery red and his eyes wild, thrust his sword into Zar's leg. He fell. His comrades pulled him back. So much blood poured from him; Zar had not imagined the human body could store so much. He knew that he would die here. He tried to crawl back but saw only darkness, only stone walls, only wild eyes and shadows and his blood pooling beneath him.

When his eyes opened, he found himself back on the ground floor of Tarath Gehena. He lay upon the obsidian table, bleeding across the engraving of the great staring eye.

Zar screamed and blood filled his mouth.

The obese, pale creature sat before him, fork and knife clutched in its hands, bloodied. More blood smeared the creature's slit of a mouth and rolled down the folds of its skin. When Zar looked down at his own body, he wept and begged and closed his eyes.

Please, Sun God, please, no, make him stop eating me, make him stop, make him give me my legs back.

Claws dug into his shoulders. He slid across the tabletop and thumped against the floor. When he opened his eyes, he saw a hooded creature clutching him, dragging him across the floor and onto the staircase. Zar's body thudded against each step, dripping, spilling, eaten away, so much of it gone, so much blood. Zar screamed and wept and begged, but still they climbed and climbed until they emerged onto the tower top.

The sky roiled red above, whirlpools of ash and blood and shadow. The hooded creature raised Zar above his head, half a man, still weeping. The creature screeched to the sky, a sound rising and shattering in Zar's ears until it cracked something inside him, and Zar could hear no more, nothing but ringing.

The world spun around him.

Wind whipped him.

He tumbled from the tower and crashed down, shattering, at Queen Solina's feet.

She looked down upon him, and her lips tightened sourly, and she turned to speak to her men. *She is beautiful,* Zar thought. *She is my beautiful queen, a deity of gold and purity.* He wept to see such light and beauty at the end.

He closed his eyes, thought of his wife and son, and walked toward the fiery halls of his lord.

ELETHOR

He lay in his bed—a mere pile of furs—and held Lyana close but could not forget the pain. She lay naked and sleeping against him, her head of fiery red curls upon his chest, and as he held her he thought: *She is beautiful, and she is all I ever wanted, and I should be happy now but this hurts too much. This is all the sadness in the world.*

He looked up at the cave's ceiling, rugged stone carved by dragonclaw into the mountainside. He looked at the walls where candles burned in alcoves. He looked back at Lyana and marveled at the milky pallor of her freckled cheek, the flame of her hair, and the warmth of her breath against him. He held her under the furs, his one hand on her thigh, the other on the small of her back. He never wanted to let her go. She was an anchor to him, and all around roiled a sea of blood and tears.

One thousand and fifty-seven.

Such a small number—a mere few trees from what once was a forest. Such a multitude—so many souls to lead, to defend, to give hope to. One thousand and fifty-seven. They survived the fall of Nova Vita. They slept in these caves and in the forest around it. They wore furs, and they ate what they caught, and they needed him, they needed their King Elethor to bring them hope, to lead them home, to defeat their enemies and bring new life to Requiem.

They need me to be my father. To be like the great kings of old. He closed his eyes. *They need me to be a man I am not.*

Lyana stirred against him. She mumbled something of poison that burned, crowds that chanted, and whips that lashed. When Elethor opened his eyes, he saw her wincing and biting her lip. She kicked under the furs, and he held her tight like holding a flouncing fish, and he kissed her head and whispered to her until she calmed. Lyana too, for all her strength in battle and fierceness by day, was afraid, was haunted, and was dependent on her king.

Sometimes Elethor envied her for her nightmares. They meant that she could sleep. He himself lay awake most nights, staring at this ceiling, holding his wife, whispering to her, trying to swallow the pain that filled his throat. Some nights the wyverns shrieked outside, seeking them as they hid under rock and leaf. Other nights his own demons called inside his head, memories of the Abyss, memories of children dead beneath him, memories of seeking his sister among the bodies.

He finally slept, but it felt like only moments passed before dawn's light fell upon his eyelids, and he opened them to see Lyana blink, the candles melted to stubs, and rain falling like silver curtains outside the cave. The sounds of the camp rose outside: soft voices, feet shuffling, and leaves rustling under boots. Lyana moaned, stretched under the blankets, and touched his cheek.

"Did you sleep?" she whispered. "You still look so tired."

I don't want to leave this bed, he thought, *and I don't want to leave this woman, and I don't want to fight this war.*

Yet he was Elethor Aeternum, King of Requiem, Son of Olasar, and he knew that he would still fly, still bleed, still roar his fire, even if he died upon the sands of Tiranor. But not yet. Not yet. This morning he lay in warmth, his wife pressed against him, the beauty of rain and leaf outside the cave that had become their home.

"Elethor," Lyana said, propped herself onto her elbow, and made to rise from the bed, but he held her fast. He pulled her back toward him and kissed her, and she closed her eyes.

They had been married for a moon now. They had wed in this forest, among leaf and rock, for the people to see, for the survivors to know that a king and queen led them, that there was still hope in the world, still light to follow. A moon had turned, a moon of waiting, of pain, of more love than Elethor had thought his heart could ever feel again, not a flame like the love of his youth, but a strong wine in autumn and warm blankets as rain fell outside. He made love to her now. They kissed as the light of dawn poured over them, and gasped, and he held her tight as she moved above him, her eyes closed, her cheeks flushed. He rolled her onto her back and lay atop her, and she felt so frail and thin, this woman who had fought in wars, survived the desert, and slain her enemies with steel—here in his bed, she felt like a doll, a flower he could trample. She buried her hands in his hair, moaning, her eyes closed, a fragile white thing, her hair still short, her every freckle as familiar to him as the stars of his fathers' constellation. Those stars seemed to burn around him, and all the lights of the heavens to flare, and he closed his eyes and tightened his fists and could barely bear this blend of joy and pain that still clawed inside him. His eyes stung.

He lay beside her, and she nestled against him. She kissed his cheek and played with his hair.

"You should have done that last night," she said. "You would have slept better."

He snorted a weak laugh. "Maybe I will sleep all day. You go lead them, Lyana."

Yet he rose from the bed. He dressed and donned his armor—old armor forged in dragonfire, dented and unpolished and feeling more heavy than ever. He clasped Ferus to his side, his old longsword his father had given him, and stared into a small mirror they had found and hung here. He barely recognized himself these days. It had been only two years since Queen Solina had led the phoenixes into Requiem, yet he seemed to have aged twenty. Where was the soft-cheeked sculptor he had been, a youth with sad eyes? He saw a hardened man in this mirror, his face gaunt and bearded, his eyes deep set.

Lyana walked up beside him, leaned her head against his shoulder, and whispered to him. She had donned her own armor—the silvery steel plates of a bellator, a knight of Requiem. Her sword Levitas hung at her side, slimmer and faster than Ferus, but just as strong and sharp.

"Let us face the day, Elethor," she said. "Let us see our people. Let us give them another whisper of hope."

They exited the cave into a forest red and gold with autumn. Dried leaves carpeted the forest floor, and moss coated the trunks of birch, maple, and ash trees. Requiem lay but a league east from here; the forces of Solina dared not yet burn this land of Salvandos, still fearing the wrath of its leaders who dwelled far in the west, guardians of this forest.

Yet if her power grows, Elethor thought, *she will burn this place too.* Birds called overhead, flying south for winter, and Elethor watched them. *They are heading to Tiranor. To Solina. Soon we will fly there too.*

People moved about the camp, clad in furs and old cloaks, leaves in their hair and mud on their cheeks. Some wore armor; these ones guarded the palisade of wooden stakes that surrounded their camp. Others wore bandages, still wounded from the war. Some lay in carts, limbs missing, flesh scarred, eyes anguished or burned away. A few men stood around a mossy boulder, praying and chanting from old scrolls. A girl was weaving blades of grass into dolls, which she then handed out to younger children.

One thousand and fifty-seven.

They had set camp here nearly three moons ago—Elethor, Lyana, and fewer than a hundred others. Their scouts had since been combing these forests, seeking more survivors. At first they would find bloodied and bedraggled Vir Requis every day, and their camp had swelled rapidly. By now few other survivors remained; Elethor's scouts had found only two—young twins, a boy and girl—over the past ten days.

Is this all there is? he wondered, looking down upon the camp. *Are these all who live from our nation?* He grasped the hilt of his sword, and his throat constricted. *Where are you, Mori?*

Once more, Solina's words returned to him, echoing through his mind as they did every day and night.

She lives, Elethor. She lives.

He closed his eyes, and his fist trembled around Ferus's hilt.

"I will fly to your desert, Solina," he whispered. "I will rain my fire upon you. If you took my sister, I will free her, and you will burn forever in my flames."

One thousand and fifty-seven. He opened his eyes and looked at them again—frightened children, wounded women, tired old men. Yet he would lead them in flight, and they would blow their fire—like the great last stand of Lanburg Fields where legendary King Benedictus had led Requiem's survivors against the griffins.

He turned to look at Lyana. She stared back with huge eyes like green wells, and he knew that she was thinking the same thing.

"Will it be enough?" he whispered.

She squeezed his hand. "I don't know." Her voice was soft, almost a whisper, but deep and haunting like ghosts in an ancient forest. "Maybe not, Elethor. But we will lead them nonetheless, and we will burn the enemy upon her towers, even if we fall in flame too."

"For the glory of our stars," he said. "For Requiem."

Her eyes dampened. "For Mori."

A scream rose from the camp, and Elethor sucked in his breath and spun his head around. He stared at the forest and the scream rose again—a scream of such terror and pain, for an instant he thought the Abyss had risen into the world.

The camp below stirred. Requiem's survivors rose to their feet and spun toward the sound. Steel hissed as Elethor and

Lyana drew their swords. His heart hammered and his old wounds blazed.

She found us. Stars, Solina found us.

The trees stirred, and Elethor prepared to shift into a dragon, to blow his fire, to burn and die. Yet it was no Tiran troops who burst from the trees, but a single, haggard man with wild hair and wilder eyes. At first Elethor thought him some mad woodland hermit; he was shirtless even in the cold, his ribs showing beneath his skin. His teeth were missing, and dried blood caked his hair. He ran barefoot toward the cave, fell to his knees, and howled to the sky.

"Stars," Lyana whispered and gasped, and then Elethor recognized the man, and his breath caught.

This man was no wild hermit.

He was Vir Requis.

He was Leras Brewer and three moons ago, he had been strong, somber, a warrior of Requiem. Elethor had sent him south to spy in Tiranor before Requiem's survivors attacked.

He returned to us a broken beast.

Jaw clenched, Elethor sheathed his sword and marched down the mountainside toward the fallen, wailing man. Lyana rushed at his side, and guards of the camp, clad in armor and holding spears, hurried forward too. Soon a ring of people surrounded Leras.

The young man—*Stars, he looks old now,* Elethor thought—lay trembling, knees pulled to his chest. Tears filled his eyes, and his toothless mouth smacked open and shut. A memory flashed through Elethor's mind, a vision of shriveled beings of the Abyss, sucking the air and smacking their gums.

Elethor's head spun. He knelt by the trembling man and touched his shoulder. Leras cowered and wailed.

"Please," he begged, "please don't touch me, please don't hurt me. No more. No more."

Lyana stood above them. She raised her head and coned her palm around her mouth.

"Piri!" she cried. "Piri, we need you and your healers! Bring silverweed!"

Elethor looked down at the trembling man. Burn marks stretched across his chest. They had tortured him—burned him, broken his teeth, maybe broken his mind. Bile rose in Elethor's throat, thick with guilt.

I sent him south. I sent him to this.

"Nobody will hurt you here, Leras," he said softly. "You are safe here. You are home. You are home. We will heal you."

Leras stared with wild, red-rimmed eyes. He reached up and clasped Elethor's cloak, fingers bony and digging. His breath trembled and his ribs rose and fell like twigs upon a stream.

"You... you must flee!" he said, voice slurred with pain. "You cannot fly south. You cannot. She... she is freeing the nephilim, my king. The... stars!" Tears rolled down his cheeks. "Flee, King Elethor! Take these people and flee north—as far as you can—and never return."

Feet stomped through the crowd, and Piri Healer came walking forward, clad in the white robes of her order. With Mother Adia fallen and the Temple destroyed, young Piri had become the closest thing Requiem had to a new High Priestess. Her dark braids were stern, her eyes sterner. Behind her trailed her pupils, a dozen young women in white silks, baskets of herbs and bandages in their hands. Piri knelt beside the wounded Leras, reached into her robes for a bottle of silverweed, and broke the wax seal with her thumb.

"Drink," she said, holding the bottle forward. "Drink and you will sleep and heal."

Elethor raised his hand, blocking the bottle from reaching the wounded man.

"Wait, Piri," he said softly. He kept his voice steady, but his insides roiled.

The young healer's eyes flashed. "My king! I—"

"Wait." His voice was harsh. He looked back at the trembling, wounded man. "Does Solina fly north? What do you know? Speak, Leras. Tell me everything."

The man's raw fingers groped at Elethor's armor, smearing blood. His eyes widened and his body shook.

"She is sending men to fetch the key. The key from..." He coughed and shook for a moment, then spoke in sobs. "From the tower! I saw the bodies. Stars, the bodies that fell from the tower. Cut, mangled, twisted. She wanted to send me in too. She pulled me from the dungeon. She wanted me inside. Please. Please! I shifted. I flew. I came here. She will free them!" His voice rose to hoarse, anguished shouts. "She will find the key and she will unlock the Iron Door. The nephilim will fly. You cannot fight them. You must flee! Fly north, King Elethor. Fly north. Never return!"

Leras's tears flowed, and sobs racked his body, and Elethor only held the man, unable to speak, barely able to breathe. His fear pulsed through his chest, and he felt the blood leave his face.

Herself pale, Piri poured the silverweed into the man's mouth, but he sputtered, unable to swallow. He hacked and laughed and wept.

"Fly," he whispered, "and never return."

His eyes rolled back, and he fell limp in Elethor's arms.

"Leras!" Piri cried. She pulled him from Elethor's arms, laid him upon the ground, and tried to revive him. She pounded his chest, poured more silverweed into his mouth, and shook him, but he would not wake. He lay with a smile—a last smile of peace—and staring eyes.

The people of Requiem stood all around, whispering to one another. Many trembled. Elethor rose to his feet and turned toward them.

"You have nothing to fear!" he called out. "Vir Requis, return to your tents and caves. You are safe here. I promise you this. You are safe."

Yet as the crowd dispersed, Elethor heard them whisper, and a few wept. As Elethor stood above the body, he realized that he had drawn his sword. Cold sweat drenched him and his breath quickened.

Lyana looked at him, eyes wide, her own hand around her sword's hilt.

"He spoke of the nephilim," she whispered. Her face was ghostly white. "The Fallen Ones. I've heard of them, Elethor." She spun and began walking through the forest. "Come. I will show you. Stars save us if he spoke truth."

Teeth clenched and sword drawn, he followed, and the man's dying words echoed in his mind.

Fly, King Elethor! Fly and never return!

LEGION

He howled in the depths. He screeched and laughed and banged against the walls until the pain twisted through him, and all around him swirled his brothers with fang and claw and horn and tongue.

"I am Legion!" His voice rose like steam. "I will bite, I will feast, I will serve. Free us! Free us, Goddess. Free us, Savior. I will serve! I will bring chaos."

His brothers and sisters filled the court around him, so thick he could barely see the walls, barely see these bricks that entombed them. Their eyes dripped pus. Their maws opened, drooling, screaming, seeking man-flesh to feast upon, craving sweet blood to suck. The nephilim climbed and twisted around the columns, scuttled across the ceiling, bled and screamed and flapped wings. A bloated, crawling nephil bit into a smaller beast, cracked his spine between his jaws, and fed and licked and laughed and screamed.

"Wait, brothers and sisters!" Legion rose among them, climbing upon scales and flesh and rusted armor. He raised his claws and howled. "Do not yet feast! Do not feed upon us, brothers and sisters. I am Legion! I will lead you to the world. I will lead you to man-flesh and sweet red blood. I will serve! She will come."

The thousands surrounded him, a sea of tooth and claw and blood, milky eyes blazing, drool dripping, hisses rising. They howled at him and climbed atop one another, mad in their pen, shaking the columns with their screams. They had been mad for so long.

"We must feast!" cried one, a lanky beast with moldy flesh, one wing torn off, and a scar that rent his rotting head.

"We must drink blood!" cried another, a shriveled twig of a creature, teeth running across her head and torso like stitches.

"No more, no more!" wept a swollen creature, flesh bubbling and sores seeping. "The pain! End the pain!"

Legion flapped his wings. Those wings blazed with agony; they had been cramped for so long, atrophying in this prison, their leather brittle and old, their bones like rusted blades. Yet he flapped them, screamed, and rose in a wake of fire until he hit the ceiling. He slashed his claws and wings, beating his brethren aside. He scuttled and descended onto his throne of bones, rusted spikes, and mummified flesh.

"See my burning crown!" he shrieked. "See the blaze of my fire! Hear my words, for I am Legion your lord!"

Around his head, his halo of fire crackled. He alone among the Fallen bore this flaming crown, for he was Legion; his mother had been the mortal Priestess Queen of the Old God, and his father had been Sharael, Demon King of the Abyss. Legion's blood swarmed with maggots, with pus, and with royalty, and upon his brow his birthright of lordship blazed. The beasts around him reached out to his crown, hissing and wailing, the firelight painting them red.

"Your pain will end!" Legion cried. "One day she will come—our savior. Hear me, Fallen Ones! Hear my howl. I am Legion! I am Prophet! One day she will open the Iron Door. One day a goddess of platinum and light will free us, and I will lead you to serve her. I will lead you to freedom! We will feast upon sweet, living blood and bones and skin and organs."

They roared around him, chanting his name, screaming for blood, spraying drool and pus and smoke. They crashed against the walls and columns, mad with hunger and thirst, eyes spinning, teeth biting at their own flesh. Not all believed him. Many roared and flew toward him through the mass, snapping teeth and lashing claws, until his servants beat them down.

"You lie!" the rebels cried, weeping blood. Their hearts beat madly beneath their brittle flesh, deep red and black. Their veins pulsed and their wounds dripped. "We hunger! We must eat one another. We must eat you!"

Legion rose tall upon his throne of the dead. He was so thin here, so frail, his skin clinging to his bones like old flesh on discarded blades of war. All around him, filling the stone court, his brothers and sisters spread and writhed and bled.

"No!" Legion cried, halo blazing. "No. We must wait. Do not weaken us. We are strong! We are Fallen. We are Chaos. We will remain strong and we will feast! She will free us. One day she will open the door, a goddess of platinum, a deity of steel." He shook his fists above him, claws digging into his palms. "I have foreseen it. I am Prophet. I will lead you out the Iron Door that seals us. I will feed you flesh and blood! We will crush the world and devour those who imprisoned us."

They roared and flew and clawed and bit and wept around him. Myriads filled this prison, crushing one another, clawing uselessly at the walls. Sometimes Legion thought them a single, writhing mass, many merged into one creature over the millennia. Behind them stood the Door, towering, solid iron, never rusting, forever sealing them here, forever burning their flesh, forever containing their madness.

"The door will open! I am Legion! She will free us, and we will crush those who sealed us, we will destroy the world, we will bring chaos and terror, and their spines will snap between our jaws, and their blood will be our wine. Hear me! Follow me, nephilim. We will be free!"

They roiled like a boiling sea and howled and begged and roared. Fangs and claws rose, red with blood, and eyes blazed, and snorts of fire burned, and wings beat as his brothers and sisters climbed one another, gasping for air to howl. Upon his throne of mummified flesh, Legion bared his fangs and laughed and screeched. He could already taste the hot blood and bones, and he shrieked so that the chamber shook—a great cry to his goddess... to Solina.

TREALE

She sailed into Irys wrapped in cloak and hood, the desert wind kissing her lips with the taste of sand.

The boat was long, narrow, and oared, and she stood upon its prow and watched the city. Her heart thrashed and she clenched her fists under her cloak's long sleeves. The delta teemed with ships around her, hundreds of them: trundling cogs laden with chests of grains, fruits, and iron ore; military longships where soldiers shouted orders as they rowed, shields and spears strapped across their backs; the creaky barges of leathery-faced fishermen, their hulls speckled with barnacles; and towering merchant ships with sunbursts upon their sails, their decks bearing bundles of silks, sacks of gems, and exotic beasts in cages. Everywhere Treale looked, sails creaked, oars rowed, men shouted, and gulls flew to nest upon masts and ropes. Reeds swayed everywhere, a field of them rising from the waters, and Treale saw at least two rafts entangled among them. Cranes, ibises, and birds she could not recognize flew overhead, squawking in a chorus. The smells of salt, seaweed, fish, and spices filled the air so thickly Treale could barely breathe.

"Please, stars of Requiem," she whispered in the shadows of her hood. "Watch over me here in this southern land of sun."

And truly a land of sun it was; Treale had never felt such heat, never seen such shimmering light. The sunlight seemed to bleach the world, fading all colors. Treale was used to the northern light of Requiem, a soft light that fell gently upon the green of summer, the orange of fall, and the white of marble columns. Here in Tiranor the sun pounded her cloak—she felt trapped in an oven—and doused the world with blinding whites and yellows. Even the water seemed barely blue, but more a bright white reflecting the sun's wrath.

Behind her, the old peddler coughed, grunted, and spat noisily. She turned to see him squinting at her and scratching his privates. His face looked like beaten leather, and his hair hung in scraggly white braids. Between her and him rose sacks of Osannan silk and wool, treasures he'd claimed to have been shipping into Tiranor for forty years now.

"Welcome to Tiranor, girl," he rasped and spat again. "It's hot and it's crowded, and if you're lucky, you'll last a day. They like Osannan silk here, but not Osannan refugees who stink of the sea. And darling, you smell like fisherman's feet and catfish guts. Now toss me that second silver coin of yours, unless you want to swim the last hundred yards to the docks."

Treale was noble born; she had spent her youth in Oldnale Manor studying dialects of distant lands. Today she spoke with the eastern lilt of Osanna, great realm of men north of Tiranor and east of her fallen land of Requiem.

"I thank you for the ride, old man, and for your warning. But I will not heed it. I survived the wars in north Osanna, even as the undead warriors who rise there slew my family and burned my village. I can survive the desert too."

The old silkmonger scratched his stubble, hawked, and spat overboard yet again; Treale did not know how any man could produce so much spit.

"The desert is crueler than any undead host," he muttered. "You should have stayed in Osanna and faced its ghosts. There you can fight on the ground with sword and shield; here weredragons swoop and rain fire from above."

Treale looked across the water at fish that leaped between barges. *Weredragons.* It was a foul word, a slur she hated. She was a Vir Requis, a daughter of noble Requiem, a child of starlight, not some filthy beast. Yet she bit her tongue and swallowed her anger. Here she must not be Treale Oldnale, a lady of Requiem, but Till the refugee from Osanna, the humble daughter of weavers come to seek her southern fortune.

But I will not seek fortune here, she thought. *I will seek you, Mori. And I will find you. And I will free you. And we will escape this cursed desert and fly away together.*

The city docks spread before them, great cobwebs of wood and rope upon the water. As the boat rowed closer, Treale watched, cloak wrapped around her and hood pulled low despite the heat. Hundreds of people, maybe thousands, scurried upon the docks and boardwalks. Treale saw sailors in canvas pants, golden rings in their ears and sweat glistening upon their bare chests; wealthy merchants, bellies ample, sauntering in plumed hats and priceless purple robes; dockhands lifting caskets, sacks of grain, barrels of wine, and cages holding exotic birds of many colors; women swaying in silks that barely covered their flesh, their navels jeweled, accepting coins from sailors and leading them into alleys; and soldiers clad in pale steel, sunbursts upon their breastplates and shields, their spears bright. Above the docks loomed five craggy towers connected with a wall. Arrow slits peered from each tower like eyes, guarding the entrance to their realm.

Tiranor, Treale thought and clasped her hands behind her back. *Scourge of Requiem. Land of sun and heat and steel. I will find you here, Mori, and I will bring you home—wherever we find a home now.*

Soon she had paid the old monger and climbed off his boat onto a rickety dock. She took two steps, her head spun, and she reeled for a moment before taking a deep breath and walking on. Her legs felt like boneless chickens. How long had she been at sea? Treale could no longer remember. It had been three moons since Requiem had burned, maybe four. The days all blended into a great nightmare of running through forests, hiding in fields, finally reaching the great plains of Osanna in the east, then hitching rides with wagons to the southern port of Altus Mare. From there, Treale only remembered countless hours in a tottering boat, gagging into the Tiran Sea and baking in the southern sun. Three moons, maybe four; was that all? It seemed ages to her.

But I still remember your columns, Requiem, she thought. *And I still remember you, Mori. If all of Requiem lies fallen, and all her people but us lie dead, I will still save you.*

Children ran across the dock, carrying baskets of oysters, and nearly knocked Treale into the water. She tightened her lips, steadied her legs, and walked on. The planks creaked beneath her, and between them, she saw silvery fish whisk between weeds. When she raised her head, she saw the city of Irys before her, a great hodgepodge of sandstone and wood.

She walked between two guard towers, following a troupe of merchants riding donkeys. Soon she was walking along cobbled streets. Multitudes of people crowded around her; even before the wars, fewer people than this had lived in all of Requiem. Women walked bearing baskets of fruits and fabrics upon their heads. One man led a small, leashed monkey, an animal Treale had only seen in books. Priests walked in white robes, chanting and bearing lamps even as the sun blazed overhead. Mudbrick buildings and wooden stalls covered the roadsides. Shops and carts sold vases, fabrics, fruits and spices, dried meats and fresh seafood, iron tools and golden jewelry, and even—Treale gasped to see it—slaves in chains. Everywhere wafted the scents of freshly caught fish, wine and beer, a hundred spices, and beyond them all the sandy smell of the desert.

"Where are you, Mori?" Treale whispered.

She walked along the streets, leaving the docks behind. She found herself between brick homes whose roofs overflowed with gardens. Palm trees lined the streets, heavy with dates, finches, and scurrying monkeys. In gardens between the houses grew fig trees and grapevines on lattices. Treale had grown up in northeast Requiem, a land of pines, birches, and maples—cold and stately trees. *This* place was lush, the hot air thick with the scents of fruit and leaf and soil.

A child ran by her, racing a barrel hoop, and nearly crashed into a group of maidens bearing baskets of grapes upon their heads. Three priests rode down the street upon white horses, swinging bowls of incense and blowing ram horns in prayer. Soldiers marched around a silo, spears clacking against the cobblestones, their faces hidden behind ibis helms. Treale's head spun. She had never seen so many people crammed into one labyrinth; the city of Irys was like a great book overflowing with countless characters.

It seemed that she walked for hours. Treale had grown up on farmlands where only a couple hundred people lived. Whenever she would visit Nova Vita, the capital of Requiem where fifty thousand had dwelled, she would think it massive; her head would spin to see those crowds. This place dwarfed Nova Vita; beside it, the old capital of Requiem had been but a humble town.

Did we ever stand a chance in this war? Treale wondered. *Was there ever a hope to defeat this southern empire where millions live?*

As if in answer, shrieks sounded above, and Treale raised her eyes to see a flight of wyverns.

There were four of them; they flew in battle formation, two attackers flanked by two defenders. Treale leaped, driven by instinct, and crouched behind an abandoned cart. Her heart hammered, her head spun, and her hand closed around the hilt of her dagger. The wyverns screamed overhead, and once more Treale was running through the forests of Requiem, bleeding and burnt, seeking a place to hide and a hope to cling to. Then the wyverns disappeared over the roofs of the buildings, flying north to sea, and Treale breathed shakily.

"I'm safe here," she whispered to herself. "I'm only Till here, Till the refugee from Osanna, not Lady Treale of Requiem. These wyverns will not hurt me."

She released her dagger, and was about to stand up, when a shout rose.

"Girl! Girl, you, behind the wheelbarrow. Come over here."

Treale's heart hammered. She rose to see soldiers staring at her from their ibis helms; she could not see their faces. Each bore a spear, a sabre, and a round shield emblazoned with a painted sun. Each wore steel plates. There were twenty of them, automatons of metal, and Treale clenched her fists to stop them from trembling. She realize that her hood had fallen off, revealing her black hair, olive skin, and dark eyes, foreign colors in this realm of platinum hair, golden skin, and eyes like glimmering sapphires.

As the soldiers approached her, Treale struggled not to tremble or flee. She thought of King Elethor, and of Mori, and of the courage of Requiem's warriors, and she bowed her head.

"My lords," she said. "I am new to this city, and I seek work. Would you know of any seamstresses looking for help?"

One of the soldiers marched up to her, grabbed her arm, and stared through his visor. She could see his eyes—blue and shrewd. He grumbled deep in his throat.

"Osanna scum," he said over his shoulder to his comrades. "I know the accent. The bastards have been overflowing the port since their Undead War started."

Treale couldn't help but breathe out in relief. Her accent, learned from flying across the border into Osanna many times in her youth, had just saved her life.

If they knew I am Vir Requis, a daughter of their sworn enemies,
they would execute me here on the street.

"Aye, my lord," Treale said and curtsied, as the daughters
of Osanna were wont to do. "The undead rise from Fidelium's
mountains and march across our realm. They slew my father; he
was a weaver. I can weave too! Would you be so kind as to direct
me to a seamstress? I will work for room and board."

The soldiers grumbled, and one laughed and whispered to
his friend; Treale caught something about how she would better
serve as a whore than a seamstress, which was all Osannan
women were good for. Treale bit her lip. Osannans were perhaps
scum to these tall, noble sons of Tiranor; scum could be spat
upon, cursed, and allowed to live. That was more than they
would offer her if they knew her true parentage.

The soldier who had first addressed her drew his sabre,
and Treale gasped, sure that he would slay her after all. When he
swung his blade, however, he slammed its flat end across her
backside. She yelped; the pain bit her like a whip.

"Be gone, scum!" he said. "Seamstress? Find a brothel
with a bed to warm, or find a gutter to clean of nightsoil. That's
all you Osannans are good for. If I see you on these streets again,
my sword will slice your neck."

He gave her a second lashing, this one against her legs,
sending her scurrying down the street. Treale gritted her teeth,
and sudden rage flared inside her. She clenched her fists. A
brothel? A gutter? She was a lady of Requiem. She could shift
into a black dragon and burn these men dead in a heartbeat. She
felt the magic crackle inside her, the ancient power of Requiem's
stars. Her fingernails began growing into claws, her teeth
lengthening into fangs.

No.

She swallowed, forcing her magic down. It fizzled away,
leaving her a mere human. If she became a dragon now, she

could kill these men, it was true... and then a thousand wyverns would descend upon her.

Find Mori first. That is what you must do now. Even if you must swallow some pride.

Shame burning across her, her backside and legs blazing with pain, she gave another curtsy.

"Thank you, my lords, you are most kind, and your generous lashing reminds me of my place."

With that, she scurried around a corner, hoping she would never encounter those men again. She walked down a narrow street and pulled her hood down again. She would be wise to keep herself concealed, she decided, especially if she met other refugees from Osanna; she could fool brutish Tirans, but if other refugees of the Undead War encountered her, she doubted her accent was accurate enough to trick them too.

As she kept exploring the city, Treale kept waiting for it to end. And yet, as she walked south, Irys kept sprawling. Was she walking in circles? When she found stairs leading up a temple wall, she climbed up, looked around from a height, and gasped. Irys spread around her for miles.

I've been walking for hours, yet I've only explored the northern port, she realized. Most of the city still lay south of her, a jumble of walls, towers, squares, and countless winding streets. *Stars, a million people must live here!*

She climbed down the wall and kept walking, barely able to grasp one place with so many lives. Wagons trundled down the street before her, their horses tossing midnight manes. Stalls selling dates, apricots, figs, and spices lined the road, and lush gardens filled the air with a perfume. Children scurried everywhere, peddlers haggled with shoppers, and a woman in motley juggled daggers.

A statue rose in a square—a sandstone man with a crane's head, twenty feet tall. In its shadow, an old man performed with wooden puppets—one puppet of a phoenix, the other of a dragon. Treale's eyes widened. She had sewn hundreds of puppets in her youth; they were her greatest love. Yet when she approached the puppet show and stood among the children who watched it, sadness crept into her. The wooden phoenix, painted bright orange, soon slew the ebony dragon, and the children cheered. Treale lowered her head.

Even the puppets here hate us, she thought, and the silliness of her thought twisted her lips into a smile. With a sigh, she turned away from the show and moved through the crowd.

Besides, I won't find Mori watching a puppet show, Treale thought. She had seen the wyverns carry Mori south. They would have come to Irys; Treale was sure of that. Solina would want the princess of Requiem imprisoned here, in the capital, in the jewel of her empire. How many dungeons would a city this size hold? Or was Mori imprisoned in Solina's own chambers, kept in a cage like some trophy pet?

She would start by searching for the city prisons, Treale decided; it seemed the most likely place to look. She was not sure how she would enter those prisons; she would have to figure that part out next.

She approached a man hawking apricots from a cart. She was about to launch into a story of an imprisoned brother, then ask for direction to the dungeon. Before she could speak, however, great horns blew across the city, a peal that hushed the crowds.

Treale felt like an icy snake was crawling down her back. She did not like this sound; it was a keen like columns crashing, like a fallen race crying from graves, the sound her heart had made when Nova Vita fell. Around her, the people stood hushed for a moment, then roared to the sky. Their faces changed; anger and fear suffused them, and they pounded the air and chanted to the

Sun God. Thousands began to move down the streets, catching Treale in their flow; she could not help but move with them.

The crowds swept forward, a simmering sea, and pulled Treale along the cobbled street. They passed under a great archway embossed with golden suns; it was large enough for three dragons to fly through abreast. Beyond the archway, the crowd swept Treale into a great square where myriads roared.

Treale stood in the throng, head spinning and breath panting. The sun beat overhead. She had never seen a square so large; it seemed larger than all of Nova Vita. She could not guess how many people filled it; they were an ocean of rage, a hundred thousand strong or stronger. A temple rose to her right, columns soaring and topped with platinum. Before her, across the square, rose a palace; it was easily the largest building Treale had ever seen, dwarfing even the fallen halls of Requiem. Its towers scratched the sky. Faceless statues guarded its doors, standing above a staircase with hundreds of steps. Soldiers surrounded the square and covered the roofs of the buildings; some sat upon wyverns, whips in their hands. Above in the sky, phoenixes circled the sun, screeching.

Treale wanted to flee this place. She wanted to shift into a dragon and fly from here, fly as fast and far as she could. Something was happening here, something dark and horrible, something she desperately wanted to escape. The square felt like a boiling pot about to overflow. And yet she stood among the crowd, hood pulled low.

If you shift now, you die, she told herself. *A thousand wyverns surround this square, and phoenixes fly above. Stay. Hide. Whatever happens in this square, you must live.*

The palace doors ahead, towering things of gold and ivory, began to creak open. The crowd roared even louder. The faces of the people swam around her, red and howling and twisted with rage. Fists pounded the air. Several people were climbing the base of a great statue of Queen Solina; Treale elbowed her way toward them, climbed onto the statue's pedestal between howling youths, and stared ahead.

When the temple doors were opened, the real Queen Solina emerged.

The crowd roared to the sun. Solina raised her arms, a deity of platinum. Soldiers in gilded armor flanked her. The procession marched across the palace's dais, stood above the stairway, and looked down upon the city. One of the soldiers held a leashed, haggard creature, perhaps a beaten dog. As the crowds roared, the soldiers lifted the creature and chained it between the towering, faceless statues that flanked the palace doors.

"Behold the weredragon!" shouted Queen Solina. "Behold our victory! We will never fall!"

All around Treale, the people of Tiranor pounded their fists and roared the call. "We will never fall!"

Treale stared, eyes dampening. This was no chained animal, no creature.

It was Mori.

Memories floated around Treale: childhood summers in Nova Vita when she played with Mori in the palace gardens; the royal family visiting Oldnale Manor in winters, and Mori sleeping at Treale's side in the great oak bed upstairs; stargazing with Mori and her brothers on autumn nights, then sneaking away from the boys to whisper of future husbands, wedding gowns, and all the other dreams of youth. And now... now this: Treale hidden in a cloak among a crowd of rage, and Mori in chains and rags, her skin sallow and lacerated.

"I will save you, Mori," Treale whispered as the crowd roared. Her knees shook. Her belly roiled. She dug her fingernails into her palms. "I swear to you, I will save you."

As the phoenixes circled above the square, leaving wakes of flame, Solina cried to the sky. The queen appeared to be in rapture, head tossed back and arms raised. Her raiment of gold and platinum shone upon her, reflecting the sun and fire.

"The weredragons burned your homes!" she cried, and the crowds roared. "They slew your sons and brothers and fathers, brave men of Tiranor who flew to banish their darkness. But we defeated them! We toppled their courts and we captured their vile princess. Tiranor lives, Tiranor grows strong, Tiranor lights the world!"

The crowd chanted, fists pounding the air. "We will never fall! Hail the Sun God! We will never fall!"

"Hail the Sun God!" cried Queen Solina. "Today is the Day of Sun's Glory. Today the light of our lord banishes the night." She turned to her guards. "Let the reptile taste our glory."

The soldiers raised whips.

Treale winced and her heart wrenched. "No..."

The whips fell and Mori screamed.

"No!" Treale cried, but nobody heard her; the crowd shouted around her.

The whips fell again, and Treale bit her lip and looked aside. Her fists trembled. Tears ran down her cheeks. She wanted to shift, to turn into a dragon, to fly to Mori and save her. Yet how could she? How could she fly with a thousand wyverns around her, with phoenixes covering the sky?

"Please," she whispered, as if Solina could hear her across the crowd. The whips fell again and again, and Mori finally stopped screaming. Her chin fell to her chest, and she hung limp in her chains.

The crowd roared as the soldiers dragged the unconscious princess back into the temple. Treale shook and wanted to turn away, wanted to run, wanted to fly, wanted to race toward the temple and leap in after Mori. She tried to elbow her way forward, but the crowd was too thick, suffocating her. She could barely breathe. Her limbs trembled, and she'd have fallen were the people not pressed against her.

"See how the weredragons suffer for their crimes!" Solina shouted, arms raised. "See how the cruel scream in pain! They tried to kill us. They tried to extinguish the sun itself with their darkness. We shall beat the creature every Day of Sun's Glory! We will find their king, who hides like a coward in the wilderness, and flay him for the sun to burn his naked flesh." As the crowds roared, Solina raised her hand high in salute, and the sun itself seemed to glow within it, a beacon of her might. "Tiranor is strong, and Requiem's last children will die under our heel!"

Treale panted, belly roiling and eyes stinging, as Solina vanished back into her temple. The doors of gold and ivory closed, sealing the queen, her men, and Mori within. As the crowd began to disperse, growling about the evil of the weredragons, Treale stood in place. She lowered her head, fists clenched at her sides. She tasted a tear on her lips.

"I'm sorry, Mori," she whispered. "I'm so sorry I left you, that I flew from battle, that I abandoned you." She trembled, remembering seeing the fall of Nova Vita... and fleeing it. "I will never find absolution from my shame, Mori, but I will save you. I promise you."

She stood in the square until the sun set and all but a few stragglers remained. Then Treale turned, walked in silence, and entered an alley between shops and taverns. The sun fell and darkness spread. Between the roofs of the buildings, Treale saw the Draco constellation, the stars of her home, and they soothed her. She missed her parents and her brothers so badly; they lay dead. She missed her king Elethor; she did not know if he too had fallen. She missed her home, Oldnale Manor; it had burned to the ground.

But Mori still lives. A last light shines. I am not alone.

Treale curled up in a shadowy corner, placed her head against her knees, and quietly wept.

NEMES

As the rain fell and the sun set, Nemes was digging a grave.

He was not a gravedigger; Requiem had employed three, and they had fallen in the war. Nor was he strong; his arms had always been thin, and others of the camp—surviving soldiers—were better suited for manual labor. But Nemes had volunteered to bury the tortured spy, for he had always loved three things above all else: solitude, corpses, and Lady Lyana.

"I have two here with me," he said softly among the trees, shoveling dirt. The camp lay far behind, and the dead spy stank beside him. "And if my Lord Legion wills, I will have the third soon enough."

He tightened his pale, bony fingers around the shovel's shaft. In the fading light, his flesh seemed gray to him, rubbery and old despite his youth; he was not yet thirty. Strands of his hair hung over his eyes, prematurely silvered—the hair of an old man. But Lyana was fair. Lyana's skin was smooth and pale like the silks Nemes's mother would dream of owning. Lyana would regret her words to him; Nemes vowed that. They would all regret how they'd hurt him; he swore that to the rain, to the worms, and to the body rotting beside him.

His arms shook. He was tired. He had never been so tired. He turned away from the grave—it was deep enough—and knelt by the body. It was a famished, scarred thing, barely better than the worms that crawled across it. Nemes touched the body's cold cheek, closed his eyes, and thought of Lyana.

"How sweet it would be to touch your cheek," he whispered. He licked his lips and imagined licking her skin.

49

"Someday I will bring you here, Lyana, into this forest, and I will tear your clothes so that I can touch all of you, see all the pale flesh of your body, and know you here upon this grave."

Eyes closed and breath fast, Nemes caressed the corpse's hair. The rain pattered around him. When a worm crawled across his fingers, he opened his eyes. The corpse stared up at him, mouth open in a toothless grin, flesh a pasty white—as white as Lyana's. This dead, decaying thing was not as beautiful as Lyana, but it was close. It was close. It could soothe him for this night.

Nemes looked around him, a snarl on his lips. And why not? The weaklings were back at their camp—lying down to sleep, or to pray, or to hug and whisper their pathetic, weakling dreams. But he, Nemes, was strong; not of arm perhaps, but of spirit, of mind, of tooth. He was a scavenger of the night. He was a vulture, tall and dark and proud. He pulled his Iron Claw from his cloak, a curved obsidian blade. He thrust it into the body's neck and pulled down, gutting the torso. His nostrils flared, inhaling the sweet smell of death.

The light faded, and Nemes lit his tin lamp. In the red light, he studied. He dissected. He placed organ by organ. He clutched the heart in his palm and breathed in ecstasy. This felt almost like that first time, years ago, when he'd been only a boy in the woods. Back then he would catch only squirrels, crush their heads, skin them, and study their innards. But squirrels were for boys, and Nemes was a man now, a vulture, a future lord to Lyana. He craved the *humans*, and he savored this human. Every piece he removed sent shivers through him.

The others, he knew, would not understand. King Elethor had always craved the beauty of sculpture. The Princess Mori had always craved the beauty of music. Lyana, his eternal love, craved the beauty of marble columns and steel blades. Their minds were so small, their worlds so dark. *This* was beauty: a smell of blood, a glimmer on bone, and the secret worlds that pulsed under skin. Nemes inhaled sharply, imagining the beauty of the organs Lyana hid under her pale skin. He vowed to someday see them too, to touch them, to study them.

He buried the man and his organs. He covered the grave in darkness. He cleaned his hands in a stream. His work was done.

He wrapped his black cloak around him, clutched his staff, and whispered the words he had learned—the words of Lord Legion. Shadows rose from the earth like serpents of smoke. Nemes welcomed them. He let the wisps caress his legs, then rise and swirl around him, until he inhaled their clammy scent. Soon the shadows cloaked him and he vanished into the night.

A thin smile twisted his lips. He had learned the words from the Old Books, the ones buried deep in Requiem's library. Only the noble house carried the keys to that chamber, filigreed works of art they bore on chains around their necks. Knowledge was power, Nemes knew, and he craved it—the power in corpses and the power in books. On many cold nights, he had crept into Princess Mori's chamber, watched her sleep, and gently lifted the key off her breast. He would spend the night in darkness, surrounded with books, studying the ancient scrolls of Lord Legion, the nephil whose voice still whispered in the night, the child of a demon king and his human bride.

"Now your shadows cloak me, my lord," Nemes whispered. "Now I slither in darkness, hidden, like you."

Nemes's fists and jaw tightened in anger. Lord Legion had fallen; he languished in a tomb, sealed from his true glory, and only his whispers crawled across the land. One day, Nemes swore, Lord Legion would rise again and spread wings in the night. One day the cruel stars of Requiem would extinguish, and their worshippers would be those crawling. Then he, Nemes, would be lord over them. He—who had emptied their chamber pots, served their wine, and swept their floors—would make them bow.

He walked through the forest, robed in shadow, snarling.

In the darkness, the memories rose again. He saw his grandfather, a bent old man, sweeping the halls of Requiem's kings, then returning home to his bed of straw. He saw his father, a meek sickly man, toil to wash, to mend, to clean, to finally die of the cough. And he saw himself, and that memory stung worst of all. He saw a lanky boy, the child of a long family of servants, a boy raised to sweep floors and wash outhouses and pick fleas from dogs, a boy who dreamed of the power and beauty of those above him.

As he poured wine at feasts, how he had dreamed of sitting at the high table with Princess Mori, with Lord Bayrin and Lady Lyana, with the beautiful and mighty! At the Nights of Seven, how he had begged to join the nobles in their gardens, to sing with them, to watch the stars... and yet he would always enter the gardens last, to clean the mess those above him had left. He remembered one night, a night of a black moon, when he dared approach the Lady Lyana, dared ask her to a ball. How her eyes had pitied him! He never forgot that look of pity; it still burned him. He could still feel her hand on his shoulder. He could still hear her soft voice rejecting him, explaining that Prince Orin had already invited her, and how sweet and lovely Nemes was, and how many girls would someday adore him.

Walking through the forest now, nearly a decade later, rage still flared inside Nemes. With a growl, he punched a tree so hard his knuckles tore and his blood sprayed. He snarled and watched the blood drip, imagining tearing Lyana's flesh open too, seeing her blood, ripping out her heart like she had done to his.

"You will regret your words," he swore in the forest as he swore most nights, as he had been swearing for ten years. "You will scream for me to forgive you. And I will not, Lyana. I will not. Not until you are fully mine—your body, your organs, your very soul." His fists trembled. "You will be mine."

He reached into his cloak and grabbed his serpent amulet, the sigil of Lord Legion. He let his blood cover the talisman. Lord Legion loved blood, he knew; Nemes was glad to give some of his.

"With your power," he vowed, "they will all bow before you. I swear it, my lord. I will make them bow."

The lord's shadows swirled around him with fury, and Nemes kept walking until he reached the camp. Most slept on the ground, bundled in blankets. Some had built huts of branches and leaves. Nemes walked between them, silent and dark. Some of Requiem's survivors were still awake, huddled together and whispering; they could not see through his cloak of shadow. Nemes moved between them, a ghost. As a servant in Requiem's palace, he had always been as an invisible man; Lord Legion let him have the true power, no longer a mere mockery.

And once you are freed, Lord Legion, your true might will bless me. They will cower before us.

The shadows danced around him, a raiment of demons. He climbed the mountainside until he reached the cave where King Elethor and Queen Lyana now ruled. A guard stood there, a young woman with golden hair, a spear and shield in her hands. Nemes walked past her; she saw nothing. He entered the cave, walked down a tunnel, and entered the chamber of his beloved.

Lyana lay there upon a bed of fur, naked in candlelight, so pure, so pale, so fragile. Her skin like marble glimmered orange in the candlelight. Tiny scars like cobwebs covered her back; others had cut her before, but Nemes would cut her deeper. Her hair burned red and wild. Elethor lay beside her, rolled toward her, and touched her cheek.

Nemes stood in the corner, silent and shadowy, and watched the two make love. His lips peeled back, baring his teeth, as the naked bodies moved together, as Lyana moaned, as the foul King of Requiem invaded her purity.

You will bow before me too, Elethor, Nemes thought, fingernails digging into his palms. *My family has served you for too long, but a new power will rise. You will watch me dissect Lyana, and I will dissect you next. You will both live through it; that I swear to you. You will both live to see your shiny, wet organs in my hands and mouth.*

He watched as they made love. He watched as they fell asleep. He then turned, left the cave, and swallowed a lump in his throat. His eyes stung and his fists shook.

No, he told himself. *No. You cried too many times as a youth. You watched your father, bent and old, die of his work, and you cried. You watched Lyana marry the cruel prince, and you cried. No more tears. No more pain. You will never weep again, Nemes.*

"But you will weep, Requiem," he whispered in the night. The rain lashed his face. "You will."

Wreathed in his lord's shadows, he shifted. He took flight as a gray dragon, his snout long and thin and sniffing, his claws pale like shattered femurs. He rose between the trees, silent as a spirit rising to the afterlife, and pumped his wings. The rain whipped him, and he flew through the night, breath pluming before him.

He flew south.

He flew to *them.*

Before him in the clouds, he could see the smoke again. In the trees below, he could imagine the fallen columns of Requiem. He remembered standing outside the city, watching the Tirans invade, attack, destroy. They were a tall people, strong and noble. In the eyes of Vir Requis, Nemes always saw pity—pity like that which Lyana showed him. He saw haughtiness—like in the eyes of the princes when they gave him his commands. He saw tears—tears like those that had filled his own eyes in his youth.

But none of those had filled the Tiran eyes. In *their* eyes nothing shone but cruel strength.

"Requiem is weak," Nemes hissed as he flew, smoke rising between his teeth. "But Tiranor is strong, and I am strong, and she is the greatest among them."

Queen Solina! He had stood in the tunnels, watching as she sliced children apart, as she gutted them and spilled their precious organs upon the floor. Their blood had splashed her, and she had licked it from her blades, and Nemes knew then, knew he had been a fool to ever worship the princes, to ever crave power in Requiem. Watching her lick the blood, he knew: Solina was the only mortal worthy of worship, the only leader of strength in this world.

"I will find you, Solina," he spoke into the night. The rain swayed and he flew until the forest vanished below him. The southern horizon stretched dark and endless ahead. "I will find you, Solina, and I will give you King Elethor, and I will give you his people, and I will take Lyana for my own. Together we will free Lord Legion. Together we will rise."

He blew fire. He roared. He licked his chops and snarled and dreamed of Lyana's pulsing heart in his hand.

MORI

She sat on the sticky floor, lowered her head to her knees, and whispered soft prayers.

"As the leaves fall upon our marble tiles, as the breeze rustles the birches beyond our columns, as the sun gilds the mountains above our halls—know, young child of the woods, you are home, you are home." Her voice trembled. "Requiem! May our wings forever find your sky."

Chains bound her arms to the wall. More chains wrapped around her ankles, pinning her legs to the floor. For the first week here, they had chained her standing; now at least they loosened the chains enough for her to sit, but her limbs still ached, and whenever she leaned backward, her lashed back blazed. Three moons had passed, and they had whipped her three times in the Square of the Sun, beating her bloody and then returning her here, to darkness, to languish and shiver and weep and pray.

And Mori prayed. She prayed to her stars. She prayed to King's Column, which she dreamed of, a pillar of marble and light rising from ruin. She prayed to the spirits of her parents, her fallen brother Orin, and all those who had died around her in Nova Vita.

"Look after me, dragons of starlight," she whispered through cracked lips. Her voice was weak and hoarse, the voice of a ghost. "I will soon fly by your side."

Her head spun, and she felt unconsciousness clutching at her. She had fainted so many times here in darkness as hunger twisted her belly, as blood seeped down her back to trickle around her feet. In her long dark dreams, she kept seeing it again and again: Solina slicing her brother open, Solina slaying children underground, Solina toppling the city Mori had loved. And she dreamed of Bayrin: her sweet, strong Bayrin, the love of her life, flying bloodied and scarred in battle, surrounded by wyverns.

Do you still live, Bayrin? Do you dream of me too?

Worse than the hunger, worse than the whips, worse than the darkness, was Mori's worry for them. Did Elethor still fly? What of her friends Lyana and Treale and all the others? Did any Vir Requis still live, or was she the last, a lingering relic of Requiem's glory, a princess shriveled into an emaciated wretch?

She swallowed a lump in her throat, twisted her fingers, and struggled to stay conscious. Keeping her eyes open was so hard here in the dark. They gave her no light in this chamber of craggy bricks, rusted iron, and blood. Torches flickered outside the door; what red light seeped around the doorframe was all she had. It was enough for her to witness her decay. Her knees were knobby now, and her thighs, which she had once thought far too rounded for Bayrin to like, now seemed skeletal to her. She wore only a tattered rag, and through it she could see her bones thrusting against her skin.

How many days had passed since they'd last whipped her? Mori did not know. Three? Ten? Days and nights lost all meaning here in the dark. Sometimes it seemed hours between the meals they fed her—cold gruel thrust roughly into her mouth with a splintered spoon. Sometimes it seemed days went by without food, and her head swam and her belly clenched before more gruel arrived. When the moon ended, they would drag her out again, and the sunlight would burn and blind her, and the whips would tear her skin.

Footsteps thumped outside the door. Shadows stirred. Keys rattled in the lock, and when the door creaked open, torchlight flared. Mori whimpered and looked away, the light blinding her. How long had she sat here in darkness, alone? It felt like ages.

"Meal time," rumbled her jailor. "You no spit up this time, lizard whore, or Sharik cram it back into your mouth."

Mori blinked, raised her head, and winced in the torchlight. Sharik, the brutish jailor, stood above her. He looked more troll than man, wide and pasty and lumpy like a bag of spoiled milk. He wore but a canvas tunic, barely better than her own rags, and carried a ring of keys on his belt. He held a club in one hand, a wooden bowl in the other.

Mori did not want to eat. The gray slop he fed her, full of lumps and hairs, left her stomach churning and her limbs shaking.

"I'm... I'm not hungry," she whispered.

Sharik grumbled and raised his club. "Club or spoon. Your choice, weredragon."

He slammed down that club now, rapping her hard on the shoulder. Mori winced, pain pounding through her. Sharik knelt, dug his spoon into the gruel, and held it out. The slop trembled, gelatinous and sludgy. Sharik glared at her above the bowl. His eyes were beady and red, moles covered his face, and stench wafted between his rotting teeth. Hairs filled his red, veined nose.

"I—" Mori began.

With a grumble, Sharik dropped his club and grabbed her jaw. His fingers, fat and pale as raw sausages, dug into her, forcing her mouth open. She gasped and sputtered. He shoved the bowl forward, slamming its edge against her teeth, and tilted it. The gruel began spilling into her mouth, and Mori coughed and sputtered.

"No spilling!" Sharik grumbled. "For every drop you spill, Sharik break one of your fingers."

Mori could barely swallow fast enough. The slime rolled down her throat, and she coughed but forced herself to keep swallowing. His fingers dug into her jaw so painfully, she thought he would snap it off. Her throat kept working. She spat out a bit, whimpering. Sharik growled and she kept swallowing, letting the sludge keep pouring. She could barely breathe and her belly roiled.

Finally the bowl was empty. Sharik pulled it back and Mori swallowed, gasped, and coughed. Her limbs, still chained to floor and wall, trembled.

"Hope you enjoyed meal," Sharik rumbled and smirked. "Sharik cook. Special recipe."

He chuckled, a deep sound, then slapped her face. Pain flared, and Mori felt her lip split. She tasted blood.

"Next time you eat silent," Sharik said and growled. "No more coughing. No more choking. Or Sharik hurt you more. Sharik cut your fingers and feed you them."

With that, he left the chamber and slammed the door behind him. Mori heard the keys jangle in the lock, Sharik chuckle, and his boots thump away.

For long moments, she could think of nothing but breathing; every breath that entered and left her lungs was a struggle. Her belly ached and her limbs would not stop shaking. But whatever foul concoction he fed her, it had kept her alive thus far; Mori tried to draw comfort from that.

Food gives me strength. Strength will let me escape. Strength will let me kill him.

Her hands were too weak to form fists, but she curled her fingers as far as they'd go.

"I will escape," she whispered. "I will kill him. I will find Solina and I will kill her too."

She kept inhaling deeply, struggling to calm the shaking of her limbs. She breathed in and out, focusing on the flow of air—rancid as it was—into her lungs, into her fingertips, into every part of her. She thought of the leaves on the birch trees back home. She thought of her friends and family. She thought of harps playing in Requiem's marble temples and of her stars. She nodded.

"All right, Mori," she whispered to herself. "It's time to try again."

Pain flared in her belly and spun her head. Every time she tried to shift in these chains, she ended up weaker, her wrists and ankles bleeding. She had come to dread these attempts, but she tightened her lips, inhaled sharply, and nodded again.

I must keep trying. I must. If I give up hope, I can only wait to die. Even if escape is impossible, even if my magic will forever fail me, I will keep trying. I will keep hope alive. Even a fool's hope is better than no hope at all.

With a deep breath, she summoned her magic.

It rose tingling inside her, bright as starlight, warm as mulled wine. She let it flow through her chest, into her limbs, and into her head, smooth and soothing like her breathing.

Help me, stars of Requiem. Light my way here in darkness.

Wings began to sprout from her back; she felt them scrape against the walls. Her fingernails began growing into claws. Her teeth began lengthening into fangs. Across her frail legs, golden scales began to appear.

I will find your sky, Requiem! Help me fly.

Her body began to balloon, and a tail began to grow beneath her, and Mori could taste the sky and starlight, and—

As her limbs grew, the chains dug into her flesh. Pain burst. Her magic began to fizzle.

No. No! Clutch it. Shift! Break the chains!

She clenched her jaw, growled, and clutched her magic, tried to keep shifting, to keep growing, to—

A yelp fled her throat.

Her limbs grew too fast. The chains tore into her. Blood dripped, and her magic vanished like birds fleeing a disturbed tree.

Her scales disappeared, her claws and fangs retracted, and Mori lowered her head. She sat shaking, and blood dripped from where the chains had bitten into her. She shivered for long moments, head spinning.

Try again. Shift! You can break the chains, you...

Yet the darkness clutched at her. She was too weak, too hurt. Too much blood had spilled. Her forehead hit her knees and Mori gagged, losing the gruel the jailor had fed her. She could not stop trembling, and she could barely breathe.

I'm sorry, Requiem. I'm sorry, stars.

She closed her eyes, wept quietly, and let the long, dark night draw her into its embrace.

SOLINA

The palace doors opened, and her guards dragged in a lanky man robed in muddy black. A hood covered his face; Solina could see only strands of dangling white hair. Sitting upon her ivory throne, she narrowed her eyes and watched as her guards, tall men bedecked in steel, shoved the man down upon the floor of her hall.

"My queen!" said a guard. His voice echoed behind his falcon visor. "We found this one skulking outside the palace, muttering strange spells. He claims he's a weredragon."

Fifty guards, ten generals of her army, and three Sun God priests filled her throne room. They all sucked in their breath. Solina leaned forward in her ivory throne. The fallen man coughed; the sound echoed in her silent hall.

"Stand up!" she barked. She rose from her throne, her jewels jingling, and walked down the stairs of her dais. Her sandals clacked against the gold and white tiles of her hall. Granite columns rose around her, the stone a mosaic of reds and blacks and whites, their capitals coated in platinum.

"My Queen Solina!" said the robed man.

He pushed himself to his feet. His hood had fallen back, revealing a smooth face that belied his long white hair; that face looked no older than her own. His eyes were shrewd, his nose thin, his mouth a red line across his pale skin. His hands, which peeked from his robes, were long and skeletal; in one, he clutched a staff.

A guard kicked the man's leg behind his knee, forcing him to kneel.

"Kneel before Queen Solina, scum!" the guard said.

The other guards goaded the man with spears. Another kick sent him facedown upon the tiles, and a boot pressed against his nape. The man coughed and hissed but did not struggle to rise.

"My queen!" he said, voice serpentine. "I only seek to serve you. I come from Requiem, I—"

Solina waved her guards back and glared down at the weredragon. Her chest rose and fell. She knew this one. She had seen him during her captivity in Requiem. He had been but a youth then, a scrawny boy who always seemed too pale, the son of the palace servants. Twice she had caught him peeking through a keyhole, watching her bathe.

"Nemes," she said, voice twisting in disgust. "I know you. On your feet."

Solina was a tall woman, but when Nemes stood, she felt short; he towered above her, thin and long and pale as a bone. His lips twitched in a mockery of a smile; those lips looked more like crawling snakes to her. She remembered the stories whispered about Nemes in Requiem: the animals he skinned and dissected in the forest, the books of dark magic he read, and the women he would leer at, Lyana foremost among them. Yes, she remembered this youth, now this man before her. She remembered him and he disgusted her.

"Queen Solina!" he said and sketched a bow, struggling perhaps to reclaim some of his lost pride. "I remember you a beautiful maiden, a rose in the thorny court of dragons; your beauty has only grown, and here I find a golden deity, a—"

Solina drew her twin sabres with a hiss, crossed them, and thrust both blades against Nemes's neck; if she pushed them but a hair's breadth closer, she'd cut his skin. He froze and his voice died.

"Silence, slithering snake," she said. "What does a weredragon, a beast of night, seek in the courts of the Sun God?"

He tried to step back from her blades, but her men held him fast. He licked his lips, tried to speak, and when his neck bobbed, her blades drew a drop of blood. He whispered hoarsely.

"I do not serve the stars of the night, those petty gods of Requiem," he said. "Mine is a different, older lord. I will help you wake him. I will help you slay the weredragons."

Solina snarled and took a step nearer. She bared her teeth and glared at him closely; her nose was but an inch from his. She drove her blades but a whisper closer, and another drop of blood dripped down his neck.

"Perhaps I shall begin with slaying this weredragon," she said.

What game did this reptile play? Surely he knew he would die in this court. She knew he was mad; all of Requiem knew that. But she had not known the depth of his madness, if he was truly so keen to abandon his life.

He licked his lips again; his tongue was serpentine, a snake emerging from its lair. He hissed his words.

"I am, my queen, but a humble servant, the son of a servant. The weredragons themselves cared not if I lived or died; why should you? But I can give you their king, the cruel Elethor. Why kill me when I can deliver him to you? For three moons now, your men have sought him in the wilderness, burning forests and fields, scouring mountains and plains—and still the weredragons evade you. I was part of their camp. I can lead you there."

Solina growled. She lifted one of her blades, keeping the other on his neck, and placed it against his cheek. A red line of blood appeared. He hissed and dared not move.

"Why?" she whispered. "Why, Nemes, do you betray your filthy kind?"

A throaty chuckle rose from him, then died when the blades cut deeper.

"They are filthy, my queen, you are right. I cleaned their filth. I watched my grandfather sweep their floors, chop their wood, empty their chamber pots, wash their clothes... and all the while, they never invited him to a feast, or a hunt, or a ball. He died alone, thin and overworked. The same happened to my father. The same would have happened to me, had you not burned their cursed court to the ground." He hissed a laugh. "The weredragons speak of their justice, their pity, their wisdom, yet they are cruel. They are weak. In Tiranor I see strength! When you invaded Requiem, I saw a proud, noble people, a strong race, a beautiful race, a race where the powerful can rise, where pity and weakness are crushed. This I seek to serve, not Requiem's cruel lords. Allow me to serve you, my fair queen, my goddess of pride and strength, and I will deliver you the Weredragon King and what remains of his court."

She stepped back and sheathed her blades. Nemes gasped and clutched at his throat and cheek where lines of blood ran. Solina nodded at her guards, and they promptly kicked Nemes down again. He lay on the floor before her, a boot pressed against his neck, spears against his back.

"Empty words," she said and spat. "Do you think I will trust you? Your kin are reptiles; you are merely a worm. I should kill you now. Guards! Hang his head upon Queen's Archway. Let the city—"

"You seek the nephilim!" cried Nemes, cheek pressed against the floor.

Her men had drawn their swords and raised them. Solina held up her hand, stopping them from landing the blows. They stood frozen, sabres held above the worm.

Solina's heart raced. She sucked in her breath and snarled. He knew. Sun God, the worm knew of the key. He knew of the

Iron Door and the creatures who lurked behind it. She knelt above him, grabbed a fistful of his hair, and raised his head. She glared into his eyes.

"What do you know of this?" she hissed.

Blood covered his cheek. He still managed to grin.

"One of Elethor's spies made it to our camp," he said. "A man you took to Tarath Gehena. He babbled. The weredragons knew not what he meant. But I do." He licked blood off his lips. "I know of the dark arts. I know of the Palace of Whispers where the nephilim languish. I know of the tower where the key to the palace is guarded." His lips pulled back, revealing crooked teeth. "I studied their art. I studied the books of Legion, their demon lord. If you free the nephilim, I can help you tame them; I speak their tongue and know their lore. With the nephilim's power, you can crush not only the weredragons, but the world itself. I ask only to stand by your side and serve you as you reign, and to serve Lord Legion. Will you accept? Will you let me serve your glory, let me watch you crush the world under your heel? I will have my revenge. You will have the greatest empire this world has known."

Solina stared down at him. What game was he playing? What weredragon trick was this? The dangers raced through her mind. He could be a spy sent by Elethor, hoping to win her favor. He could be planning to lead her into a weredragon trap. He could be an assassin, waiting to catch her alone. He could be insane. Solina knew enough of weredragons to never trust them; she would not trust this one.

Unless...

Unless there was some way he could prove his loyalty, prove his worth. Solina narrowed her eyes and nodded.

Yes, she thought. *Yes, a weredragon would do nicely. If he dies, he dies. And if he lives... I will be too strong for an empire of reptiles to hurt me.*

"Stand him up!" she shouted to her guards. "Chain him. Collar him. We leave for Tarath Gehena—right now." As Nemes struggled, and as her men clasped him in chains, Solina smiled. "The weredragon will prove his loyalty. The weredragon will retrieve the key."

At once Nemes began to object, sweat upon his brow. "My queen! I... I am not a warrior, merely a priest of Lord Legion. I can help you speak with the nephilim, but to fetch the key, perhaps a soldier or—"

"Gag him!" Solina said. At once her men silenced him.

She walked across the hall toward her towering doors of gold and ivory. When she snapped her fingers, more guards stepped from between her columns to march behind her. The weredragon's chains rattled, and a thin smile twisted Solina's lips.

When her guards opened the doors of her hall, she stepped outside and stood above the palace stairway. The Faceless Guardians, the great statues of her dynasty, towered at her sides. She gazed down upon her realm. The Square of the Sun spread below her, its cobblestones golden in the sunset. The Sun God's Temple rose to her left, scratching the sky, while Queen's Archway rose before her across the square, golden sunbursts shimmering upon its bricks. Beyond the square rolled countless houses and streets, finally fading into desert and delta. And there in the west, beyond dune and mountain, rose the tower. There awaited her glory.

The sun dipped in the sky, a melting ball of orange. Its light caught the platinum capitals of the columns surrounding the square. They burned like a ring of torches, like the light of her heart, and like her glory that would soon bathe the world.

BAYRIN

He rocked on his heels, rolled his eyes, and blew out his breath.

"Lyana!" he said. "You've been reading for ages. Will you tell us what the book says?"

She sat before him on the rug, huddled against the cave wall. The ancient codex lay open before her, a tome the size of a suckling pig. Lyana raised her eyes from the pages, glared at him, and held her finger to her lips.

"Shh!" she said and returned her eyes to the book.

Bayrin groaned. "Lyana! Merciful stars, you heard what the spy said. War and destruction. End of the world. Toes stubbed left and right. Will you *please* quit your pleasure reading, stop shushing everyone, and tell me what the book says about these Falling Ones?"

Lyana groaned too, an enraged sound like a mother bear disturbed in her cave. She bared her teeth at him.

"Bayrin!" she said. "It's the *Fallen* Ones, or *nephilim* in their tongue. And maybe if you had spent fewer years chasing tavern wenches, and instead learned to read and write, you could study this book too."

He raised his hands in incredulity. "I know how to read and write!"

"Scribbling rude limericks on alehouse walls doesn't count, Bayrin. Now *please* shut that blabbering hole in your face and let me read."

Bayrin let out the longest, loudest sigh of his life. He turned to face Elethor, who stood at his side in the cave.

"Do you see, El? Do you see what I've had to put up with all my life? Bloody stars, since becoming queen, her tongue's only grown sharper; you could slice a wyvern to ribbons with it, no sword necessary."

He expected Elethor to laugh; his friend would always laugh whenever he'd mock Lyana. And yet today Elethor only stood solemnly, face frozen, staring down at the book.

Stars, Bayrin thought, *you can barely even see his face anymore behind that dreadful beard of his.*

Where was the Elethor he had known, the young man who'd laugh or groan at his jokes? Where was the Lyana who'd leap up to punch him, not just glare and bury her nose in a book? Bayrin would welcome groans and punches over this tense silence, this... this wait for an evil he didn't understand.

Stars, Mori, I miss you, he thought and closed his eyes. A lump filled his throat. He would have given the world to have her here now—to hold her, kiss her, never let her go. The beauty of silver rain on autumn leaves, of stars in purple sunset, of Requiem's fallen columns; all paled by the love, beauty, and goodness of Mori. He thought of her pink lips that would kiss him, her gray eyes looking up at him in wonder, the smoothness of her hair, and the purity of her heart as he held her against him.

Where are you now, Mori? Do you too have a cave to hide in, somebody to talk to?

Elethor believed her a prisoner in Tiranor; others whispered that the princess lay dead among Nova Vita's ruins. Bayrin knew that she lived; he refused to believe anything else. And if she *was* Solina's prisoner...

Bayrin clenched his fists. *If you hurt her, Solina, I will crush you in my claws, and I will burn down your city with my flames.*

He shook his head wildly.

"That's it!" he said. "I've waited long enough. I want to fly. I want to burn." He walked around the book, sat down by Lyana, and shoved her aside. "Let me see what this storybook of yours says."

"Bayrin!" she began and launched into a lecture, but he ignored her.

He stared down at the cracked old parchment. A baker's boy had saved the book, an ancient tome titled *Mythic Creatures of the Gray Age*, when fleeing the city. Upon its pages appeared illustrations of a thousand beasts: griffins, dragons, undead warriors, and every other creature that had ever walked, slithered, or flown. Lyana had the bestiary open to a chapter titled "Nephilim".

On the left page sprawled an illustration of a battle. In a valley stood an army of knights and archers. Toward them swarmed a host of rotting, twisted giants. Each stood thrice the height of a man. Each wore motley pieces of armor over rotten, scaly flesh. Some were bloated, their skin oozing; others were lanky and covered in spikes and horns. All bore tattered wings tipped with claws. A crimson serpent appeared upon their shields and helms, their sigil.

"Merciful stars," Bayrin said. "Ugly bastards, aren't they?" He leaned down and squinted at the opposite page. Lines of text appeared there, nearly too small for him to read. "What's it say here, Lyana?"

Sitting beside him, she groaned. "I thought you said you could read, Bayrin."

"I can! But these letters are so small and faded, and they're written in the tongue of Osanna, which only old priests and shriveled-up scribes can read anyway."

"Well *I* can read it, and the only thing shriveled up here is your brain. I'll read it for you; if you squint any harder, your eyes will be sucked into your skull." She shoved him aside, cleared her throat, and began to read from the page, translating the words as she went.

"Ten thousand years ago, the children of darkness emerged from their Abyss, crawled upon the earth, and took human wives. Thus were born the nephilim, the Fallen, the spawn of darkness dwellers and human wombs. Tall as giants they grew with rotted flesh, blazing eyes, and wings like black banners. They roamed the land, and their cries shook the mountains, and their claws tore down the walls of cities.

"The Ancient Ones, the desert dwellers whose daughters birthed the nephilim, raised a great host. They drove the nephilim into the Palace of Whispers, their great fortress in the desert, and sealed them in a deep chamber. An iron door they wrought for the prison, which they locked with an iron key.

"The fathers of the Fallen, demons of the Abyss, raged at the shame of their children. They took the iron key into Tarath Gehena, a dark tower, and placed guardians around it, so that none will see the shame of their fallen spawn."

When she finished reading, silence fell upon the room. Elethor stood frowning down at the book; he had not spoken all day. Lyana hugged herself.

"I don't get it," Bayrin said and furrowed his brow. "If you wanted to seal these critters, why even make a key? Why not just... build a door that cannot open, or destroy the key—why hide it in some tower?" He sighed. "Of course some madwoman like Solina would eventually seek this key. Didn't the Ancients have any sense?"

Lyana glared at him. "They had more sense than you, Bayrin, and so do most bricks. They didn't use a regular door. The nephilim would smash through it. They used a magical door, a Door of Sealing; nothing can break through those. The Ancients lived ten thousand years ago, before Tiranor and Requiem even existed, and they crafted many magical artifacts. If you had ever paid any attention to your tutors, instead of

scribbling naked ladies into your books, you'd have known that."
She reached into her pocket and drew a filigreed key, identical to
the ones Elethor and Mori wore around their necks. "Seen this
key before, Bayrin? That's right. The key to Requiem's library,
Chamber of Artifacts, and... the Gates of the Abyss." She
shuddered and pocketed the key. "Doors of Sealing exist in
Requiem too, though their history predates our own. Without a
key, they're forever closed."

"Somebody should have used one of these keys on your
mouth," Bayrin muttered. "Seal it shut forever." He sighed. "So,
what do we do now? Fly south and try to grab the key before
Soli? Or do we fly north and hide like our spy Leras politely
opined?"

For once, Lyana had no answer. She looked up at Elethor;
so did Bayrin. The young king stood above them, silent, staring at
the book as if he hadn't heard the conversation. Dark circles
hung under his eyes, and his brow was creased.

Damn it, Bayrin thought, *he's too young for wrinkles, too young to
look so tired.* His friend was not yet thirty but lately, with that
ridiculous new beard of his and long sleepless nights, he looked
ten years older.

"What do you think, El?" he asked softly. He rose to his
feet and stood by his friend. "What do you make of all this
mess?"

For a long moment, Elethor remained silent and stared at
the book. When finally the king looked up, Bayrin lost his breath;
a deep, haunting pain lived in Elethor's eyes, a demon's shadow
twisting underwater. For three moons now, Bayrin had never
stopped thinking of Mori, and her memory tore at him; looking in
Elethor's eyes, he knew that the king felt the same pain for
myriads of souls, for all those who had died in Nova Vita under
his reign.

"We cannot run," Elethor said. His lips were pale, his voice ghostly. "We cannot run now, or we will always run. If Solina awakes the sleeping nephilim, her wrath will flow across the world; there will be no more places to hide." He gripped the hilt of his sword. "We must fly south. We must burn her land and topple her court. But not alone. With the nephilim, Solina will crave the world entire, and the world entire must fight alongside our banners. Dragons. Salvanae. Griffins. Men. We must fight as one or the world will fall."

Lyana sighed, a deep sigh that clanked her armor. "Elethor, the world abandoned us," she said and touched her husband's arm. "We tried to rouse them. We begged for aid when wyverns flew. Our friends forsook us. Where were the salvanae when acid flowed? Where were griffins when Solina murdered our children? Where were men when our columns fell? We are Vir Requis; we have no friends in this world. All we have is our fire, our claws, and our roar."

Bayrin nodded and pounded his fist into his palm. "Damn right! We fly alone. To the Abyss with everyone else. I'm going to roast Soli's backside myself."

Elethor turned away from them, walked toward the cave's entrance, and stood staring outside at the rain. From below rose the sounds of the camp: babes crying, children playing, and elders praying. The soft light limned Elethor and silvered his armor. He stood silently, one hand on the pommel of his sword.

"No," he said finally, not turning back to face Bayrin and Lyana. "Too many died. Too many voices are silenced. A thousand live here, a last light for our race. How many more hide in the wilderness? Another thousand? A hundred? Even if Solina empties her land of wyverns, if she wakes the nephilim, they will slaughter us in the desert. We cannot face this threat alone." He turned back toward them. "Bayrin, my friend, fly west from here. Fly west, take this book with you, and raise the salvanae to our cause. Lyana, my love, fly east and rally men and griffins to our banner. Our neighbors did not fight the wyverns, it is true. They will fight to stop Solina from unleashing the nephilim, or the world will burn—their lands too."

Bayrin bit his lip and tugged at his hair. "I don't know, El. I don't know. Flying to raise help will take a while. If Solina is working to find this key, we can't waste time." He blew out his breath. "But I'll fly west if you ask me."

Mori might be hiding out west. Will I find her in the golden halls of the salvanae?

Lyana gripped her sword and raised her chin. "And I will fly east—to the courts of men and the isles of griffins. If aid lies in the east, I will bring it here."

They left the cave. They stood outside above the forest, and the rain pattered against their armor. Bayrin looked at his companions: his friend and king, tall and gaunt Elethor, all the joy and life gone from his eyes; his sister, now his queen, her hair fiery and her fists clutching her sword and dagger. A lump filled his throat.

I love you, Elethor, he thought. *I love you, Lyana. More than I can ever tell you.*

He opened his arms. They crushed him in their embrace. For long moments the three stood silently in the rain, holding one another. The rain was cold and their breath plumed warm against their cheeks. The lump refused to leave Bayrin's throat and his eyes stung.

If you hide in the west, Mori, I will find you. Wherever you are in this world, I will bring you here. I promise, Mori. I promise.

Nemes

They had left their wyverns below the mountain. This was holy ground; they would not profane it with beasts that drooled acid. They walked. It seemed like they walked for hours. The trail coiled up the stony mountainside; they must have climbed a league high. All around them rolled the desert, lifeless and golden, nothing but endless sand and rock.

The sun dipped below the horizon, a shimmering drop of blood, then vanished. Only their torches now lit the night, and still they climbed: a golden queen, fifty men in steel, and a prisoner robed in black. Step after step. Mile after mile. And still the mountain loomed.

They had chained his arms. The rusty iron chafed his skin, and Nemes bit down hard against the pain. He could endure some pain, some humiliation. For a hundred years, the weredragons had shamed his family, forcing them to clean plate, floor, and chamber pot. What was one more night of chains for a lifetime of glory?

I will fetch you your key, Solina, he thought and gritted his teeth. *I am no weakling, no craven like Leras. I will fetch the key, and I will stand by your side as you release the nephilim, as you crush the weredragons, as you rule the world. I will be no servant then, but a lord of your court.*

The night and trail stretched on.

It must have been midnight when they reached the mountaintop. Clouds covered the sky. A hot wind blew and their torches crackled. There above them loomed the tower, a coiling shard of obsidian like a rotten nerve. The torchlight flickered against it, and Nemes bared his teeth and hissed.

The night was hot, but an iciness flowed from this tower; it invaded his cloak, cut his skin, and froze his very bones. He felt his talisman burn against his chest; the iron serpent cried out for its lord. This tower itself, Nemes realized, was like a serpent of stone, rising from the earth to scream at the sky. His breath came fast. His blood pounded in his ears.

"Yes," Nemes whispered. "Yes, my lord! I come to serve you here. I come to seek your treasure. I am Nemes! I am your dark blade to thrust."

His head spun. For years in the Weredragon Court, he would study the books of Lord Legion. He would twist the animals of the forest to please his lord. He would suck and chew their innards to taste Legion's truth. He would study the Old Words and learn the dark magic: to cloak himself in shadow, to move in silence, to see where others were blind. And all the while, the stars of Requiem burned him, the cursed Draco Constellation that had doomed him to servitude. Yet here... here no stars shone. Here the power of Legion reigned.

Nemes fell and kissed the ground. Tears filled his eyes.

"I serve you, Fallen Lord!" he cried. "For years I sought you, Lord Legion, and now I kiss your holy earth. You will rise!"

Somewhere behind him, Solina spoke in disgust. "Stand him up. Toss him in. I'm tired of his whining."

Hands grabbed Nemes's shoulders and tugged him to his feet. They yanked his arms up, unlocked his chains, and shoved him forward. Nemes stumbled, looked over his shoulder, and hissed at the men. His wrists blazed with pain as the blood flowed back into them.

"You will show this place respect!" Nemes said. He snarled at the soldiers; fifty of them stood behind him, clad in steel, faces hidden behind their falcon visors. "You walk on holy ground, and

I am the servant of Lord Legion. One day you will bow before me—and before him—or your bones will be his feast."

For an instant the guards hesitated. Nemes hissed again, savoring the taste of power, the scent of their fear. Then Solina marched toward him. Her eyes flashed, and her scarred lips twisted in a snarl. She grabbed a sabre from a guard and thrust it into his hands.

"Fetch me the key and you can hiss like a snake," she said. "For now you are still a worm. Go! Enter the darkness."

He stared into her eyes; he guessed that few men dared to. For a moment the two stared in silence, neither one blinking—a desert queen and a dark priest, for a moment locked in silent struggle.

Finally he snorted and tossed the sword down. It clattered against the ground.

"I need no blade," he said. "Return me my staff; it is more powerful than any shard of steel."

Still Solina dared not break the stare. Silent, she walked toward a soldier, grabbed the staff from him, and tossed it at Nemes. He caught it in one hand. Only then did he looked away, bowing theatrically.

"I shall see you again, my queen, with the key in my hand and the power of Lord Legion at our doorstep."

The guards made to drag him into the tower, but Nemes glared at them, a glare of all his simmering pain, rage, and lust. It held them back. Nemes straightened his back, smoothed his robes, and raised his head. He walked toward the tower. The doorway loomed before him.

Heart thrashing, he stepped inside.

He walked through darkness. The sounds of wind and men faded behind him, leaving only silence. Shadows parted before him, wisps like serpents of smoke. Nemes found himself in a round, stone chamber.

An obsidian table stood here, piled high with platters of raw, bloody ribs. The bones looked human and flesh still clung to them. An obese, naked man sat at the table, his back to Nemes. As the man feasted, grunting and huffing, blood and gobbets of flesh flew.

Nemes gripped his staff tight, lips curling in disgust, and a grunt fled his lips. The feasting man froze, squealed, and spun toward him.

Nemes gritted his teeth, struggling not to faint.

This was no man, he saw, but some creature of pale, fleshy rolls, his eyes mere slits. The creature's mouth opened, revealing sharp teeth and chunks of half-chewed flesh. Blood smeared his cheeks. He gave a shrill cry that Nemes thought could shatter glass.

"The key!" Nemes demanded. He gripped his staff, hand shaking. "Where is the key?"

The creature stared at him, blood dripping from his mouth. Slowly he raised a pudgy, clawed hand and pointed to the shadows, where Nemes could just make out a second doorway. With that, the creature returned to his meal. When Nemes looked at the table, he grunted in disgust. The bones *were* human; a severed head rotted among them.

Nemes stared, sucked in his breath, and found that his mouth was watering. He craved a taste. He craved to crack the bones in his mouth, suck the marrow, and feast. But there would be time for that later. Once he freed the nephilim, the earth itself would be his table, and the flesh of the world would lie rotting before him, ripe for the feeding.

Nemes turned away. He stepped through the second doorway and onto a staircase. The stairs wound upward, a corkscrew of bloodied bricks, and brought him into a second chamber.

A pile of raw, writhing flesh lay curled up here, draped in sagging gray skin. Nemes raised his staff, stepped forward, and frowned down at the wriggling mass.

The creature leaped up. Teeth shone and eyes blazed.

Nemes leaped back, swiping his staff. The wood *cracked* against bone. The creature fell into the corner, scampered up, and howled with two bloated heads. It looked like a furless, muscular dog, but its two heads were humanoid—the wrinkled heads of waterlogged corpses. Black drool like ink filled its mouths. The creature raced toward him again, claws clattering against the floor.

Nemes snarled and swung his staff. It hit one of the dog's heads. The second head latched onto Nemes's shoulder, and teeth drove into him, stinging like a thousand fires.

He screamed. He drove his staff into the biting head. The creature squealed but would not release him. The second head bit his left arm, and blood spilled to the floor.

No. No! I have not flown through fire and rain and sand to die here.

He looked around the chamber. Would there be room enough? Would the tower collapse around him? The teeth drove deeper and he screamed again. He had no choice.

Nemes summoned his magic, the ancient magic of Requiem that blessed even him, the kingdom's lost son. He shifted into a dragon.

Gray scales rose across him, hard and smooth as bones. The canine creature howled and fell to the floor. Wings sprouted from Nemes's back and slammed against the walls. He ballooned like a leech sucking blood. Horns grew from his head and hit the ceiling. A tail flailed beneath him. He filled the chamber, barely able to move. The two-headed dog whimpered below him; it now seemed no larger than a rat.

Nemes spewed his fire.

The white flames crashed against the dog, and the creature screamed, a scream like children dying, like demons burning. It

79

writhed. Its skin melted. Its blood boiled. Nemes kept blowing his fire, and the creature blazed, but still it squirmed and screamed and begged. Soon nothing remained of it but bones, but it would not die.

Nemes snarled. He let his flames die. He slammed down his claws and crushed the burnt, bony remains. He felt them moving under his foot, and he ground them down. Bones snapped and finally the creature's screams died to a whimper... then went silent.

When he shifted back into human form, Nemes groaned. His shoulder and arm were a bloody mess. He doffed his cloak, examined the wounds, and felt faint. As his heart thrashed, the blood pulsed and spurted. Head spinning, Nemes rummaged through his cloak's pockets, produced his old leather pouch, and pulled out string and needle. He had used these tools often: sewing little creations from the animals he caught in the forests, mismatching heads and bodies and legs, creating new animals that were stronger and more beautiful. Today he sewed himself, fingers coated with blood. When his wounds were sewn shut, they reminded him of his creatures, of the snakes with the heads of squirrels and the ravens with bat wings. He tore off strips of his cloak, bandaged the stitched wounds, and licked the blood off his fingers.

He looked around the room, seeking the key. Nothing but blood and burnt remains were here, staining the brick walls and floor. A doorway led back to another staircase; the stairs wound up into shadows. Nemes left the room and kept climbing.

When he entered the third floor, he felt the blood leave his face. Disgust rose in him. The stench of rot filled his nostrils and roiled his belly.

Rusted blades rose from the room's floors, walls, and ceilings like iron brambles; old blood coated them. Among this rusted maze, a woman's corpse sat in a chair, swarming with worms. Nemes had once dug up a week-old corpse; this woman reminded him of that maggoty old flesh. Her head hung low, the flesh so rotted, the skull peeked through. Her eyes were gone; larvae squirmed in the sockets. Jagged growths sprouted from her like horns, mimicking the spikes that rose from the floor; they were colored a sickly green and sprinkled with white splotches.

The woman was dead, but her belly was slashed open, revealing a fetus that squirmed and sucked for air. The coiled, red creature raised his eyes, stared at Nemes, and let out a wail. Sharp teeth lined his mouth, and his eyes burned red. The fetus tugged dangling veins inside the womb, and his dead, rotten mother rose to her feet. The fetus grabbed and tugged other veins; his dead host began to shuffle forward.

Nemes wanted to shift into a dragon, to burn the aberration down. Yet he could not; the blades thrust out from every direction, filling the room with rusted metal. If he shifted, they would pierce him like an iron maiden. He hissed and raised his staff. The fetus screamed, eyes blazing, and moved his dead mother forward like a puppeteer. The fetus tugged a vein, and his mother swung a clawed hand.

Nemes parried with his staff. The corpse's claws scratched grooves into the wood. The fetus shrieked and drove his host forward. The rusted horns that grew across the mother, diseased tumors like blades, thrust toward Nemes. He leaped aside, dodging the mother's growths, only to scratch his thigh against a blade that rose from the floor.

A throaty, bubbling chuckle rose from the fetus. The little beast licked his lips in delight. He tugged the veins mightily, and the mother lurched toward Nemes, claws swinging and horns thrusting.

Nemes sidestepped, sliced his cloak on another blade, and swung his staff. The wood cracked against the mother's head. The corpse's neck ripped and centipedes fled from it. The head dangled. The fetus howled in rage. The babe drove the corpse forward, and a rusted growth—one that sprouted from the mother's chest—drove into Nemes's shoulder.

Nemes grunted, wound blazing, and kicked. His foot hit the fetus inside the sliced womb. The creature screamed, bit at his boot, and Nemes screamed too; the small teeth pierced his skin. He swung his staff again, hitting the mother's dangling head. The blow tore the rotted head off, and the mother crashed down. The rusty blades that rose from the floor pierced her chest. Blood gushed. The fetus screeched.

"You *killed* her!" cried the parasite inside the fallen body. His voice was shrill, demonic, a voice like wind through canyons and demons in the deep. "You *killed* my mother!"

Nemes could barely move. He stood panting, wounds blazing and blood dripping. Around him spread the brambles of blades. The fetus rose from the womb, dripping mucus. His umbilical cord ripped. The red, writhing creature leaped up, flew through the air, and grabbed onto Nemes's torso.

"You will be my new host!" the fetus screamed. He began slashing at Nemes's stomach, ripping his cloak and tearing his skin. "I will enter you. Let me in. You will be my mother!"

Nemes screamed. He grabbed the slimy parasite. He tried to rip it off, but the beast was too slippery, too squirming. The fetus began to bite at him. With bloody fingers, Nemes held the snapping head back. Such strength filled the creature; he was strong as a grown man.

"I will live inside you!" the aborted fetus screamed.

Nemes stumbled toward a wall bristly with blades. He pitched forward toward the spikes. A blade impaled the fetus and blood poured.

"Mother!" the babe cried. "Mother, it hurts, it stabs us! Why does he kill us?"

Nemes stumbled backward, clutching at his wounds. The fetus remained upon the wall, skewered on the blade. The creature writhed. He wept. Suddenly he seemed to Nemes not a demon spawn, but a human child, scared and hurt and dying.

"Mother," the babe whispered... and then his head slumped. He hung still like a slab on a meat hook.

Nemes limped toward a door in the back. His head swam and he trembled with blood loss. He trudged upstairs, holding the wall and smearing blood across it. He entered the fourth floor of the tower.

A choked gasp fled his lips.

No horror—not the obese diner, not the twisted dog, not the fetus in his host—could prepare Nemes for this.

Tears filled his eyes.

"No," he whispered and fell to his knees. "Please, no."

Lying on the floor before him, gasping and bleeding and pale, was his father.

The old man opened his mouth. His teeth were gone. His lips were dry. He tried to speak, sputtered, and whispered.

"S-son." He lifted a skeletal hand. Sweat covered his brow. "Son, please... please save me."

Nemes crawled toward his father and touched his forehead. It was blazing hot. His father was feverish, so frail his skin draped across his bones. His eyes were sunken, and a dry cough rattled in his chest. He wore only canvas breeches and he trembled.

"Father!" Nemes said. He doffed his cloak and wrapped it around the old man. "I'm here. Your son is here."

His father tried to smile, then coughed and grimaced. Blood stained his lips; more speckled his chest. He touched Nemes's cheek with shaking, twisted fingers.

"My son. You must take the key. You must take it from me. You—"

Coughing seized him, and he spat more blood.

No, Nemes thought. His fists clenched. *No! This cannot be. Cannot!*

"I saw you die!" Nemes said, tears burning in his eyes. "You died in the courts of Requiem. You died with a broom in your hands. The cruel king and princes did not even know; they did not care. I buried you! I buried you myself." He raised his head and howled at the ceiling. "What cruel mockery is this? How dare you show me this illusion!"

Tears burned down Nemes's cheeks. His father wiped them away, smiling thinly. His hair had once been dark and thick; now it was white and wispy, nearly all gone from his scalp.

"I live again," the old man said. "I died; it is true. He brought me back to life. Lord Legion. The prophet of the Fallen. He breathed new life into my lungs, and filled my heart with blood to pump, and placed me here. For you, Nemes. For you. To give you the key so you may free him."

Nemes shook as he held his father. The man felt so frail in his arms, his bones so brittle, likely to snap in an embrace.

"I will take you out of here, Father," he said. "I promise. Once we give the queen the key, she will reward us. We will be powerful, no longer servants. You will never serve again, I promise you." He let out a sob. "You will live in a palace of gold, and King Elethor will serve you, a slave in irons."

Nemes snarled, imagining it. With the gold Solina gave him, he would build a great hall, a palace larger than the fallen court of Requiem. He would build a throne for his father and force cruel Elethor to kneel before it, to clean the floors, to beg for mercy from the whips. He would build a dungeon for Lyana, chain her underground, and invade her body whenever he pleased. He would hurt her—like she had hurt him—and make her beg. The key would give him that.

"Where is it, Father?" he whispered. "Where is the key?"

The old man struggled to speak. Only a hoarse gasp left his throat. His body trembled and his veins pulsed. Nemes could feel the man's heart fluttering like a trapped bird. His father's skeletal hand rose, then pointed down at his belly. He tried to speak again, but only coughed and trembled.

"What is it, Father?" Nemes whispered.

His father pulled open the cloak, revealing his pale torso. He grabbed Nemes's hand, pulled it down, and placed it against his stomach.

Nemes sucked in his breath. His eyes stung.

"Please, Nemes," his father whispered. "Take it out. Cut it from me. Take the key."

Beneath his father's skin, hard inside his belly, Nemes felt the outline of the key.

"No," Nemes whispered. Tears blurred his eyes. "I cannot."

"You must." His father clutched his wrist. "Lord Legion will bless you. Cut the key out. Let me die again. My death will free me from this prison; I will die in your arms, knowing that you will rise to glory." Tears streamed down his wrinkled cheeks. "My son—the first of our family to rise to greatness."

Nemes clenched his jaw. His breath shook. *No. No!* He could not. How could he? To kill his father? The vile court of Requiem had killed his father! The man lived again; how could Nemes kill him for his vainglory?

He howled to the ceiling. His roar shook the tower.

"No! I cannot. I will not!" He shook his fists. "Do not ask me this! Please, Lord Legion. I beg you. I serve you. Anything but this! Do not ask me to prove my loyalty this way."

A low, rumbling laugh rose from the floor, bubbling up from the depths like tar. The walls trembled and dust rained. The tower itself was laughing, Nemes realized; it was a living thing, a demon of stone and dark magic and blood.

"Please," Nemes whispered.

A rumble shook the floor. The bricks creaked. A screech ran through the walls, rising as a voice, a shriek, a cry of endless darkness and wonder.

"You will prove your loyalty, Nemes of Requiem!" rose the cry of the tower, a sound like steam from a kettle. The walls pulsed. Blood dripped between the bricks. "You will slice him open. You will dissect him. Why do you think, Nemes, that you spent years in the forest, spent years cutting open your animals? For this! For this day. To free me. To free Lord Legion and his Fallen Horde. Slice him! Dissect him! Cut the key from his innards and raise it in glory!"

Nemes's breath shook. His hands trembled. His eyes burned with tears. He reached to his belt and drew the Iron Claw, the blade he'd used in the forest so many times.

"Forgive me, Father..."

He sobbed as he drove the blade down.

His father screamed.

Nemes wept as he worked.

When his father lay dead, Nemes stood and raised the bloody key and screamed.

"I passed the test!" His tears mingled with his blood. "I have the key! I am Nemes, a servant of Legion! The nephilim will swarm again, and the weredragons will die. They will beg and weep and I will crush them for their sins!"

He left the chamber, laughing and weeping, key held high. As he descended the stairs, he uttered the Old Words, and the shadows of his lord cloaked him. The smoky serpents writhed around him, a new cloak, a mantle of his glory. Soon the nephilim themselves would flow around him.

He passed the chamber where the mother lay dead, her babe impaled. He passed the chamber where the dog lay crushed and burnt. He entered the ground floor where the obese diner hissed and glared and smacked his lips. Nemes approached the demon, thrust his Iron Claw forward, and sliced the creature open from collarbone to navel. He laughed as bloody snakes fled the beast, leaving its sagging skin like creatures hatching from an egg. Now it was Nemes who feasted at this table. Now it was Nemes who ruled this tower and its secrets.

He stepped outside into the night, laughed, and raised the key. Lighting crashed into it, lighting the desert. Nemes saw Solina, her men, the endless leagues of sand and rock. Wind shrieked, blowing back his hair.

"The key, Nemes!" Solina shouted in the storm. She reached out for it. "Hand me the key and the trophies of Tiranor will be yours."

He stood in the tower doorway, laughing, the wind roaring. The shadows swirled and laughed around him.

"The key!" he said. "You want the key."

And why should he share it? Why should he, Nemes, give this desert queen her prize?

I can free the nephilim myself! This power can be mine, not hers. Why should I still serve? For years I knelt! For years I groveled. Now Nemes can rule; with the nephilim, no power could oppose me.

"The key, Nemes!" Solina demanded.

He laughed and snarled. "Why should I give it to you? Will you beg me, Solina? Will you kneel and—"

She leaped toward him.

Her blade flashed.

Nemes tried to pull back. She was so fast. She was a streak of gold and steel.

He screamed.

When her blade severed his arm, blood sprayed in a mist. His arm tumbled. His hand still clutched the key when it hit the ground.

"You will die for this!" Nemes screamed, clutching the stump.

Solina knelt by his severed arm. She wrenched the key free from his fingers.

"Chain him up!" she shouted to her men. "Drag him in irons to Irys. He will see the glory of the nephilim before we hang him to die upon the walls."

The guards stepped toward him, chains in their hands. Nemes hissed and turned to flee. He fell. His blood spurted. Hands grabbed him, yanked him up, and Nemes screamed before his eyes rolled back and darkness spread across him.

My glory... my power... I promised it to him.

"I'm sorry, Father," he whispered. "I'm sorry..."

Demons laughed, and dark claws grabbed him, and his soul sank into a long black night.

TREALE

"Pomegranates, fresh pomegranates, grab one to eat!" cried the boy.

He stood upon the banks of the River Pallan, a scrawny thing with deep golden skin, holding a basket laden with the red treasures.

"Grab a pomegranate, a copper a fruit!" he shouted.

Around the boy, a dozen other children stood upon the boardwalk, hawking their own wares from baskets. Behind them, longships rowed up and down the river, laden with more baskets and crates of goods.

"Carobs, dried carobs!"

"Fresh oysters, grab them while they're fresh!"

"Seashell bracelets for fertility! Wear them in bed for healthy babes!"

Treale stood upon the cobbled boardwalk, shaded under the awning of a chandlery. She wore her dark cloak draped around her and hid her midnight hair and eyes—foreign in this land of platinum hair and blue eyes—under her hood. The scents of the foods filled her nostrils. Her stomach growled and her mouth watered. She had not eaten in... how long had it been? She could barely remember; certainly she had eaten nothing since landing in Irys yesterday. Fingers trembling with hunger, she reached into her pocket, fished around, and produced a single copper coin. It was all the money she had in the world—not enough for a nice fish or crab, even if she had a place to cook them—but perhaps enough for a pomegranate.

She walked onto the boardwalk, leaped back as a peddler came trundling down upon his donkey-drawn cart, and kept moving. When she reached the boy hawking pomegranates, she held out her coin in her palm.

"I'll have one if you please," she spoke from the shadows of her hood.

The boy took the coin, squinted at it, and Treale felt faint. This was a coin from Requiem; she had smoothed its surface, effacing its image and lettering, but would the boy still recognize its origin? Would he sound the alarm and shout "Weredragon, weredragon!" for the city to hear?

"It's good copper," Treale said. "An old coin, but solid metal and pure. Feel its weight. That's worth two pomegranates. You have to sell me two."

Her legs trembled with hunger as the boy squinted at the coin. Treale had never felt so lowly. Only moons ago, she had been a lady of Requiem's courts, and now... now she trembled before a boy half her age, so weak with hunger she nearly wept.

Finally the boy nodded, pocketed the coin, and offered her the basket of fruit. Not a moment later, Treale crouched between a brothel and a shoemaker's shop, scooping seeds from a split pomegranate and eating so fast she nearly choked. When her meal was done, she stuffed the second pomegranate into her cloak's pocket. Though her stomach still rumbled with hunger, she would save the second fruit for later.

"It might be a while until you find more food, Treale Oldnale," she whispered to herself. "The days of feasting at the side of kings are over."

She rose to her feet, pulled her hood low, and began walking down the street. People crowded around her: loomers bearing baskets of fabrics, barefoot children scuffling with wooden swords, mothers nursing their babes, and bare-chested masons lugging packs full of bricks. Shops and stalls lined the roadsides. A child on a donkey knocked into a stall, spilling a thousand live crabs that scurried across the cobblestones. The crabmonger shouted and began a futile chase for his catch; Treale managed to grab one crab and stuff it into her pocket for later. The clang of hammers on anvils rose from smithies, laughter and grunts rose from brothels, and screams rose from surgeons' shops where tongs pulled teeth and needles stitched wounds. The sun pounded the city; the air felt like thick soup rank with the scents of fish, oil, tallow, and dried fruits.

Treale's head still spun to see so many people; they seemed to her like ants scurrying through tunnels. She missed the open spaces of Oldnale Farms: the rolling fields, the sunset over the forests, and the clear skies where she would fly with her brothers. And she missed Nova Vita, capital of Requiem where her friend Mori had lived: its wide streets, its marble columns that soared between birches, its music of harps that rose from silver temples.

That land is gone, she thought and her eyes stung. *The farms have burned, and the city has fallen, but you still live, Mori. There is still some starlight in the world.*

She made her way through the crowds, her black robes searing hot and swirling around her, until she reached the mouth of an alley, and before her spread the Square of the Sun.

The cobbled expanse stretched out like a sea of stone. Columns surrounded the square, and upon each capital, a wyvern perched and snarled. Soldiers marched here, their helms shaped like cranes and falcons and eagles, their breastplates glimmering with golden sunbursts. Their spears clanked against the cobblestones and their songs echoed inside their helms. Beyond the soldiers rose the monuments of Tiranor's glory: the great Queen's Archway, two hundred feet tall, its limestone engraved with sunburst reliefs; the Temple of the Sun, its columns capped with platinum; the great statue of Solina, fifty feet tall, from whose pedestal Treale had watched Mori beaten; and the Palace of Phoebus upon a great dais, its doors flanked with stone guardians, its glory tapering into the Tower of Akartum, the tallest steeple in Tiranor and perhaps the world.

Treale swallowed. *This is the most dangerous place upon this world,* she thought. *This is the heart of Tiranor's wrath and might. This is where I must walk.*

She took a deep breath, wrapped her cloak tight around her, and entered the square.

After only three steps, she held her breath and looked around, ready to scurry back into the alley. Yet the soldiers kept marching, and the wyverns kept their vigil upon the columns, and crows circled above and cawed as ever. Treale swallowed again, reached under her cloak, and grabbed the amulet she wore—a golden sheaf of wheat, the sigil of her house. That house had fallen, but Treale was still an Oldnale, and the touch of the gold soothed her. She kept walking.

She moved along the outskirts of the square, staying near the columns that ringed it. She tried to keep staring ahead toward the palace, but couldn't help it; as she passed near a column, she peeked up at the wyvern that perched upon its capital. The beast glared down, and a glob of its drool fell to burn a hole into the ground. Its tail flapped, but its wings remained still.

Sweat dripped down Treale's back. She remembered those wyverns swarming across Nova Vita, felling dragons from the sky. She wanted to shift into a dragon, to burn them, to kill as many as she could before they took her down.

Requiem will have its revenge, she swore. She clutched her amulet so hard it nearly pierced her palm. *That I swear to you, Solina. I will not forget your crimes. But not now. Not this day. Today is for Mori.*

She was halfway to the palace when the guards spotted her. Falcon helms turned toward her, creaking together. Spear shafts slammed against cobblestones. Perhaps sensing the men's unease, the wyverns atop the columns shifted and ruffled their wings. Treale froze, hood pulled low. Her heart thrashed and she clutched her amulet tighter.

Be brave, Treale, she thought. Her throat constricted and she could barely breathe. *Be brave like King Elethor. You fled the last danger; today you will be strong.*

A guard detached from his phalanx and came marching toward her. He bore a round shield, and a red cape fluttered behind him. Treale fought down the urge to flee, though her knees shook and she had to force her breath through clenched teeth.

"What do you seek here?" the guard called.

Treale curtsied in the manner of Osanna. "I seek the weredragon, my lord." She spoke with her best Osannan accent, knowing she would never pass for a Tiran. "I come to see the beast."

When the guard reached her, he tugged her hood back. He cursed, and behind his falcon visor, his eyes narrowed. Her black hair, olive skin, and dark eyes were as foreign in this land as hippopotamuses—beasts that filled the Pallan—would be in Requiem.

"Osannan dog," the guard said. "You scum have been washing up on our shores and swarming our streets."

Treale let out a shaky breath. *Thank the stars.* Her accent had fooled him; he thought her a daughter of Osanna, that war-torn land of eastern men, and not a child of Requiem. Tirans perhaps hated the former, but they slaughtered the latter.

"My lord." She gave another quick curtsy. "I might be scum from the sea, but even scum hates the wretchedness of weredragons." She forced a snarl. "The weredragons burned my village in Osanna. They killed my father. He was a jailor in our land. Now I seek to be a jailor too—not in the ruins of my

Osannan town, but here in this land of southern glory. You keep
a weredragon imprisoned beneath the palace; I saw it chained and
whipped yesterday. If you'll have me, I will join your rank. I will
help you guard the beast, shackle it, and whip it too." She
clenched her fists. "I would enjoy beating it bloody."

The guard widened his eyes, silent for a moment, then
burst out laughing. Treale stood, barely daring to breathe. It was
a long moment before the guard could speak again.

"You!" he finally said. "You—a dog from Osanna, a land
of flea-ridden woolmongers—want to serve in the Palace of
Phoebus?" He raised his spear. "Find yourself a brothel to
spread your legs in. That is all your kind is good for, whore. Be
thankful we even let you do that much; I say we should butcher
your kind like weredragons." He raised his visor, revealing a
leathery face, and spat at her feet. "Kneel and clean the
cobblestones of my spit; that's what you Osannan scum are
worth."

Treale stood frozen, rage flaring within her. She was a
daughter of a great lord. She had flown by the King of Requiem
in battle. She was a warrior, a woman of starlight, a—

You are alone, a voice whispered inside her. *Your home is
gone; your father is dead and probably your king. Whatever nobility you once
claimed is lost.*

She bit down on her anger. If saving Mori meant giving
up some pride, well... she had enough of that pride to give.

She knelt. She cleaned the cobblestones with the hem of
her cloak. She clenched her jaw and tried to ignore the burning in
her eyes.

When she rose to her feet, she bowed her head and spoke
softly.

"I will clean for you in the dungeon, if you let me. If I
cannot stand there as a guard, let me serve you as a maid. I can
clean. I can cook for jailors. But one thing I insist upon." She

raised her eyes and met his gaze. "I want to work near the
weredragon's cell. Her people burned my village. I will watch her
suffer and I will hear her scream."

The guard looked over his shoulder at his phalanx, then
back to Treale. He reached into her cloak, cupped her breast, and
squeezed hard. Treale sucked in her breath and froze, daring not
move. She wanted to shift, she wanted to burn him, she wanted
to run... yet she could only stand here frozen between her pride
and Mori.

"Yesss," the guard said slowly, crushing her in his hand.
"Yes, I think we might just find you some work underground.
There are many cobblestones there for you to clean."

He released her, and Treale gasped with the pain, and her
legs shook.

Think of King Elethor, she told herself. *Think of how you lay
by his side, kissed his cheek, and flew with him. Think of the courage he gave
you.*

"Th-thank you, my lord!" she said to the guard. "I... I will
serve Tiranor as best I can."

He snorted. "Yes, we'll make sure that you do. Quite
often and quite well."

He grabbed her arm, digging his fingers so deep Treale
gasped and thought he'd tear her skin. He began dragging her
across the square, moving closer to the palace. Treale struggled to
match his wide strides; when once she fell, he dragged her until
she could walk again.

*Think of King Elethor. Think of how you kissed his cheek. Think
of the stars of Requiem; they shine here too.*

Soon the palace loomed above them. The staircase rose
hundreds of steps, ending with towering doors of ivory flanked by
faceless statues, each larger than a dragon. Above this gateway
rose walls and towers of limestone; the steeples clawed the sky.
Treale was expecting a long climb, but the guards dragged her past

this staircase toward a pathway alongside the palace. They walked along walls lined with archers. Fig and carob trees rose to her left; to her right rose the stone of Tiranor's center of power.

Finally they reached a small archway filled with a wooden door; a back entrance. More guardsmen waited here, spears crossed. The leathery-faced guard dragged Treale through the doorway and into the palace.

They moved through chambers and halls. The tiles gleamed white, and golden filigrees covered granite columns. Treale was hoping to see more of the palace; if any in Requiem still lived and hoped to fight, they would need the layout of this place. The guard, however, soon dragged her onto a staircase that plunged underground.

They descended for what seemed like miles, coiling deeper and deeper into darkness. Candles lit the rough walls. The steps were so narrow and craggy Treale nearly fell. Outside the palace, the sun had pounded her, and the heat had coiled around her like serpents. Here, as they descended, the air grew so cold that Treale shivered. Stairs led to tunnels, then stairs again, then doorways and more tunnels. This place reminded her of the labyrinth beneath Nova Vita where she and Mori would read books; these halls were just as dark and twisting. But Requiem's tunnels had also been warm and dry and safe. This place reeked of mold and echoed with distant screams.

Finally, after what seemed an hour of plunging, they reached a hall lined with cells, and those distant screams exploded like demons of sound.

Solina's dungeon, Treale thought and shivered.

"Sharik!" shouted the guard who held her arm. "Sharik, damn you. Come, boy. I have a treat for you."

At first Treale was sure the guard was calling his dog. When a burly, bald man came trundling up the tunnel, Treale realized: This was Sharik, and she was the treat.

"Sharik here, Sharik want treat," rumbled the man. "Give to Sharik!"

He had but three teeth, and moles covered his pasty lump of a head. He was wide and fierce-looking as a bull; a golden ring even pierced his flat nose. He wore a tattered canvas tunic, and a ring of keys jangled on his belt. His flesh was lumpy and pale like old turnips; Treale doubted the man had seen sunlight in a year.

The guard shoved Treale toward him, and Sharik caught her. The brute dug yellow, cracked fingernails into her arm. His breath assailed her, scented of rot. His nose sniffed at her cheek, and his tongue thrust out. Treale pulled back an inch, narrowly dodging the wet appendage.

"Give this one a job, Sharik," said the guard and laughed. "Have her empty your chamber pot, mop the blood off the floors, or even warm your bed at night if you please. I'll come for her some nights; on those nights she's mine. Do you understand, Sharik?"

The bullish man drooled and huffed. "Sharik likes treats."

He reached into Treale's cloak and tried to grope her. She struggled in his grasp, and he shoved her, then backhanded her. Pain exploded. White light flashed. She hit a wall, and Sharik raised his fist again.

"Sharik, no!" said the guard. "I want her beautiful. Do not scar this one. She is my gift to you; keep her pretty."

Sharik snarled, but when the guard reached for his sword, the jailor lowered his gaze and grumbled under his breath. His fingers still dug into her arm, so strong she thought he might break her bone. When the guard turned to leave, Treale almost wanted to call after him. *No, don't leave me here, don't leave me with this man, with these screams, with this smell of blood.* Yet she remained silent. Mori was somewhere here in this nightmare; Treale would stay, and she would save her.

"Come," Sharik grumbled, his voice like cascading stones. "Follow Sharik. Work for you."

He pulled her down the hall, trundling like a bear. Treale dragged behind him, and as they passed along the cells, she nearly gagged. She bit down on a scream.

Stars, no... how could such terror exist? Stars, how could such evil lurk in this world?

Prisoners filled the cells, broken and shackled and turned into wrecks of humanity. One man hung from chains, his legs cut off and the stumps still dripping. In another cell, children hung upon the walls, their skin burned off, their eyes pleading and their mouths gagged. In a third cell, a jailor was busy stretching a man on the rack; the prisoner howled, his arms dislocated. Treale wanted to close her eyes. She wanted to weep. She wanted to fall and curl up and never look at these horrors again. Yet she forced herself to look. Somewhere, in one of these cells, Mori languished.

Stars, Mori, I'm so sorry. Now Treale could not help it; tears streamed down her cheeks. *I'm so sorry you are here.*

Yet where *was* the princess? Before Treale could find her, Sharik pulled her into a cell. This one was empty. Chains hung from the ceiling and fresh blood and hair covered the floor. For a moment, Treale was sure the jailor would imprison her here, and she made to flee, but he grabbed her and grunted.

"Clean!" he said. "Clean cell. Clean floor."

He stepped back into the hall, grabbed a bucket and rags, and shoved them at her.

"Clean! Clean and you eat later. Clean floor."

When Treale hesitated, Sharik grabbed a whip from the wall. Before Treale could react, he landed a blow across her shoulder. She yelped. The whip lashed through her cloak and tore her skin.

"Clean!" Sharik said. "Clean floor. Make clean for next prisoner."

Her welt blazing, her eyes still damp, Treale knelt. She grabbed a rag and dipped it into the bucket of water. She began to scrub.

"Faster!" Sharik said and his whip landed again. Treale yelped, her back blazing, and cleaned faster.

"When I'm done cleaning," she said and dared to look up, "I want to see the weredragon. I—"

The whip landed a third time, blazing against her from shoulder to tailbone. Treale arched her back and yowled with the pain. Sharik grumbled and clenched his fists.

"Speak again and Sharik take your teeth. Clean. Faster."

Treale cleaned. She did not speak again.

When the cell's floor was clean and the rags bloody, Sharik grabbed her by the hair. He yanked her up and dragged her out into the hallway. Treale yelped, her hair tearing in his paws, but he only tugged harder. He dragged her into a second chamber, closed the oak door, and locked it behind them.

This must have been his home, though it was barely better than the prisoners' cells. The chamber was rough and bare. It contained only a straw bed, a table laden with candles and dirty dishes, a chamber pot, and a chest of old rags.

"You sleep on floor," Sharik said. "Sleep!"

He raised his whip. Treale clenched her fists behind her back. She was a slight woman, thin and short and not very strong, and he was thrice her size. But she was young, she was fast, and she could fight him. There was no room to shift here, but she could grab his whip and strangle him, or gouge out his eyes, or....

No, she told herself. *Even if you can defeat him, Treale Oldnale, he'd holler and guards will swarm here. Save Mori. Even if you must give up some pride. You might sleep on a floor this night, but Mori sleeps in chains.*

She lay down on the floor like an obedient pup, hugged her knees, and looked up at Sharik. He stared down at her, his feet by her head, their nails cracked and moldy. Finally he grunted in approval, lolloped toward his bed, and climbed in. Soon the man was snoring like a saw, his drool seeping.

Treale rose to her feet. Her heart raced. The candles still burned upon the table, casting soft light. She tiptoed toward the bed and stared down at Sharik.

His keys.

They still dangled from his belt, each one longer than her hand. If Mori languished in this prison, one of these keys would open her cell. Holding her breath, Treale reached toward the ring of them.

Sharik snorted and rolled over, burying the keys under his girth.

Treale cursed this dungeon, cursed the gods, cursed every grain of sand in this desert and every brick in this dungeon. She reached around the brute, but he would not stir. She tried to roll him over; he would not wake or move. He kept drooling, and his snores kept rising, and the keys remained trapped.

Finally Treale fell to the floor, closed her eyes, and trembled. She was so weak, so tired; she could barely summon the will to breathe. Her belly ached with hunger. Sharik had never fed her as promised, and she felt too weak to crack open her second pomegranate. Her wounds blazed. Worst of all, the images of the prisoners would not leave her: their anguished eyes, their broken flesh, their seeping blood. Again and again, she saw Mori outside the palace gates, frail and screaming as they beat her.

"I will find you, Mori," she whispered into the darkness. "If not tonight, then tomorrow, or the day after, but I swear to you, I will find you, and I will free you."

She looked up at Sharik again; he had not budged, and his snores rose louder than ever. Treale wanted to try to move him again; with all her strength, perhaps she could roll him onto the floor, but what if he woke and beat her? He would soon roll over on his own, Treale told herself. After all, how comfortable could it be, sleeping on his keys? She had to wait but a moment longer. Maybe two moments. Maybe...

Her eyes closed. Blackness tugged at her. She lay, curled up and shivering, and slumber pulled her into a deep, dark nightmare of mangled bodies and shrieking falcons of steel.

SOLINA

She flew through the night, a phoenix of crackling fire and claws of molten steel. The desert streamed below her. She opened her beak and cawed to the darkness. She was fire. She was gold. She was might. She called to her lord the Sun God, and his glory rose from the eastern dunes to kindle her empire. The sand and clouds burned with his might. She flew through the dawn, a bird of beauty, a light to banish the darkness.

She had brought this fire to Requiem; the weredragons had doused it with their dark magic. She had brought wyverns and acid to their halls; they had fled.

But they cannot fight the nephilim. They cannot flee my long arm. Their halls are fallen; their skulls will be mine.

She had left her men in Irys, her oasis jewel. Today she flew alone. Today was a day of her glory.

I was born for today. You will see my power, Elethor. You will see my light.

The agony rose inside her, twisting like demon claws in her womb. A child had grown there, a life she had created with Elethor. The small light had died; her soul had extinguished with it. In her dreams, he cried to her, her son of golden skin and blue eyes, a paragon of light, a holy son—a gift to the world.

For you, she thought. *For you I burn. For you I conquer. They killed you, my son. The weredragons killed you, and I will slaughter them all, and it will not be enough. For you I raise this army; in your memory the nephilim shall rise.*

She screamed to the sky, wings showering flame.

The mountain rose before her in the south, an edifice of stone under a yellow sky. It rose taller than the peaks of Amarath Mountains where she had crushed the Weredragon Army. It rose taller than the great mountains of Ranin where she would make love to Elethor in their youth. It rose like her empire, undying, eternally strong.

When she flew closer, she saw that towers, archways, and walls covered the mountain, ancient beyond reckoning, faded into mere hints of their past glory. Steeples, once topped with battlements, now rose crumbling like melted candles. Archways, once gleaming in welcome, now rose craggy like the mouths of caves. Walls, once bright with soldiers and banners, snaked across the mountain like the faded trails of goats.

This had been a great fortress once—an entire city, a palace that had housed myriads. Thousands of years had passed since the Ancients had raised it. This was all that remained: rugged boulders, snaking trails, echoing chambers. In the rains and winds of time, the fortress had melted into the mountain like a corpse's flesh melting into the earth.

The sun crackled overhead. Heat waves rose from the endless dunes. Solina flew toward the mountain, a comet of fire. As a phoenix, her wings were two hundred feet wide; she was a beast of wrath. And yet the mountain dwarfed her. She felt like a mere spark by this stone edifice.

A great archway loomed upon the mountainside, as tall and wide as Queen's Archway back in the capital. Shadows loomed beyond. When Solina flew near, her flames lit a hall carved from living rock.

She shrieked—an eagle's cry that echoed down the mountainside—and flew through the doorway.

Walls of stone streamed at her sides. Her flaming wings beat, sending dust flying to reveal chipped mosaics of coiling serpents and manticores. The firelight leaped against the walls. The hall drove into the mountain, its ceiling a hundred feet tall.

The nephilim will emerge from this canal like a child from its mother's womb. I will be their mother.

She landed upon the dusty mosaic. She shifted into human form. Her flames writhed around her, then gathered into the amulet she wore around her neck. She clutched the amulet in her hand and raised it, casting its light against the grand hall of the Palace of Whispers.

Once this place had been beautiful. Once the Ancients had lived here, a people of golden light. Statues rose here, faded now with the years, showing a people slim and fair, their heads oval, their eyes almond-shaped, their hair flowing. Once the limestone statues had held blades; today but stumps of rusted metal remained.

"Once you ruled this world," Solina whispered to the statues. "But you sinned. You lay with the demons of the Abyss. You birthed the nephilim. They destroyed you, but I will rule them." She clenched her fist around her amulet. "You buried and sealed them. You tried to hide the shame of your spawn. They were your children and you shackled them. I will free them. I will rule what you imprisoned."

She walked deeper into the hall and entered a doorway. A dark corridor loomed before her, and she walked upon limestone tiles, her sandals clattering. Her light shone upon walls covered with silver runes and faded murals. The Ancients had drawn their wars here, a hundred feet tall upon the walls of their palace. The murals rose around her, painted in faded blacks, golds, and reds.

Solina saw hordes of men, great armies in steel, tossing spears and shooting arrows at their enemy. Painted nephilim charged across the walls, life-sized, thrice the height of men. The giants lumbered, bat wings spread wide, fangs and claws painted a faded blood red. Men died between their teeth and under their feet, crushed and devoured. Solina raised her amulet high, shining her light. The painting of a great nephil covered the ceiling, spines dangling from its jaws, a flaming halo around its head. Solina smiled to imagine the nephilim walking again, feasting upon the weredragons' backbones.

She explored the Palace of Whispers for hours. She climbed staircases and gazed upon shadowy halls. She moved through chambers where stood hundreds of statues, stone armies of sandstone and gold. She walked down winding halls lined with dozens of doors, labyrinths like the veins of a giant. The palace seemed endless. Solina thought that all the people of Tiranor, two million souls, could reside within these halls and think them roomy. This was not merely an abandoned palace, but a city.

No, not even a city; an entire kingdom, she thought. She walked through chambers where thousands of sarcophagi rose, tombs for ancient kings and warriors. She moved deeper and deeper into the mountain. She thought that the sun outside must have set. She thought that she could walk here for days—for years.

Finally, after what seemed like eras of wandering, a shriek shattered the silence.

Solina froze.

The scream was mournful, echoing, a cry like a dying star. It rolled through the palace, torn in agony, a call of ancient pain, of lingering torment, of fallen ones begging for revenge. She had heard such screams in Requiem when toppling her halls. She herself had screamed that way when the weredragons murdered her child.

Now the nephilim screamed, and Solina smiled.

"I am coming to you, my children," she whispered.

The scream died and echoed. A hundred screams then rose together, a chorus of screeches, groans, and wails. The palace reverberated. Dust rained as bricks shifted. A column cracked.

"I come to you, fallen children!" Solina shouted.

Her voice echoed down dark halls. She walked under vaulted ceilings, her light shining in the dark. The screams rose.

"Free us!" they screeched.

"The pain! End the pain!" they cried.

"Enough, enough!" they howled. "The pain must end!"

Solina raised her arms as she walked, casting her light upon halls as large as her entire palace in Irys. A grin spread across her face. She followed the screams through the darkness.

"I have the key, twisted ones!" she called. "Your savior comes to you!"

The screams swirled. The creatures wept and laughed and roared and shrieked.

"Savior! Savior!"

"We will crush bones, we will drink blood!"

"Legion will lead! Legion will kill!"

The Palace of Whispers trembled around her. A statue of a priest fell and shattered. Cracks spread along the ceiling. The screams of the nephilim raced like demons through the halls, so loud Solina could barely hear her own cries.

"Ten thousand years you languished here!" she shouted. "Today I free you, Fallen Ones. Today you will drink the blood of the world that tortured you!"

The palace echoed and shook with their cries.

She descended a coiling staircase. The screams rained against her. She crossed a dark hall lined with statues. The voices wept and begged. She reached an iron door that shone a deep gray; it towered taller than dragons. The screams crashed like falling empires.

"I have come, nephilim!" she shouted and laughed. "I come to free you!"

Red light and shadows scurried around the door. Claws reached under the doorframe, scratching at the iron. Blood dripped through the keyhole and between the hinges.

"Free us, free us!" they begged.

"End the pain!"

"End the hunger!"

Solina drew the key from her belt. It thrummed and gleamed in her hand, so hot it nearly burned her. A force was tugging it toward the lock; Solina barely kept it in her hand.

"I am Solina Pheobus!" she howled above the screams. "I am Queen of Tiranor! I am the Destroyer of Requiem! I free you, nephilim. You will follow my light to flesh and bone and blood!"

The red light streamed across her. Her key flared like a rising sun. Screaming and laughing, Solina placed the key into the lock.

She twisted.

Light and blood and sound exploded.

The Iron Door blazed like sunrise, then shattered into a million shards. Howls and stench rose. Shadows leaped. From the darkness, the nephilim swarmed.

Solina raised her arms above her, dwarfed by the giants, but shining bright with the light of her lord.

"Serve me, nephilim! I am Solina! I free you."

They spilled into the hall, weeping and shouting and swirling. They stood fifteen feet tall, giants of shriveled flesh, patches of scales, and diseased eyes. Their fangs tore at the walls. Their claws slashed. Their great wings, wide as the wings of dragons, beat the air. Their armor was rusted, their blades chipped, their chain mail hanging in shreds, yet still Solina knew: This was the greatest army the world had seen.

"We rise!" one shouted and wept tears of blood.

"We walk again!" cried another, a bloated beast with lines of teeth like stitches crossing its face.

They kept spilling from their prison, filling the halls, swarming across the caverns. A cry rose among them, a cry shriller and louder than all others, a screech like boiling oceans.

"Bow before Queen Solina!" The voice echoed. "I am Legion! I foresaw the savior. Bow before the Queen of Light!"

All around, the nephilim fell to their knees, wept, clawed the air, and screamed. They trembled. They kissed the floor.

"Hail Solina!" they cried. "Hail the prophet Legion! We rise!"

From the shadows of the prison, a great nephil emerged, taller than the others, reeking and rotten. He was an androgynous beast, a thing of ruin, but Solina deemed him male. A halo of fire burned around his brow; he alone among the beasts bore this crown. Solina knew this one from the old, whispered tales. He was Legion, spawn of a mortal priestess and a demon king—ruler of the nephilim.

Beneath his burning halo, strands of yellow hair dangled from his scarred head, caked with blood. Milky-white eyes burned in his face between oozing boils. He had no nose, only two slits for nostrils. Drool, blood, and sharp teeth filled his maw. His skin was rotten and torn, but muscles shone and rippled beneath it. His claws were long as swords and jagged black. Rust covered his armor and a great blade, taller than two men, hung at his side. He howled to the ceiling, arms raised and drool spraying.

"Hail Solina!" he cried. "I am Legion. I am Leader. I am Prophet. I serve you, Golden Queen! We are nephilim; we were fallen. We rise! We rise!"

They swarmed through the palace. They carried Solina upon their shoulders. They flapped wings, and clawed at walls, and shattered columns, and wept and praised her name. They flew to daylight. They flowed from the palace like a swarm of wasps from a nest. They filled the desert sky and howled at the sun. The land shook beneath them, the palace trembled, and the sand burned.

"Rise, nephilim!" cried Solina, caught in the storm of them, flying upon their glory. "Fill the world with your might! I will lead you to food. I will lead you to dragon bones and scales and blood to drink. Fly, nephilim! Fly north, fly to Requiem, and you will feast!"

The roared and sang and wept.

They flew.

Solina laughed and raised her arms and the sunlight bathed her.

MORI

She walked upon marble tiles, fallen birch leaves crunching underfoot and scuttling before her like orange mice. Marble columns rose around her, glowing like moonlight, and beyond them Mori saw the forests roll across hills, kindled red and gold and yellow with fall. She walked in Nova Vita, she thought, but she saw no houses, no snaking streets or smithies or forts, only mist, birches, and gliding leaves.

"Requiem," Mori whispered. Tears stung her eyes at the purity of her home.

These were the courts of Requiem. Mori knew these marble tiles, these columns, and the Oak Throne which stood before her in a beam of light. Here had her father ruled, and Elethor after him, yet Mori heard no flap of dragon wings beyond the columns, no sounds of mothers calling for children, no clank of armor or song of harps. She heard only the crunch of leaves, the distant song of birds, and the wind through the trees. The marble seemed purer than Mori had ever seen it; no scratches marred the floor or columns, and the letters engraved into them—spelling old prayers of Requiem—appeared crisp as if freshly chiseled.

Mori kept walking, approaching the beam of light where the Oak Throne rose upon a dais. Her breath caught. A figure stood before the throne! Though daylight shone through the mist, strands of starlight seemed to cloak the figure ahead. Mori clutched her luck finger and kept walking, and the figure of light descended from the dais and moved toward her.

When the figure drew nearer, emerging from the light, Mori saw a woman in golden armor, her hair a cascade of blond curls. Mori recognized the sword that hung from her side, its hilt jeweled and its scabbard filigreed with silver leaves; this was Stella Lumen, the sword Mori's father had borne, the sword Solina had broken.

"Queen Gloriae's sword," she whispered.

In her childhood, Mori had spent many hours praying in Gloriae's Tomb to the great marble statue of Requiem's legendary queen. Gloriae had defeated Dies Irae, the tyrant. Gloriae had raised Requiem from ruin and rebuilt this temple. Gloriae was her ancestor, the heroine of her childhood. Gloriae—not a statue or a legend from scrolls, but a woman of flesh and blood—now stood before her.

Mori knelt.

"My queen," she whispered.

Then she knew: This was not Requiem, or at least, not the Requiem she had known.

I died in the darkness of Solina's dungeon, she thought. *My body hangs from chains underground. My soul has risen to the starlit halls of my ancestors, and now I kneel before the soul of my great queen.*

She felt a hand on her shoulder, soft and warm as spring's morning light. Mori rose and stood before her queen, the woman who had founded Nova Vita three hundred years ago. Gloriae's eyes were green as deep forests, and her face was pale.

"Fly," the queen said.

Mori lowered her head. "I cannot."

Gloriae placed a finger under Mori's chin and lifted it. Her face was blank, the face of a statue, but an urgency filled her eyes.

"Fly," she whispered.

Mori looked up, expecting to see the vaulted ceiling she had always known. Instead she saw the sky awhirl with white clouds, a painting all in blue and white. A few of the columns were missing their capitals, and Mori realized: These were not the starlit halls of afterlife after all. This was the court of Requiem long ago, back when Queen Gloriae was rebuilding it, before the roof had even been raised. The sky of Requiem still shone upon the new Oak Throne. This was not her afterlife; this was a whisper of her past.

Mori turned to the east, looked between the birches, and saw two figures cloaked in light. Here were the other heroes of the great war, the founders of Nova Vita: Agnus Dei, clad in green, a woman of black curls and kind brown eyes; and Kyrie Eleison, Prince of Requiem, a young man of yellow hair and winking eyes, Mori's ancestor. They stood in the starlight, smiling softly upon her, waiting for her.

We will fly together through starlit halls, their voices whispered in her mind. *But not this day. Your tale does not end here.*

"Fly," Gloriae said again, and the queen held Mori's hands, sending warmth and love through her. "Become the dragon. You bear the golden scales like I do, a color of royalty and dawn. Become the golden dragon and fly. Find our sky. Find the light of stars in the dark."

Mori tried to shift here in the temple, to soar toward the sky, but pain blazed around her wrists and ankles, and her breath rattled in her lungs. She was so weak. She was so hungry, so hurt.

"I can't," she whispered. "I am chained. Iron binds me."

"And I wear steel and gold," said the queen, gesturing at her armor, "and I bear Stella Lumen, a shard of metal and light, the sword of my mother Queen Lacrimosa. And yet I can shift."

Starlight cascaded, the song of harps played, and the woman of golden curls was gone; instead a golden dragon stood before Mori, eyes green and sad.

A golden dragon, Mori thought. *Like me.*

"But... your armor is a part of you," Mori said, standing small and thin before the great golden beast. "I can shift with my gown too, and with a good book that I love, if I hold it close to my breast. But I could never shift with armor, nor a sword, not like Lyana can." She placed her hand upon the golden dragon's head. "You are a great warrior, Gloriae! You fought the armies of Dies Irae himself and slew so many. You can shift encased in steel; I cannot."

Yet why could Lyana shift in armor? Mori wondered. She had seen the knight shift with sword, shield, and helm; they all melted into her dragon form, then reappeared when Lyana became human again. Yet Mori had seen the knight once try to shift while holding a harp, a musical instrument she had never mastered; Lyana had become the blue dragon, and the harp had clattered to the floor.

Gloriae nodded, as if she could read Mori's thoughts.

"We can shift," the golden dragon said, "with what is *ours*, with what is *us*. My armor is a part of me, a steel skin. A book is a part of you, a piece of your soul upon parchment."

Mori stood in the court of Requiem, clad in a white gown, yet when she raised her wrists, the skin was red and raw; she could feel the chains around them, even here in this hall of light and ghosts.

"Will these chains be a part of me?" she whispered.

With silver light, Gloriae returned to human form. Softly the queen embraced Mori; her armor was cold, but her hair and arms were warm.

"We are part of you," Gloriae whispered into her ear. "We are with you. Always, daughter of Requiem. We fly with you even in your darkest hours. Surrender to the shackles. Let these chains become like arms of steel. They imprison you. They will let you fly."

The queen kissed Mori's forehead, lips warm and soft, and white light flowed, and for a moment Mori saw nothing but the glow of stars.

When the light cleared, she saw the dungeon again: the bloody floor, the brick walls, and the door before her. Once more she sat here in shadow, her arms shackled to the wall behind her, her ankles chained to the floor.

"Was it a dream?" she whispered, throat dry and voice raspy. Had she truly seen the spirit of Queen Gloriae and the great Kyrie Eleison and Agnus Dei? Had she seen a light from the starlit halls or a light from the past?

Mori lowered her head; it felt too heavy to hold up. Her stomach clenched, her back blazed with pain, and her eyes stung. She missed that hall of marble. She missed those birches. All lay burnt now, all was fallen.

We are with you, their voices whispered in the darkness, and Mori thought she could feel the warmth of starlight. *Always, daughter of Requiem. We fly with you even in your darkest hours.*

Mori closed her eyes, tightened her lips, and tried to shift.

Pain racked her body. She trembled. Golden scales began to appear across her. Her limbs began to grow, and claws sprouted from her fingers. Wings unfurled from her back. She could almost imagine the sky of Requiem, all blue and white and cold around her.

The chains bit deep, shoving Mori back into human form.

She sat trembling, head lowered, and coughed and blinked and gasped for breath. She could not stop shaking, and she tasted blood on her lips. Her eyes stung.

"I can't do it," she whispered. "I'm sorry, Gloriae. I want to fly with you. I want to go home."

She shook for long moments, ravaged with pain and weakness. Her skin felt hot; perhaps she was feverish. She closed her eyes and tried to breathe like Mother Adia had taught her: a slow breath in, a moment of healing, a slow breath out. She breathed again and again, letting the air—even the fetid air of this dungeon—flow through her body, soothe her trembling, and ease her pain. She imagined that she breathed the air over Requiem, the sky of her youth, a sky she vowed to find again.

She took one more great breath, filling her lungs, and tried to shift again.

She could see the sky. Clouds trailed across blue fields. Dragons flew there, hundreds of them—blue, green, gold, and a dozen other colors, all undulating on the wind, smoke trailing from their nostrils, wings gliding. She felt her own wings move behind her, and she raised her head, ready to soar.

Once more, the chains bit, and her magic fizzled.

She sat chained and trembling.

She thought of her books from the library of Requiem—books of adventures about brave knights, beautiful maidens, and dragons who flew to distant lands of wonder. She thought of her gowns, her harp, her dolls—the things she could always shift with, draw into herself, extensions of her body and soul.

She thought of these chains, things of cold metal, of pain. *They imprison you. They will let you fly.*

How long had she lingered here in the dungeon, shackled, wasting away? Several moons? Several years? These chains were parts of her now; she could barely remember a time without them.

They've become extensions of my arms. They've become like steel wings. They are part of me.

She tried to imagine that she'd been born shackled, that she would live and grow old and die in these chains. They were as parts of her as her clothes, as her old books, as her very bones.

They are me. They will shift into me, and I will take these irons into myself.

With a deep breath, she mustered her magic.

Wings thudded from her back.

Scales clanked across her.

With a pain like thrusting daggers, the chains flowed into her body.

Mori screamed.

The walls cracked. Her body ballooned and her head hit the ceiling. The chains snapped from the walls and molded into her, driving like steel demons as her magic spun. Smoke filled her nostrils, and her tail flailed beneath her, and she was a dragon, a frail and thin golden dragon trapped in the cell, freed, unchained, fire in her maw.

Always, daughter of Requiem. We fly with you even in your darkest hours.

Mori shook. She clawed at the door, again and again, until the hinges tore. She was weak, but her claws were still sharp, and the door splintered and tore apart.

Frail and wheezing, the golden dragon tumbled out from the chamber into a hallway. Shouts echoed and boots thudded. Mori could barely raise her head. She looked up to see Sharik rushing her way, a club in his hand.

Always, daughter of Requiem. We fly with you...

She tried to blow her fire; she could muster none. She was so weak. Only sparks left her maw. Sharik reached her, and his club swung, and Mori raised her claws. The jailor howled and Mori once more was flying over Nova Vita, wyverns all around her, as crossbows fired and spears dug into her flesh.

BAYRIN

Bayrin stood in the forest camp, stuffing his supplies into his pack, when Piri Healer marched up toward him, raised her chin, and announced: "Bayrin, I'm flying with you to find the salvanae."

The camp bustled around them. Over a thousand Vir Requis had been hiding here in Salvandos, several leagues west of the border with Requiem, since Nova Vita's fall. The forest spread around them, leaves red and gold and crunching underfoot, giving way to a chalky mountain that rose like a wall. Elders were tending to pots of simmering stew, children ran playing with wooden swords, and guards in muddy armor patrolled the palisade of sharpened spikes that surrounded the camp.

They had been living here for several moons now, and Bayrin had done his best to avoid Piri during this time. Packing his things today, he had congratulated himself on avoiding her until his very last day here... and now as she stood before him, chin raised and arms crossed, he cursed under his breath.

"Piri," he said and glared, "I fly alone."

She glared back with those lavender eyes he used to marvel at, and which he now hated. She was a tall woman, taller even than most men, and Bayrin had always felt uneasy around women this tall. She wore the white robes of a healer, the hems muddy, and her dark hair fell across her shoulders in two braids. When she scrunched her lips, Bayrin couldn't help but remember kissing those lips four years ago, and the memory sickened him.

"Bayrin Eleison!" she said and placed her hands on her hips. "You know the old saying: Those who fly alone die alone. I'm not letting you fly alone to seek aid from the salvanae. I'm going with you, like it or not."

Bayrin groaned so loudly he blew back a curl of his hair. It had been *four years* since he'd kissed her, and since then, it seemed Piri followed him everywhere. Before the wars, she would sneak into Castra Murus, barracks of the City Guard, and try to slink into his bed at night. Whenever he would pass her in Nova Vita, she would gaze at him lovingly, sending him fleeing. Even here, in this camp, she had been giving him longing looks for moons now, and he had barely avoided her.

Looking at those flashing, lavender eyes, Bayrin sighed. It was not that he hated Piri; truly, he did not. But stars, why did she have to pursue him so urgently?

So I kissed her. So what? They had rolled around in the hay a few years ago, and she had demanded marriage. Not a week had gone by since their first kiss, and Piri had already planned what they'd name their children. Bayrin had tried telling her he was too young for marriage—and certainly too young for children. He had tried to avoid her since. Yet year after year, she pursued him, tried to kiss him again, even tried to lie with him, and nothing could dissuade her.

"Piri," he said and frowned. "No. Just no. I know why you want to fly with me, and it won't work."

It was her turn to snort. She rolled her eyes. "Bayrin, don't you get a big head. Do you *truly* think I'm still infatuated with you? I'm long over what happened between us; not every girl in camp loves you, Bayrin Eleison, despite what you might think." She raised her nose at him. "I want to fly with you because I know Salvandos. I've visited Har Zahav before, the mountain where the salvanae live, to train as a healer. You need me as your guide. I've spoken to King Elethor about this, and he quite agrees. Ask him if you like; he will command you fly with me."

Bayrin sighed. He could just imagine Elethor's grin. On many nights back in Nova Vita, Bayrin would complain about Piri's onslaught, and Elethor would howl with laughter. Whenever Elethor—just a young prince then—would see Piri in the city streets, he would point her toward Bayrin and wink as the young woman began her pursuit. One time, when Bayrin had been hiding in an alehouse, Elethor had smuggled Piri inside under his cloak, then laughed for days about the mugs Bayrin had broken trying to flee the place.

"Of course Elethor would say that," he muttered.

He grabbed his longsword and buckled it to his belt, careful avoid Piri's gaze. As he was packing his pan, cutlery, and tinderbox, she kept standing with hands on hips, merely staring. As he was counting his rations—strings of sausages, sacks of oats, and jars of preserves—she began tapping her foot.

"Are you quite ready, Bayrin Eleison, or are you going to wait until the nephilim kill us all?"

He groaned, slammed an apple into his pack, and sealed it shut. He straightened, slung the pack over his back, and glared at her.

"I'm ready," he said. "Are you ready? To shut your mouth, that is?"

"Very clever, Bayrin." She nodded at his sword. "Why take a blade? Surely you could slay an enemy without it; they'll groan to death at your jokes."

She hefted her own pack, which hung across her back. Bayrin grumbled. He couldn't help but notice how the pack's straps pulled her silk robes taut, exposing her curves, or how her lips twisted as she smiled. A memory pounded through him: Piri four years ago, sneaking into his chamber and doffing her cloak to stand nude before him. They had made love three times that sweaty summer night.

With a grunt, Bayrin shoved the memory aside.

It's Mori I love, he thought, and sadness flowed over his memories of Piri's kisses. Mori—pure and beautiful, the love of his life. *Stars, Mori, I won't forget you, not now, not ever. I will find you, and when I do, I'll never let you go again.*

Eyes stinging, he shifted into a green dragon. He kicked off the earth, crashed through branches, and soared into the sky. He began flying west and shouted over his shoulder.

"If you want to fly with me, Piri, you better fly fast. I wait for no one."

The trees shook as she soared, a lavender dragon with silver horns. Her body was long and slim, her scales were bright, and fire flicked between her teeth. She flew like an arrow. Bayrin cursed, turned his gaze back west, and flapped his wings mightily.

He'd always been a fast dragon—not as fast as Mori, perhaps, but close. He flew now with every last bit of strength, determined to lose Piri over the wilderness. The forests streamed below him, an endless sea of red and gold. Mountain peaks rose ahead, white against the sky and cloaked in clouds. Bayrin dived between them on the wind, the scents of autumn in his nostrils. He flew toward a valley and streamed over a lake. His reflection raced across the water; the reflection of a lavender dragon raced there too.

Bayrin looked over his shoulder to see Piri close behind. Blasts of smoke rose from her nostrils. She snarled at him and beat her wings mightily.

"Bloody stars!" he cursed, turned his head back west, and flew with new vigor.

For a healer, she's damn fast.

"You can't escape me, Bayrin!" she cried behind him. "I'm just as fast."

She had the speed; Bayrin had to admit that. But did she have the endurance? He snarled and flew faster than he'd ever flown. The lake ended and forests of oaks and maples rolled below him. He flew until his wings ached, and his lungs felt ready to collapse, yet whenever he glanced over his shoulder, he saw Piri mere feet behind him. She panted, and her eyes were narrowed to slits, but she kept flying.

How many leagues did he fly? Bayrin couldn't tell; dozens perhaps. His body ached. He remembered flying across the northern sea with Mori, seeking the Crescent Isle, and the memory stung his eyes.

I wish you were flying here with me, Mori. We will fly together again. I promise you.

The sun began to set, and still the blasted lavender dragon flew behind him. Bayrin wanted to keep flying, but smoke rose thickly from his maw, and he was weary, so weary he wanted nothing more than to crash down and fall asleep.

Bloody stars, I'll lose the damn girl tomorrow, he thought and began to dive down. He spotted a clearing between trees where grass grew along a stream. He spiraled down, landed upon the grass, and shifted into human form. It was cold—damn cold—but still sweat drenched him. He knelt by the stream and drank deeply.

Piri landed by him, claws digging into the grass, and shifted too. She panted, and sweat dampened her hair and robes. She too approached the stream, knelt so close by him that their bodies touched, and also drank. She glanced at him, mouth dripping, and flashed a grin.

"Good flight." She reached up and tousled his hair.

He turned aside with a grunt, trudged away from the stream, and lay upon the grass. He was too weary to eat supper, and besides, eating meant having to stay awake around Piri. He turned his back toward her, placed his head upon his pack, and pulled his cloak over him as a blanket. He paused long enough only to kick off his boots, then closed his eyes.

Her voice spoke softly beside him. "Bayrin?"

He ignored her.

She spoke softly again, and he felt her fingers in his hair. "Bayrin, are you sleeping?"

He grumbled under his breath, keeping his eyes stubbornly shut, though he could feel her looking at him. The woman was a leech! He had never met anyone so clingy. He did not want to speak to her. He did not want to remember her kisses, those warm kisses that used to intoxicate his youth. He did not want to remember her lithe, naked body pressed against him, the warmth of her as they made love, her teeth biting his shoulder, or...

Stop it. He ground his teeth. *Stop thinking about her, Bayrin. It's Mori you love. It's Mori you are sworn to protect. Just ignore Piri.*

He lay still for long moments, pretending to sleep, and she did not speak again. Finally he heard her lie down behind him. She wriggled in the grass, and he felt her pressed up against his back. Her arm reached over him, and she nestled close under his cloak.

He groaned.

"Piri!" he said. "What are you doing?"

She cuddled against him, arm draped over him. He could feel her breasts press against his back, and her hand strayed down, moving dangerously close to the very last parts he wanted her near. He sucked in his breath.

"I'm trying to sleep," she whispered, her lips touching his ear. "I thought you were sleeping too."

He wriggled in the grass, moving away from, placing a good foot of space between them.

"Well, sleep away from me!" he said and closed his eyes tight.

He heard her stand, walk around him, then lie down on his other side. When he opened an eye, he saw her facing him. She wiggled closer to him, so close that she pressed against his chest. She sneaked under his cloak, draped an arm and leg over him, and cuddled.

"But I'm cold and I forgot my cloak at the camp," she said.

"Not my problem, Piri."

His cheeks flushed. *Stars damn it.* Her body against his was affecting him, like it or not. She pressed close against him, felt his arousal, and smiled.

"Please, Bayrin? I don't want to freeze to death." She closed her eyes, still smiling, and nuzzled her cheek against his cheek. "I'm just going to sleep. I know you still love Mori. I'm not going to do anything, I promise. Just... sleep..."

Her voice softened, and soon she was breathing deeply, sound asleep against him.

Bayrin cursed inwardly. He cursed Piri. He cursed Elethor for sending her here. He cursed the desert of Tiranor, and he cursed his own blood for boiling. Piri mumbled in her sleep and cuddled even closer, pressing hard against him. Stars, how would he possibly sleep like this?

He sighed. It would be a long night. It would be a long quest.

TREALE

She was stoking the fireplace in Sharik's small, craggy chamber when she heard shouts, ran into the dungeon corridor, and saw the golden dragon.

Her breath died and for an instant Treale froze, eyes stinging and fingers trembling.

She had been working in this dungeon for six days now, serving her master, Sharik. For six days she had swept his floor, stoked his fireplace, cooked his meals, and—she cringed to think of it—emptied his chamber pot and washed his foul tunics. For six days she had cleaned up after his work, mopping blood and gore from under the bodies he tortured. For six days he would grumble, fondle her, slap her if she met his eyes, and spit upon her. For six days she had tried to grab his keys—but whenever she inched close, she earned another smack that left her head ringing, and at nights his girth would cover his treasure.

And Mori was so close! Treale had heard the princess whimper down the hall, and she longed to run to her, to whisper under the door, to comfort her, to let Mori know she was here. And yet how could she?

During the days, Sharik kept her at his side. She would mop blood from cells where prisoners hung, their flesh lacerated, their skin peeled. She would collect the fingers he severed and burn them. She would bring water and food to whimpering or screaming mouths, trying to keep these broken bodies alive.

And yet the chamber at the hall's end where Mori lay... that was forbidden. In that chamber lay Tiranor's greatest prize, the Weredragon Princess herself. Only Sharik brought food and water to that chamber. Only Sharik mopped the blood from that floor. Even at nights when Sharik slept, Treale could not approach Mori's shadowy cell. During those long cold nights, Treale languished in her own prison—locked with Sharik in his room, forced to sleep on the floor by his chamber pot and gobs of drool.

And now—after six days of blood and screams that would forever haunt Treale—Mori's chamber door lay shattered across the corridor, and Sharik ran toward the frail dragon that emerged from it.

With a gasp, Treale began running too.

This corridor was narrow, but the golden dragon was frail enough to fit, her scales dulled and her wings limp. Mori tried to blast Sharik with fire, but only sparks left her mouth, and only wisps of smoke left her nostrils. She tried to lash her claws, but Sharik's club swung down, and Mori whimpered and fell against the wall.

Sharik raised his club again, prepared to shatter the dragon's head.

With a scream, Treale leaped and clung onto the jailor's back.

"Treale!" Mori cried.

Sharik howled and bucked beneath her, and Treale screamed and clutched his throat, trying to choke him. His club flailed and slammed against a wall. He swung the club backward, and pain blazed across Treale's shoulder. She yowled. She thought the blow might have shattered her bone. She slid off Sharik's back and slammed against the floor. The club swung down, and she rolled aside. The club cracked the floor by her, and Treale kicked, hitting Sharik's leg.

He crashed down atop her, and Treale gasped and yelped. His weight was immense; he was thrice her size. His hand reached out, fingers thick and clammy, and clutched her throat.

Treale gurgled for breath. She clawed at his hand, but it was like clawing a slab of ham. She drew blood but could not break his grip. Stars floated before her eyes. She thought her neck would snap. Sharik snarled above her, drooling onto her face; his eyes were mad. Treale kicked, again and again, hitting his belly; it was like kicking a soggy old mattress. He seemed not to feel the pain, and his fingers kept clutching her throat, and blackness spread across her vision.

Her eyes rolled back.

Goodbye, Mori, she thought. *Goodbye, Requiem. I'm sorry. I failed you, Mori. I failed.*

Sharik howled.

The fingers loosened around her neck.

Treale gasped for breath, a gasp she thought could swallow the world. The blackness pulled back from her eyes like curtains, and stars exploded across the dungeon. She struggled to her feet, clutching at her throat and hacking, and saw Sharik howl. Mori's horns had gored him; they pierced his back and emerged bloody from his chest. The blood soaked his tunic and sprayed Treale's face.

His club lay fallen. Treale grabbed it and swung. The wood *cracked* against Sharik's skull. She felt the blow reverberate up the club, up her arm, and into her shoulder.

Sharik tilted, head caved in, and crashed to the floor. He lay still, dead eyes staring, blood pooling beneath him.

Behind him, the slim golden dragon mewled, and her magic left her. Where a dragon had stood, pressing against the corridor walls, now lay a frail, scarred woman with pale skin and wispy hair.

Treale leaped over Sharik's body and knelt over Mori. She cradled her princess in her arms, and her tears splashed against Mori's cheek.

"Mori," she whispered, holding her princess close. "Mori, I'm here. I've come for you. I'm going to get you out of here."

Mori felt so thin in her arms, barely more than skin and bones. The princess smiled softly, a ghostly smile, and her eyelids fluttered.

"Treale," she whispered. "Are you really here? Is this a dream?" She reached up with a frail arm—stars, it was nothing but skin and bone!—and clung to Treale's shoulder. "Treale, I saw them! I saw Queen Gloriae, and Kyrie Eleison and Agnus Dei—the heroes from the old scrolls. They fly with us."

Treale's throat still throbbed with pain, and her arms shook with weakness, but she gritted her teeth and struggled to pull Mori to her feet. Other guards often patrolled these dungeons; they could appear any moment.

"Come, Mori! Stand. We have to go now. We have to run."

She looked around, waiting for guards to appear. Boots thumped somewhere above and screams echoed through the chambers. She growled as she pulled Mori to her feet. The princess could barely stand; she leaned against Treale, her arms around her shoulders.

"You have to walk as fast as you can," Treale said. She began to take slow steps down the hall. "Lean on me and let's get out of this nightmare."

Yet Mori did not move. She looked back at Sharik's body, a lump of warty white flesh and oozing blood.

"Wait," the princess whispered. "We need to free the others."

Treale hissed between gritted teeth, whipping her head back and forth. *Stars damn it!* she thought. The shouts of guards still echoed above; no doubt they had heard the fight, and they would burst into this corridor any moment. And yet... Mori was right, she knew. Other screams echoed here: the screams of prisoners who filled the cells, hanging from the walls, skin lashed and bodies broken.

We can't leave them here, Treale thought.

She moved back to Sharik's body. For six nights, he had lain snoring upon his keys; it took dying for him to lie upon his other side, the keys exposed. Still holding her princess, Treale grabbed the ring of keys and wrenched it off Sharik's belt.

"Come on, Mori!" she said, keys in one hand, club in the other. "Hold onto me and walk, and we're going to get everyone out of here."

She began moving down the corridor, heels digging into the floor, breath rattling and body aching. The screams rolled above, and boots still thumped, and steel clashed. Yet still the guards did not appear. What was happening in the upper chambers? Treale did not have time to guess. It sounded like a hundred soldiers were clanking above her; she knew she had only moments before they arrived.

Mori limped by her, arms around her neck, and Treale stumbled toward one cell. She thrust the keys into the door's lock. The lock clanked, and the door opened to reveal a cell with three prisoners.

The men lay upon the floor, bloodied and whimpering. Sharik had dislocated their arms upon the rack. They trembled, pale and sickly and coughing, blood upon their backs. For a moment Treale could only stand, breath wheezing, head spinning.

How can we do this? Guards shouted above. Hundreds filled the palace, and thousands filled the city. Scores of prisoners filled this dungeon, and most were too ill, frail, and wounded to walk; she could not carry them all.

Did I travel to Tiranor only to die in darkness? Did I survive the fire over Requiem, and fly through smoke and blood, to fall with my princess underground?

Treale tightened her lips. *No. No, I will not die here.* She knelt by the prisoners, somehow holding her club, her keys, and Mori. She growled. *We will not die like rats in Tiranor's bowels. We will find our sky. We will fly over Requiem again.*

"You must stand!" she said to the prisoners. "Stand and flee! Move, now, before guards arrive."

The prisoners crawled, struggling for breath, struggling to rise. One managed to stand, leaning against a wall, then fell and mewled. The others could not even do that. More wails rose from the other chambers, and voices cried out to her, begging for freedom, begging for death. Tears stung Treale's eyes, and she let out a frustrated yowl.

"How can I do this, Mori?" she whispered. The princess still leaned against her, so frail she could barely support her own weight. "How can we free them? There are so many... so many wounded..."

The prisoners were crawling toward her, bloody hands outreached, when a shriek pierced the dungeons.

It was a shriek like shattering glass, like rending souls, the primordial cry of ancient evil. It was so loud, the dungeon shook and dust rained, and Treale dropped club and key and covered her ears. The prisoners moaned and fell. The floor shook and cracks raced along the wall. Mori winced and also covered her ears, and the shriek kept flowing, rising to an impossible pitch, so shrill Treale thought her eardrums might rip.

When finally the shriek ended, Treale turned to face the cell door. She raised her club. Outside in the hall, a shadow was stirring.

Stars of Requiem, be with me.

The torchlight flickered madly outside, casting shadows and red light across the floor. Something was moving in the hall. Snorts rose and a stench like rotten flesh and mold invaded Treale's nostrils. A long shadow fell across the corridor outside the doorway, and the shriek sounded again, so loud Treale fell to her knees and winced and thought her skull might crack.

"Treale," Mori whispered. She trembled against her.

"Be strong, Mori," Treale whispered back. Her heart thrashed and her chest rose and fell. "Whatever walks outside, we will face it."

Was a wyvern crawling in the corridor? No, impossible; wyverns were too large to fit down here. Was it a phoenix? No; she would have felt the heat. Some beast, some evil, crawled outside the cell. Its breath snorted as if sniffing for flesh, and claws clanked against the floor, and the shadow neared, and finally the creature appeared at the doorway.

Treale froze. Such terror pounded through her she couldn't even scream.

She had faced wyverns in battle over Ralora Beach. She had seen the death of her parents. She had sailed from Osanna to Tiranor and survived for days in these dungeons, witnessing the blood and gore and agony of Tiranor's torture. Yet she had never seen anything that filled her with such pounding, twisting, screaming terror. Her teeth clenched, sweat drenched her, and her knees felt soft as wet cloth.

"Stand behind me, Mori," Treale whispered. Without removing her eyes from the creature, she knelt, placed Mori upon the floor, and straightened again. She raised her club with shaking, clammy hands.

The creature regarded her, one eye bright yellow, the other milky white and swollen. It crawled on hands and knees, body long and lanky, its bones thrusting against leathery skin. It looked almost like a man, but far too large; Treale guessed it would stand fifteen feet tall, if it had room to straighten. Leathern swings sprouted from its back, and its claws were long and thin. As it stared at her, its lips pulled back to reveal fangs like daggers.

When its tongue lolled, drool dripped and sizzled against the floor.

"Stand back!" Treale warned and raised her club. Her knees shook, but she snarled and stayed standing. "You will not enter this place."

Its tongue licked its chops, long and wet like a sea serpent. Its white eye spun madly, the size of a melon, oozing pus.

"Fleshhhh," it hissed, eyes blazing. "We must eat, yes, we must lick blood, we must suck marrow. Fleshhh."

Quick as a spider, it scuttled on hands and knees into the chamber.

Treale yelped and leaped back. She swung her club, and it clanged against the demon's shoulder. The beast barely seemed to notice. Its head whipped from side to side, taking in the cell, like a starving man stumbling upon a feast and for a moment overcome, not sure which dish to devour first. Mori crawled into the corner, face pale, and Treale stood over her, club trembling in her hands. The beast gave them a stare, then looked back at the prisoners who mewled upon the floor. It finally seemed to make up its mind.

It pounced onto one prisoner, a man with dislocated arms and severed fingers, and began to feast.

Treale winced and Mori yelped. Blood and entrails splattered. The prisoner gave a last scream, then died as the beast fed. It ate greedily, claws lashing and teeth ripping flesh, then turned and pounced upon a second prisoner. The man screamed as the creature sucked up his entrails. The third prisoner, back lashed and legs broken, whimpered and began crawling away, but the demon leaped upon him too, and more blood splashed.

"Come on, Mori!" Treale cried. She grabbed the princess and pulled her up. "Run, Mori!"

As the demon feasted upon the third prisoner, crunching bones and sucking organs, the two young women stumbled out into the hall.

A second shriek, coming from ahead, tore through the dungeon. Walls cracked and dust rained. Treale screamed and Mori whimpered. More shadows stirred, and a second beast scuttled into the dungeon, licking its chops. This one's flesh was so rotten, it hung in tatters, revealing white bones. It crawled forward, long and rail thin. Its nostrils flared, and with a howl, it burst into a cell where children hung from a wall. The beast began to feast, splattering blood. The children screamed and died between its teeth.

"Nephilim," Mori whispered, her arms around Treale's shoulders. Her voice was weak, and her arms shook.

"Demons?" Treale whispered.

"Half demons. I read about them in my books. Their fathers were demons from the Abyss who took human brides; these are their spawn." She began to limp forward again. "Hurry, Treale!"

They rushed down the corridor as the nephilim screeched and slurped and feasted behind them. As they passed by cells, they saw that the prisoners had already been devoured. The doors lay shattered, and only bits of hair and bloodied chains remained beyond them. More screeches rose above; the dungeons were swarming with these creatures.

"More flesh!" rose cries behind them. "We must drink more blood! We crave more bones, comrades, and marrow to suck."

Treale's feet slogged through blood. The nephilim screeched behind her. Every step seemed a mile long. The staircase rose ahead; it would lead them out of darkness. It was only ten paces away, but seemed the distance of seas and forests. She walked on shaky legs, Mori leaning against her.

The shrieks swirled behind her, louder now. "More blood! More flesh to suck!"

Shadows danced. The torches flickered madly. The staircase was only five paces away now. When Treale looked over her shoulder, she saw the nephilim emerge from the chambers, maws bloody. They tossed their heads back and howled, and the dungeons shook.

The prisoners had only whetted their appetite, she realized. *And we're the main course.*

She yowled, clenched her jaw, and kept trudging forward. Mori was frail, but she seemed so heavy now; Treale's limbs were too weak, too thin. The creatures began scuttling behind them, claws clanking against the stone floor. Treale yowled and tried to run, but her feet slipped in the blood, and she crashed to her knees. Mori whimpered and fell beside her.

"Blood! Flesh! Fresh sustenance, comrades, fresh bones to snap!"

The two nephilim came charging toward them. Treale screamed and leaped to her feet. Was this corridor too small? Would the walls crush her? Would she crush Mori?

The nephilim snapped their teeth.

"Stand back, Mori!" Treale shouted, summoned her magic, and shifted.

Her body ballooned, becoming the dragon. Flames crackled in her maw. Her scaly flank shoved against Mori, pinning the princess to the wall. Treale howled, a black dragon trapped in the corridor like a clot in a vein. The nephilim screamed before her, and Treale blew her fire.

The flames exploded through the dungeon, crashed against the nephilim, and roared into the cells lining the corridor. The half demons shrieked, stones shattered, cracks raced along the ceiling, and bricks tumbled. Treale kept blowing her flames, and the beasts kept screaming. A chunk of the ceiling crashed against

Treale's back, and she howled. More stones slammed against the nephilim, and she heard one's spine snap. She kept roaring her fire, emptying every flame inside her, until the beasts lay burnt and broken and still.

Panting, head twisting with pain, Treale shifted back into human form. Smoke and flame filled the dungeon; she could barely breathe. She knelt above Mori, and tears filled her eyes. The princess lay on her back, eyes closed.

"Mori!" Treale called, lifted the princess in her arms, and shook her. "Mori, wake up. Stars, Mori!"

The princess lay still in Treale's arms. *Stars, did I crush her? Did I kill her?* She placed her ear against Mori's lips. A shaky sob fled Treale's own lips. Mori still breathed! Some life still filled her.

"I'm going to save you, Mori," she said.

She wrapped Mori in her cloak, then roared with pain as she lifted the princess. She was not much larger than Mori. And yet here in this dungeon, weakened and wounded, she slung Mori across her shoulders and began to climb the stairs.

Step by step, growling with effort, Treale carried her princess out of the dungeon. Screams rose above her: both the shrieks of nephilim and the cries of men. Treale kept climbing. The stairs seemed to twist forever, finally leading to corridors that twisted and chambers where blood flowed. Down one hall, she glimpsed a nephil scuttling and shrieking for blood; she heard more racing through the palace above her.

It seemed hours before Treale found the back door that led outdoors into sunlight.

The sun nearly blinded her, and for a moment Treale saw nothing but light; she had been underground for six days now. When she blinked, she saw the sky swarming with nephilim. Hundreds flew there, maybe thousands, lanky bodies twisting and coiling, black wings flapping. They shrieked and howled at the sun.

"Hail Queen Solina!" they cried. "Hail Legion! We are free! We will feast! We will devour dragons!"

Treale stared, frozen, and her eyes burned.

The world is overrun. Can we ever flee such evil?

She sniffed and tightened her grip on Mori; the princess still hung across her shoulder, wrapped in a cloak, unconscious and breathing softly.

"We're leaving this city," Treale said.

She began to trudge away from the palace, and soon she walked down an alley where people fled, pointed at the sky, and whimpered in corners. If anyone even looked Treale's way, they saw her carrying only a thin bundle wrapped in cloth, perhaps some kindling for a fire.

"We are leaving this cursed desert, Mori, and we are never coming back."

Her legs shook, her back blazed with pain, yet Treale kept walking—step by step, breath by breath. She would cross the desert afoot if she must. Soldiers raced around her, shouting and pointing at the nephilim who swarmed above. Children wept and families rushed into their homes and peered from windows.

Treale kept walking, Mori across her shoulder, the screams of the nephilim shaking the sky.

MORI

The world spun around her.

Mori remembered little of leaving Irys, capital of Tiranor: only the scent of sand, the shriek of beasts above, and Treale carrying her across her shoulders. The young squire was a slight woman, and yet she had carried Mori through the entire city of sprawling squares, cobbled alleys, and throngs of people.

Stars, I'm so thin, Mori remembered thinking in a daze. *I'm skin and bones.*

Beasts of claws and fangs soared overhead, scuttled down the streets, and cried to the sun. Soldiers ran and somewhere above Solina laughed, flying upon the king of the Fallen, a twisted beast crowned with a flaming halo. Treale was sweating beneath her as they sneaked outside the city walls. The desert sands swirled around the squire's feet, and finally they rested beneath an ancient, smoothed statue of a falcon that rose from the dunes.

"Here," Treale said, reached into her pack, and handed her a waterskin. "Drink."

Sweat, sand, and blood coated Treale, and she panted and wiped damp hair off her brow. When Mori held out her arms to grab the waterskin, they seemed so thin to her, mere twigs compared to Treale's arms. Her hands trembled as she clutched the skin, and Treale had to help her drink. It was good, clear water, the best she had drunk in moons.

"I can't see very well," she said softly. The sun blazed overhead, and shadows fell only when nephilim scudded across it. The world seemed fuzzy and far too bright; it was like looking through sunlit glass.

Treale took a pomegranate from her pack and cracked it open against her knee. She handed half to Mori.

"Your eyesight will improve," she said firmly. "Eat, Mori. Eat and you'll grow strong again."

Her voice didn't waver, but Mori saw tears in the young woman's eyes. She looked down at her pomegranate. Looking at the bright red color helped her focus her eyes, and she blinked a few times. She scooped seeds out and ate them, then closed her eyes and sighed. They were the sweetest, most wonderful, magical things she had ever eaten; they exploded in her mouth and shot healing energy through her. Her body shook with it.

A shadow fell over them. A nephil screeched above and swooped so low, its wings raised sand around them. The creature overshot them and soared over the city ahead, crying to the sun. More followed, a flock of rot and screams, their wings spreading their stench.

"We shall feed on dragon bones!" they screeched. "We shall drink dragon blood! Hail Solina. Hail the Golden Queen!" They beat their wings and swirled across the desert sky. "We are free! We will eat dragon flesh!"

Treale huddled closer to the old falcon statue that rose above them; the sand below and the limestone beak above formed a hollow. Mori pushed herself back and huddled by her friend. She began to shiver.

"How did Solina free the nephilim, Treale?" she whispered. "My books said the Ancients imprisoned them years ago."

The squire placed her arms around her, pulled her close, and held her. She too was shaking. Sand stung the welts on Mori's back, mingling with the pain in her belly and head. She watched as the beasts dived and cried overhead.

"Don't worry about those creatures, Mori," Treale said, holding her. "I'll get you out of this desert. I promise. We're going to fly north to a beautiful forest, and we'll find lots of food there, and we'll live there together." Her tears fell. "I promise. Do you believe me?"

Though Mori shook and her own eyes dampened, she nodded.

"Will Elethor be there?" she whispered. "Is Bayrin waiting in that forest too? And Lyana? They're waiting in that forest for us, right?"

Treale hung her head low and said nothing. A tear streamed down her cheek.

Mori bit her lip. "I thought not," she whispered.

With a sniff, Treale raised her head, looked into her eyes, and pulled her into a soft embrace.

"I pray that they live, Mori," she whispered. "But if they're gone... if you and I are the only ones left... then we must survive. We must escape and we must live alone. You understand, right?"

Mori nodded, a lump in her throat. "We will live, Treale. We will get out of this awful place." Her lip trembled, and the statue shook behind them with the shrieks of the beasts above. "We'll find that forest, and we'll find lots of food and water, and we'll survive."

Treale sniffed again and knuckled her eyes. "Can you fly, Mori?"

"I don't know. Let me eat a little more. Let me catch my breath. And then we'll try to fly. If I can't, will you let me ride you—you a dragon and me a human?"

Treale laughed through her tears. "You'd fall straight off! But if you can't fly, I will hold you in my claws, and I promise to be gentle."

They finished their pomegranate, then some bread and cheese Treale had pilfered from the dungeon, and Mori felt some of her strength return. The world still seemed too bright, and her limbs too shaky and weak, but she managed to push herself up to her feet.

"We'll walk a little farther," Treale said. She pointed ahead. "See the mountains there in the west?"

Mori squinted, able to see only a tan smudge. She nodded. "I see them."

"None of these creatures fly there. But we will. We will rest there among the stones for the night, then keep going. The swamps of Gilnor lie a few days northwest. We'll find more food there—fish and frogs to eat—and we'll find shelter under trees." Treale's voice trembled as she spoke, but she clenched her fists and plowed on. "We'll fly north from the swamps. A few days' flight will take us to the forests of Salvandos. That's where the true dragons live, and they can protect us. We can be there this moon, if we fly fast enough."

"The salvanae!" Mori breathed.

She had read many books about them. True dragons of old, they had no wings, no limbs, and no human forms; they flew as great chinking serpents, wild in the forests and mountains, forging no metal and plowing no fields, yet studying the stars and singing many old songs. Mori had seen a salvana once—the priest Nehushtan, a wise old dragon who had visited Requiem a year ago.

She lowered her head. Memories of Requiem flowed over her, as powerful as whips: Lacrimosa Hill where she had stood with her brother, the library with the leather books, and her canopy bed where she would laugh with Bayrin. Her trembling returned, and tears filled her eyes, but she knuckled them dry. She could not panic now. She could not weep now. They were still in danger; there would be time for tears later.

"Let's go," she said. "We'll walk to the mountains as humans so the nephilim don't see us. We'll fly from there. I'm strong enough."

They began the journey. Mori walked with her arms slung across Treale's shoulders, and the young squire held her waist and helped her every step. The nephilim kept swarming above, screaming of the dragons they'd eat. If they saw Mori and Treale, two haggard women, they did not see them as prey. When one landed in the desert before them, and hissed at them, Mori nearly fainted with fright. The nephil, however, only tossed its head, spraying drool, and took flight again.

"Dragons!" it screeched. "Solina will feed us. We will feast upon them!"

Mori tightened her lips and kept walking toward the mountains. "Come on, Treale. Let's hurry. I reckon Solina told these creatures they can only eat prisoners and dragons, not her people. They must think we're Tirans. But once they get hungry enough to forget orders... I want to be far away."

They seemed to walk forever. The sand burned Mori's bare feet, and the sun pummeled her. When evening fell, she looked behind her. The city of Irys was distant now, a patch of stone under the red sky. Nephilim still bustled above it, cawing and swirling, landing and soaring. None now flew over Mori and Treale; they were safe from them here.

When Mori looked west toward the mountains, she let out a sigh. They still seemed so distant, leagues and leagues away, no closer than they had ever been.

"Once we get to those mountains, we can fly," Treale said. "We'll be far enough from the nephilim. They're staying at the city, and they won't see two dragons from there."

Mori nodded. Yet how far was enough? She felt weak, and her eyes rolled back. When she blinked, she found herself sitting in the sand, legs splayed out.

"Oh, Mori," Treale said softly, knelt, and touched Mori's forehead. "I'm sorry; I pushed you too hard. We'll rest for a bit here, okay? We'll keep walking toward the mountains later, and then I can fly and carry you."

Mori nodded, head spinning. Treale let her drink some more; there were only a few sips left, and Mori left the last one for Treale, yet the squire insisted that she was not thirsty. They nibbled on more bread and cheese as night fell. The sun dipped behind the horizon so fast here in Tiranor, not a slow melting sunset like the northern ones of Requiem, but a plunge into darkness. The stars emerged overhead, piercing bright, millions of them. The Draco constellation shone in the north—the stars of their home.

"Can we sleep a little, Treale?" Mori whispered. "I'm so tired. So tired. Can we sleep just for a little?"

Treale nodded. Nothing but leagues of sand surrounded them, but thankfully the wind lay low, and the dunes did not swirl. Treale laid out her cloak, lay down upon it, and Mori lay beside her.

With the sun gone, it grew very cold very fast. The day had been so hot, and sweat had drenched the two women, and the sun had burned their skin. Now it felt like winter, and Mori shivered. She clung to Treale, sharing her warmth. Weariness tugged on her as tightly as chains.

"Mori?" Treale whispered. "Do you remember my canopy bed in Oldnale Manor, the one we'd sleep in as children? Remember how we'd hide under the blankets, pretend it's a palace, and read books? Let's pretend we're sleeping there now."

Mori smiled, remembering that great bed with its oak posts, soft mattress of feathers, and woolen quilts. She imagined that she lay there again, and slowly the beating of her heart eased.

"Thank you, Treale," she whispered. "Thank you for coming for me."

They slept embraced, their breath mingling.

They woke to a dawn of shrieks and rot.

Mori opened her eyes and shivered. She had not expected to sleep this long, yet the morning rose around her, and she still lay by Treale. The desert shook around them. Nephilim swarmed above, their wings tossing the sand into clouds. Mori coughed; the sand entered her nostrils and mouth. Treale woke at her side and coughed too, and they could barely see through the sandstorm. The shadows of the nephilim shot overhead, wings beat, stench flared, and shrieks cracked the air.

"We seek dragon blood!" they howled. "We will find the dragons, and we will feast! We fly to blood and organs and sweet marrow. We rise, we rise!"

Mori and Treale lay huddled together. The sand rose and stormed around them. The horde seemed to swarm forever, blasting their faces and fluttering their hair and cloaks with beating wings. Finally the last nephil disappeared overhead, leaving the sand and stench to settle. Globs of nephil drool and pus littered the desert like boils upon patchy skin.

Mori rose to her feet and stared north. Her heart thrashed against her ribs, and her legs shook. She shielded her eyes with her palm and stared after the dwindling nephil army.

Stars, she thought and her breath quickened.

"Treale!" she said. "Treale, they... they seek dragons!"

The young squire pushed herself to her feet. Sand filled her long black hair, painting it yellow. She shook that hair and patted sand off her tunic.

"I heard!" she said. "Bloody stars, trust me, I heard; they've been screaming about that for two days now. That's why we're walking in human forms, isn't it?"

Mori wheeled toward her, and a smile spread across her face. She grabbed her friend's shoulders. "But Treale! Don't you understand? How did I not see this earlier? If they seek dragons, that means others still live! More Vir Requis survived, not just you and me!"

She trembled and panted, still grinning. *Bayrin! Bayrin might be alive! And my brother Elethor, and my friend Lyana, and maybe more—many more.*

Of course, if they did live, they were in grave danger. Solina had summoned these new beasts to hunt them—just like she had summoned the wyverns and phoenixes. But still, they could be *alive*. That filled Mori with such joy that she lifted her chin and began walking again, not even waiting for Treale.

"Mori!" Treale said behind her. "Wait *up*. Mori!"

But Mori would not wait. She kept walking, head high, biting her trembling lip.

They're alive. I know it. They have to be. Otherwise Solina would never have sent these beasts to find them.

Treale rushed up beside her, buckling her cloak and tossing her pack across her shoulders. They walked through the sand, stepping around the globs of nephil drool.

"Mori, please," Treale said. "I... I hope they're alive too, but... I don't want us to get our hopes up. Okay, Mori? You understand, right?" She looked down at her feet. "Mori, we both saw the wyverns destroy Nova Vita. It was a slaughter. I don't know if anyone else escaped. It could be Solina lied to these nephilim, or maybe only a very, very small handful survived in the mountains where the miners work."

Mori stopped walking and turned to face her friend. She sniffed and tightened her fists.

"Bayrin is alive," she said. "I feel it. I know it. Elethor and Lyana are alive too. They are great warriors and... stars, Treale. Solina wouldn't wake this horde of demons for a few miners. She sent them to catch Elethor! He's always been the one she wanted. This whole war started because of this... this unholy obsession she has with him. Elethor is alive, and if he's alive, I bet he kept Lyana and Bayrin close to him. We'll find them, Treale." A tear rolled down to her lips. "I won't stop looking. I believe."

She looked behind her; the city was distant and the nephilim had left it. She looked ahead; the horde had disappeared over the mountains.

Now we fly.

Mori summoned her magic and shifted.

Her wings wobbled. She tried to take off, flew a few feet, and dipped. Her claws hit the sand, and she kicked off again, flapped her wings with all her strength, and rose into a tottering flight. It took several heavy strokes to fill her wings with enough air and rise higher. She dipped again, snarled, and finally managed to rise and glide.

I will find you, Bayrin. I will find you, Elethor and Lyana. I swear.

Yet as she flew, she wondered: If truly she found Bayrin, would he even recognize her now? Whom would he find when he held her in his arms? Not the old Princess Mori, the timid girl whose lips he would kiss, who would laugh at his jokes. No; she could barely remember that Mori anymore. She did not know who she was now. A princess of Requiem? A famished prisoner, her back scarred and her mind forever haunted? In the dungeons of Tiranor, had something broken deep inside her, something that could never heal? She did not know.

"You are Mori," she whispered as she flew. "You are Mori, Mori, *Mori*."

She might not know what that name meant anymore, whether it was the name of a princess, a prisoner, or a survivor, but she would not forget it. She would cling to herself. She would hang onto that name like a rope, for below her spread an endless pit and the reaching claws of monsters.

She flew over the mountains, their peaks carved from tan, bare rock. Treale flew at her side, black scales shimmering under the sun. The Tiran Sea shone blue and white to the northeast; distant beyond that horizon lay the ruins of Requiem, too far to see from here. When Mori looked northwest, she could just make out a green haze: the swamps of Gilnor. Beyond them lay a wilderness of forests where lived the salvanae, the true dragons... and safety, and hope, and a dream.

They flew toward that distant green patch, two dragons in an endless sky.

ELETHOR

The southern swarm grew, a stain upon the sky, and the distant shrieks rose.

Elethor stood upon the mountain, clad in plate armor. His leather glove creaked as he gripped his sword's hilt. He stared south. Fall was fading into winter, and the forest trees were nearly bare now; the branches and trunks of birch, maple, and beech grew dark from carpets of orange and red. Cold wind ruffled Elethor's hair and stung his face. Clouds veiled the sky and a drizzle fell.

"With rain and wind," Elethor whispered, "with bare trees and bare hearts; thus did winter find us."

It was an old poem. He could no longer remember the poet, but he remembered Mori quoting those words every winter by the fireplace. She would shudder, and he would laugh, muss her hair, and tease her for fearing the wind and rain and coming cold. She would smile hesitantly, and they would drink mulled wine and stoke the fire.

Yet now the storm does rise, and we are bare before it.

The dark cloud was spreading, still leagues away but moving fast. Thousands of beasts seemed to fly there, black and red and crying into the wind. Even from here, Elethor could detect their stench; they smelled like rotten corpses. They were mere specks from here, but when he squinted, Elethor could see beating wings, glints of sun on armor, and lanky limbs.

Nephilim. The spawn of demons and mortal mothers. He gripped his sword tight. *Stars, Solina, what have you done?*

He looked below the mountainside to their camp. A thousand souls lived there—people who depended on him, people he had protected for moons now, people who might die this evening. They could hear the distant shrieks; as they moved between the trees, the survivors cocked their heads, listened to the southern cries, and began to whisper. A few men drew swords.

Elethor snarled, fear gripping his heart like claws. He stared at the spreading shadow. It was buzzing and shimmering, a foul tapestry. How long before it reached them?

He missed Lyana and Bayrin so fiercely his chest tightened. He did not relish the thought of fighting without them, yet they had flown west and east, seeking aid.

Will you fetch aid for a pile of corpses?

An old man walked up the mountainside, clanking in armor. A scar rifted his creased face, and braids filled his white beard. A patch covered his left eye, and his gnarled hands clutched a sword and shield.

"Garvon," Elethor said and nodded his head. The old man had fought in the City Guard for forty years; he was one of the only guards to survive Nova Vita's fall.

"My king." The old man's breath rattled. He spat, then turned to stare south. His eyes darkened and he grumbled. "Bloody bollocks, what are those?" He covered his eyes and squinted. "Wyverns? Stars, there's an army of them."

Elethor shook his head and spoke softly. "Not wyverns. Nephilim."

Garvon grunted and stared at him with his one narrow, shrewd eye. "Nephilim? My king, they're only a legend. Don't tell me you believe—"

"I believe what I see, Garvon, and those are no wyverns." Elethor inhaled deeply. "They're flying our way. They know we're here."

Garvon flexed his fingers around his sword hilt. "They're just scanning the forest. We've seen Solina patrol here before. We're hidden under the trees; they won't find us."

Elethor looked down at the camp. A moon ago, leaves had covered these trees, and not even wyvern eyes could see through their cover. Today the branches were bare. From here upon the mountainside, Elethor could see huts and tents. They had covered their dwellings with woven curtains of leaf and vine, but that would not fool seeking eyes.

"These are no scouts, Garvon. This is an army, as you said." He grunted. "Solina would not invade Salvandos with an entire army; she would not risk angering the salvanae. Not unless she knew we were here." He began walking downhill. "We evacuate. At once."

"My lord," Garvon began, chin raised, "I say we stay. We fight. We slay them upon the—"

"The days of fighting are over," Elethor said, still walking downhill. "At least until Lyana and Bayrin return with aid. We flee to the temple."

Garvon muttered as he walked downhill, breath snorting and armor clanking. "That temple might make us miss the nephilim. I prefer fighting beasts I can see, rather than ghosts. Beasts you can cut and burn."

They had discovered the temple three moons ago, a network of ruins a few leagues north in the forest. Elethor had wanted to set camp there, to hide among its fallen statues, crumbling archways, and dungeons. The others—everyone from Garvon to Bayrin and Lyana—had adamantly refused, quoting old tales of the ghosts who dwelled in those ruins.

The Ancients built those temples, Lyana had warned, *and some say their ghosts still haunt the place. Let us hide among trees, not old stones that still whisper.*

Yet now these trees were naked, and stones could protect them, even if they had to share those stones with spirits.

He reached the foothills and entered the camp. The distant shrieks rose louder now. The survivors stood still, staring south. Children raised wooden swords as if, with enough courage, they could slay any enemy. Wounded men lay legless in carts, faces pale. Mothers clutched babes to their breasts.

One thousand and fifty-four souls. The last lights of Requiem.

Elethor climbed onto a fallen log. He gripped Ferus's hilt so tightly his fingers ached. The people came to stand around him, forming a ring in the forest. Elethor looked from face to face. They were pale. They were afraid. These were not fighters; nearly all their fighters had died in Requiem. These were elders, children, mothers, wounded.

"People of Requiem!" Elethor said, looking from face to face. They stared back silently. "Queen Lyana and Lord Bayrin have flown to fetch aid; they will return with it, I promise this to you. But now we must move. Now we must flee danger. I will lead you north through the forest, and we will hide among the ruins of Bar Luan. We will find safety there until help arrives."

The people exchanged dark glances. They whispered prayers and curses. One old man drew his sword and a child whimpered. They had all heard stories of Bar Luan, the fallen temple of the Ancients. In a thousand bedtime stories, they had heard of the ghosts who wandered there, the spirits that sucked the blood of the living, and the old pain in the rocks.

Yet what choice do I have? Elethor thought. *We can face old stories. Or we can face beasts that fly upon the sky.*

The distant shrieks rose higher—cruel, inhuman shrieks, high-pitched like shattering glass. A stench wafted on the wind, scented of corpses. A child began to cry, and a few of the wounded whimpered. A young woman cursed and drew a chipped sword.

"Be calm!" Elethor said. "Danger approaches; the enemy flies from the south. We will hide in the temple, and we will find safety there. I promise this to you. I swear it on the name of my fathers. Now move! Walk in human form. Stay under the trees and wear your cloaks of leaf and vine. Move silently, move fast, and stay under the cover of the branches. The temple is three leagues away. Follow me now!"

He stepped off the log. The ring of people parted, and Elethor began walking north. His heart pounded so madly he thought that, were he not wearing a breastplate, it could leap from his chest. He walked silently, lips tight, hand still gripping his sword. Around him, the people glanced at one another uneasily.

"Follow, now!" Garvon hissed, moving from survivor to survivor. "Do not pack. Leave your things! Move—no, leave your supplies. Move!"

Behind them in the south, the nephilim shrieked. Elethor marched among the trees, leaves and twigs snapping under his boots. Behind him the people walked, faces pale, clutching spears and swords or simple staffs they had carved from fallen branches.

Please, stars, don't let them see us, Elethor prayed silently. *Let us live until Bayrin and Lyana return.*

They moved through the forest in single file, silent. These people had fled the phoenixes into the tunnels under Nova Vita, then the wyverns; they knew how to move silently and swiftly. Strings of leaves covered their heads and cloaks, red like the forest around them. Eyes darted. Voices whispered. Fingers twisted around weapons.

"Legion, Legion!" rose a distant shriek behind them, curdling Elethor's blood. "You promised flesh! You promised dragon bones. We hunger! We thirst!"

Elethor gritted his teeth. Around him, the survivors whispered and a few mewled. The shrieks still sounded distant—leagues away—but louder than the crash of columns.

"We must feast! We must drink dragon blood." The cries rolled across the sky, loud and shrill as snapping bones. "Where do dragons hide?"

Requiem's survivors watched the skies, clung to one another, and raised their weapons.

"Keep moving!" Elethor hissed. "Garvon, keep them moving."

A hundred men and women served in their new army, a force Elethor had dubbed the Camp Guard; old Garvon led them. These soldiers, clad in dented armor and bearing longswords, moved along the line of survivors, rallying them forward. They kept moving through the forest. Elethor quickened his walk to a run; the others ran behind him.

"I am Legion!" rose a cry from behind. The stench of rot blazed. "I am Prophet. I lead you to dragons! A camp, a camp! Dragons were here. Dragons are near! I smell them, brothers and sisters. I smell sweet dragon blood to drink, and bones to crack, and marrow to suck, and meat to lick, and souls to break. Dragons flee! Dragons will die."

A shadow shot above the branches overhead. The survivors bent, wailed, and pointed. The shadow circled, then soared again, and Elethor snarled.

Stars save us.

He had seen illustrations of nephilim, those spawn of demons and their mortal brides, great lanky beasts with bat wings. In real life, they were more hideous than anything an artist could draw. The nephil above looked, Elethor thought, like a strip of dried meat, its fingers clawed, its mouth full of teeth like swords. A halo of flame encircled its head. The creature howled, and trees shattered, and the survivors covered their ears. The sound was so loud Elethor shouted through his clenched jaw. The scream pounded through his chest; it felt like it could snap his ribs.

"Shapeshifters, shapeshifters!" cried the creature. More shadows shot overhead. "Humans walk, humans smell like dragons. Feast upon them! I am Legion. I am Prophet. I bring you blood and bones!"

Three nephilim swooped, crashed between branches, and landed on the forest floor before them.

Elethor snarled, shifted into a dragon, and blew a stream of fire. Around him, men of the Camp Guard shifted too and blew their flames. The nephilim screeched and burned, and a fourth one swooped from above. Its claws reached out, grabbed a child, and ripped her apart. Blood spattered. People wailed.

"Shift and fly!" Elethor shouted. "Fly, Vir Requis! Into the sky."

They screamed. They wept. They shifted into dragons—elders, mothers, youths. A few Vir Requis were mere babes or toddlers, too young to shift; their mothers carried them in their claws.

Elethor crashed between the branches into the sky. Thousands of nephilim swarmed and howled. At his left, one swooped and grabbed a young red dragon. The nephil ripped off her head and swallowed it; the dragon's body returned to human form and crashed down. At Elethor's left, a nephil crashed into a silver dragon, slashed its claws, and gutted the dragon as easily as a fisherman gutting his catch.

"Fly, Vir Requis!" Elethor shouted. "Fly north. Fly to the temple!"

He could see Bar Luan perhaps a league away, rising from the forest. A few staircases, a crumbling archway, and craggy walls remained from what was once a sprawling complex; these remnants would have to serve them now. Dragons began flying toward it, blowing fire over their shoulders at pursuing nephilim. Elethor rose, blew a flaming jet at a beast, and ducked to dodge its tumbling body. Thousands of the creatures covered the southern sky, swarming forward.

"Fly, Vir Requis!" he howled. "Hide in the temple." He roasted another nephil, a scaly beast clad in rusted armor, and rose higher. "Camp Guard, rally here! Hold them back. Battle formations, here!"

A clanking white dragon rose ahead, horns long and eyes red—Garvon, chief of the Camp Guard. A gash ran down his side, seeping blood, but still he fought, blowing fire at nephilim above. A dozen other dragons, wearing the great dragonhelms of the Camp Guard, rose around them and blew their fire.

"Hold them back!" Elethor shouted. "Let the others flee. Flame the beasts!"

Behind him, the women, elders, and children were fleeing north. Before him and his fellow soldiers—less than a hundred dragons—the nephil host spread. Thousands of beasts, maybe tens of thousands, covered the horizon. They screeched to the heavens, and the trees below cracked and fell, and boulders rolled. The earth itself seemed to shake.

Hovering in midair before the swarm, Elethor bared his fangs and growled. Around him, his fellow dragons beat their wings and smoke rose from their nostrils. Elethor's heart pounded, and fear and rage throbbed through him, tingling from his tail to his horns.

"Soldiers of Requiem!" he said to the dragons around him, a mere handful of warriors before the swarm. "You will hold your ground. You will hold the beasts back. You will buy our people time to flee to safety."

Behind him, Elethor heard the survivors of Requiem fly farther; they would soon reach the temple. Before him, the countless nephilim screeched and soared and circled in the air. They flew in no battle formations like wyverns or phoenixes; this was a mob of devilry.

"Legion!" they howled. "Legion! Prophet of the Fallen!"

The great nephil, their champion, rose from flame. His halo of fire screamed. His body was lanky; his ribs pushed against skin like dried parchment. He howled to the sky, teeth long and thin and white, and his wings sprayed fire as he rose. His cry was so shrill it raised boils across the nephilim around him.

"I am Legion, I am Prophet!" he screeched. "I have led you to freedom. I lead you to dragons. Feast upon them!"

The thousands of beasts howled, beat their wings, and shot forward.

The dragons roared their flames.

LYANA

She crouched between the roots of fallen trees, stared downhill, and cursed.

The Tiran camp sprawled a mile away, covering the scorched earth. Sooty palisades, carved from uprooted trees, encircled a mass of tents and huts and campfires. Thousands of men swarmed there. Many were soldiers, clad in breastplates of pale steel, suns upon their shields. Others were masons; they bustled across scaffolding, raising walls of stone.

They are building a fortress here, Lyana thought. *A great barracks in the heart of Requiem.*

She growled and clutched her sword Levitas. Once fields had swayed here. Once House Oldnale had plowed this land, growing barley and wheat and sweet peas. Today the farms were gone, the earth scorched. The old bricks of Oldnale Manor, where her squire Treale had lived, lay in wheelbarrows within the Tiran camp; those old stones of Requiem were now growing into the Tirans' fort.

"I swear to you, Treale," Lyana whispered, crouched behind the roots of the fallen tree. "I will avenge you. I will return to this place someday, and I will burn those who defile your home."

A screech rose from the camp, and Lyana winced. Even here, a league away, the sound throbbed through her chest. She pulled her cloak tighter around her, narrowed her eyes, and snarled.

A dozen nephilim guarded the camp below, patrolling the palisades of sharpened spikes. Each stood as tall as a dragon, dwarfing the Tiran men. Their bodies were emaciated, dried flesh clinging to bones, yet their claws and teeth were long and white; Lyana could see their glint even from here. Bat wings beat against their backs, stirring ash beneath them. Lyana had been traveling across the ruins of Requiem for ten days now, and she had seen their destruction everywhere: their drool upon forest floors, corpses of animals torn apart, and trails of the rot they leaked.

Lyana longed to fly down there. She long to test these beasts in battle—to see how fast they flew, to blow her fire upon them, to kill them upon the land they infested. Yet she could not—not here, not alone.

We need more than dragons now. We need the men of Osanna, and the griffins of the east, and the salvanae of the west. We need aid or the world will fall.

With a grunt, she turned away from the roots and began moving downhill, away from the camp. Her cloak fluttered in the wind, revealing the armor she wore underneath: the ancient, silvery armor of a bellator, a knight of Requiem. Her scabbard and helm bore engravings of the Draco constellation, the sigil of her order.

The bellators have fallen. I am the last of their number. She walked down into the wind. Dry leaves fluttered around her boots and her cloak billowed behind her. *Yet I still serve my stars. Now. Forever. Until my last breath.*

She walked upon the scorched earth, moving between fallen trees and dead cattle until those stars glowed in the sunset. Smoke still blew above Requiem, hiding all but the dragon's tail above, yet still Lyana gazed upon those lights, and she prayed to them.

"I still fight for you, stars of my fathers." She drew Levitas, ancient sword of her order. "I still fly under your light."

As the sun dipped below the horizon, she shifted into the blue dragon and took flight. Nephilim patrolled this land; she had seen countless of the beasts while walking across Requiem, peering at them from between trees and boulders. In the darkness she could fly silently, fire in her maw, sky beneath her wings. She dived through the cold, long night.

The land soon changed below, the scorched fields giving way to lush dark forests. Forts rose from the trees, their battlements alight with torches. After days of ash and soot and mud, Lyana was leaving the ruins of Requiem; she flew now over the eastern lands of Osanna, ancient realm of men. It was a vast land; Lyana had visited here before as an envoy of Requiem, but she had seen only small parts of the kingdom. Osanna stretched from northern Fidelium, mountains where the undead rose from tombs, to the southern port of Altus Mare, whose ships navigated the Tiran Sea and sailed east to Leonis, land of griffins.

She flew for hours, crossing forests, mountains, and fields, before finally spiraling down to a silver lake under the moon. There she lay upon grass, drank from the water, and slept until the dawn.

She awoke to see two cloaked archers pointing arrows at her.

With a snarl, Lyana leaped up and began to draw her sword.

"Freeze!" shouted one of the archers, voice ringing deeply from the shadows of his hood. "Release your sword or you'll die before you draw the blade."

Lyana bared her teeth at the men. Both wore green cloaks, and beneath their hoods, brown scarves covered their faces. Leaves and vines covered them, and swords hung from their belts. One man was short and squat, his wide shoulders tugging at his cloak; the other was tall and lean. Something about them seemed familiar, though Lyana could not place them.

She growled. "I am Lyana Eleison, Queen of Requiem, and—"

"We know who you are," said the taller, leaner man, the one with the deep voice. "Release your sword."

Both men drew their arrows back farther; the bowstrings creaked. With a grunt and hiss, Lyana released her sword's hilt, letting the blade fall back into its scabbard. The two men stepped forward and grabbed Lyana's arms.

Lyana growled, tugged herself free, and shifted.

She took flight, a blue dragon with fire in her maw.

Below her, the two men shifted too and soared, bronze dragons with long white horns.

"Stars!" Lyana shouted, beating her wings. The grass below swayed, and waves raced along the lake. "You're Vir Requis. How dare you threaten your queen?"

Seeing them as dragons, she finally recognized these two. She had seen them in Requiem's northern mountains; they were brothers and miners of iron ore. The older, taller one was named Grom Miner, she remembered. The younger, squat brother was named Gar.

"We are no longer in Requiem, Lyana Eleison," said Grom; his scales were a slightly deeper shade of copper. "And you are no longer our queen, if indeed you wed the Boy King Elethor in your exile. All titles are forsaken in the ruin of the world, and every dragon is master of himself now. We will take you to our camp, and you will answer to our new lord."

Lyana snarled, and fire flicked between her teeth. These two dragons were burly and long, far larger than her own short, slim form, yet she knew that she could kill them. She was fast. Her fire was hot. Her claws were sharp. She had trained to fight in Castra Draco, garrison of Requiem's fabled Royal Army. These two had perhaps grown strong from digging mines and hauling ore, yet Lyana had slain phoenixes and wyverns, and she could slay these two.

And yet... and yet they were still her kin. They were new survivors when she had thought none existed. She spat her flames into the lake.

"You call yourselves your own masters, fellow dragons of Requiem," she said. "Yet now you speak of serving a new lord. Are you free dragons or servants?"

Gar Miner—the younger brother—spoke for the first time. He was a shorter dragon than his brother, but burlier. He spoke in the high voice of a man just leaving his youth.

"We are free dragons," he said. "Yet we choose to fight for the Legless Lord. You will follow us. You will answer to him, and you will have a choice to serve him too, or you may leave these lands and find your own fortune."

Lyana growled deep in her throat. She had not come here to Osanna for this; she had flown seeking aid from the king of men, and then from the eastern griffins. And yet here hid more survivors of Requiem, perhaps many more. She could not forsake this chance to meet them, to bring them back to Elethor's camp.

"Show me to your lord," she said.

Grom Miner nodded and growled. "We walk. In human forms. We live in Osanna, and the cruel Queen Solina still dares not invade this land, yet we've seen her beasts fly overhead as scouts. We walk hidden. We walk quietly. We will not fly as dragons again."

The bronze brothers descended and shifted back into human forms upon the lakeside. Lyana landed beside them and shifted too.

"Follow," said Grom. He turned and began walking into the forest.

Lyana snarled at him. She was Queen of Requiem; she followed no one. And yet Grom was walking among the trees already, and his younger brother Gar was caressing his bow. Growling, Lyana followed, and the three moved through the forest.

They walked for a long time, and the forest thickened. The oaks grew twisted and tall here. Moss covered the boles and mist

floated between them. Back in Salvandos in the west, where
Elethor ruled his camp of survivors, the autumn leaves had fallen
and covered the forest floor. Here they still grew bronze and
dulled gold, metallic and hard and barely rustling. Lichen hung
from gnarled branches, brushing against Lyana's cheeks, and the
air smelled of loam and stagnant water. She could not see the sky
or sun—the canopy was thick as a roof—yet the brothers seemed
to know their way. They walked assuredly, boots crunching
branches and twigs.

Lyana guessed it was near noon when a stench rose on the
wind, twisting her gut. Flies buzzed. With a snarl, she drew her
sword, but the brothers only snickered.

"No need for blades here, my *queen*," Grom said, speaking
the last word as an insult. He led them around a boulder and
pointed at a thick oak. Upon its trunk, tied with ropes and chains,
hung the corpse of a nephil.

"Stars," Lyana whispered.

Nausea rose in her. She had never seen one of the beasts
so close before. Patches of dank scales covered its flesh like
lesions, and its claws curved, long as sabres. Its bloated head
bustled with insects; the eyes were already gone. Worms crawled
upon its cleaved skull, and dried entrails hung from its slashed
belly. Half the body was burnt with dragonfire, the other half
lacerated with claws.

Squat young Gar smirked. "Figured we'd leave the bastard
here—a warning to his comrades. I killed this one myself." He
thrust out his broad chest. "Burned him dead."

Lyana spat in disgust. "Bury it," she said. "It stinks."

"We want it to stink, *your highness*," Gar said. "Let its
brothers smell it. Let them smell their death on the wind and
know that more death awaits them here."

Lyana whipped her head toward the brothers and glared.
"You are a boastful couple." She growled. "You hide here in

disguise, and you dare not shift and fly, yet you brag of slaying nephilim. Do you know how many of these creatures fly in Requiem, seeking us? Thousands. *Tens* of thousands. Armies of them muster, and more keep flowing north from the desert. You burned one? Swarms of them will fly here; they will cover the world. Do you think the stench of one will deter the rest?" She marched toward Gar, grabbed his collar, and bared her teeth at him. "You are a foolish boy, and when this corpse's comrades arrive, you will die squealing." She twisted his collar tight, constricting his breath. "I've seen many boys like you die squealing."

The young miner paled, and for an instant his lips shook. Then he raised his chin, shoved her off, and smoothed his tunic.

"Be silent," he grumbled, though his voice shook slightly. "Follow. We're almost there."

They walked past the corpse—Lyana nearly gagged as the flies buzzed near her—and moved down a leafy slope toward a stream. The water rose past their ankles, and beyond it stood a hill with trees so thick, they had to push branches aside and climb over roots and boulders. Finally, below the hill, Lyana saw the camp.

Her heart leaped and tears dampened her eyes.

"So many," she whispered.

Only a thousand Vir Requis lived with Elethor in the west; Lyana had thought them the only survivors of Requiem. Yet here lived many more—this camp was twice the size of the one Elethor led, maybe larger. Children ran playing around boulders, holding dolls woven of leaf and grass. Young women whispered around campfires. An old man stood upon a boulder, leading a congregation in prayer. A palisade of spikes surrounded the camp, and men stood guarding it, armed with spears.

A tear streamed down Lyana's cheek, and her legs trembled. "So many still live."

The brothers tried to grab her arms and lead her. Lyana wrenched herself free and began marching toward the camp, holding her head high. She let the wind billow her cloak open, revealing her knightly armor. At times like these, Lyana missed her old mane of fiery red curls; it used to draw people's attention like a beacon of fire. Solina had sheared that hair last year, and now only a finger's length grew upon her head. Today these embers, a memory of a great flame, would have to do.

"My lady!" Gar cried behind her. "I mean, Lyana! I mean—newcomer. Halt! We will escort you into our camp."

Lyana ignored him and kept marching. She made toward a gateway in the palisade where two guards stood, bearing cracked shields and makeshift spears. They wore old, dented breastplates; one from the armories of Requiem, another stolen from a dead Tiran and still bearing the Golden Sun of Tiranor. When Lyana tried to march between them and into the camp, they moved closer together, making to block her way.

"Move!" Lyana barked and shoved them back. When they tried to grab her, she glared and bared her teeth at them. "I am Lyana Eleison, Queen of Requiem, your mistress. If you touch me, I will cut off your hands."

She gripped her sword's hilt and drew a foot of steel; it gleamed and the guards hesitated. Not wasting another moment, Lyana strode into the camp.

"Who leads this place?" she called out. "Bring him before me."

All around her, people abandoned gardens, wheelbarrows, toys, harps, and weapons. They began to gather around her, staring and whispering to one another. She heard her name spoken in awe. She knew these faces; she had seen them labor in Requiem's fields, dig in her mines, and forge steel in her smithies. She saw no nobles; the last lords and ladies of Requiem had fallen. Here were the commoners of Aeternum's Kingdom.

"Who leads you?" she repeated. She stepped onto a tree stump and wheeled her head around, seeking a ruler. "Bring him to speak with me."

Grom approached her, tall and grim, his ill-fitting armor clanking beneath his cloak. He cleared his throat and smirked.

"It will be... difficult to bring the Legless Lord here. I think you will find it easier if we took you to him."

Lyana gripped her sword tight and frowned. She was queen to these people; would she approach this Legless Lord, a son of Requiem, as an ambassador? She grinded her teeth.

"Very well," she said. "If truly this *lord* of yours— and I use the term lightly—has no legs and cannot approach me, take me to him."

She did not like this. These people had missed her coronation in the wilderness of Salvandos, yet they still knew her as the Lady Lyana, a knight betrothed to their king. And yet they did not bow before her.

I will find no loyalty here, she thought. *Titles still mean something in the west, where King Elethor protects his people; here they are forgotten.*

The brothers led her down a dirt path between gardens, tree stumps, and rows of game hanging from poles. A hall rose ahead, built of boles still rough with bark and the stumps of felled branches. Those branches, still leafy, formed a rough roof. The structure looked long enough to house a dragon.

They stepped through its makeshift doors, which were carved of branches and rope, and into a shadowy chamber. The air outside was cold and wet; inside the hall was hot and stuffy and scented of pine. A campfire burned upon the earthen floor, its smoke rising through a hole in the roof.

"My lord!" called Grom, standing at Lyana's side. "We have found another survivor. She is Lyana Eleison, once a lady of Requiem's courts; we found her by the eastern lake."

A cough sounded behind the campfire; a man sat there, hidden behind the flames. The coughing went on for a long moment, then ended with a wheeze. Finally the man behind the fire spoke, voice raspy.

"Bring her closer, Grom. Let me see her."

Grom and Gar grabbed Lyana's arms yet again. She tried to shake herself free, but the brothers gripped her firmly, and they pulled her forward. She grunted but walked with them; she was more curious to see this man than to fight his minions. They walked down the hall and around the fire, and there she saw the Legless Lord.

He was an older man; she guessed him sixty years old, maybe older. His cheeks were stubbly, his long hair grizzled. He wore a brown leather tunic and sat in a chair of twisting oak roots—a mockery of Requiem's old throne which had stood in its palace. Upon his knees, the man held a sword with a dragonclaw pommel; forged in dragonfire in Requiem's Castra Draco, Lyana thought. His legs ended below those knees, and cloth wrapped the stumps.

"Lyana," he rasped. Coughs seized him again, and he brought a handkerchief to his mouth. It was a moment before he could speak again. "Lyana Eleison, once a lady of Requiem; I am glad to see you survived the carnage. Welcome to our camp."

"Dorin Blacksmith," Lyana said, eyes narrowed. She recognized this one. He had forged steel in Nova Vita smithies, and he had served in the City Guard during the war, though last time she had seen him, he had walked on two legs. "I too am glad to see you live; I fought with you against the wyverns. I saw you slay two. You fought well, my friend."

The blacksmith hacked a laugh, then coughed again. "Yes, I slew more than two. The last one did this." He swept his hand across his stumps. "You have emerged unscathed, I see, though perhaps with less hair."

She took a step closer to him, shaking off the brothers' hands.

"Dorin," she said, "King Elethor lives. He reigns in exile, leading a camp of a thousand Vir Requis. We still fight. We will assault Tiranor and we will slay her queen. Fly west with me now, join King Elethor, and we will rain fire upon the enemy."

Coughs interrupted Dorin's sigh. He dabbed his lips with his handkerchief. "Damn smoke and damn ash." He cleared his throat; a rough, rusty noise. "Since the fires in Nova Vita, my lungs are ruined." He hacked again, then *tsk*ed his tongue. "Do you see the ruin of war? My lungs. My legs. These ragged, haunted people I lead. That is what your King Elethor brought us; that is what he will bring those who still follow him." He shook his head. "Fly west to join the boy on another adventure? I think not. We've had enough of war; now is our time to grow gardens, to build halls, to find a new life here in the east. Requiem is fallen, my child. Her columns lie smashed, and her halls shattered; her cry is silenced. Let us find new spring here—in Second Haven—a new kingdom for the children of Draco."

Lyana raised her eyebrows. "*Second Haven?* A new kingdom?" She grabbed the man's shoulders. "Damn it, Dorin, Requiem still lives. Requiem is not a piece of earth; she is starlight, and she is the magic inside us. King's Column still stands; Requiem still roars. You are one of her children, and Elethor Aeternum is still your king."

Grom and Gar grabbed her and tugged her back. Lyana snarled, spun, and kicked at them. She hit the elder on his shin, and he raised his fist. Lyana leaped back, drew her sword, and nodded to him.

"Go on," she said softly. "Go on, Grom Miner. Make your move. You can soon become a Legless Servant to your Legless Lord."

The lanky miner rubbed his shin and spat. He looked at Dorin, hesitating. The Legless Lord grumbled and raised his hands.

"Brothers!" he said. "Leave her be. Lyana! Sheath your sword; we draw no steel in this hall."

She raised that sword higher. "You look upon Levitas, sword of Lord Terra Eleison, a Light of Requiem. I draw and raise my steel where I please, Dorin. You were a blacksmith once; you should show more respect to a blade of legend."

He sighed again, breath rattling like dice in his lungs. "I was a blacksmith; that is true. And these two brothers were miners; they are guards now. You were a knight; now you are a guest. Requiem has fallen. Her legends are nothing but burnt scrolls. Lower your sword; its history means nothing in Second Haven."

Lyana growled. "Nova Vita has not lain fallen for a year, and you forsake all memory of her halls and heroes?" She spat at his feet. "You fought nobly for Requiem over her capital; now you defile her. You may stay here, Dorin Blacksmith, upon this mockery of a throne you have carved. I lead these people west—with or without you."

She turned and marched back toward the door. She trudged out into the camp, stepped onto a boulder, and raised her voice.

"Children of Requiem!" she called.

Women planting seeds, men carving spears, and children weaving baskets looked up, pausing from their work. Lyana raised her sword so the light caught it.

"I am Lyana Eleison!" she shouted. "I am wed to King Elethor Aeternum, son of Olasar, descended from Queen Gloriae. I am Queen of Requiem. King Elethor still lives! Requiem still fights. Join me west, and—"

Pain shattered against her nape.

Lyana fell from the boulder and hit the ground.

She flipped over and tried to raise her sword, but a boot pressed down on her wrist. The brothers stood above her, and behind them sat the Legless Lord in a wheelbarrow.

"Tie her up!" the grizzled old man shouted. "Guards, tie her to the tree."

Lyana kicked and nearly freed herself, but more men rushed forward. She leaped and tried to shift; they grabbed her legs, and one man swung a club. Pain exploded across her, her magic fizzled, and blood dripped into her eye.

She hit the fallen leaves.

Men leaped onto her, and dirt filled her mouth, and she couldn't even scream.

ELETHOR

Behind him, the dragons fled toward the temple ruins—mothers, children, elders. At his sides, a hundred dragon warriors flapped wings and blew fire. Before them, the army of nephilim spread, covering the sky and horizon, a buzzing horde of countless demons.

As their wives, children, and elders escaped, Elethor and his dragons shot forward, roaring fire.

The nephilim crashed against them.

Elethor howled and blew his flame. The fire crashed against one nephil, and the beast screeched and fell. Two more nephilim flew at him, one from each side. Elethor spun and clubbed one with his tail, driving his spikes into its rotted flesh. The second nephil crashed into him and grabbed hold like a great spider clutching its prey. Teeth bit into Elethor's back, and he roared. Claws ripped at his flank.

He dipped in the air, twisted his neck, and bit into the nephil. It felt like biting mummified flesh. The beast opened its mouth and screeched; the sound was so loud and shrill that when it faded, Elethor heard nothing but ringing. He flamed the beast, and when it screeched again, the call washed over Elethor like white light.

It fell. More swooped from above. There must have been ten thousand.

Stars, give me strength. Let me hold them back just long enough—long enough to let the others flee into the temple, to hide among its stones and shadows.

"There, my Lord Legion!" rose a voice from the mass of nephilim—the rumble of a dragon's voice. "The brass dragon! That one is their king. Feast upon him, my lord!"

Elethor flamed one nephil, clawed another, and looked up toward the voice. He growled and rage flared within him, spilling between his teeth in rivers of fire.

A gray dragon flew ahead between the nephilim, his eyes red, his mouth open in a gloating, snaggletoothed grin. Elethor knew this one.

"Nemes," he growled.

So that is how they found us.

Roaring, Elethor beat his wings and rose higher. He blew flame and flew through the fire, shooting toward the traitor.

Nephilim crashed into him. Teeth bit and claws swung; he felt them tearing off scales. He roared and blew fire in a ring. They surrounded him, a cell of putrid flesh and rotting eyes. Their wings blocked the sky. Their sores oozed pus. A claw lashed his wing, tearing a rent through it.

"Nemes!" Elethor shouted. He barreled forward through the beasts, seeking the gray dragon. He had never felt such bloodlust, such a craving to kill and destroy his enemies; today he hated Nemes more than Solina herself.

"Elethor!"

Garvon's gravelly voice rang out. The burly white dragon rose and tugged at him, pulling him back into a ring of other dragons. They blew fire, holding back the beasts.

"Garvon, he betrayed us!" Elethor said. "Nemes—the gray dragon. Help me find him."

He whipped his head from side to side, seeking the traitor, but saw only nephilim. The trees below cracked and fell under their shrieks. The half demons chewed severed limbs of Vir Requis, tossed their heads back, and swallowed greedily. When he glanced behind him, Elethor saw his people vanish into the distant temple, scurrying into its crumbled halls and secret tunnels. He looked back south, seeking Nemes again, and growled.

I will find you yet, Nemes, and I will burn you with my fire.

He spun and began flying north to the temple.

"Fly, warriors of Requiem!" he shouted. "Fall back to the temple. Fall back!"

They flew around him, bloodied and slashed and panting. They blew fire over their shoulders, burning nephilim, yet the swarm spread for miles; they seemed endless. Elethor beat his wings madly. A nephil swooped from above, and claws thrashed, and Elethor banked. He soared, flamed the beast, and clawed another dead. More rose below them, and Garvon rained fire upon them.

A hundred dragons had remained to hold back the swarm; perhaps twenty still lived. They raced over the collapsing forest toward the temple. Every moment, another one fell. Nineteen remained. Then eighteen. Soon only a dozen. In death, their magic left them, and they crashed into the trees—torn apart and splattering blood upon the fallen leaves of autumn.

Finally Elethor and his surviving warriors reached the temple. The ruins spread below them like the scattered bones of a stone giant.

Nobody knew the age of Bar Luan; books from a thousand years ago called these ruins ancient. Walls carved with reliefs of men and beasts rose from the forest, crumbling and mossy, chunks of them missing as if giants had chewed upon them. Some walls cradled dark archways with stairs that plunged into darkness. Others lay fallen. Great stone faces, carved larger than dragons, stared stoically from some walls that still stood; other faces lay fallen and overgrown with moss and vine.

The roots of great trees clutched these ruins, twisting over them like woody tentacles or the wax of melted candles. Years ago, paved roads and courtyards had spread here; today trees and roots broke through the cobblestones, casting them aside like discarded dice. Years ago, pyramids had risen here from the trees; today only one remained standing, its stairs so chipped they would send climbers tumbling.

Bar Luan, Elethor thought. *House of ghosts.*

They called it a temple; it looked more like a city. Ten thousand people could have lived here, maybe twice that many. Elethor thought the place nearly as large as Nova Vita.

"Go, into the doorways, into the halls!" he shouted. Dozens of doorways filled the walls, leading to chambers and dungeons. They were small passageways built for the Ancients, a people short and slim; the nephilim would not fit through.

Elethor dived toward one doorway, a narrow opening with a lintel shaped as a stone lion. Before he could land, two nephilim swooped and crashed into him, shoving him against cracked cobblestones.

Elethor writhed beneath them. He whipped his tail, hitting one beast. It screeched, deafening him. Again ringing rolled over him; he could barely hear anything else. The second beast bit, driving teeth into Elethor's left shoulder, the one already scarred from wyvern acid. He bellowed, kicked, and rolled. They slammed into a wall, sending it crumbling. The nephil roared, and Elethor beat his wings. He rose ten feet and rained his fire, catching the nephilim before they could rise. They blazed, screeching and kicking, knocking into walls and statues. Stones cascaded and fallen leaves burned.

Elethor looked around him; he could see one last dragon land, shift into human form, and run into a doorway between hanging roots. The rest had either hidden in the ruins or lay dead.

Above the ruins, thousands of nephilim blocked the sky.

Elethor growled, resisting the temptation to fly at them; he still craved to roast Nemes. Instead he shifted into human form and ran toward the doorway.

Nephilim swooped behind him.

Their claws scraped against the cobblestones.

Elethor leaped into the doorway and rolled.

Behind him in the courtyard, the nephilim shrieked. They bit at the doorway. Their claws reached into the darkness, each as long as Elethor's sword. He drew that sword and slashed at them. He cut one finger off—it was longer than his arm—and black blood sprayed him. Their teeth snapped at the doorway, their eyes blazed, and rocks tumbled.

Elethor retreated deeper into darkness. The walls were built of rugged bricks overgrown with moss. The ceiling was low, only a finger's length above his head, and the doorway only five feet tall; the Ancients must have stood hardly taller than children. Elethor walked around a bend, moving out of the doorway's line of sight. When he stepped a few more paces into darkness, he bumped against something soft.

He turned to see two children kneeling in the shadows, a boy and a girl with muddy blond hair. Elethor recognized them as twin children from his camp.

"Aw da monstews outside?" asked the girl; she looked to be about five years old.

Her brother raised a wooden sword. "I'll protect you."

Elethor knelt by the children and examined them for wounds; they were bruised and muddy and scratched, but otherwise unhurt. When he looked behind him, he could no longer see the doorway, but he could still hear the nephilim shrieking. The twins clung to him, one clutching him from each side. They shivered.

Nemes, Elethor thought. His old servant. A Vir Requis. *How could a son of Requiem do this?*

As the children embraced him, Elethor's head spun with rage. Solina had betrayed him, but she had always been a daughter of Tiranor; this was a stab in the back, and Elethor swore that someday, somehow, he would reach Nemes and slay him.

The nephilim shrieked outside. The temple shook and dust fell from the ceiling. The rage and darkness of an ancient horde howled outside, and Elethor held the twins close, shut his eyes, and struggled to breathe.

BAYRIN

He woke up with a stiff neck, Piri still cuddling against him.

Merciful stars, he thought and sighed. His every part ached, and he had barely slept with the girl clinging to him.

It's an amazing discovery, he thought. *A creature for one of Mori's bestiaries—half woman, half leech.*

"Up, up!" he said. "It's morning."

He struggled to rise, but Piri only mumbled, scrunched her lips, and wrapped her arms more closely around him. She kept sleeping. For such a slim young thing, she was surprisingly strong, pinning him down.

"Piri Healer!" he said with a groan. "Stars, get *off.*"

The girl was intolerable. Throughout the night, whenever he would crawl away from her, she would snuggle closer, trapping him in her embrace. Whenever he did fall asleep, moments later she would mumble or kick her legs, waking him. And now dawn had risen, and still he could not extricate himself.

Bayrin groaned and let his head fall back onto his pack. He looked up at the sky. Clouds rolled there beyond the branches of maples. It would be a long day of flight, and Bayrin knew his wings would ache, but anything was better than lying here.

"Merciful stars, Piri, will you wake up?" he said. He grabbed her arm and tried to pry it off, but she clung tight.

A distant cry sounded.

Bayrin frowned.

He raised his head and stared. In the distance between trees, he could just make out dark forms in the sky. Shrieks rose, closer this time.

Oh stars.

"Piri!" he said. "Wake up!"

The screeches rolled across the sky. Long figures were flying there like dolls made from sticks, distant but moving fast. A stench of rot wafted through the forest.

Nephilim.

"Piri, Piri, wake up!" He shook her. "I really think you need to wake up now, Piri!"

She scrunched her lips, squeezed her eyes tightly shut, and mumbled. "What, Bay? I'm sleepy."

He managed to pry her arms off, leaped up, and stared east. *Damn it.* A hundred of the creatures flew there, moving straight toward them, and their cries rolled across the land.

"Bay?" Piri sat up and rubbed her eyes. "What's that sound?"

He grabbed her and pulled her to her feet. "Look!"

"Hey!" The young healer wrenched herself free. "Watch who you tug, Bayrin Eleison! I—"

Her eyes fell upon the approaching nephilim and she paled. She grabbed him and pulled him down. They ran at a crouch, grabbed their packs and blankets and pots, and scurried behind a fallen log.

"Bloody stars, Piri," he whispered, "I think you could have slept through the Griffin War."

She elbowed him. "Shush! And stay down." She tugged his cloak over them; leaves and twigs were still woven into it. "Be quiet for once, Bayrin."

"Me?" He bristled. "I—"

She dug her elbow sharply into his stomach. "Shh!"

They crouched under the fallen tree and stared between its branches. The stench of the nephilim flared. Two years ago, after the phoenixes had crushed a building in Nova Vita, Bayrin had helped dig up the ruins. Beneath a fallen wall, they had revealed a rotted corpse, and the stench had nearly knocked him down. These nephilim smelled the same way, but the stench was older somehow: rotten flesh mixed with old leather, dust, and mold on cold stones. Their wings beat, sending leaves flying across the forest floor. Their mothers had been human, and their bodies bore humanoid shapes, though their ribs thrust out like those of birds, and their limbs were stretched like men pulled off the rack. Patches of scales clung to their skin, not bright like the scales of dragons, but rotten like lesions of leprosy. Their faces were bloated like waterlogged corpses about to burst. They screamed to the sky and their claws caught the sun and blazed. Their flesh was perhaps rotten, but those claws still looked sharp and hard as freshly forged blades.

Bayrin grabbed his sword and growled. A hundred or more of the beasts flew above. If they saw him and Piri, could the two flee fast enough? These creatures swarmed as fast as swooping dragons. Bayrin pushed himself deeper under the branches.

He waited for the nephilim to overshoot him and disappear westward. But they circled above like a murder of crows, and their nostrils flared, sniffing as loudly as steam rising from smelters.

"Dragon flesh!" they cried, and their drool rained. "We smell dragon flesh, comrades! Crunchable bones, and blood to sip, and sweet organs to suck on, yes comrades. Dragon flesh hides here! Sweet bone and vein!"

Piri cursed and whispered at his side. "Bayrin, they smell you!"

He peeked between the branches and his stomach sank. The nephilim began to dive down. It happened so quickly, Bayrin barely had time to gasp. A few landed ahead, scattering leaves with bony, clawed feet like those of vultures. One landed behind him, mere feet away, and its swollen head thrust down. Its nostrils flared, and its milky white eyes widened. It opened a mouth full of razor teeth and howled, blowing back fallen leaves.

With a roar, Bayrin leaped forward, drew his sword, and sliced the creature's eyes.

It shrieked.

Blood splattered the leaves.

"Fly, Piri!" Bayrin shouted, leaped, and shifted. His wings beat and he crashed between three nephilim who still flew above. One dived screeching behind him, and he spun and flamed it.

"Piri!" he cried, rising higher and blowing fire.

"Bayrin, here!" she shouted. She flew ahead, her lavender scales flashing between the rotten beasts. She blew fire, flaming two.

He shot toward her. They soared higher. They flew back to back, blowing fire in every direction. The nephilim screeched and surrounded them. One rose from below, and Bayrin knocked it aside with his tail. Another slammed against them from above, and claws tore at Bayrin's back. He roared and gored the beast with his horns.

"Piri, follow me!" he shouted. "I'm breaking through."

With a great roar, he shot forward, claws slashing and fire blazing. A nephil clawed his flank, and he howled. He barreled through them, revealing the western horizon, and shot forward. Teeth bit him. More claws cut him. He kept flying, screaming and blowing his fire.

He glanced over his shoulder and saw Piri flying beside him. Behind them, a hundred nephilim screamed and followed.

Clear cries bugled ahead.

Bayrin looked back to the west, and his breath left him.

Beautiful, he thought. Tears came to his eyes. *Stars, it's beautiful.*

Over the forest flew a horde of salvanae, true dragons of the west. They had no human forms like Vir Requis; they lived feral in the woods and mountains, wise and ancient beings. They had no limbs or wings; they coiled upon the air like serpents upon water, a hundred feet long. Scales shimmered and chinked across them. Their horns were long and bright, and their beards and mustaches fluttered as they flew. Their eyes were like crystal balls, spinning and glowing and topped with long white lashes. A thousand or more flew there, a tapestry woven of silver and gold. As they charged eastward upon the wind, they bugled their cries again, sounding like trumpets of silver from castle towers.

"Bloody stars, the cavalry's arrived!" Bayrin shouted.

He shot toward them, Piri at his side.

Behind them, the nephilim screeched to the sky. The earth shook below. Trees shattered. A boulder cracked. Bayrin screamed with the pain; the sound thudded against him and left his ears ringing.

The salvanae ahead trumpeted again, and this time, their voices pealed with rage. They stormed forward, serpentine bodies undulating upon the wind, beards fluttering. The nephilim screamed, beat their tattered wings, and reached out their claws. The two armies drove toward each other over the toppled forest.

"Up, Piri!" Bayrin shouted.

He soared in a straight line, teeth grinding. Air beat his face. His head spun. Darkness spread across his eyes. Piri flew at his side, growling.

Screams exploded below them as the armies clashed.

Bayrin spun in the air and swooped. Below him, the salvanae were trumpeting their cries. Lighting shot from their maws to slam into nephilim. The beasts burned and screamed. Their claws tore into the salvanae. Scales showered like spilling jewels, and the blood of true dragons rained.

Bayrin blew his fire, drenching a nephil below him. Piri swooped at his side, and her own fire took out another beast.

The sky blazed with battle. Lightning bolts flew everywhere. Fire blazed. The bodies of salvanae and nephilim fell around them, and the forests below caught flame. One nephil shot forward, and its maw opened so wide Bayrin thought its head would split in two. It drove teeth into Piri's shoulder, and she cried out; suddenly she sounded so young to Bayrin, a mere girl.

He roared and drove forward. He leaped onto the nephil, bit down, and tore into its neck. Its scales cut his mouth. Its rotten flesh oozed. He spat out a chunk and bit down again, and the nephil shrieked, releasing Piri. She dipped in the sky, blood streaming down her shoulder.

The nephil turned toward Bayrin, half its neck missing. Black blood spurted from it, and it laughed, a bubbling laughter full of dragon blood. Its eyes were mad, burning with sickly white light.

"Mortal child," it hissed through its laughter. "You do not know what you face. Legion rises! The Fallen rise! Your souls will scream in our darkness. We—"

Bayrin bathed the creature with flame.

It shrieked and fell. When its body hit the forest, it cracked open like a rotten fruit.

Bayrin dived and flew toward Piri. She was wobbling, still aflight but barely higher than the trees. Blood coated her shoulder. He nudged her with his wing, and she gave him a weary smile.

"You saved me, Bayrin."

He looked above him, waiting for nephilim to swoop. He found only salvanae above, and when he looked over the forest, he saw bodies everywhere, two hundred or more; about half of them were the nephilim, their corpses leaking pus and blood. The rest were golden and silver salvanae, the light dimmed from their eyes, their bodies hanging from the trees like the discarded skins of great snakes.

Piri landed in a clearing, shifted into human form, and clutched her wounded shoulder. Bayrin rushed toward her, and she gave him a wan smile.

"My hero," she said and kissed his cheek. "I'm never letting you go now."

Despite the horror, fire, and blood around them, Bayrin rolled his eyes.

The salvanae spiraled down above them like streamers. Soon they hovered a few feet above the clearing, scales chinking like coins. They blinked their crystal eyes, and their long white lashes fanned the grass. Their beards hung low enough to brush the ground. One of them, a dragon of white scales, lowered his head and blinked at Bayrin and Piri. He exhaled through his nostrils, fluttering his mustache and blasting the two Vir Requis with air.

"Children of Draco!" the salvana said. His tufty eyebrows pushed down over his crystal eyes. "A great evil followed you into our realm—an ancient curse. You have brought the Fallen here! We have heard their tales. Our forefathers whose souls fly among the Draco stars have fought these beasts before; they are the spawn of demons. Why have you brought this curse into our land?" The salvana tossed his head back and cried in mourning. "My brothers are slain! Salvanae have fallen! Curse this day."

Bayrin reached into his pack and began rummaging for bandages.

"Save your curses for later," he said. "My friend is wounded, and I have a feeling more of these nephilim are on their way." He looked up at the salvanae. "Queen Solina of Tiranor freed them. She cursed this land, not us. I am Bayrin Eleison of Requiem. Take me to your halls, and I will speak with your leader, the priest Nehushtan." He looked at a dead nephil which leaked blood upon a tree. "Our trouble with these bastards is just beginning."

LYANA

She sat tied to a tree when the nephilim lumbered into the camp.

The tree was an ancient oak, twisting skyward as tall as a palace, and its roots rose around Lyana, coiling and smoothed like the Oak Throne of Requiem's fallen hall. The tree grew in the southern corner of the camp behind piles of firewood; she could see nobody from here other than a distant guard in a tree.

It was seven days since she'd entered Second Haven, and she had spent these days sitting upon these fallen leaves, her wrists bound behind her back and tied to the trunk. The rope was ten feet long, just enough to let her sneak into the bushes when nature called, but too short to reach the huts, gardens, and people of the camp. Twice a day, the bronze brothers would bring her game and wild berries and oats. She ate at her tree. She slept at her tree. She wondered sometimes if she would grow old and die at her tree.

The seventh morning dawned clear and cold; winter was almost here, and the sun seemed small in the pale, cloudless sky, unable to warm her. Lyana shivered in her cloak and gave the ropes a good morning tug, but once again could not break them.

"Here," said Grom, the elder of the bronze brothers, who came trudging through the fallen leaves toward her. "Eat, dog."

He tossed a bowl of stewed greens and venison her way, spilling half onto the ground before her. Lyana glared, wrists bound behind her back. With a growl, she leaned down to grab the food in her mouth. Grom stood above her, smirking.

Before Lyana could take a bite, she heard the shrieks.

The sound tore across the camp, and Lyana winced and yelped. Grom covered his ears. It sounded like steel scratching along stone, like mountains shattering, like ancient souls torn in two. The camp shook with it. The shriek died for an instant, leaving Lyana's ears ringing, and then ten more cries answered it, and Lyana screamed.

Grom fell to his knees and clutched his ears.

"Grom!" Lyana shouted. "Free me. Nephilim. Free me!"

He looked up at her, gasped, and turned to flee. He kicked the bowl of food as he went.

"Grom, damn you!" Lyana shouted. "I will rip your guts out and feed them to the beasts!"

Shouts and screams sounded through the camp. Lyana leaped to her feet, ran ten steps, and the rope yanked her back. From here at her tree—stuck between a palisade on one side, a copse of oaks on the other—she could see nothing. She tried to shift—she had tried it a thousand times these past few days—and failed again, the ropes tugging her back into human form.

"Grom!" she screamed. "Damn you! You will hang for this in the court of my king!"

Fire blazed and heat washed Lyana. Ahead above the trees, she saw dragons take flight. A few were tough, hardened warriors roaring fire. Others were elders missing teeth. A few were youngsters, barely larger than horses. She could catch only glimpses of them between the branches. She saw a nephil shoot above, baring its fangs. She heard a dragon scream.

"Grom!" she shouted.

Screeches rose. Claws grabbed the trees before her and yanked them out. The roots pulled from the soil like hair pulled from a scalp, showering dirt. A nephil stood before her, holding an oak in each hand. The beast tossed back its rotted head, howled at the sky, and threw the trees aside.

Then it saw Lyana, its white eyes widened, and it snarled. Drool splattered. It came lolloping toward her on clawed feet.

Lyana stood with legs parted, rocking on her heels. Her wrists were still bound behind her; the rope which tethered her to the tree stood taut, a good ten feet long. She narrowed her eyes, staring at the approaching beast, and bared her teeth.

The nephil reached her and slammed down its claws.

Lyana leaped aside.

The claws slammed into the earth, digging ruts. The beast thrust its maw forward, teeth jutting out like rusted blades.

Shouting wordlessly, Lyana leaped back, allowing the rope to spin her around the tree like a tether-ball. She placed the trunk between herself and the nephil.

"God damn you, Grom," she muttered. If only she could fly! Stars, if only she had unbound wrists and sword in hand!

The nephil screeched, shaking the earth, and raced around the oak. It thrust down its jaw, and Lyana leaped back again. Its teeth dug into the earth. It raised its head and howled, a shattering sound that splattered drool and earth and dry leaves.

Lyana pressed herself close to the tree trunk, narrowed her eyes, and nodded at the rotted giant. The rope which ran between her wrists and the trunk lay loose at her feet.

With a howl, the nephil lashed its claws.

Lyana leaped forward, tightening the rope between herself and the trunk. The nephil's claws severed it.

Shouting hoarsely, Lyana ran through the camp. The nephil raced behind her. Its jaws lashed down, and she rolled. Its teeth missed her by inches. She leaped up and tried to shift, but could not; she was free from the tree, but the rope still bound her wrists behind her back.

Dragons and nephilim howled above her. Children ran through the camp. Lyana scurried forward. She looked over her shoulder and saw her nephil leap skyward like a giant, rotten grasshopper. The beast came plunging down toward her, and Lyana screamed and turned her head aside.

Fire blazed.

Through squinting eyes, Lyana saw a legless red dragon—Dorin Blacksmith!—crash into the nephil an instant before the beast could hit her. Dragon and nephil tumbled, rolled through the leaves, and crashed into a tree.

Lyana leaped up, whipping her head from side to side. The battle raged around her, nephilim and dragons slashing and biting and burning.

A blade. I need a blade!

Her eyes fell upon Grom.

"The poor fool," she muttered.

The miner lay in human form, his legs bitten off, his eyes staring lifelessly. He still clutched a sword in his hand—*her* sword, the ancient blade Levitas. The leaves around him soaked up his blood.

She ran toward him, turned backward, and crouched. She ran her wrists against Levitas, cutting the rope.

Three nephilim flew above, howled, and came swooping toward her.

The rope fell off her wrists.

Lyana grabbed her sword, shifted with it, and soared.

A blue dragon, she roared her fire, bathing the creatures. She shot through her own flame, lashed her claws, and crashed between the blazing nephilim. They fell around her, burnt and lacerated.

Lyana soared higher, rising from flame. Dragons and nephilim fought around her. She slew one beast with a blast of fire, then spun and swooped, the sun at her back. She crashed between the treetops into the camp, swung her claws, and ripped the head off a charging nephil.

Wails rose behind her. Lyana landed and spun around. A nephil was chasing a group of toddlers too young to shift. The children leaped under a fallen bole, which the nephil began to slash at. Still in dragon form, Lyana charged and leaped onto the nephil's back. It bucked, and she dug her teeth into its shoulder.

Gooey blood filled her mouth. The nephil screeched and she pulled it backward, allowing the toddlers to flee. She crashed onto her back, the nephil writhing above her. Lyana pushed her tail down, thrust herself up, and tossed the nephil forward. When it spun toward her, she flamed it and it fell.

She looked around the camp, panting. The battle was over.

The nephilim all lay dead, their corpses oozing pus and black blood thick with worms. Some lay burnt, others slashed with claws, their entrails dangling and their innards bustling with cockroaches. Many Vir Requis lay dead too, a hundred or more; they were torn apart, limbs strewn, heads severed. Some were half-eaten, and their blood stained the teeth of the fallen nephilim. Huts and trees burned, and living dragons flew between them, patting down the flames with tails and wings.

Lyana's head spun. She shifted back into human form and clutched her sword. Her hand trembled and her breath shook in her lungs.

War. War and blood and death again. She gritted her teeth, forcing down the horror. *You are Lyana Eleison, Queen of Requiem, ruler to these people. You will not panic. You will not faint. You will stay strong.*

A hoarse cry rose through the camp. Lyana drew her sword, for an instant sure a nephil still lived. She looked up to see Gar Miner walk through the camp, the younger of the bronze brothers. He howled and wept, carrying the body of his fallen brother.

"Dead!" he cried. "My brother is dead!" The short, burly miner looked at Lyana and his eyes blazed. "She led them here.

Lyana Eleison arrived in our camp, and these beasts followed her." Tears ran down his cheeks. "She murdered my brother!"

He lowered his dead brother to the ground, knelt over him, and wept.

Around the camp, people muttered and stared at Lyana. One man, his arm lacerated, spat and glared. Two young men grabbed spears, and Gar rose to his feet and grabbed a club. They began to advance toward Lyana, stepping over corpses, and blood coated their boots. Lyana snarled and raised her sword.

"You accuse your queen of treason," she said softly. "Come lay this charge before my sword; Levitas will cut your lying tongues from your mouths." She spat toward them. "I've slain more of Solina's beasts in this war than you have thoughts in your skulls. If you accuse me of treason, I will slay you too."

They kept advancing toward her, raising their weapons. Ash and blood covered their faces.

"You are no queen in Second Haven," said Gar. He limped; a gash ran down his leg. "You are a stranger here, and you've brought only blood to this camp. Your blood will be the last shed here."

The men charged toward her.

Lyana growled and raised her sword.

"Cease this madness!" rose a shout over the camp.

A legless red dragon dived down from above, wings raising a cloud of fallen leaves and dirt. Snorting smoke, Dorin landed by the combatants. He shoved his head between them, nudging Lyana away from Gar and his comrades. He blasted more smoke from his nostrils and grumbled. When Gar tried to step around him, Dorin slapped him back with his wing, and the miner's club thumped to the ground.

Dorin shifted back into human form. He lay legless upon the leaves, his grizzled hair and beard matted with dirt and soot. He grumbled and pushed himself up onto his elbows.

"Gar," he said and coughed. Soon his entire body shook as he hacked. "Gar, fetch me my seat. Go, son."

The young miner still shed tears. He looked at Lyana. He looked back at his dead brother, and a sob racked his body. Finally Gar stormed into the wooden hall—half its roof had collapsed—and emerged carrying the mock Oak Throne carved from roots. He placed it upon the forest floor, grabbed Dorin under his arms, and lifted him into the seat.

The Legless Lord sat in the forest, and slowly the Vir Requis of his camp gathered around. Many clutched wounds.

Dorin shouted, voice hoarse. "People of Second Haven! Hear me. Hear your Lord Dorin. This camp is lost; Queen Solina knows we are here, and she will send more of these beasts our way. We must leave this place."

All around, men and women wailed, whispered, and looked from side to side. Gardens lay trampled. Huts lay fallen. The palisades were smashed.

Lyana lowered her head. She knew what these people were thinking.

They spent moons building this place, she thought. *They believed their life could spring anew here—a new city for the children of Requiem, a new haven. Now they relive the destruction of Nova Vita. Now again they are refugees.*

She stepped toward Dorin and bowed her head.

"Lord Dorin," she said softly; for the first time, she gave him the honor of a title. "You fought nobly. You saved my life." She held her sword before her, blade pointing down. "Fight by my side. Fly with me to Confutatis, capital of this kingdom you hide in, and speak with me to the king of men. Let us Vir Requis form an alliance with Osanna." She raised her sword. "We will not just flee. We will not hide. We will *fight*."

Dorin stared up at her from his seat, eyes narrowed and shrewd. His lips tightened and he clutched the armrests.

"How can we fight such evil?" he said, voice low.

She grabbed his shoulder. "We fly south. We fly to Tiranor. Solina is sending her wrath north, emptying her lands. We will fly to those lands and rain fire upon her." She tightened her fingers around him and stared into his eyes. "Fly with me, Dorin. The days of hiding are over. Fly with me, sound your roar, and blow your fire with mine. A dragon needs no legs, only fire and wings."

He glared up at her, lips tightened and trembling. Finally he coughed, spat sideways, and stared back at her.

"I will not serve you as some man-at-arms." His fists shook around his seat's armrests. "My sons served your husband, the Boy King Elethor. They fell upon his towers. I flew for Elethor. I lost my legs in his service. No, girl. My days of serving Elethor are over. Requiem is fallen, and he has no titles in these lands, nor do you."

Her lip curled. "Requiem did not fall. She lives in the west, in Salvandos, among tree and stone, a light in our hearts."

Dorin snorted. "Then let Requiem remain in the west." He swept his arm around him and spoke louder. "This is Second Haven! This is a free realm. Look at our banners upon the trees; they fly still." He looked back at her with narrowed eyes and spoke softly. "But yes, Lyana. I will fly with you. And I will rain fire upon those who destroyed our camp. I will not bend the knee before King Elethor even if I still had knees to bend. Let Requiem and Second Haven fly together, two free nations aligned, and together we will crush this desert queen."

Lyana stared at him silently. The man still spoke treason. To secede from Requiem meant to hang from her walls.

She lowered her head. *Yet those walls are fallen. And I cannot fight this entire camp, nor will I kill my own people.* She heaved a sigh. *Bloody stars, but Elethor will kill me when he hears.*

She nodded. "We fly together, Dorin. Requiem and Second Haven. Let us seek what allies we can in these eastern realms—men and griffins who will fight at our side." She gripped her sword and snarled. "And then we will set the desert aflame."

ELETHOR

She lay nude beside him, golden in the dawn. The light cascaded through the window, dappling her with pale mottles. She smiled at him—the smile that showed her teeth—a smile so rich and full and singing of purity, and a smile so rare these days, so precious to him. Her platinum hair cascaded like a moonlit river, hiding her breasts, so pale it was almost white, and Elethor ran his fingers through it. He touched her nose, marveling at the golden freckles he loved, and ran his hand over her body, tracing her curves from shoulder, down her ribs, into the deep valley of her waist, and finally up the hill of her hip. He had caressed her landscape countless times, and every time he lost his breath at its beauty.

"Solina," he whispered her name. Daughter of sunlight, the name meant in her tongue. Sun of his life.

They lay in his bed upon blankets of green and silver wool—the colors of Requiem. Around them stood the statues that filled his small house upon the hill: marble elks with antlers of gold; a wooden turtle with jeweled eyes he had carved for Solina; and statues of Solina herself, nude or clad in flowing robes of marble.

"They are all away," she whispered, leaned forward on her elbow, and kissed his lips. "Today is ours."

He looked outside the window above and breathed in the clear air. *A free day. A day for us.* His father, his brother, the Lady Lyana, even his little sister—they had all flown to distant Oldnale Farms for a feast. The courts of Requiem had emptied; only he, Prince Elethor, remained to rule.

*But I intend to spend the entire time here in bed with this very
beautiful, very naked woman.*

He ran his hand again over her curves, from waist to hip
and back. She reached under the blankets, sneaked her hand into
his pants, and closed her fingers around him. She smiled softly
and kissed him. They had made love last night for what seemed
like hours; in the dawn, he loved her again until she screamed and
scratched his back so violently, he bled.

A day for us. A free day. A perfect day.

They held each other close in bed. They closed their eyes
under the soft light, and they slept again, and they did not wake
until noon.

Finally Solina rose from the bed, walked to the window,
and stretched before the trees that rustled outside, nude and
golden and drenched in light. She was a work of art to him,
greater than any statue he could sculpt. She looked over her
shoulder at him.

"Wake up, sleepy," she said. "I'm hungry."

She stepped toward the bed, pulled the blanket off him,
and wrapped it around herself. He rose with a grunt, embraced
her, and kissed her head. They held each other closely for long
moments before breaking apart, stepping into his pantry, and
rummaging for food.

They filled a basket with bread rolls, a jar of preserves,
smoked sausages, a slab of butter, a wheel of tangy cheese, and
hard yellow apples. They took their meal outside and sat upon
the grass beneath the cypresses. She wore nothing but the blanket
wrapped around her shoulders; he wore only his woolen trousers.
Below the hill where Elethor had built his home rolled the city of
Nova Vita: the palace of marble columns, the domed temple, and
the cobbled streets that snaked between birches.

That palace is empty now, he thought. *The day is ours: a day of
sunlight, a day of peace, a day of Solina.*

"What will we do today?" he asked as they ate. "Walk through the forest? Go swim in the lake? Maybe visit the library and read old books?"

She yawned magnificently. "Too hard." She lay back on the grass, and her hair spread out around her like molten white gold. The sunlight danced upon her face. "I'm just going to lie here all day." She reached out, grabbed him, and pulled him back. "And you will lie here with me."

He lay on his back watching the clouds, and she nestled against him, and soon she slept again. He kissed her forehead and held her in his arms, and her breath danced against his neck. He closed his eyes, Solina warm against him.

This is the best day of my life, he thought. *Here and now, this is perfect. This is all I ever want. Never let this end.*

A shriek tore the day.

Elethor opened his eyes and found himself in darkness. Solina slipped into shadow, and he tried to grab her, and his heart ached at her loss, and then the shriek sounded again and he covered his ears.

He rose from the cold stone floor and looked upon a shadowy, dusty tunnel. His body ached, and dried blood covered his left arm. At his side, children cowered and held one another. The shriek sounded again, coming from far above through walls of stone—the nephilim circling above the temple ruins.

Elethor clenched his jaw. His dream faded, the last warmth of sunlight and Solina's embrace falling into a deep, throbbing cold.

He grimaced. He had slept in his armor, and every muscle and joint in him groaned. The mossy brick walls pressed close around him. The root of a great tree thrust down through the ceiling, splitting the room. Behind the root, a dozen more Vir Requis huddled—the young twins and ten others who had scurried inside. They had been hiding here for six days now, drinking what rainwater dripped through the ceiling and eating only what supplies they had carried in their packs and pockets.

The screech sounded again from outside, a cry torn in agony. The tunnel where they hid shook and moss rained from the ceiling's bricks.

"Something is going on out there," grumbled Garvon. The leathery, one-eyed man huddled against a wall, his white beard caked with mud. "I don't like this."

Elethor frowned and found himself agreeing. The past three days had been eerily silent. They had heard nephilim pacing and grunting outside, sometimes shrieking in rage. They had heard other Vir Requis shout from their own hideouts in abandoned cellars and halls. But this—this cry of agony—was new.

"Something is hurting them," Elethor muttered. "That is no scream of rage or hunger. It's a scream of pain."

Were the other Vir Requis emerging to fight? No; he heard no dragon roars. Did Bayrin return with the salvanae or Lyana with griffins? Elethor could not hear them either; salvanae bugled and sang in battle, and griffins let out eagle cries.

Garvon rose to his feet. His hoary head nearly hit the ceiling. He drew his sword with a grunt.

"Get ready," he said and spat. "They're planning something."

The nephilim screeched again, and a new stench flared from outside, one of blood and sour milk and worms. Elethor could not see outside from here—the tunnel curved, sealing them in shadow. He began walking toward the bend. He had to look outside, to see what new devilry festered there.

Garvon grabbed his shoulder. "I go first."

The old man shoved Elethor back, trudged around him, and walked down the tunnel toward the exit. Elethor drew Ferus, his old longsword, and walked close behind. The stench invaded his nostrils as violently as demons thrusting into mortal women.

The crumbly doorway stood before them, lichen hanging from the lintel. Elethor frowned and Garvon muttered. For the past three days, nephilim had stood here, reaching claws and teeth through the doorway like cats pawing at mouse holes. Today Elethor saw sunlight through the doorway, no claws or teeth blocking the exit. The screeches rose outside, and the stench of blood and rot swirled so powerfully Elethor nearly gagged.

Garvon kept advancing toward the doorway, sword raised. Elethor walked close behind. Soon they stood in range of thrusting claws; Elethor saw their grooves cut into the walls and floor.

"Careful, Garvon," he said.

The old soldier froze, spat, and cursed. Elethor looked over Garvon's shoulder into the forest. He felt the blood leave his face.

"Stars," he whispered.

The nephilim stood in a ring outside between fallen statues, crumbling walls, and trees that grew from cracked flagstones. Between them lay a howling nephil. She was a female, Elethor saw; her rotted breasts hung loose like bags of sour milk, and her shrieks sounded almost human.

They are half human, he remembered with a chill, *the spawn of demons and human mothers.*

The female nephil dug her claws into the earth, tearing stone and root. Her screams rose. Her legs lay open, and blood sprayed from between them. She gave a great howl, and a warty head began to emerge from her womb. The mother screeched. Her spawn's head burst out, coated in blood and mucus, and screeched.

"Stars damn it, oh stars damn it," Elethor hissed through clenched teeth.

The nephil spawn thrust its claws out, tearing the opening wider. Its mother wept and screeched, and the nephilim around her roared and reached for the heavens. The spawn fell into the dirt, coated with blood, and bit off its umbilical cord. It stood the size of a man, its wings limp and dripping, its flesh already rotten and covered in boils. It wailed and leaped onto its mother. It grabbed onto her breast and began to feed, not drinking milk but tearing into the flesh, feasting like a wolf upon prey.

Garvon growled low in his throat. "Bastards."

More blood gushed from the mother.

Another spawn began to emerge, wailing and clawing and biting its way out. Soon the second beast began to feast, ripping into its mother's flesh. Across the forest ruins, more shrieks sounded, followed by the shrill wails of spawn.

"They're small enough to enter the tunnels," Elethor said softly.

Garvon stared at him, teeth bared. "They're too young; they're babes."

"Babes who are tearing apart grown nephilim and eating their flesh." He grabbed his shield from over his back and slung it onto his arm. "Garvon, I—"

A squeal rose outside, cutting off his words. One of the spawn leaped off its mother, face smeared with blood, and stared right at them. Its eyes burned with white fire. Its lips pulled back, revealing long teeth like daggers. It came racing toward them, squealing and snapping its jaws.

Garvon cursed and raised his sword.

The spawn reached the doorway, leaped into the tunnel, and crashed onto the old man.

Elethor yowled and thrust his sword, but could not reach the spawn without cutting Garvon too. The old soldier screamed and hacked at the creature; it was nearly as large as him. Garvon fell. The spawn opened its jaws wide, bit down, and tore into

Garvon's head. With thick claws, it cracked the skull open and began to feast.

Elethor screamed, heart thrashing, and thrust his sword.

The blade slammed into the spawn's chest, and blood sprayed.

The beast writhed upon the sword. It lashed out its claws, mewling. Elethor raised his shield, and the claws slammed into it, scattering chips of wood. Screaming hoarsely, his boots sticky with blood, Elethor pulled his blade back and swung it down. He cleaved the demon open from collarbone to navel, and centipedes fled from its body to scurry across the floor.

Elethor gagged. His head spun. The spawn fell dead, and Elethor stepped toward the doorway and chanced a look outside. He cursed. More demon spawn were racing across the forest and leaping into burrows, doorways, and tunnels. Among the ruins, other pockets of surviving Vir Requis fought. They swung swords from under fallen statues and collapsing roofs. Beyond an expanse of trees rose a crumbling hall; great stone faces stared stoically from its walls, mossy and green with vines. Nephil spawn were climbing the walls and trying to crawl into holes and windows. Fire blasted from within, roasting the beasts; dragons hid inside.

Shrieks sounded ahead. Elethor snarled. Two demon spawn came racing toward his tunnel, eyes blazing and teeth stained with blood.

Elethor raised his sword. The two nephil infants crashed into him, jaws snapping; they were nearly his size.

He roared and shoved one back with his shield. The other lashed claws, scratching across his breastplate and raising sparks. Elethor drove his sword's crossguard into the beast, and its skull cracked, and it howled. The demon behind his shield began biting at the wood, and Elethor drove forward, crushing the beast between his shield and the wall. Another spawn came racing from the forest and leaped onto him, and Elethor crashed down. Within an instant, three of the beasts were atop him, biting and slashing, and one's claw broke through his breastplate to scratch his chest. Elethor screamed and saw nothing but their rotting faces.

A blade whistled overhead. Steel crashed into a spawn's head, crumpling it like a tin mug, and the creature fell. Elethor leaped to his feet, swung down his sword, and slew another. At his side, he glimpsed one of the survivors, a boy of fourteen named Yar. The boy was trembling but managed to swing his sword again, stabbing another spawn. They swung their blades together, and soon the last of the creatures lay dead.

Yar shook, bent over, and gagged. Elethor placed a hand on the boy's shoulder. The corpses lay stinking; cockroaches and worms fled from them.

Elethor stepped over the corpses and looked outside. Across the forest, more female nephilim were falling over, howling and tearing down trees, and spawning their vermin. Hundreds of the infants shrieked.

At least, Elethor thought wryly, *we didn't meet any ghosts.*

"We can't fight them," Yar whispered, trembling. "So many. Hundreds."

Elethor grunted. "We're trapped in here." He stared at the youth. "Yar, carry the toddlers with you; they are too young to shift. Fly behind me. We're breaking out."

The youth trembled and clutched his sword before him. "There are thousands of nephilim out there. Where will we go?"

Elethor stared outside into the forest; he could see the vermin emerging from rotten wombs, crawling to the breast, and feasting upon the meat. In moments, they would be racing here to feast upon Vir Requis too.

He clenched his fist. *Damn you, Solina. Damn you, Nemes.* With Garvon dead, Yar was the only survivor in this huddle old enough to fight; the others were mere children. *There is no more safety here.*

"Yar," he said, "listen carefully. There is a wide hall among the ruins—about five hundred yards from here. There are stone faces on the walls, and the roots of trees clutch the place, sending trunks up through the ceiling. Don't look outside now! Some Vir Requis hide there, and they hide as dragons; I saw their fire blasting out the windows. Our burrow is too small; we cannot hold back these spawn with our swords. The great hall is wider. We can crouch there as dragons and join our fire to those who already hide there."

Yar's hands shook around his hilt. "My lord, five hundred yards... stars, we'll never make it. They'll tear us apart."

Ahead in the forest, the fresh spawn raised their faces from the bloodied torsos of their mothers, stared toward the tunnel, and hissed. With screeches, they came racing toward them.

"They'll tear us apart here," Elethor said. "Yar, get the others! Follow me to the hall!"

Snarling, Elethor raced outside into the forest, shifted into a dragon, and blew his fire. The nephilim howled and swarmed toward him.

BAYRIN

Bayrin had heard tales of Har Zahav, the mythical golden mountain of the salvanae. In old books, he had read how Kyrie Eleison and Agnus Dei, the great hero and heroine of Requiem, had visited this place to summon the salvanae to aid them. Those books described a volcano of pure gold rising from the forest, above it a sky full of the true dragons. In countless illustrations, tapestries, and paintings Bayrin had admired the scene: the two Vir Requis, among the last of their kind, flying to the golden hall under a sky of coiling, glittering salvanae with flowing beards and crystal eyes.

During the journey here, Bayrin had imagined himself like Kyrie Eleison, the old prince of Requiem, and imagined Piri as Agnus Dei, the fiery warrior-princess. He had imagined them too flying among wise salvanae toward a mountain of wonder and magic.

Now Har Zahav rose before him, the golden mountain of legend, and Bayrin's eyes dampened at its glory lost. Nephilim had flown here. Whatever beauty had once shone here had fallen to their rot.

"Stars," Piri whispered, flying beside him. Her eyes dampened. "Stars, Bayrin, we're too late."

A battle had raged here not long ago. The pines lay smashed and burnt below. The mountain did rise ahead—triangular and golden like in the paintings—but blood and ash now coated it, and the corpses of both salvanae and nephilim lay upon its slopes. More bodies littered the forest below: salvanae torn into segments, the glow of their eyes dimmed, and nephilim charred with lighting, their corpses bustling with maggots.

"When the wyverns attacked last year, we found no allies," Bayrin said softly. "The world did not believe that Solina could threaten it too. Stars, Piri. Look at this world now."

Those salvanae who had first found Bayrin and Piri in the forests now flew around them. At the sight of their bloodied mountain and the corpses of their brothers, the salvanae tossed back their heads and cried with grief. Their calls rang out like mournful bells, like forests weeping, and their tears fell as rain into smoldering fires.

"Salvandos!" they cried. "Salvandos, land of the true dragons! We will avenge you, land of Draco. Your beauty rivaled the light of stars, Salvandos! You were brighter than sunlight, sweeter than wine."

Gliding beside him, her lavender scales glimmering under the veiled sun, Piri looked at Bayrin with soft eyes.

"Are the other salvanae all dead?" she whispered.

Bayrin looked ahead across the smoldering forests to the mountain. He squinted and then breathed in relief.

"Look, Piri," he said and pointed a claw. "Some still live."

A group of salvanae rose from the mountain, their scales splashed with blood. They coiled skyward, wailing in grief, then dived down the mountainside toward their slain kin. Flying serpents, they had no limbs or wings, and Bayrin caught his breath, wondering how they would lift the bodies and carry them to burial. The salvanae opened their mouths wide, tears in their eyes.

Piri gasped and looked aside. "Stars, Bayrin! They... stars! They're eating them!"

As he glided toward the mountain, Bayrin stared with disbelief. Piri was right. The living salvanae took the tails of their fallen into their mouths. They began to swallow the fallen like snakes swallowing their prey. As they ate the dead, more salvanae coiled above, singing songs of mourning. The clouds parted, and rays of light fell upon the golden mountain, and the song rose like the keen of harps. Bayrin knew he should be horrified. *Stars, they're cannibals!* And yet, as he glided upon the wind, this act—the consumption of the fallen—seemed not obscene but deeply sad, deeply respectful.

"It's a last honor," he whispered. "The fallen will become part of the living. Their blood will live on."

When the bodies were gone, the salvanae rose—heavier and rounder—into the air. They coiled toward the top of their golden volcano and vanished inward into darkness.

Above the mountain floated a great, golden salvana with a flowing white beard. He came flying across the charred forest toward Bayrin and Piri; they met above golden, bloodied foothills.

"Children of Draco," said the salvana, and his eyes shone with tears.

Bayrin recognized him; here was Nehushtan, High Priest of Salvandos. Bayrin had seen the wise old dragon in Requiem; Nehushtan had visited Nova Vita a year ago to meet with Elethor.

Sudden rage filled Bayrin, erupting from his nostrils with puffs of smoke. He wanted to slash his claws at the old salvana, to slam him against the mountain, to burn him dead.

When the wyverns attacked, you abandoned us! he wanted to shout. *Elethor begged you for aid, and you refused. Look at you now! Look at your dead.*

He fumed, unable to speak. Nehushtan only looked at him, tears in his eyes. When Bayrin looked into those great, glittering orbs like crystal balls, his rage faded. Such sadness lived in those eyes, such regret.

I am sorry, those eyes seemed to say to him, and starlight swirled inside them. *I am sorry and I will forever mourn.*

Hovering in midair, Bayrin snorted smoke and looked aside.

"Nehushtan," he said. "I am Bayrin Eleison, a son of Requiem, and this is Piri Healer, a daughter of our stars. We come on behalf of King Elethor and Queen Lyana. Let us fly into your hall. Let us speak." He looked over the bodies of nephilim that still littered the mountain and forests. "We have much to discuss."

Smoke rose from scattered fires. Ash painted the sky. The stench of rot filled the air. Salvandos burned, and the salvanae above wept, their tears falling as rain to wash the blood and soot. Bayrin thought back to that day eight years ago when Solina had fled Requiem, scarred and screaming of vengeance. Now that vengeance burned the world.

Nehushtan turned and began flying around the mountainsides, and Bayrin and Piri followed. Upon the western slope, they found more bodies, blood, and rot. Hundreds of nephilim lay dead upon the foothills like great insects swept down a river. A great hole loomed open in the mountainside, its rim showing the marks of claws and teeth. The mountain was not solid, Bayrin saw, but hollow; through the hole, he saw salvanae coiling among orbs of floating light. They seemed to fill the mountain like ants filling a hive.

Beard flowing like a banner, Nehushtan coiled through the air, flew into the hole, and vanished into the mountain. Bayrin glanced at Piri, and she looked back, eyes sad. They flew side by side, heading over the bodies and through the gaping hole. They entered the hall of Salvandos.

The mountain's innards loomed around them, a cavern the size of a city. Glowing orbs floated through the hall, casting their light upon golden walls and burrows. The place indeed seemed like a great hive; salvanae coiled through the air, flowing from and into round passageways. Far below upon a polished floor, a pile of nephilim lay dead and burnt between fallen boulders. Several dead salvanae lay around them, torn apart.

Nehushtan flew upward and crashed between a cluster of floating orbs, sending the balls of light flying. Bayrin and Piri flapped their wings, rising after him. He led them to a wall of pods like a honeycomb. Thousands of the alcoves covered the wall; the heads of salvanae peeked from some, their eyes blinking and their beards hanging.

Nehushtan hovered before one pod. He turned to look at Bayrin and Piri and nodded.

"You will spend the night here," the old priest said. "Inside you will find sweet fruit and sweet water, and you will rest." His lips pulled back, revealing sharp teeth, and his brows pushed low; suddenly his face was terrible, a mask of rage. "And tomorrow, children of Draco... tomorrow you will fly with the hosts of Salvandos. Tomorrow we will fly to blood and death and song. Tomorrow we fly to war."

With that, the true dragon flew away into shadow.

The entrance to the pod was round and narrow; it could perhaps fit a slim and long salvana, but not a bulky dragon of Requiem. Bayrin clung to the opening with his claws, shifted into human form, and climbed in. He looked over his shoulder to see Piri do the same.

The pod was long, round, and narrow—a cozy little nook. Standing here in human form, Bayrin felt like a small forest critter nesting in a hollow log. Fresh leaves carpeted the floor, and the walls were carved of smooth stone. In the back lay clear, round vessels holding fruits, wine, nuts, and leafy greens. At first Bayrin thought these made of glass, but when he lifted a sphere, it burst and spilled berries into his hands.

Bubbles, he thought and began to eat. The berries too burst when he ate them, spilling juice down his throat. He began tearing into the other bubbles and feasting.

"Come on, Piri!" he said through a mouthful of almonds. "It's good."

He looked over his shoulder at her... and the rest of the almonds fell from his gaping mouth. She stood naked before him, holding her cloak in one hand. Her body was tall, lithe, and tanned. She let the cloak drop and took a few steps toward him.

"Bayrin," she said softly. "Forget about your belly for now. Take me instead."

He sighed and rose to his feet. She took his hands and smiled at him, a smile that began seductively but ended trembling, and her eyes dampened.

"Piri!" he said and touched a tear on her cheek.

She placed her hands in his hair and kissed him deeply. Her lips were soft and full, and her tongue sought his, and her naked body pressed against him. For a moment Bayrin closed his eyes, overwhelmed with the warmth and softness of her.

Then he broke their kiss and looked aside.

"Piri, I can't," he whispered. "I'm sworn to another."

She touched his cheek, tears in her eyes. "I know, Bay. I miss Mori too. She was my princess and my friend. But... it's been moons now. We lost so many in Nova Vita. I loved Mori, but we have to move on; we have to realize she is gone. I am so sorry for your loss, Bay, but..." Her tears flowed. "But *I* love you. *I* need you now. I've loved you for years, Bayrin—since our first kiss four winters ago under the stars. You remember that night, don't you? Will you not return my love now, here, as the world burns?"

She tried to kiss his lips again, but he turned his head, and her kiss landed on his cheek.

"Bay," she whispered, held his head, and turned it toward her.

He stepped back and held her waist, keeping space between them. He stared into her eyes.

"Mori is still alive," he said, unable to keep anger away from his voice. "I know it. I can't betray her." His voice softened and he held her hands. "Stars, Piri, you are beautiful. You are kind and brave and you are..." He couldn't help but look down at her naked body, then up again, and a sigh fled his lips. "Stars, but you *are* perfect. But I can't. Not while there's still a chance Mori will return."

She nodded, tears on her cheeks, and closed her eyes.

"Then hold me one last time," she whispered. "Please, Bay. Hold me just once and hold me tight, because I'm so scared."

He held her close, his arms around her, and she laid her head upon his shoulder.

Behind her, a figure stepped into the pod. A voice rose, high and hesitant.

"Bayrin?"

He looked over Piri's shoulder.

His breath died.

At the doorway, clad in a white cloak, stood Mori.

ELETHOR

He flew across the temple ruins, roaring fire.

"Vir Requis!" he shouted. "Fall back to the main hall! Fall back! We gather in the Hall of Faces."

That hall, once the central temple of Bar Luan, rose at the back of the ruins. Over thousands of years, the rest of the complex had fallen to the encroaching forest; roots, trunks, and branches had gradually broken down Bar Luan's outer walls, smaller homes, and statues. The great Hall of Faces, however, still stood. Its walls were pockmarked and green with moss. The great stone faces upon those walls, each as large as a dragon, were smoothed with countless winters of rain and snow. Holes gaped open in the walls, punched by tree roots or the slow pummeling of the years.

Today fire blasted from those holes, burning the spawn of nephilim. Some dragons hid inside that great hall; there was safety there, Elethor thought. But many Vir Requis—hundreds of them, perhaps—still hid across the rest of the complex. These ones crouched in human forms. They hid under fallen statues, inside the small stone homes of ancient monks, or in tunnels that had once led to cellars. These hideouts had protected them from the fully grown nephilim; those beasts were too large to enter burrows where humans could fit. Now, as Elethor flew above the ruins, the spawn of nephilim scuttled across the ruins like cockroaches, entering every hollow and hole and feasting upon what flesh they found. Hundreds swarmed.

Three nephilim took flight from a craggy wall and flapped toward him. Their claws reached out, and their teeth snapped.

Elethor doused them with fire. More nephilim soared from the ruins below and crashed into him. Elethor swiped his tail and crushed one's head. Another clawed his legs, and Elethor howled and flamed it.

"Vir Requis!" he shouted. "Fly with me! To the hall!"

A few Vir Requis burst out from their hiding places. Three children—just old enough to shift—emerged from a cellar, shifted, and took flight. Nephilim screeched and swooped toward them. From under a statue rose a silver dragon; she clutched her babe in her claws, a boy too young to shift. Three youths ran from inside a crumbled old home, took flight, and roared fire.

"To the Hall of Faces!" Elethor howled. "Enter through the windows at the back."

He flamed another nephil. To his left, three dragons soared. Nephilim crashed into them, claws swinging. One of the dragons screamed, then fell as a bloodied human girl. Beneath Elethor, three graybeards ran from a cellar, swinging clubs at nephil spawn. One old man fell, and the spawn leaped onto him, and blood sprayed.

The nephilim covered the sky. More kept rising from the trees. Elethor cursed and began flying toward the temple, spraying his fire.

"Fly!" he shouted. "Vir Requis, to the hall! Follow!"

Dozens of dragons soared around him, blowing their flames. Walls of fire rose around them. Nephilim tried to break through. They blazed and screeched and fell. The trees below kindled, and smoke filled the sky. Elethor coughed, barely able to see. More dragons kept rising from below. More nephilim crashed into them, biting and clawing. One crashed onto Elethor's back, and its teeth scraped his shoulder, and he roared and bucked. He slammed his tail like a scorpion, driving its spikes into the nephil; as the beast fell, he flamed it.

"To the Hall of Faces!" he cried. "Enter the windows."

He began circling the great, crumbling temple. Through holes in the walls and ceiling, he saw hundreds of Vir Requis inside. Most huddled in the center of the temple in human forms. The rest stood as dragons at the walls, blasting fire from windows, archways, and holes.

"We're sending people in!" Elethor shouted at them through a hole in the roof. "Make room!"

The dragons inside nodded, pulled back from one window, and opened a path for survivors. At once, the nephil spawn began clattering up the wall outside toward the window. Elethor swooped and whipped his tail, shoving them off. He blasted flames against the wall, burning the others.

Teeth bit into his wings, and he dipped several feet. Spawn covered him, biting and clawing. Elethor growled and shook, but they clung to him. He crashed onto the forest floor, and the brood crawled over him like ants over a discarded piece of fruit. Elethor roared and rolled and blew flames, but the spawn seemed endless.

Roars sounded above. A yellow dragon dived, shifted into human form, and leaped onto Elethor's back. It was Yar, the youth who had shared Elethor's tunnel for six days. He began swinging his sword, knocking the spawn off.

"Yar, shift and blow fire!" Elethor shouted. "Help me hold them back."

The boy nodded, leaped, and shifted back into dragon form. He and Elethor stood flanking the window, blowing flames at the encroaching spawn. Two walls of fire spread from the temple across the complex, creating a corridor.

Dragons dived into the corridor of fire, shifted into humans, and began leaping through the window into the temple. Soon a dozen had entered, and more kept landing between the streams of flame. Elethor dug his claws into the earth; he had maybe a few more breaths of fire in him before he would need rest.

Three young dragons landed in the corridor, shifted, and began running toward the window. An adult nephil swooped from above and tore into them. Its claws ripped them apart and the beast howled, tossing limbs aside like a child tossing toys.

Elethor growled and turned his fire toward the beast, crossing his flames with Yar's. The nephil shrieked and burned. More came flying from Elethor's other side, and more spawn began crawling atop him. He roared and fell back against the temple, cracking the wall, and tore the beasts off. He looked up to see thousands fly toward him; they covered the ruins.

"Yar, get inside!" he shouted. "Into the temple."

The yellow dragon growled at his side, clawing at demon spawn. "Not without you, my king."

"Go now, Yar! I'll hold them back. Go!"

He trundled toward the boy, shaking spawn off his back, and whipped his tail, knocking more beasts off the yellow dragon's back.

"Go!"

Yar blasted fire at the sky, catching a diving nephil, and shifted. He leaped through the window into the temple.

Elethor stood outside the walls, alone with the nephilim. The covered the ruins before him: the forest floor, the trees, the crumbled walls, and the sky. He could see nothing but them, a tapestry of the Abyss. Their eyes blazed, burning white. Their tongues lolled, raining drool. Some had swollen, distorted heads that leaked pus. Others had gaunt, long faces lined with spikes. Some had nothing but great mouths full of teeth, their entire heads made only of jaws.

"Elethorrr...," one hissed, a great nephil that hovered among them. Its wings spread wide, and it sat upon a throne of flame. A halo of fire wreathed its brow, shrieking like a storm,

and blood coated its maw. It was the largest among them, a
leader of darkness.

"You will leave this place," Elethor called to it, standing
before the temple window. "You will return to the Abyss."

The nephilim tossed their heads back and howled. They
laughed and snapped their teeth and beat their wings. Severed
heads and limbs cracked inside their jaws. Their leader rose
higher upon a throne of fire. Its halo blazed white-hot.

"I am Legion!" it screeched, its voice so loud and shrill,
Elethor roared in pain and trees cracked across the ruins. "I am
Prophet! I serve the great Queen Solina. I have feasted upon the
sons of dragons. I will feast upon their king! Your doom is near,
King Elethor of Requiem. Your blood will be my wine, and your
spine will feed my children." It howled, pus and blood spraying
from its maw. "The time of the dragon ends, King Elethor. Your
kingdom is fallen. The world burns and we, the Fallen, feast. The
nephilim rise!"

All around Legion, the thousands of nephilim repeated the
cry. "We rise! We rise! We feast!"

How can we fight such evil? Elethor thought in a daze. His
head spun. He felt weak. He could barely cling to his magic.
*How can we fight countless of these demons, creatures risen from ancient evil?
How can Requiem survive such malice, such might?*

He thought of Lyana, his wife, the love and light of his
life. He thought of Mori, his sister whom he had vowed to find.
He thought of all those people who had died under his banner,
and those who still lived behind him.

*I am still their king. Even now. Even as our light fades. If we die
here, let us die with a roar that will sound across the world.*

He sounded his roar. He blew his fire at the Prophet of
the Fallen. The blaze crashed into Legion, and the nephil
screeched to the sky.

Elethor shifted into human form and leaped through the window. He rolled into the temple and the arms of fellow survivors. At once two dragons thrust their heads to the window and shot fire outside, holding the swarm back.

Elethor lay in human form, bruised and cut and bleeding. He struggled to his feet and looked around him. His breath left his lungs and the weight of mountains seemed to lie upon his shoulder.

So few still live.

Several hundred Vir Requis huddled here, bloodied and bruised, clinging to one another. This was all that remained of his father's nation. Dragons stood along the walls and clung to the ceiling, blowing fire outside, holding the nephilim back.

But they will break in, Elethor thought. *They will break these walls and they will tear us apart—elders, mothers, children. They will feed the horde and King's Column will fall.*

"Come back to us, Lyana," he whispered, voice hoarse. "Come back to us, Bayrin. Bring what aid you can. We cannot wait."

He didn't even know if his friends could find them now. If Bayrin and Lyana returned to their abandoned camp, would they know to head to Bar Luan? Were they alone here, and no aid could reach them?

The sun set outside. Darkness covered the world. The nephilim howled and slammed against the walls. Dust and moss fell and babes wept. Fire blew. Elethor shifted back into dragon form and replaced a young dragon at a window. He blew his fire, not knowing if they'd last the night.

LYANA

They flew north across the plains, heading toward the ancient capital of Osanna, and found it burning.

Lyana had been to this place, the legendary city of Confutatis, many times. She had flown here with her father to visit the king of men, a wise old grandfather with a flowing white beard but pitch-black eyebrows. The people of Osanna had no magic; they could not become dragons like the children of Requiem, but rode horses and shot arrows, forged steel and wove silk, wrote ancient books and studied the stars. They were an ancient race—their history stretched back as far as Requiem's—and wise.

As a youth, Lyana had read many stories of Confutatis, the White City: how the twins Osira and Osari had founded the city, carving its first bricks three thousand years ago; how Confutatis grew from a simple village of farmers to a great metropolis of towers, amphitheaters, castles, and a million souls; and of course, how the tyrant Dies Irae conquered Confutatis, forged his center of power here, and led the griffins from this place to destroy Requiem, leaving only the Living Seven among the ruins. Confutatis was a city of ancient secrets, of old blood, of steel and light and stone. For three hundred years now, the priest-kings of the Earth God had ruled here, honoring a strong alliance with Requiem—an alliance Lyana was depending on.

And today... today when she needed this city's strength most, she found its walls crumbling.

She still flew several miles away, and shadows still cloaked the world; dawn had just begun to rise. But dragon eyes were sharp, and Lyana snarled. A hundred nephilim encircled the city, tearing down walls and towers with claw and tooth. Arrows rained upon them from the battlements. More nephilim flew above, dipping to claw at soldiers who manned towers or ran along snaking streets. Three nephilim barreled into one of those towers, a great spire of marble and gold; it crashed onto the streets below, burying men beneath it.

Stars, Lyana thought, *is no place upon this earth safe anymore?* Solina's arm had grown long enough to cross desert, sea, forest, and plains, even to this distant northern city.

She turned to look at the dragons who flew around her. Dorin flew to her right, an old red dragon with no back legs, his wings whistling with holes. At her left flew Gar, the young miner, a burly bronze dragon with fire in his jaws. Behind them flew the survivors of Second Haven: three thousand men, women, and children. Their eyes widened with fear, and they blasted fire.

Lyana raised her voice and cried to them.

"Soldiers ahead!" she shouted, smoke fuming from her nostrils and mouth. "Women and children behind. Battle formations—like we drilled. Go!"

Wings creaking, Dorin snarled at her. His eyes blazed.

"You will lead our last survivors to die upon the walls of a foreign city?" He turned to the dragons behind them. "Dragons of Second Haven! This is not our war. We have come for aid; we find death. Fly back! Back to the forests! To—"

Lyana slammed into him, shoving him into a tumble. He glared and snapped at her, and she pulled back and hissed. Flames sparked between her teeth. She and Dorin circled each other in the sky, glaring and snorting smoke and flames.

"You have played your little games of dominion, *Legless Lord,*" she said, spitting out the last words mockingly. "Yet Confutatis still stands; she is besieged but still fights. We will fly to her aid."

She looked back at the battle. Trebuchets swung upon the city walls, tossing boulders onto the Fallen Horde. One boulder crashed into a nephil, crushing the beast upon the plains like a great insect. Other nephilim still swooped above the city, lifting men from towers and feasting upon them. Arrows thrust out from the creatures, but seemed barely to faze them; their hunger was too great. Some soldiers of Osanna upon the walls, tall men clad in steel, saw the dragons and raised a cry.

"Requiem!" they cried. "Requiem flies to our aid!"

The nephilim screeched, turned, and saw the dragons too. They raised their arms and howled, and a city wall cracked, and the land itself shook. Dozens of the creatures began flying south toward Lyana, Dorin, and the thousands behind them.

"We flee now!" Dorin said, glaring at Lyana. "That is my order; these are my people."

Lyana looked back at the dragons; they hovered in midair, torn between their queen and their new lord. She looked at the nephilim; they flew across the plains, bat wings beating, teeth bared and glinting in the small morning sun.

"Dorin," she said softly. "Dorin, I led your son in battle."

His eyes narrowed. He sucked in his breath. Smoke plumed from his clenched jaw.

"He was brave," Lyana said softly as the nephil horde approached. "He was among the bravest dragons I knew. He charged into the host of phoenixes, and... I could not save him. But he saved me. He saved many."

Dorin hissed and flames shot from his mouth. "You will not mention my son! You—"

"Dorin, do not flee from this battle. If truly you lead these people, you must fight for them." She looked back at the nephilim; they flew only a mile away now. Her jaw twisted into a crooked smile. "We can take them."

Dorin stared at her. He stared at the dragons behind him. He stared at the enemy and grunted. Finally he bucked and roared.

"Dragons of Second Haven! Leave none alive!" He blew his fire, clawed the sky, and charged toward the horde. "Slay them!"

A hundred dragons, warriors of Second Haven, sounded their cry and charged.

The nephilim crashed into them.

Lyana blew fire. She slammed her tail's spikes into one nephil's head, punching through its skull. Her claws slashed another. Three nephilim crashed onto her, clinging like spiders onto their prey, and teeth punched through her scales. She roared and clawed at them, dipping in the sky. Another soared from below and slammed into her belly. The beasts enveloped her, crushing her and biting, and she howled.

Stars damn it.

With a deep breath, she shifted into human form.

She slipped between their claws and tumbled toward the ground.

Wind roared. The nephilim shrieked above and swooped. Before she could hit the ground, Lyana shifted back into a dragon and soared, shooting fire. Her blaze caught the swooping nephilim and she knocked between them, clawing their burning forms. They fell around her, blood and worms spilling from their wounds.

She soared to fight among her comrades. The dragons flew back and forth, blazing their fire. These ones had survived the phoenixes, the wyverns, and the attacks on Second Haven; they were scarred and battle-hardened, and they killed with grim intent. Nephilim fell before them, blazing.

A few of the beasts dipped, flew beneath the warrior dragons, and crashed into the women, children, and elders.

Screams rose. Claws dug into dragon flesh. Dragons returned to human form and tumbled, and nephilim caught them in their jaws and feasted.

Lyana howled.

"Circle the group!" she shouted to her fellow warriors. "Above and below!"

She swooped, slashed a nephil's swollen head, and flew under the mothers and children. Nephilim swarmed her way; she blazed them with flames, and above her, the young dragons screamed. At her sides flew the other warriors, circling the weaker dragons, forming a shield of scale and flame around them. The nephilim kept charging at them. The dragons kept blowing their flames.

Finally only three nephilim remained. They howled, spraying fountains of saliva. One reached out and grabbed the leg of an old, female dragon. He pulled her from the protective ring and bit deep, and the old dragon returned to human form. The nephilim tore her apart and fed upon her.

Lyana roared and charged at them. Fire blazed at her side; Dorin flew there, howling. The two dragons—blue and red—crashed into the feasting nephilim, clawing and biting and thrusting their horns. The beasts fell dead, and Lyana roared to the sky.

She looked back at her people. Some had fallen; their bodies lay upon the fields below. Most still flew, scales splashed with blood and soot. Heart hammering, Lyana whipped her head back toward the city. Dozens of nephilim still flew above the walls, insects above a prized morsel.

"To Confutatis!" Lyana cried and roared a pillar of flame. "Slay the beasts upon the walls and towers!"

Three thousand dragons streamed toward the city, raising a roar to shake the earth. Lyana flew at their lead, blowing fire and howling, a hoarse cry of rage, of pain, of loss—a cry for the death of her parents, for the fall of her palace, for the fading light of her people. She flew to aid others. She flew to slay her enemies. She flew as queen, as a woman haunted, as a blue dragon with so much fear and pain inside her that she could never heal. She shot over the city walls. Above the towers and streets of Confutatis, she crashed into nephilim and slew them with fire and claw.

When all the creatures lay dead, diseased corpses strewn across streets and roofs, Lyana landed upon a steeple that rose among cobbled streets, dwarfing the houses and shops beneath it. Her fellow dragons landed upon roofs, towers, and walls around her, panting and tossing their heads to scatter their smoke. Around them across the city, soldiers ran in armor, cheering and crying for Requiem.

We slew them, Lyana thought, snarling and baring her teeth. *We slew the bastards, and we will slay Solina next.*

She kicked off the steeple and rose into the sky.

"Dragons of Requiem!" she shouted. "We've secured the city. We've shown our strength! We—"

Shrieks rose in the south.

Lyana's heart froze.

Hovering in midair, she turned to see a bustling swarm cover the southern horizon.

They had slain a hundred nephilim. Ten thousand more now cried for blood and stormed toward the city.

Merciful stars.

Below Lyana, Osannan soldiers ran along the streets, drawing swords and arrows; they heard the distant shrieks. Around her upon the towers, walls, and roofs of the White City, her fellow dragons snarled and stared. They were weary. Blood coated their scales. So much of the city lay fallen around them, towers smashed and walls fallen and houses crushed—the work of but a hundred nephlim. Now thousands flew from the south, and Lyana trembled and spat flames.

"Stars bless us, Requiem," she whispered. She landed back on the steeple. She could not win this fight, she knew. Not with only three thousand dragons, most of them elders and children. Not with only men living in this city, soldiers so small and frail by the cruelty and might of the Fallen Horde.

So here my life ends, she thought, *far from Requiem and far from my king—here, upon the white walls of Osanna's Jewel, will I die with fire.*

The screams rose from the south. The eyes of the nephilim blazed. Their wings rose and fell like a cloud of locusts. All around Lyana, dragons snarled upon roofs and men drew arrows upon walls.

Dorin perched upon a temple's dome beside her. He looked at her, and his eyes were weary; so much pain and whispers of blood filled them.

"Lyana," he said softly. She had never heard him speak softly before. "Lyana, you are brave, and you are strong, and you fought well. But now we must flee. We have shown our honor here, but this is not our war."

She glared at him, and her claws dug grooves into the steeple.

"This is Solina's horde!" she said. "These are the beasts that ravaged our camp. Here is our war—it flies toward us."

Dorin sighed and gestured at the city that sprawled around them. "In Confutatis? City of men? We are Vir Requis, Lyana. These are not our walls to die upon. This is not our city to protect."

"Our walls fell!" She snapped her teeth. "Our city, which we protected, burned. I will make my last stand here if I must. If here is my end, I will make it an end for poets, and I will rise to the stars knowing that I died fighting my enemy, not fleeing into the wilderness to die alone and old many years from now, still haunted by my cowardice."

Dorin shook his head, and smoke streamed between his teeth. "Cowardice, Lyana? Is it cowardice to seek life when death looms with certainty? Is it cowardice to survive, yes—to flee—when there is no chance of victory? No; I call that prudence. Your valor will have you die upon walls not yours. What honor is there in that? How will your death protect those of our people who still live? I would rather live as a man than die as a dragon. In the forests we survived."

"Until the horde found us," she said. "How much longer do you think we can hide? The nephilim cover the world; stand and fight them here, Dorin. With me."

And yet... and yet her words tasted stale to her. She wanted to roar them with conviction, to rally his heart and hers. But was this valor truly foolishness? Was his wish to flee not wisdom? And had she—Lyana herself—not fled from Nova Vita as its walls fell and the dead burned upon its streets?

The nephil army was close now, so close that Lyana could count the teeth in their jaws. She flapped her wings and rose higher, and flames filled her maw. She growled and her wings sent dust flying across the city below.

Maybe I am foolish, she thought. *Maybe he is wise, and I am but a headstrong soldier dreaming of glory. Let him flee then; let him survive. But I am Queen of Requiem, and the scourge of my people flies before me, and I will roar my fire. If I must stand alone, I will die with my fire and the song of my stars—foolish perhaps, but I am a warrior, and I will die as one.*

The Fallen Horde stormed across the fields, a tapestry of claw and fang, a night of rot and malice. Dorin grunted, gave Lyana a last glare, then took flight and began to flee north. A few dragons began to follow him.

Be strong, Lyana, she told herself, staring south as the horde approached. *Be strong and you will soon fly to your parents, to Orin, to all those who fell.*

Darkness covered the city.

From the east, like a sun rising, sounded the cries of new dawn.

Lyana turned her head, looked eastward, and tears filled her eyes.

"Hope," she whispered. She raised her voice and roared to the city. "Griffins! Griffins are coming! Dragons of Requiem, rally here! Griffins fly to aid."

Flocks flew from the dawn, half eagles and half lions, great beasts the size of dragons. Sunrays rose around them. Lyana had never been to their home, the mythical Leonis Isles across the sea. She had seen only one griffin before, Prince Velathar who had visited Requiem a year ago. Now thousands flew from the rising sun, a golden dawn aflight.

Seeing the host, the nephilim wailed and covered their eyes with their claws, blinded and hissing. A few turned to flee. Others howled and faced the sun.

The two hosts crashed above the ancient walls and towers of Confutatis.

Lyana soared and blew her fire.

BAYRIN

"Mori?" he whispered.

Inside the golden mountain of the true dragons, he stood in his pod, embracing a very naked Piri. Before him at the doorway, Mori stood with wide eyes and trembling lips.

Bayrin gasped and froze, barely able to breathe. How could this be? How could Mori be here? She looked almost like a ghost, so frail and pallid Bayrin thought he might be seeing a spirit. She was thinner than he'd ever seen her, her cheekbones prominent, her eyes large and gray, her arms sticklike and neck too thin. Her skin was milky white and dark circles surrounded her eyes. And yet it was her, and she was alive, and she was beautiful and fragile and *real*.

Still embracing him, Piri looked over her shoulder and saw the princess. She gasped, pulled away from Bayrin, and grabbed her cloak from the floor. She covered her nakedness and retreated to the back of the room, eyes wide and mouth hanging open.

"Mori," Bayrin said, and his eyes stung, and his heart thrashed. He took a step toward her. "Stars, Mori, are... is it really you?"

She looked at him, frozen. She looked toward the back of the room where Piri stood, cloak wrapped around her. Mori's eyes dampened. She turned, shifted into a golden dragon, and flew away from the pod.

Bayrin leaped out into the darkness. The cavern of the golden mountain loomed around him, its walls lined with countless more pods like a beehive, its empty spaces lit by flowing orbs of light and the shimmer of salvanae scales. He shifted and flew, seeking Mori, but salvanae flew everywhere—thousands of them. He could not see her.

"Mori!" he shouted, flying inside the mountain. He knocked through a cluster of floating orbs; they scattered, tossing light and shadows. "Mori!"

He glimpsed a slim golden tail behind a group of salvanae. He flew in pursuit. Salvanae streamed everywhere around him, flying serpents moving so quickly they appeared as streams of light. As he flew, Bayrin kept having to dip, rise, and skirt the coiling creatures.

"Mori!" he cried out. "Stars, Mori, come talk to me."

He barreled through a group of salvanae; they bugled in surprise and scattered. He dived between floating orbs and saw her there. She flew away from him, descending deeper down the mountain into shadow.

"Mori!"

He dived after her, calling her name. She flew beneath a cluster of salvanae elders who crowded around glowing runes, their eyelashes beating and their beards dipping as they prayed. Stars, she was still so fast! Bayrin flew after her, incurring clucking tongues and grunts from the salvanae elders. He saw Mori soar toward a wall of more pods. She approached one pod, shifted into a human, and ran inside.

Heart pounding, Bayrin followed. His claws grabbed the pod's rim. He shifted into human form and crawled inside like a bee entering its hive. This pod looked much like the one he shared with Piri: long, round, and simple. Fresh leaves covered its floor in a rug, and bubbles of food and wine lay upon them. Mori sat by the far wall, her back to him.

Bayrin approached her, walking gingerly upon the carpet of leaves. When he reached her, he knelt and hesitantly touched her shoulder. She cowered at his touch and huddled deeper into the corner.

"Mori," he whispered. "Stars, Mori, I... I can't believe you're here! I missed you. Mori?"

She looked over her shoulder at him. Tears filled those huge gray eyes Bayrin had dreamed to see joyous.

"Bayrin," she whispered. A tear rolled down her cheek.

He embraced her, but she felt wooden and stiff, and she did not return the embrace. She was so thin, so pale. Bayrin closed his eyes. This was not how he'd dreamed of meeting Mori again. For moons, he had wanted nothing else, and his fingers still shook with the shock of it. In endless dreams, she would run toward him and crash into his embrace, and they would kiss and laugh and tell stories of daring escapes. Not... not this, just silence and Mori so still in his arms, a porcelain figurine.

"Mori," he whispered again. "I'm so glad you're here. Stars, I missed you, Mors." His voice cracked and his eyes dampened. "You don't have to tell me what happened. Not now or ever, if you don't want to. I'm just so glad you're here. I'm not going to let you go again—ever, not ever, Mori. I'll never let you out of my arms. If we have to, we'll just stay like this forever."

She looked up at him, blinking tears from her eyes. "Is... I saw Piri. Is she...?"

Bayrin found himself weeping. He hated showing such emotion; hated it! He had not cried since he was nine and Lyana had kicked him too hard. Today he could not help it. And yet he laughed—he laughed through his tears until his chest shook.

"Piri! Stars, Mori, the girl in crazy. You remember how she used to follow me around, right?" He kissed her cheek. "I love you, Mori. Only you. Now and always. Nothing happened between Piri and me. She tried to seduce me; I refused her. You've always had a talent for showing up at just the wrong

moment! Remember how you once walked into the armory just
as I was, uhm... testing Lyana's dress?"

"You were going to put it on!" she said, and now a soft
smile trembled on her lips.

"I was not! I was only holding it against me to see if... I
accidentally stabbed it with my sword."

She laid her head against his chest.

"I know," she whispered. "I know, Bay. I believe you."

He did not have to ask if she meant the dress or Piri. He
leaned back against the wall, and Mori wriggled until she nestled
in his arms. He held her very close for a very long time, and they
said nothing more.

A hole upon the mountainside, a remnant of the nephil
attack, gaped open not far outside their pod. Through it, Bayrin
could see into the wilderness. The sun began to set, casting rays
of orange light upon the forest. In the evening, the priest
Nehushtan flew to their pod, coiling and chinking, and
summoned them to a council.

"We will meet under the stars and discuss the evil that stains
the world," he said, his tufted eyebrows curved in sorrow.

Bayrin and Mori followed him in dragon forms, and they
flew out the mountain and above the forests. Sunset gilded the
land, and Bayrin looked at Mori as she flew. She looked back and
gave him a soft smile, and despite the ruin of the world, and the
evil that still lurked in the desert, Bayrin was happy.

Mori is here. There is still light in the world.

Nehushtan led them to a grassy hill that rose from a forest
clearing. Ten great stones rose here, each larger than a man,
arranged like the Draco constellation. Night fell, and blue runes
glowed upon the stones, and the true stars shone above. Fireflies
swirled around the henge, adding their glow. All around the hill,
the forest rolled into shadow, the trees mere black hints like
charcoal etched onto obsidian.

Above several stones hovered elder salvanae. Their eyes glowed silver and gold in the starlight. Their bodies coiled behind them like banners in a breeze. Their beards were long and their brows furrowed, and their breath steamed in the night.

Upon a pair of stones perched two dragons of Requiem—unlike the salvanae, they had stockier bodies, four legs, and wings. Even in the dim starlight, Bayrin recognized Piri's lavender scales; it was a rare color in Requiem. The other was a slim black dragon, and Bayrin gasped when he recognized her.

"Treale Oldnale!" he blurted out, hovering above the henge. "Bloody stars, I haven't seen you in ages. Where the Abyss have you been?"

She raised her chin at him. "Probably having a rougher time than you, Bayrin Eleison. Now sit down and don't be rude. We have a council to attend."

Blinking in amazement, Bayrin landed upon one of the boulders. His tail flicked against the grass below, and a silvery rune glowed upon his perch, warming him. Mori landed upon another stone, and the high priest Nehushtan flew to hover above another. All the stones were now occupied, the stars shone, and the council began.

"An ancient evil has fallen upon our land," said Nehushtan. He blinked, and his great white lashes fanned the grass below. "Thousands of winters have passed since blood spilled in our land, and we were young. We saw the demons of the Abyss rise to crawl upon the earth, and we saw them choose mortal brides. We watched, weeping, as their spawn grew into rotted giants, as the Fallen Ones—the nephilim—roamed the world, neither men nor demons, half-breeds torn in anguish. We watched them burn trees, smash rocks, and feast upon living flesh. We fought them. We slew them. Now they rise again, and we weep, for our sons and daughters have fallen and now fly among the stars."

The salvanae all looked up toward the Draco constellation and sang prayers, for the true dragons—like the Vir Requis—worshipped the stars of Draco.

They too are Draco's children, Bayrin thought. *They too are dragons. They are cousins to us Vir Requis—different from us, but sharing our light.* He sang their prayers with them.

As they sang to the stars, he looked at Mori. She sat beside him upon a boulder engraved with a crescent rune. She was looking skyward, and the starlight glimmered in her eyes and upon her scales. Warmth filled Bayrin in the cold night. He reached out his tail and coiled it around hers. She looked at him softly and nodded, and their tails braided together in a warm grip.

Other dragons spoke next. Treale spoke of seeing Solina raise these beasts in Irys, capital of her desert realm, and send them to feed upon dragon flesh. Piri spoke too, talking of King Elethor and his camp in the eastern forests where a thousand Vir Requis lived. Finally Bayrin himself spoke, describing Elethor's wrath and plans to invade Tiranor and slay its queen. Only Mori did not speak, but every time the word *nephilim* was uttered, she gave his tail a squeeze.

The salvanae elders talked too. They talked as the stars wheeled above: of Solina's evil, of the souls of the fallen, of the sadness in their hearts. They bugled to the sky their rage and mourning.

Bayrin listened to them pray, talk, and sing, and slowly fire grew inside him. He mourned too—for his slain parents, for his fallen friends, for his kingdom that lay in ruins. Yet perched here upon this stone, he found mostly rage inside him—a rage against Solina's cruelty and the murder of so many. Finally he could bear it no longer. He released Mori's tail. With three great flaps of his wings, he rose to hover above the henge, and he blasted fire skyward.

"Hear me!" he said. "We have mourned here for hours, and the stars have turned; soon dawn will rise. I'm done weeping! Solina brought death here. She bought blood and misery. I say we repay her in kind." He blasted more flames; they danced against the dragons' scales. "I am a warrior of Draco. You can fight too. Fly east with me to King Elethor and his camp. We'll join our forces there, and we'll fly south as one... and we'll slay this mad queen upon her desert." He sounded his roar. "What say you?"

At his right side, Piri and Treale both snarled, flapped their own wings, and tossed their heads back. Lavender and black dragons, they blew pillars of fire skyward. Heat blasted Bayrin to his left, and he turned to see Mori roaring her own fire. Bayrin joined his fire to theirs. Four flaming pillars crackled and spun and blasted heat, and the dragons of Requiem sounded their roars.

The salvanae looked at one another, and their bushy eyebrows furrowed. They were peaceful beings, wise and ancient and sad, and yet now their lips peeled back, and their fangs shone, and they became terrible to behold. A fire burned in their eyes, and lightning crackled in their maws, and for the first time, Bayrin saw them not as old wise priests, but as warriors.

They tossed back their heads and roared their wrath, and they shot lighting to the stars.

"We will fly!" they cried. "We will fly! We will avenge our brothers. We will fly!"

Their roars seemed to shake the forest, and Bayrin grinned as his flames flowed.

Yes, he thought. *Yes. To fire. To blood. To ruin. To the desert and to Queen Solina.*

"We will fly!"

SOLINA

In the bowels of the Palace of Whispers, she sat in a hall of stone and shadow. Nephilim swarmed around her. They scuttled across the dusty mosaic floors, clung to the ceiling like bats, and climbed the limestone columns. Three knelt beneath her, heads downcast and wings splayed out; they formed her new throne, a seat of living rot and scale and bone. The spine ridges of two beasts formed her armrests, and their claws formed the legs of her chair; a third nephil rose behind her, a backrest of scales and boils, and its head drooled and hissed above her own.

"Children!" Solina cried, her voice ringing across the hall. "Feast! Feast upon the bones."

They howled and fed upon the bones of prisoners she had tossed them, cracking them open to suck the marrow. This chamber, here in this desert palace, loomed thrice the size of her throne room in Irys; ten thousand nephilim fit inside it. They roared all around, drooling and screeching and clawing the floor and walls. Solina imagined that their cries carried to every hall, tunnel, and chamber throughout this great palace—an edifice the size of a city. Their cry would ring across the desert too—across the world.

"Do you hear it too, Elethor?" she whispered. "Do they scream for you?"

The nephilim that formed her throne cawed and writhed, and she stroked them. They drooled and their white eyes narrowed. She had sent Legion himself, king of these beasts, to fetch her beloved. She had sent more to every corner of the world: to the wilderness of Salvandos where true dragons flew, to the plains and cities of Osanna where men rode upon horses and knew no magic, and even to the distant isles where griffins flew.

"You will find no place to hide, Elethor," she said, stroking the nephilim she sat upon. "In every corner of this world, my children will hunt you. Any allies you enlist, my children will kill them. You cannot stop them. You cannot hide from me." She clenched her fists and grinned. "I will *bring you here.*"

She stood upon her throne of living flesh and raised her arms. All around her, the Fallen Horde flew in a storm, wings beating and teeth snapping.

"The flesh of the world is ours!" she called. "The bones of your enemies will be your prize! We will never fall!"

They howled around her, a myriad of demons, bodies lanky and rotted like corpses, wings full of holes, mouths full of blood. They roared and praised her name, and the chamber shook.

"Hail Solina! Hail the Golden Goddess! We are free!"

She walked down a nephil's spine as if descending stairs, crossed the hall between the beasts, and left the chamber. When she closed the doors behind her, she could still hear them sing her name and growl and feast.

Solina walked down a corridor of shadows. She gripped her twin sabers at her sides, and her lips tightened. She had her power. She had her glory. But one thing she still missed; one prize she would still claim.

She walked through the palace for a long time.

She walked down hallways where dust and cobwebs covered old murals of beasts and men. She climbed chipped staircases lined with statues of slender, solemn Ancients, their heads oval and their eyes staring. Finally, after what seemed like miles, she stepped through a doorway into the Hall of Memories.

She stood before the great, dark cavern and a shiver ran through her.

The chamber was vast, larger even than her throne room; she could have fit a palace in here. Columns surrounded the chamber in a ring, supporting a shadowy, domed ceiling. Below the doorway spread a black pit; the bases of the columns faded there into shadow. Solina had tossed stones into that pit before and could not hear them hit the bottom; perhaps there was no bottom and the darkness led to the Abyss itself.

In the center of the chamber, a great stone well rose from the darkness like a tower rising from a moat. A bridge crossed the pit, leading from the doorway where Solina stood to the towering well. She began to walk. The stone bridge was narrow, barely wide enough for her to cross. On both sides loomed the pit; cold air rose from those shadows to sting her cheeks. The columns that surrounded the chasm frowned upon her, ancient sentinels of stone. The hall was so silent Solina could hear her own heartbeat.

Finally the dusty, chipped bridge led her to the towering well.

The well was wide—wide enough for a dragon to swim in—and pale bricks formed its rim. It seemed less like a well from here, and more like a pool upon a tower top. Water rose to the brim, silver and opaque and perfectly still. A staircase led from the edge down into the water.

Solina stood above the pool. She lowered her head, and the cold wind played with her hair. She breathed deeply, in and out, again and again. All around her lurked the shadowy pit.

The place of my heart. The innermost whispers of my soul.

She stepped onto the staircase that led into the pool. When her sandals touched the first step, the water rose over her ankles, cold and warm at once, both soothing and stinging like a memory of lost love. She kept descending, taking each step slowly. The water rose to her knees, stung the jewel at her navel, and finally rose to her neck. She raised her head, closed her eyes, and took a deep breath. She descended the last step, and the water covered her.

When she opened her eyes, she saw feathery white light. A warm breeze caressed her skin and hair. Slowly the light parted like silk curtains and she saw it.

A tremulous smile touched her lips and tears stung her eyes.

"Home," she whispered.

Marble statues filled the small room, carved in her likeness. Tapestries hung from the walls, and plush rugs covered the floor. Upon shelves stood the wooden statuettes he would whittle: deer, leaping fish, and her favorite—a turtle with emerald eyes he had carved especially for her. Upon a table stood a plate of bread rolls, a bowl of apples, and a jug of wine. His bed stood under a window, topped with quilts and pillows, the place where they would kiss, love, sleep, and whisper all the whispers of their hearts.

Outside the windows the day was clear and warm. Birches and cypresses rustled upon the hill, and the scent of jasmines wafted. Only scattered white clouds filled the blue sky. Birds chirruped and bees bustled around the honeysuckle. It was spring in Requiem, a day of peace, of warmth, of him and her.

A day for us. A free day. A perfect day.

The cruel King Olasar, his pitiful daughter Mori, the haughty Lady Lyana and Prince Orin—they were all gone to Oldnale Farms far in the east. Nova Vita was theirs, just hers and Elethor's—a spring for their love, a spring to lie in bed and hold each other, to sit upon the hill and watch the trees, to be free, a day of no fear, no hurt.

She looked around his chamber. Marble statues. Shelves with books and geodes and his carvings. The table with the bread and wine. His bed of quilts. And silence. Waiting. A loneliness like a house after death.

"I created this for us, Elethor," she whispered. She tasted her tears. "You remember. It was the best day of our lives. A day for us. A perfect day."

She had found this old place in this old palace: the Memory Pool, a place where she could weave her dreams. The Ancients, it was said, would enter this pool to return to their childhoods in old age, to revisit old ghosts before the great journey to the world beyond. Solina had only bad memories from her childhood, memories of the dragons slaying her parents, of captivity in the hall of the Weredragon King. But this memory... this memory from only a decade ago... this was pure. This had been—*was!*—her one perfect day, the one perfect piece of her soul.

"You remember, Elethor." She lay upon his bed and looked up at the ceiling. Cracks spread there like cobwebs, but they were beautiful to her; she knew each one. "You remember how we lay here. We made love three times that night, and you were *so lazy* in the morning. You didn't want to wake up. Do you remember?"

She was weeping. Her tears flowed down her cheeks and dampened the quilt.

Why did such pain have to fill this world? Why had so much fire burned her? She was but a mortal, but a frail woman, and she had walked through fire, blood, and death. She had fought the dragons and slain them, and she had raised beasts from the desert, and she had done great things upon this earth.

"But this is all I ever wanted, Elethor. This day again and again and again. A day for us. A perfect day. I will bring you here to this Palace of Whispers, to this Memory Pool, and you will be here with me." She clutched the blankets. "We will be here forever."

She turned her head aside, blinked the tears from her eyes, and pulled a blanket over her. She felt so cold and she longed for his embrace. She looked outside the window at the clouds that glided, and she missed him so badly that her insides ached and she could barely breathe.

LYANA

Corpses littered the city. Thousands lay dead here, Lyana thought—tens of thousands. She flew over Confutatis, her heart a block of ice.

The ancient capital of Osanna was home to a million souls, a great labyrinth of white stone and cedar. Its walls had stood for thousands of years, and its towers kissed the sky. Today holes peppered those walls; in some parts they had fallen completely. Towers lay smashed, crushing houses and streets beneath them. Everywhere she looked—in gardens, squares, and streets—dead nephilim lay rotting, cut with griffin talons, pierced with arrows, or burnt with dragonfire. Many griffins lay dead too, their wings torn off and their bellies slashed. Vir Requis lay dead in human forms, indistinguishable in death from the corpses of Osannans; many of this city's people had fallen too, bitten apart by the feasting horde.

The stench of rot and blood filled the sky. Outside in the fields, living dragons and griffins stood side by side, digging mass graves and shoving piles of bodies into them. Flies buzzed and crows feasted.

Again you bring death, Solina, Lyana thought as she circled above the city like one of the crows. *Again you bring blood. But now not only Requiem knows your evil, Solina. Now the world will fight you with one great cry. You have kindled a fire you cannot tame.*

The sun set upon a city of blood and tears.

Bells of mourning rang in the night.

Lyana found a cobbled square beneath an archway, curled up in dragon form, and slept dreaming of white demon eyes.

Dawn rose, and three monarchs met in the Palace of Osanna. Upon his throne of giltwood sat King Shae, elderly ruler of Osanna, his beard flowing and white, his eyes sad and wise beneath black brows. Before him stood Vale, the Griffin King, his breast mottled white and his yellow eyes solemn. Lyana stood there too, Queen of Requiem, clad in her silvery armor, her sword upon her waist and her helm upon her head. Three rulers of three great kingdoms; they stood silently as funeral bells rang across the city and echoed in the palace hall. They stood here alone.

It was Lyana who spoke first.

"King Shae," she said. "We must attack Tiranor. Join your forces to mine and let us strike the desert." She pounded fist into palm, then turned to the Griffin King. "King Vale, most noble of beasts! The nephilim attacked your homeland too. Now fly with us. Let griffins fight with dragons; let talons and claws join in war. Together we will topple the halls of the desert queen."

She had expected a long day of arguments, of pounding fists, even of pleading.

Instead she got two nods, one from each king.

In the hall of Osanna, she closed her eyes, clutched trembling fingers behind her back, and whispered.

"Thank you."

She left the palace with more fear in her belly than during the battle.

Fire and blood will cover the world, she thought. She stood outside the palace doors, shifted, and took flight. *No place is safe now; no land will be spared death.*

Lyana had never been particularly pious. Her mother had been a priestess. Her friend Mori had spent hours in the temple, singing old songs and praying to the stars. Lyana had always preferred drilling with her sword, or roaring her fire, or polishing her armor; her weapons and strength had been her gods. Yet today she flew outside the city, walked through forests in human form, and prayed.

"Please, stars of Requiem," she whispered among the naked trees. The first snows of winter glided and clung to her cloak and hair. "Please, stars, do not let the light of the world go out. I am afraid. I am afraid for my husband. I am afraid for Mori and for Requiem." She closed her eyes and clenched her jaw, and pain dug through her. "I am afraid for myself. I miss my parents and I'm so scared."

Tears filled her eyes. She could not remember when she had last cried. She spent all day here in this forest, and when night fell she looked up at the stars, and sang to them softly, and clutched her sword's hilt so tightly that her fingers ached.

"I am Lyana," she whispered to those distant lights, the constellation Draco, stars of her fathers. "I am Queen of Requiem. I am your daughter. I will walk in your light, stars; this I swear. Light this long, dark night."

She slept among the trees in dragon form, curled up as snow coated her blue scales. Dawn rose pale around her, and icicles filled the forest, and Lyana took flight. Osanna rolled cold and glimmering around her, but when she looked south, Lyana could imagine the desert, and there the sand was hot and the sun burned her.

LEGION

Legion licked his chops and snapped his teeth and slashed his claws. He grinned and howled and tasted the blood of dragons.

"We are strong!" he said, his cry rising and tearing the air and cracking trees and boulders. He flapped his wings and rose upon fire. "We feed! We feed!"

Across the ruins, the Fallen Horde roared, swirled across the sky, and covered the ground, an endless swarm. His children screamed and laughed and flew around him, thousands of his spawn torn from the wombs of his wives. Already more nephilim rutted in the dirt, and rotted wombs swelled, and more beasts burst through flesh to feast upon their mothers.

"The world imprisoned us!" Legion cried. They answered his call with thousands of screams. "Now we kill. Now we eat. Now we drink blood. We are the nephilim! We were the Fallen. Now we rise! We rise!"

Countless screams shook the world, boulders rolled, trees fell, and the ruins crumbled below.

"We rise!" the nephilim howled. "We rise!"

Legion flew around them, blood roaring, halo flaming, tongue licking, wings beating. He rose. He rose! He fed. He ate! He killed. Solina freed him! He was a god. He was Prophet. He was Legion.

"The dragons cower!" he shouted. "The world trembles. We are strong! We are Nephil. We are Enemy. We are Nemesis. Our jaws will crush their spines!"

As he flew drooling, he caressed his belly. His own womb swelled, and he felt the vermin kicking and biting inside, drinking his blood and eating his innards.

Soon, precious spawn, he thought. *Soon you will burst from me too, and you will eat my flesh, and you will grow to lead this swarm.*

He landed upon the roof of the crumbling temple. Blasts of fire burst from within. The flames sprayed from every window and hole. One flame blasted not two feet from Legion, clawing at the sky, and heat baked him. The vermin bustled inside his womb, and Legion heard their muffled screams.

Yes, Legion thought, *yes, the fire burns us, my vermin. But not for long. They are weak. They are afraid. We will eat them, and their blood will nourish us.*

He spread his wings wide, curtains of black leather, and raised his claws. His halo blazed and screamed. He howled to the sky of nephilim, and they swirled above and around him, a storm of rot.

"Tear down these walls!" he shouted. "Drag the beasts out and rip them apart! Feast, nephilim. We rise! We rise!"

They howled around him and the ruins shook.

"We rise!"

ELETHOR

"Break down the walls!" the beasts screeched outside. "Break them down!"

They huddled in the darkness—a few hundred Vir Requis, perhaps the last of their kind. They were ashy, bloody, and famished. They crowded together, mothers embracing weeping children, youths clutching swords, elders whispering. Around them rose the walls of the ancient temple—mossy bricks, roots and branches pushing between them, as old and brittle as the scrolls of ancient scribes.

Outside the horde cried for blood. White eyes like smelters blazed at every window and hole. Claws tore at every brick. The ceiling was crumbling, and through it the Vir Requis saw no sky, only more fangs and blazing eyes and claws that thirsted for blood. Countless of the creatures swarmed there; they covered the sky, the forest, and the ruins, breeding and multiplying until it seemed the world itself would crash beneath them.

Elethor shifted into dragon form, moved toward a gaping hole in the wall, and replaced a weary silver dragon who blew fire there. The silver stepped back and shifted back into human form—a weary, gaunt woman. Elethor placed his maw into the hole and blew his flames, driving back the nephilim who clawed and bit there. His flames roared and crackled, flowing over his vision, but in his brief pauses for breath, Elethor saw the horde and fear clutched him.

Thousands. A hundred thousand. More. They covered the sky and land, a mass of scale and rot; he saw no end to them.

Elethor howled as he sprayed his fire. He could not hold them back much longer. They had moments before they grew too weary for fire, before these walls fell and the demons drowned them.

Finally his fire was drained. He pulled back, panting, and another dragon replaced him. Elethor shifted back into human form and stumbled into the center of the room. His people crowded around him, wailing and staring from wall to ceiling.

At every window, doorway, and hole, dragons stood blowing fire. No more than a dozen dragons could fill this crumbling hall; if more Vir Requis shifted, they would crush one another.

Bricks shifted.

Claws drove past stone.

A hole crashed open in the southern wall, showering dust. A nephil's arms reached inside and slashed, lacerating a Vir Requis child. The boy fell, his belly sliced open. Elethor screamed and swung his sword, cutting the nephil's arm. Black blood showered, and the arm withdrew. At once Yar, the young yellow dragon, leaped toward the new opening and roared fire. The nephilim outside shrieked.

"The ceiling!" somebody shouted.

Elethor looked up to see bricks shift. Fangs burst between the stones, and a hole gaped open, raining rock and dust and moss. A nephil's jaw thrust in, snapping, and Vir Requis screamed.

"Burn it!" Elethor shouted, and one Vir Requis—an old graybeard—shifted and roared fire at the ceiling.

Claws thrashed at the northern wall, tearing a window wider. A nephil reached into the hall, claws lashing, and a woman fell, her arm severed.

Elethor shifted back into dragon form, raced toward the new opening, and blew more fire. The nephil screeched.

Elethor's flames were weak now, mere sparks. He was too weary. When another dragon replaced him, Elethor could barely stand. He shifted into human form and looked around him.

"Mama," whimpered a child and clutched her mother.

"Stars of Requiem," whispered an old woman, holding her husband.

And so it ends, Elethor thought. His armor felt so heavy; such a weight to bear. *So does Requiem fade away, a small lingering light crushed under darkness.*

He looked up. Claws and teeth lashed at the ceiling, tearing stone from stone. All the terrors and evils of the world were digging in.

"Requiem," he whispered. "May our wings forever find your sky."

These were the ancient words of his people. Now the survivors repeated them as the claws tore the walls. A hole cracked open in the ceiling, and bricks rained, and a sickly red light fell. The nephilim shrieked and cackled.

No, Elethor thought. He snarled and drew his sword. *No, we will not fade like a guttering candle. We will die in a great pillar of flame.*

Yar stumbled toward him, panting and coated in sweat; another replaced him at the window. He stood by Elethor and bowed his head.

"My king," the boy said.

No, not a boy, Elethor thought. *He is a man today.*

He clutched Yar's shoulder.

"Yar, you fight nobly for Requiem." He looked up at the ceiling where claws tore brick from brick. He lowered his voice. "Yar—fly with me."

Yar followed his gaze. The ceiling was trembling. Bricks and dust and moss fell, and the nephilim howled there, eyes blazing.

"To the sky," Yar whispered.

"To death," Elethor said. "To glory. To our starlit halls."

Yar bared his teeth, nodded, and clutched Elethor's shoulder. "We will fly, my king. We will fly there together."

The temple shook and the shrieks nearly deafened them. King Elethor gave the orders, and the dragons pulled back from the walls, and the survivors crowded in the center of the hall. All around them the walls shook, the claws reached in, and the shrieks echoed. Elethor held his sword high.

"Vir Requis!" he shouted, voice nearly drowning under the screams of the horde. "We fly now. We find our sky. Shift, dragons of Requiem, and sound your roar! Let the sky shake with the song of dragons!"

In the darkness of night and demon siege, after seven days of hiding in shadow, the dragons of Requiem emerged from their temple and crashed into the sky.

Elethor led the charge, a brass dragon with rippling scales and bright horns. His fire rose before him, a pillar of flame to lead their way. At his sides flew his soldiers, battle-hardened dragons with dented scales and broken claws, and their fire rose like the columns of afterlife. They shot through the collapsing roof and soared into a sky of demons. The nephilim spread endlessly into the night; thousands upon thousands covered the sky, a sea of rot and scale and blazing eyes.

The dragons soared upward, flames and claws carving their way. Behind Elethor and his warriors flew his people, the elders and mothers and children, and they too roared and blew their flames. The dragons of Requiem rose, a few hundred souls in an endless ocean, and all around them the darkness closed in.

Requiem! We will find your sky.

To the stars that hid above beyond the cruelty of Solina. To that sky. To the white halls of afterlight. They flew to glory and death.

"To death!" his warriors shouted at his side. "To fire!"

From the east, dawn broke and distant cries answered their call.

Elethor turned and saw light blaze over the battle, overflowing him with white. The eastern cries rose, and the nephilim howled in fear, blinded with the light, their dark scales bleached. They hissed and clawed at one another and wailed to the sky. Elethor looked into the light, and his eyes watered.

"Lyana."

She flew from the dawn, a blue dragon with sunrays bursting around her. She sounded her roar, the song of Requiem, and blew her fire. She charged toward the nephil horde. Behind her from the light emerged more dragons—thousands of them in every color, all blowing their flames, a great host of Requiem roaring its song.

Tears filled Elethor's eyes.

More Vir Requis live. Lyana found them. We are not alone.

The nephilim howled, heads whipping from side to side. Some turned to flee. Others screeched and cowered. Some bared fangs and raised claws. Lyana and her dragons crashed into them, and the world exploded, and beams of dawn blazed through the Fallen Horde like spears of light.

Eagle cries rose in the north, and Elethor turned to see a griffin host—ten thousand beasts or more—their fur and feathers golden in the morning, their beaks wide and their talons outstretched. Riders sat upon them, clad in the armor of Osanna, bearing bows and spears. This host too charged toward the nephilim, ablaze in light and crying for battle. The nephilim wailed and fluttered before them, pierced with arrows.

From the west rose a keening song, clear and cold as winter dawn.

Elethor turned and lost his breath.

"Salvanae," he whispered.

The true dragons flowed from the west, wingless and long, coiling and uncoiling in the sky like serpents upon water. Their beards fluttered like banners. Their crystal eyes shone. Their scales rippled and they trumpeted their song. Among them flew several Vir Requis, flapping wide wings, and Elethor wept in the sky.

A golden dragon flew among them.

Mori. Mori.

From the west, the salvanae crashed into the nephilim, and lightning flowed from their mouths, and their teeth bit the demon host. The nephilim howled in fear. They scattered. They fled. They died and fell upon the scorched earth.

The battle raged through the dawn and day, a tapestry of light and darkness, a song of blood and fire. The armies of the world crashed over the ruins of Bar Luan, and nephilim rained dead, and finally the survivors of the horde turned to flee. Screeching and licking their wounds, those nephilim who still lived flew southward, and the griffins and salvanae chased them and slew them over the forest, so that only a handful escaped bloodied and wailing to their desert queen.

When the sun began to set, Elethor landed upon the ruins of the world, his scales dented and chipped. Nephil corpses piled around him, hiding the forest; countless rotted and bustled with flies, and even the crows would not touch them.

He looked toward a crumbling wall that rose from the carnage. A golden dragon perched atop it, gazing upon the battle with soft eyes. Elethor flew and landed upon the wall too, and the golden dragon looked at him. Elethor's limbs shook and his eyes stung.

"Mori?" he whispered.

She shifted into human form and stood before him, as pale and wispy as a ghost, and her hair fluttered in the wind. Her gray eyes stared up at him, huge pools like oceans under clouds.

Elethor shifted too. They stood upon the wall, and he touched her cheek, not sure if she was real or a spirit.

"El," she whispered. "El, we saw the ghosts! The ghosts of Bar Luan! We arrived at your forest camp, and they were fleeing the nephilim, and they summoned us here. Ghosts are real!"

Right then, Elethor did not care about the dead, only the living. He blinked tears from his eyes. He pulled his sister into his embrace and almost crushed her, and he rocked her in his arms, and he whispered her name again and again.

A cackle rose beneath the wall.

His sister still in his arms, Elethor turned and looked down. Upon a pile of nephil corpses lay a bloodied, laughing man. His left arm and both his legs were severed. Blood oozed from his stumps, caked his long white hair, and covered his face, and yet still he laughed hoarsely and coughed.

Elethor growled.

"Nemes," he said through clenched teeth.

The traitor looked up at him, spat blood, and laughed some more.

"You have failed, Elethor," he said, blood in his mouth. "My Lord Legion has left this place; you could not kill him. He returns now to his palace in his southern empire, and he will return, mightier than ever before." Nemes had only one hand left, but he clenched that fist as if clutching onto life itself. "You will bow before him!"

Gently, Elethor removed his arms from his sister, climbed off the wall, and stood before the hacking man. He drew his sword and held it above Nemes.

"You did this, Nemes," he said, chest tight. "You caused this death. You were a son of Requiem! You lived under my roof."

The wretched, dying man spat blood and hissed. His eyes blazed. "I *served* under your roof—like a worm crawling through the dirt. My father served you, as did his father; our backs nearly broke from bending to you and yours." He spat more blood, spraying Elethor's boots. "But now I bow before Legion, a great lord of darkness. Soon you will bow too, and your back will break, but that will not save you, *boy king*. You will beg and plead for mercy, but my Lord Legion will lock his jaws around your spine. He will snap you in two before devouring you." Nemes snorted and swept his one arm across the battlefield. "Who do you bring for aid? Griffins? Dragons of the west? Pathetic creatures. Do you think they can hold back the darkness that rises in the south? You have tasted but a bite from Lord Legion's feast. His greatest power still lurks in the desert, and he is coming for you, boy king. You cannot hide from him, only die. Only die."

Elethor growled and placed his sword against Nemes's neck.

"Soon you will be silent," he said. "You have betrayed your people, Nemes; for this *you* will die."

Silence fell over the battlefield. Elethor was vaguely aware of more Vir Requis coming to stand behind him: Bayrin, Lyana, Treale, and others. They stood silently, watching.

Nemes hacked more blood and laughed again. "I'm already dead, boy king," he said. "So are you. You don't know it yet. But you will. When the jaws of my lord close around you, you will." He coughed blood. "Go on, boy. Go on. Kill me. You were always a coward. You cannot even do this. But I am strong, Elethor, more than you can imagine. I—"

Elethor drove his sword down, piercing the traitor's neck.

He pulled his blade back, stumbled away, and Mori crashed back into his embrace. Bayrin wrapped his arms around them, and Lyana followed, then the others. They stood together, wounded and burnt and bloody survivors upon a mountain of corpses.

Holding his sister, wife, and friends, Elethor looked south. The ruins and bodies stretched for miles, but beyond them hung a cloud and dark mist.

Solina waits there, he thought. *That is where we fly. Into darkness. Into the very lair of madness.*

He held his friends and family close and shut his eyes, and the pain grabbed him like demon claws.

BAYRIN

He walked through the ruins of Bar Luan, calling her name. Ash covered his face and he shouted himself hoarse, but could not find her. He shifted, flew as a dragon over the carnage, then landed and turned human again. He walked among the dead—so many men and beasts rotting and bloody.

"Piri!" he shouted. "Stars damn it, Piri! Where are you?"

A few others had joined him. Treale walked among bodies across the ruins, armor sooty, also calling the healer's name. Many others searched for survivors: mothers cried the names of their children, wives called for husbands, and even griffins cawed and searched for their fallen comrades. Bayrin moved among the crowds in a haze. His heart would not slow down nor his fingers stop trembling.

"Damn it, Piri!" He shouted himself hoarse. "Piri, where are you?"

Clouds roiled overhead, and rain began to patter. Blood ran in rivulets between the corpses. Rainwater streamed off fallen trees and walls. Bayrin walked around a great, smashed carving of a stoic face—it was large as a dragon—and over the roots of a fallen tree. Dead nephilim lay around him.

"Piri!" he shouted, seeking her in the mud and ruin.

"Bayrin?"

Her voice was so soft, so timid and afraid, that tears leaped into his eyes.

He ran toward her voice. He found her beneath a fallen wall. The stones buried her up to her chest. She looked up at him, only one arm free, and smiled softly. Her head lay in the mud, rainwater flowing around it. Blood soaked her healer's robes.

"Stars, Piri. Hang on."

Bayrin trembled and grabbed the fallen wall. He shouted and grimaced, but it would not move. Piri lay there, watching him, the sad smile never leaving her face. Blood matted her dark braids.

With a growl, Bayrin shifted into a dragon, grabbed the wall with his claws, and pulled at the bricks. The wall crumbled in his claws; it was like grabbing sand. He roared, eyes stinging, and tossed the bricks aside until he revealed her body.

Oh stars.

He shifted back into human form and knelt above her, tears in his eyes. Her body was broken. Every bone in her must have snapped. Bayrin blinked, barely able to see. He touched her cheek.

"Piri, you're going to be fine. I'm going to take you home."

She raised her good arm. It trembled. She touched his cheek and smiled and whispered. He had to lean down to hear her words.

"Bayrin," she whispered. "Bayrin, do you remember Requiem?"

He smoothed her hair. "Of course, Piri."

"I'm flying there now, Bayrin. I can see them." Tears flowed from her eyes. "I can see the columns again, all in silver and moonlight, and I can see my parents there and all those I could not heal." She trembled in the mud and rain. "Bayrin, do you remember how I sneaked into your room once? Remember how surprised you were? And how we kissed, and you said that I was so beautiful?"

He laughed through his tears. "I'll never forget."

She laughed too, a weak, broken sound. "It's a good memory. I never forgot it." She sniffed, eyes red. "It was my best day. I love you, Bayrin. I love you. No! Don't say anything back. I know, Bay. I know." She caressed his cheek. "Be with her, Bayrin. Take care of Mori and be happy with her. Protect her. Promise me."

He nodded and whispered, throat tight. "I will."

"Will you hold me, Bay? One last time?"

He held her in the mud, her head against his chest. She held him with one arm and smiled softly, and her breath died. She stared over his shoulder, and he held her against him, and he wept for her. He placed her down, kissed her forehead, and closed her eyes.

"Goodbye, Piri. May the song of harps lead you to our starlit halls. You will find Requiem's sky. You will fly home."

He shifted into dragon form. He lifted her body gently in his claws. He flew with her. He flew for hours until he found a hill far from the battle, a sanctuary where he could not see or smell the death. Pines rose twisting here, their needles rustling in the wind and coating the ground, and pinecones lay strewn and glistening in the rain. Between the pines he could look west to distant, lush forests, a river, and a lake where deer herded. A quiet place. A peaceful place. A place of pine, water, and memory.

He buried her there and placed his sword upon her breast, a sigil of honor for a soldier of Requiem. He rolled a boulder onto her grave, and with his dagger, he engraved it with her name, a birch leaf, and the Draco stars. He whispered.

"Goodbye, Piri Healer, a daughter of Requiem, a healer of starlight."

He flew back to their camp, found Mori, and held her, and they stood silently together for a long time.

ELETHOR

He stood upon the mountain, the wind ruffling his hair, and gazed upon a host like a frozen sea. Snow swirled through the air, coating the mountainsides, pines, and wrath of wounded nations.

Below him in the valley stood the survivors of Requiem, all in dragon forms—over three thousand of them, joined from his camp and Second Haven. Every Vir Requis old enough to fly and breathe fire stood here in the snow, smoke pluming from their nostrils, frost upon their scales.

East of them stood a host of griffins, over twenty thousand strong, snow in their fur and rage in their eyes. King Vale stood at their lead upon a boulder, the greatest among them, his head raised and his talons like great swords.

Beyond the griffins, an army of salvanae coiled above a frozen lake, as large and mighty as the host of griffins. The true dragons hovered, their long bodies undulating like waves, scales chinking like purses of jingling coins. Their beards were long, their eyes blazing, their breath fuming.

Finally, in a field of grass and stone, stood the soldiers of Osanna. Fifty thousand rallied here, each warrior bearing a sword, spear, and bow. Their breastplates and shields sported engraved bull horns, the sigil of Osanna's Earth God, a deity of all things growing and good and a nemesis of Tiranor's flaming lord. These warriors would ride to battle upon the beasts that flew. From the backs of griffins and dragons, they would shoot their arrows and toss their spears, and when they landed in the cities of Tiranor, they would draw swords and fight the enemy in streets and halls.

"A hundred thousand men and beasts," Elethor said softly as snow swirled around him, coated his beard, and frosted his armor. "Will it be enough?"

He turned to look at Lyana who stood at his side. She reached out, took his hand, and squeezed it. Their leather gloves creaked.

"All free nations fight against the evil in the south," she said. "It will be enough, or we will perish. But fly south we must. I would rather die charging into evil than waiting for it to come."

Her hair, shaved off in her captivity last year, now grew several inches long. It fell across her brow and ears, little cascades of orange curls kissed with snow. Her eyes, green as a spring forest, stared deeply into his. Fields of freckles spread across her pale face; Elethor knew and loved every one.

He looked south over forest and mist, imagining the desert. *Tiranor*, he thought. So many times, Solina had lain in his arms, or walked with him through the forests, or stood with him upon the hill, and spoke of her desert realm. She would describe dunes kissed golden with dawn, oases lush with palms and birds, and towers of limestone that rose capped with platinum. She spoke of the dragons burning those trees and toppling those towers, and how one day she would restore her land to glory. She spoke of a magical realm of secrets, a desert paradise of pomegranate wine, figs sweet as honey, smooth myrrh and chinking gold—a land of beauty, of wonders, of ancient wisdom.

"We will live there together someday, Elethor," she had whispered so many times in the halls of Requiem, her eyes rimmed red and her fingers clutching him desperately. "It will be our place, our secret land of magic. We will rule there together, queen and king of the desert, so far from the dragons who hurt us."

Elethor had never been to Tiranor, the land that Solina's heart had always beaten for. Now he would see those towers, those oases, and those statues and steel and treasures.

And we will burn them. Stars, Solina, we will burn your land and burn you. He clutched his sword so tightly his fist trembled. *You drove me to this, Solina; now Tiranor will rise in flame.*

"The north has mustered!" he cried to his army, palm coned around his mouth. "We have gathered our hosts, and we will crush the desert. We fly at dawn tomorrow. Rest tonight, northern warriors. Tomorrow we fly to victory!"

They cheered, a hundred thousand warriors roaring for victory and vengeance and flame. But Elethor only stood, jaw squared, chest tight. He could not roar with them. He could not find joy in this; the fires of war had never lit his heart, and even now, with so many dead behind them, he could not summon the flame that drove Solina, that drove these warriors below the mountain. He held Lyana's hand tight and looked at her. She looked back up at him, lips tight, and nodded.

"I fly by you, my king," she said. "Tomorrow and always. Our wings beat together, and our fires will light the long, cold night."

He spent that night in a tent the men of Osanna had brought upon griffinback. The tent was wide, its walls woven of thick green cloth, and they had set a bed, a table topped with candles, and a tall bronze mirror within it.

Elethor stood before that mirror and gazed upon himself. It had been moons since he had looked at his reflection. Tonight he barely recognized himself. Two years ago, when Solina had invaded Requiem with her army of phoenixes, he would look into his mirror and see a thin, pale young man with soft cheeks—a boy who pined for his lost love, who shunned the court, who hid within his walls, sculpting his desire over and over. Today, Elethor did not find that boy staring back from the mirror. He was not yet thirty, but looked older; his beard had thickened, his body had grown gaunt and hard, and lines marred his brow. Instead of the soft woolen tunics of a prince, he wore the steel plates of a soldier. Mostly his eyes had changed; they were sunken, hard, and dead as the ruins of a fallen kingdom.

I look ten years older than I should, he thought. *And I have the eyes of an old man.*

Lyana came to stand by him and placed her hand on his shoulder. She was barely taller than that shoulder, and so thin, but her eyes stared into the mirror with all the strength and grief of an aging, hardened warrior. If he was a battered longsword forged in dragonfire, she was the blade of a knight, scarred with a thousand nicks but strong as the steel of ancient heroes.

She helped him unclasp his armor, piece by piece. She placed his pauldrons on the table, then his greaves and vambraces, and finally his breastplate. When he stood before her in his damp woolen tunic, she placed her hands on his shoulders. She stood on her toes, her eyes still haunted, and kissed his lips.

He began unclasping her armor, buckle by buckle. He moved slowly at first, placing every piece of steel aside. But soon his fingers grew rough, and she gasped as he pulled at the straps, tore her breastplate off, and tossed it aside with a clang. His chest was too tight. His heart pounded with too much pain. He clenched his jaw and swallowed, forcing the terror down, and tugged the lacings of her tunic. Fabric ripped in his fingers, and he let out a hiss that felt almost like a snarl, and tore at her clothes.

She winced and sucked in her breath. "El..."

He put one hand on the small of her back and pulled her against him. He tugged at her clothes almost violently until she stood naked, and his eyes stung, and his heart thrashed against his ribs, and his fingers trembled, and he kept seeing them—kept seeing the demons tear at the walls, pull brick from brick, slash his people apart until their blood gushed and their limbs fell.

"El, please," she whispered.

He realized that he was grabbing her so tightly his fingernails had cut her. He released her and took a shuddering breath. She stood before him, naked in the candlelight, her hair a pyre of flame. The scars of war covered her flesh, but she was beautiful to him. He sat on the bed, and she stood before him, and he reached up and touched her cheek with trembling fingers.

"Lyana," he whispered. "I..."

I'm afraid, he wanted to say. *I can't stop seeing the blood. I want to roar in rage and fly to battle as a hero, but I can't stop my chest from hurting, or my stomach from feeling so cold and tight.*

But he could say none of those things, and he knew she understood. He saw it in the softness that filled her eyes, and he felt it in her fingers as they touched his hair.

He pulled her onto the bed, and placed her on her back, and when he climbed atop her and loved her, he closed his eyes, and he could barely breathe. But he made love to her—no, not love, but something rougher this night, something that felt more like a battle, like a war against demons, and sweat drenched him, and he *hurt* her. Stars, he hurt her until she gasped and bit into the blanket and cried.

When it was over, and he lay beside her, he found that tears filled his own eyes, and he pulled her against him and held her so tight he nearly crushed her.

So many died. So many gone. So many will still die as we fly into the southern horde.

She kissed his lips.

"I am yours," she whispered. "In bed. In battle. In the glory of our halls when we rebuild them—or in the starlit halls of our fathers. You are my king. You are my husband. You are my love." She held him tight and closed her eyes. "We fly together, Elethor; always."

They slept holding each other through the long, cold night.

TREALE

She stood upon the cliff, the wind in her hair, and looked at her king. Treale had dreamed of this for so long—to finally stand beside him again. He was so close now she could reach out and grab him, yet he had never seemed farther to her, not in all the forests and deserts she had hid in.

Once more they stood upon Ralora Beach. Last year she had stood here with Elethor and three thousand dragons, a green army awaiting the southern fire. Today a hundred thousand warriors covered the cliffs, hills, and beach: griffins, salvanae, soldiers of Osanna, and dragons of Requiem. Last year Solina had lured them here, allowing her forces to crush Nova Vita. Today Elethor had decided the queen's fall would begin in this same place.

You are thinking of her now, Treale thought, looking at the young king. He was staring south, the wind ruffling his dark hair. *You are thinking of Solina, the one you loved, the one you vow to kill. But I am thinking of you, Elethor. I am thinking of the night I kissed your cheek, and I am standing here beside you, and you cannot even see me.*

Treale lowered her head, and the wind played with her long black hair, scented of the sea. She closed her eyes. So many nights she had dreamed of him! When she had lain curled up in charred forests, fleeing the wyverns, she had pretended to still lie by his side like that night upon the hill. When she had huddled in alleys in cruel Irys, or crawled over dunes that burned her, or trekked through the swamps of Gilnor to seek sanctuary in the north, she had thought of him. She would remember talking to him about her puppets, and kissing his cheek, and sleeping all night by his side under the stars, feeling safe by her king. And then... and then after all those long moons, she had met him again! She had returned to him. She had flown with true dragons and fought by his side, driving the nephilim from the ruins of Bar Luan.

And he had gone into his tent.

And he had taken Lyana into his bed.

And her heart had been broken; it still felt like shattered clay in her breast.

Oh, he had given her a compulsory embrace, and squeezed her shoulder, and thanked her for saving his sister. He had kissed her forehead, then pulled Mori into his arms again and nearly crushed her, and not a moment later he was walking with his soldiers and talking of battles, and Treale had remained standing in the ruins, cold and alone.

You have Mori now, she thought, looking at him. *You have your sister whom I saved. And you have your wife, whom I serve. And you have me, Elethor. You have me always; you had me since that night upon the hill. And still I wait for you. Still I stand by your side, but do you see me here?*

She walked across the cliff, moving closer to him, until she stood a foot away. Lyana stood at his other side, clutching her sword and also staring south. Mori stood beyond her, clad in armor—Treale had never seen the princess in armor before—and hugging herself. None seemed to notice her.

"My king?" Treale said softly. He seemed not to hear her, and she touched his arm. "Elethor?"

He seemed to wake from a dream. With a quick draw of his breath, he turned toward her, and his face softened.

"Lady Treale," he said.

Not his love, she thought. *Not his wife or sister or even a friend. A lady. A cold title for a court.* Her eyes stung and she blinked. She wanted to grab and shake him, to yell at him: *Don't you remember that night? Don't you remember how you told me your story, and I told you mine—about the puppets, and Oldnale Farms, and... I kissed your cheek, Elethor, and we slept side by side. And now I am only a lady, this... this cold warrior like the thousands of them?*

But she could say none of that. Not with his wife by his side or even with Mori there. So Treale only swallowed and spoke soft words.

"I will fight by your side, Elethor," she said. "I will not leave you. I promise. You have my fire—always."

She lowered her eyes, the shame burning through her. *Of course,* she thought. Of course he was so cold to her. She had abandoned him in battle last year. When the wyverns had flown toward Nova Vita, she had defected. She had left his army despite his orders, had flown to Oldnale Farms and found her parents dead. She had deserted him; of course he would not show her the warmth he showed Lyana and Mori.

I'm a traitor to him, she thought, and her throat constricted. She looked away lest he saw the tears in her eyes. *I saved his sister, but he still remembers my sin.*

The wind blew, and she lowered her head.

The invasion of Tiranor began with rain, wind, and beating waves. The dragons of Requiem took flight first, three thousand in all—all Vir Requis old enough to shift into dragons and fight. Today they were all soldiers. They roared and their scales clanked and their wings thudded, rippling the sea. Upon every dragon's back rode a soldier of Osanna, clad in steel and armed with bow, spear, and sword. Their bull horn banners streamed, and their shields caught the sun. They shouted for their land, and the dragons roared, and they raced across the sea into a horizon of rain and cloud.

Behind them, the salvanae and griffins took flight too, a great host nearly fifty thousand strong. Upon their backs too rode soldiers of Osanna, clinging to their saddles. The army soon covered the sea like a great cloud, shimmering and snorting and rippling the water beneath them.

Never had the world seen so many beasts fly together, Treale thought. Poets would sing of this day until the world fell.

She flew, a slim black dragon with fire in her nostrils. Upon her back rode an Osannan soldier, a young man with a stubbly face, an impish grin, and a shock of brown hair.

"Stop dipping so much!" he shouted down to her. "By the Earth God, you do wobble when you fly."

She growled over her shoulder and found him grinning.

"Be quiet, Jadin," she said and gave him her best glare. "Stars, you farm boys do whine a lot."

He snorted. "I haven't seen my farm in a year now. I'm a soldier; don't you forget it. If we meet any nephilim, it'll be my bow shooting at them."

It was her turn to snort. "And my fire. I think they will barely notice your puny little arro—OW!"

He had dug his heels deep into her flanks. Treale grumbled and cursed. She was a dragon of Requiem! It was ridiculous that she should wear a saddle like a horse. And yet the Osannans had insisted, saying something about how otherwise, they would fall and drown in the sea. Flying with Jadin upon her back, Treale did not think that would have been so tragic.

"If you do that again," she said, "I'll bite your legs off."

He flashed a grin. "I'll stop if you stop wobbling."

She grumbled, looked back forward, and beat her wings with grim intent. She tried to forget he rode her. It would be a long flight. The sea stretched for many leagues between southern Requiem to the northern shores of Tiranor. Even flying at top speed, it would take hours to reach Tiranor, perhaps all day.

Jadin began to sing old, rude limericks—something about the beasts he'd slay, the women he'd bed, and the gold he'd plunder. Treale grumbled and snorted fire and kept flying.

She looked to her left. Elethor flew there, Lyana and
Mori at his sides.

The royal family of Requiem, she thought. *The man I love. The
man so close and so far from me.*

Behind them, the army spread like a great tapestry, a
league long. Treale looked over her shoulder at them, so many
dragons and griffins and men. She imagined this army sweeping
across Tiranor, claiming city and fort; the world had never known
such might. And yet...

Fear pounded through her. She had seen the nephilim.
She had seen them slay so many. She had seen the Lord Legion
rise, a great beast all of scales and horns and rot, his halo flaming
like a sun. Could they truly kill this dark god? Even with all their
might, could this northern alliance truly defeat Solina, or would
they crash against the shores of Tiranor?

A growl rose in her throat.

Perhaps we fly to death, she thought. *But I will fight by my king.
I will never more abandon him. I will show him that I've grown brave.*

She narrowed her eyes, snarled, and flew.

They flew for a long time.

Dawn turned to noon, and the sun burned above; already
it felt hotter than the sun of Requiem. They kept flying. Treale's
wings ached and she snorted smoke. Her lungs blazed. She
wanted to slow down—her body screamed for it—but when she
looked around her, the other dragons still beat their wings
mightily. Treale growled and kept flying.

"Stop wobbling!" Jadin said on her back. "Treale, darling,
are you getting tired?"

"Tired of hearing your voice, boy," she said. "Save it for
your battle cries."

The noon sun trailed down in the sky. When Treale
looked behind her, she saw that the army's formations had
loosened. Griffins, salvanae, and Vir Requis now trailed behind

her, the slower flyers dragging like a wake. King Elethor, however, flew far ahead of her now; Treale could see his brass scales glinting hundreds of yards ahead. By his side, she saw Lyana's blue scales, Bayrin's green ones, and Mori's gold.

I will fight by their side.

Treale snarled and flew faster.

"That's more like it," Jadin said. "Go, little dragon, go!"

Treale's breath ached. Her eyes stung. Her wings screamed with pain. The sun hung low in the sky when finally she saw rocky beaches ahead leading to a dead, golden desert.

"Tiranor," she whispered.

She drew flame into her throat, bared her fangs, and shot forward. Soon she flew by her king. Elethor was staring ahead with narrowed eyes, and smoke streamed from between his teeth. She gave him a nod and a grim smile; he returned the same.

"I fly by you, Elethor," she said, fire flickering in her mouth.

He growled and stared forward, and his claws flexed. "Be strong, Lady Treale. Be brave. We fly together." He looked at her and his eyes softened, and Treale could weep, because she saw that he *did* remember, that he too had never forgotten that night. "Stay safe, Treale. You are among the bravest, strongest dragons in Requiem, and you will make me proud this night."

I love you, Elethor, she wanted to say. *I love you always; from that night upon the hill until today and every day after this one. Always. Always.*

Yet she did not have to utter those words; in his eyes, she saw that he knew, and that though he was wed to another—though he loved Lyana with all his heart—he loved her too. That soothed her. That would give her strength this night.

Lyana came to fly at their side, flames snorting from her nostrils. Bayrin and Mori joined them, flying so close their wings almost touched. Behind them spread thousands of other dragons, the last of their kind, and as the sun fell, their flames lit the darkness.

They streamed toward the Tiran shore.

The sun dipped into the sea.

From the dunes of Tiranor, a dark host rose, and countless nephilim soared, screeched, and flew toward them.

LYANA

The sky burst with the demon horde.

The beasts swarmed from the sands, myriads like clouds of locusts. Lyana roared, beat her wings, and drove forward. Her fellow dragons roared at her sides, and behind them cried the griffins and salvanae. The beasts ahead shrieked, their voices so high-pitched and deafening, the dragons' riders screamed.

Stars save us, Lyana thought, fear chilling her. *They knew we were coming. They knew where we'd land. These are no mere sentinels patrolling the border; this is an army bred to crush our invasion.*

"Hang on tight, Wila!" Lyana shouted to the woman who rode her, a young captain of Osanna. "This is going to get rough."

She stormed forward. The nephilim shot toward her, eyes blazing and jaws snapping and bat wings wafting their stench.

The two armies crashed above the beach.

Dragons slammed into nephilim. Fire exploded and rained and shot in pillars everywhere. Claws lashed and fangs bit, and from the backs of dragons, a rain of arrows whistled, red shards in the firelight.

"Lyana, your left!" Wila cried from her back.

Lyana banked and saw a nephil swoop her way, claws outstretched. Wila shot her bow, and an arrow slammed into the beast; it bucked and shrieked and kept swooping. Lyana roared her fire, and the nephil blazed.

Lyana banked again, narrowing dodging the flaming beast as it fell. Wila screamed and held out her shield, and the nephil's claw scraped against it before the beast crashed against the beach below. Lyana soared and blew more flames. More nephilim fell before her. Claws and teeth shone everywhere.

Stars damn it! Lyana thought. With Wila on her back, she could barely fly properly. She could not soar straight up, or spin, or whisk like a bee between the swarming enemies; Wila would fall. Lyana gritted her teeth and flew onward, lashing her claws and blowing her flames as Wila shot arrows.

"Crash through them!" Elethor roared somewhere above her. "Past those cliffs—land above them!"

Lyana looked up, seeking her husband. The sky was burning. Dragons, salvanae, and griffins flew everywhere, crisscrossing and scattering and regrouping and all roaring their cries. Nephilim crashed against them—some of the beasts swung curved, rusted blades—and blood splattered. Bursts of dragonfire exploded. When howls sounded in the south, Lyana looked to see new combatants arriving: hordes of burly wyverns blowing acid and phoenixes crackling with fire. They too crashed into the battle. The sands below turned red with blood. Bodies rained and piled up and drifted into the sea. Lyana couldn't even see the sky, only beasts and men screaming and killing.

This should not have happened, Lyana thought in a daze. Her eyes blurred. *They knew. They were waiting for us. They are too many.*

For an instant Lyana froze, barely able to fly, barely able to breathe. She had fought many battles. She had slain Tirans in the Phoenix War when they first invaded her land. She had walked through the Abyss and fought its creatures. She had defended Nova Vita even as it crumbled under wyvern acid. She had fought hordes of nephilim above cities and temples. And yet this... Lyana had never seen a battle like this. Hundreds of thousands of creatures flew and died here, spreading for a league around. To call this a battle, she thought, diminished its magnitude; here was a great song of blood and flame and carnage.

I never knew, she thought, eyes stinging. *I never imagined. We should have run. We should have hidden. We will burn the world from this place.*

"Lyana!" Elethor shouted. He dived toward her, blew fire over her shoulder, and a nephil shrieked behind her.

She snarled. She soared. She fought.

The battle raged through the night—a night of dragon wings and fire and rot. The dead covered the beaches and cliffs. They bobbed upon the water like thousands of fallen leaves. When dawn rose, it rose upon a world drenched in blood. When the battle finally ended, there were no songs of victory: there was only weeping, screaming, and everywhere the dead and wounded.

Lyana landed upon the cliffs of Tiranor. She shook so badly Wila nearly fell off her back. When the woman dismounted, Lyana shifted into human form and stood trembling.

Stars save us, she thought, looking over the beaches below.

"We won," Wila whispered. Blood splattered the soldier's pale face, and she clutched an arm that still sizzled with acid.

"Nobody won this slaughter," Lyana replied and leaned against her, so weary she could barely stand.

The hosts of the enemy lay dead, but so many of their own lay among them. Tens of thousands of corpses covered the beaches: piles of nephilim bustling with gulls and crabs, men and women slashed with claws and burnt with fire, and salvanae and griffins torn apart.

Among the dead, thousands of wounded screamed and wept and begged. Men clutched at stumps or spilling entrails, calling for their mothers. Young women—torn from their homes into a war their brothers could no longer fight alone—lay burnt and swollen and screaming. Healers in white robes rushed among them, trudging through puddles of blood, but there were so many hurt, so many dying; every moment, another screaming warrior fell silent, voice forever lost.

Elethor landed beside Lyana, brass scales charred and chipped. He shifted into human form. Blood splattered his armor and sweat dampened his hair. He took Lyana's hand and they stood together, gazing down upon the landscape of death.

ELETHOR

He walked along the beach, blood sluicing around his boots. The dead rose in hills around him, stinking under the pounding sun. Crows and gulls flew everywhere, picking at the flesh. Nephilim lay broken and burnt, their foul innards leaking from their mouths. Griffins and salvanae lay in heaps. Men and women too lay dead, torn apart into mere hints of humanity.

"Elethor," Lyana said softly at his side. "Are you sure?"

He nodded. "We'll find one here."

They kept walking—him, Lyana, and a dozen of their men. The tide was rising, grabbing bodies and pulling them to sea, then tossing them back ashore covered with seaweed and salt. Crabs and flies bustled across severed limbs and heads and burnt corpses.

Wounded Tirans, their armor and bodies broken, writhed in the sand among the dead. Half were wyvern riders, their mounts dead beneath them, slashed with griffin talons or burnt with dragonfire. The rest had flown in phoenix forms; bolts of salvana lightning had crushed their magic and charred their bodies. Most were dying, barely able to whimper, common soldiers with no ranks upon their shattered armor.

They will know nothing, Elethor thought.

"El," Lyana said softly. "Should we heal them? We can't just... just leave the wounded here to die. We—"

"First we will find what we seek," he said. "Then we will heal whoever we can."

They kept moving through the bloody sand, at times climbing over the corpses of beasts. Finally Elethor found what he sought and stopped walking.

The Tiran officer lay on the beach, clutching her slashed stomach. Blood seeped between her fingers. Her breastplate was shattered—it showed the form of dragon claws—but upon her pauldrons Elethor could still see golden suns. This one was of high enough rank to serve him. He knelt by the woman.

"You are a captain," he said to her.

Blood covered her lips. The sides of her head were shaven, revealing sun tattoos, and several rings pierced her lips and brows. The hair that grew from her scalp spread out around her, platinum stained red, and more blood splashed her golden skin.

"I..." She licked her lips and coughed. "I will not talk."

Elethor tightened his lips. Rage flared in him. She would not talk? He would make her talk. He would stab at her wound. He would stab her eyes. He would hurt her until her bones cracked, and she screamed, and—

No. He clenched his jaw and looked away. *No, I will not torture a prisoner. I am not Solina. I will not let that rage overcome me.*

He looked back at the wounded officer. She lay clutching her belly, and her blood kept trickling; so much of it already soaked the sand.

"We can heal you," he said. "You need not die here, bleeding in the sand among the corpses of your comrades. We can give you silverweed to ease the pain, bandages, and water to drink. But you must tell me what I need to know."

She gave a weak cackle, spitting blood. "My queen was right." She laughed hoarsely, a hideous sound, and blood stained the rings piercing her lips. "She told us this King Elethor was a weakling, a soft boy. I never imagined how soft you were." She managed a snarl. "But we are strong, boy king. We will never fall.

The Tiran empire rises, and Queen Solina leads her to glory. You will *die*, weredragon, you and all your kind."

He leaned down; their faces were but inches apart. He stared into her mocking blue eyes.

"We will die, Tiran? We crushed you at this beach. We claimed your shores. We drove you out of our lands, and now we drive into yours. Who is weak, Tiran? I, a king who conquered, or you, a wounded soldier in the sand?"

She laughed, and more blood trickled down her chin, and her armor clanked as her chest shook.

"Drive into our lands? Weredragon, you have seen nothing of our strength. You fought but a drop from our ocean, and this drop ravaged half your forces. Do you think you can move beyond these shores?" She coughed a laugh. "The might of Tiranor still awaits you, weredragon. I wish only that you live to see it all, but you will be crushed too soon. Even as you linger here, my queen breeds new hosts. Even as I lie dying, she gives life to a million more nephilim."

He bared his teeth and glared. "My father burned Irys to the ground and killed its monarchs; I will do the same."

The Tiran spat blood at him. "You are not fighting Irys now, boy. You fight the Palace of Whispers, a god of stone, a city in the mountains. You will crash against its walls. From within its chambers, Solina will send forth her wrath, and you will die, weredragon. You will die screaming and begging to worship her."

He rose to his feet and wiped her blood off his cheek. He turned to Lyana and his men.

"I've heard enough," he said. "Fetch healers; treat her as well as you can. If she dies, bury her with the rest."

He shifted into a dragon, took flight, and soared above the cliffs. Before him, plains of rock and dry scrub rolled for leagues, finally giving way to dunes and distant southern mountains. Heat rose in waves. Even in winter, the sun pounded the Tiran landscape; it baked Elethor's scales and blinded him.

When he looked east, he could just discern a distant green line leading to a delta—the Riven Pallan and the city of Irys, capital of this land. They still lay a day's flight away. When he looked west, Elethor saw the desert roll to distant tan mountains against a white sky, mere hints of color from here. Somewhere in those mountains rose the Palace of Whispers, he knew, the ruins where Solina lurked and bred her beasts.

He looked down at the desert below him. His camp spread here, a league from the sea. Whoever had survived the slaughter upon the beach bivouacked upon the plain. Griffins stood to one side, frozen like sentinels of stone. Salvanae hovered around the camp, coiling and chinking, their beards dipping into the sand. Soldiers of Osanna were erecting tents and campfires, and the scents of sausages, breads, and wine filled the air.

Finally, the Vir Requis camped to one side, the smallest of the hosts. They stood in human forms, gazing south upon the desert, solemn and silent. Most of them were not soldiers; they were mothers, fathers, brothers, sisters. They were the few who'd survived the attacks on Nova Vita and the slaughter in Bar Luan. They were the last light of Requiem, and they stood here wounded and gaunt and grim, and they comforted Elethor even more than the might of griffins or the wisdom of salvanae. They were his people, and their fire burned deep and hot within them.

As the sun set, spreading orange and red fingers across the desert, Elethor met with his generals upon a rocky hill.

At his right stood Lyana, clad as always in her silvery armor, her helmet upon her head, her sword and dagger hanging from her belt. Beside Lyana stood her squire, the young Lady Treale; she wore armor engraved with a sheaf of wheat, the sigil of her house, and the wind played with her long black hair. To Elethor's left stood Princess Mori, clad in the armor they had forged her, its steel engraved with a two-headed dragon, sigil of House Aeternum. Bayrin stood there too, the wind in his red hair.

Elethor looked upon them—a wife, a sister, his dearest friends. His heart gave a twist. Suddenly he loved them so much that it hurt. These were the dearest people in his life, the people who had flown through fire and blood for him. There were none braver in the world, he thought.

I wish you were here with us, Orin. I miss you, brother.

He thought of those who had died in this war: his brother, his father, Deramon and Adia, Piri Healer, and so many others. So many extinguished lights.

But we still fight for you. Your light still guides us—always.

Before him upon the hill stood his allies: the Griffin King Vale, his fur kindled with sunset; wise old Nehushtan, High Priest of Salvandos; and King Shae, his beard white and flowing, ruler of Osanna. Between the allies stood a table topped with candles, wooden carvings of griffins and dragons, and a parchment map of the desert. Standing over the map, Elethor looked at his companions one by one. They stared back in the sunset. He took a deep breath and began to speak.

"We invaded Tiranor with a hundred thousand warriors. Twenty thousand of them died upon the beaches." He lowered his head. "Their memory will light our path. We will forever sing of their sacrifice and courage in our halls."

The others bowed their heads and whispered prayers. A few had tears in their eyes. When the moment of prayer ended, Elethor spoke in a deep, firm voice.

"We cannot rest here long," he said. "We won a battle, but Solina is not idle. Already she musters new forces; we must continue our assault with all the might and speed we can muster. We believe that Solina lurks here." He tapped a western mountain upon the map. "The Palace of Whispers—a great fortress built into a mountain, once the domain of the Ancients, now a lair of her devilry. She is... creating, summoning, or breeding nephilim there. It won't be long before she hears of our invasion and strikes our camp."

Bayrin snarled and pounded his fist against the map. "Then let us fly to her! We'll attack that mountain with everything we've got. Soon it'll be called the Palace of Solina's Blood... and Guts." He tapped his chin. "Yes, Guts too; I like that."

Elethor was about to reply, but to his surprise, it was Mori—shy, timid Mori who never spoke in their councils—who replied first. Her voice was soft, and her lips trembled, but she clutched her luck finger tight and spoke for all to hear.

"We must attack Irys too." She looked at the map and spoke as if to herself. "Maybe Solina now lives in the mountains. But Irys is where her palace is, where the capital is, where she..." Mori swallowed and reached out to clutch Bayrin's hand. "We have to attack it. We have to burn it down."

Bayrin held her hand tight and pulled her closer to him. Mori bit her lip and said no more.

"Princess Mori is right," Elethor said and nodded. "We will attack Irys too. The city still holds the garrisons of her men, phoenixes, and wyverns. It still holds her palace, her greatest symbol of power. We must topple that palace, crush her forces there, and cut off the capital from the rest of this desert."

Lyana spoke up, chin raised.

"Irys gets its supplies from the river," she said. She ran her finger along the map, tracing the Pallan down from Irys in the north. "It snakes many leagues down to here, its sister Iysa." She tapped the map at the southern city. "Here in Iysa is where Solina forges her steel, grows her grains, and mints her coins. The supplies flow up the river on a thousand ships." Lyana snarled. "We will boil the river. We will burn all ships along it and crush southern Iysa. Without the river and her southern sister, the capital will dry up and die like an old fruit."

Elethor nodded. "We'll have to guard the northern sea too. Solina still commands many forces in the ruins of Requiem—wyverns and riders, men-at-arms, warships, phoenixes, and hordes of nephilim. These forces will not sit idle in Requiem's ruins when Tiranor itself is under attack. They will fly to Solina's aid. We must prevent them from returning into the desert."

For a long time the council talked. The sun disappeared and the stars emerged, brilliantly bright above the desert. No moon shone. The camp slept below. And still the council talked.

Finally at midnight, Elethor rolled up the map and nodded.

"We all know our tasks." He looked at the wise salvana who coiled before him, crystal eyes glimmering. "Nehushtan, you will guard the northern seas, preventing Tiran aid from the north. Take with you five thousand salvanae; you will need them to patrol the coasts."

The High Priest nodded. "The dragons of Salvanados shall keep the coasts secure. This I vow to the stars of Draco that shine above. They bless us this night. We will succeed, King Elethor."

Next Elethor turned to look at Lyana, and he felt some of his fear melt. His wife looked up at him with her green eyes—eyes that for years had taunted him, that for years he hated to see, yet which now spoke of her love, which now lit his heart.

"Lyana," he said. "You I will send south. Fly along the Pallan; burn any ships that sail north. Fly until you reach southern Iysa and burn her smelters, her mines, and her shipyards. Take with you a thousand dragons and ten thousand griffins; bear on your backs soldiers of Osanna to fight among the streets.

Nehushtan will cut off Irys from the north; you will crush the south."

Lyana nodded and held his hands. "I will not let you down, my king. We will take Iysa and the river."

Mori spoke up again, chin raised. Her lips trembled but her voice was strong. "And I will attack the capital of Irys." She clutched the sword that hung at her side. "I will fly there. Bayrin can fly with me. We will burn them." A strange fire lit her eyes; Elethor had never seen such fire in her. "We will burn their palace, and burn their soldiers, and burn them all." She nodded, face pale. "We will burn them all."

Elethor placed a hand on her shoulder. "Are you sure, Mori?" he said softly. "You can fly south with Lyana if you want; she will keep you safe."

Mori shook her head. "No, El. I'll do this. I... I have to. I want to fight in Irys; that is where my battle lies." She held his arm. "I promise you, El, I will fight well. We will take the city."

"And I'm going with you!" Bayrin said. He placed an arm around Mori's waist and pulled her close. "Just don't fly so fast you leave me behind."

Elethor smiled softly; seeing his friend hold his sister close comforted him. If anyone could keep Mori safe, after all, it was her personal guardian.

"Yes, Bay, you will fly with Mori to Irys," he said. "And you will take with you twenty thousand griffins, dragons, and men." His voice hardened. "The Palace of Phoebus must fall."

Mori nodded. "It will fall."

Elethor turned to look west. In the darkness of night, he could not see the distant mountains where Solina lurked, but still the shadows chilled him. He thought of that day long ago—*their* day, a perfect day in his home upon the hill—and he thought of Solina slaying children in Requiem, kidnapping Mori, and screaming that she would slaughter them all.

You wait for me there, Solina, in darkness. You vowed to light the world; now you lurk in shadow. We will meet again in the mountains. No more words. No more memories. Now we meet with flame and steel and blood.

He spoke softly. "And I will fly to the mountains. I will lead a host against the Palace of Whispers. And I will kill Solina."

For the first time in the council, young Lady Treale spoke. "And I'm going with you."

Her eyes shone in the moonlight. Her lips tightened. Elethor remembered that night upon the hill when those lips had kissed him, when those eyes had seemed so warm and comforting in the night. Her kiss had given him strength then, though he had never dared tell her that, and even now, looking upon those lips, those dark eyes, and her flowing black hair soothed him.

"But Treale," he said, "you squire for Lyana. Will you not fly south with her? Will you not fight at her side?"

The squire looked over her shoulder at Lyana, then back at Elethor. She raised her chin higher and shook her head.

"Lyana is no longer a knight, but a queen," Treale said. "And I'm a warrior. My lord, I..." She lowered her head. "When the wyverns attacked, I... I let you down. I am so sorry, my lord. I fled from battle then." She raised her eyes; they shone with tears. "But I will not let you down again. You are my lord, my king, my guiding star. Let me reclaim my honor. I will fly by your side, King Elethor, and I will sound my roar, and I will slay our enemies. For you, my king." She drew her sword and knelt before him. "My sword and flame are yours."

The council dispersed in the night, each member retiring to a quiet place to rest until dawn. Around the sleeping camp, salvanae circled in vigil, their bright eyes piercing the night.

Elethor stepped downhill toward a tent of lush, crimson fabric. He stepped inside to find beds soft with quilts, tables topped with untouched meals, and candles casting their flickering light.

His family shared the tent with him. Mori and Bayrin nibbled a cold dinner, then lay down in a plush bed; the princess slept with her head upon her guardian's chest. Treale, like family to them, curled up in her own bed and slept clutching her sword to her breast.

Elethor could not eat nor drink. He removed his armor, lay upon his bed, and stared at the tent walls. The pain still clutched his heart; it had not left since Solina had returned to Requiem two winters past. Perhaps this pain had not left him since Solina had fled into her exile nearly a decade ago.

Lyana slipped into bed with him. She huddled close, wrapped her arms around him, and her lips touched his ear.

"Will you sleep?" she whispered.

He looked aside and saw the others sleeping. He looked back at Lyana.

"I will sleep," he whispered. "Lyana, this... this might be our last night together. I don't know what tomorrow will bring."

She touched his cheek. "It might be our last night," she agreed. "But I don't think it will be. We've survived this long, and now we are strong. Now we fly with aid. We will win this, El."

He held her close and shut his eyes. They stung; he dared not open them lest they shed tears.

"I love you, Lyana," he whispered, holding her like a drowning man. "I am so sorry, Lyana, for the man that I was. For the man who pined for Solina. For the man—no, the boy—you tried to reach, but who pushed you back. I remember myself in Nova Vita before this all began—a dour youth who shunned you, who shunned the court. And I'm ashamed." His throat tightened. "Will you forgive me for those years, Lyana?

For those years I yearned for Solina and forgot about you, about my family?"

She kissed him. "Only if you forgive the woman I was then—the woman who would pester and lecture you. Stars, I drove you crazy!"

He laughed, opened his eyes, and saw her smiling mischievously. He mussed her hair.

"Oh, I'll never forgive you for that," he said. "What was it I called you once? Intolerable and overbearing?"

"And supercilious," she said with a grin. "I think you called me that too. Big word for you, El. I was impressed."

He gave her a mock shove, then felt the coldness between them and pulled her back into his embrace. She laid her head upon his chest, and he stroked her hair.

"Goodnight, Lyana," he said softly.

She raised her head, kissed his lips, and cuddled against him.

"I love you too, Elethor," she whispered. "Always."

The candles guttered into darkness, and they slept.

SOLINA

She lay in his bed under the quilts. She paced his room and caressed the marble statues he had sculpted. She lifted the wooden turtle he had carved for her, kissed its head, and placed it back upon the shelf. She stepped outside and gazed upon the trees. She dreamed. She missed him. Loneliness clawed at her and stung her eyes.

I am so sad without you, she thought, pacing his chamber again and again like a prisoner in a cell. *I am so alone. I want you with me.*

But it was time to leave this place. It was time to rule. To conquer. To slaughter his people and bring him here—to warmth, to memory, to light.

To me.

She stepped toward the door of his chamber, placed her hand on the knob, and closed her eyes.

I wish I could stay here forever. She was young here, only twenty-three and still bright with youth, and her face was unscarred, and no pain or hatred or death filled her heart. *A perfect day.*

She tightened her lips, twisted the knob, and opened the door.

She stepped out of memory and into the chamber.

She walked up the stairs, emerging to the rim of the well. All around her spread the Hall of Memories, its columns rising from darkness to the shadowy domed ceiling. The pit surrounded the well, spreading all around her like a moat around a tower. Once only shadows and wind had filled this pit. Today her glory festered here.

"My children," she whispered.

The spawn of nephilim filled the pit, biting and mewling and clawing at one another, their bat wings beating and their eyes leaking pus. Each was the size of a man already, and they were growing larger every day, the strong feeding upon the weak. They writhed in the pit like a pile of maggots. A million or more rotted here. The strongest rose to the top, teeth bloodied and bellies bloated with the flesh of their brothers. For a mile deep they festered, stinking of decomposing flesh and blood and nightsoil.

"You will rule the world someday," Solina said softly. She stood upon the bridge, looking down at them. They reached out to her, claws shaking and glimmering with blood. They hissed her name.

"Sssolina... Sssolina..."

Mature female nephilim clung to the columns around the pit. Fifteen of them screamed here, bellies bulging and contracting and birthing more spawn into the pit. Blood poured down their legs, and nothing but wounds now spread between their thighs, and still their spawn burst out screaming and hungry to fall onto the million others.

Lord Legion himself clung to the sixteenth column, father of his brood. He licked his lips, gazed upon his wives and children, and gave a toothy smile. His drool rained.

"My queen," he said to her, bowing his horned head.

"Your brood is strong, Legion," Solina said to him from the bridge. "They will consume the world."

The great nephil hissed. Twenty feet tall, his body like a blackened cadaver, he spread out his bat wings, lovingly embracing the stench of his spawn. He inhaled and licked his chops.

"*He* will lead them when I'm gone," Legion said. "*He* will be the greatest among them, a devourer of the weak, a conqueror of dragons."

Solina smiled and placed her hands upon her belly. She could almost feel her son wriggle inside. She could almost hear him screech.

The weredragons killed my child with Elethor, she thought and closed her eyes. *But Lord Legion has given me a new heir, and he will be greater. He will rule this world.*

She still ached from the night she had allowed Legion to know her. Her belly gave a twist, and Solina gasped. That was his son. That was the demon child within her. His claws tugged at her womb, still too weak to break through.

But soon, my child, she thought. *Soon you will emerge into this world and be my heir, a great king the world will cower from.*

She opened her eyes and looked back at Legion.

"Keep mounting the females," she told him. "Again and again. We need more. I want them pressed against the ceiling until they crack it. Very soon, Legion, we will have enough to cover the sky of the world."

He nodded, fangs bright with drool.

"For you, my queen, I will create a mountain of spawn."

She nodded and crossed the bridge. As she left the Hall of Memory and marched toward her throne room, she caressed her belly and smiled.

LYANA

She flew across the desert, fire in her belly. Behind her flew ten thousand warriors, a swarm of dragons and griffins bearing archers on their backs. They flew low. The desert raced below them, boulders blurring into streaks. The sun pounded above. The air whipped them and screamed in Lyana's ears.

"Here we are, boys," Lyana called over her shoulder. "Stay low and burn those sails!"

The River Pallan stretched across the desert ahead, a scar of blue and green rifting the land. It flowed several leagues away; they would be there in moments. Reeds, palm trees, and fields of barley grew alongside it. Upon the water rose hundreds of white sails, each emblazoned with the Golden Sun of Tiranor.

These waters will boil, Lyana thought, *and the trees and sails will blaze.*

She looked to her left. Far in the north, she could just make out a sprawling patch of brown and green. Distant white towers rose from it, mere twigs from here. There lay Irys, capital of Tiranor, a hive of a million souls. A second army flew toward it, a cloud in the northern horizon; Mori and Bayrin flew there with thousands of warriors.

But that is their battle, Lyana thought and looked back east. *Here is mine.*

The Pallan flowed so close now, Lyana could count the sailors' shields. She growled and filled her maw with flame.

"Burn every last ship!" she shouted to the dragons, griffins, and soldiers who flew behind her. "Sink them all."

She streamed forward, leaving the desert to dive over fields and trees. Irrigation canals stretched below her like blue cobwebs, and farmers dashed to hide in their homes. Behind Lyana, her dragons roared, her griffins shrieked, and their riders—men and women of Osanna—sounded their war cries.

Lyana reached the water. She banked and dived to skim southward along the river. Rushes and palms billowed at her sides, bending under the flap of her wings. Ships rowed and sailed beneath her, and she bathed them with flames.

As her fire rained, arrows soared. Lyana roared. Arrows clattered against her scales. One shot through her wing, and another slammed into her back leg. Upon her back, Wila of Osanna fired down her own arrows, screaming the battle cries of her people. One of her arrows pierced a Tiran sailor upon a ship, sending him plunging into the water.

Around Lyana, dragons and griffins swooped to tear and burn the ships. Arrows flew in both directions, fired by both northern riders and Tiran sailors. Several griffins crashed dead into the river, their necks pierced with arrows. The ships rocked madly and sails blazed. One dragon screamed, arrows in her neck, and shifted back into human form; she crashed into the water.

Lyana rose higher, arrows whistling all around. The river stretched before her, a great stream that flowed into the southern horizon; it ran for so many leagues it could take days to clear. She snarled and dived again, raining fire on more ships. More arrows flew. One scraped Lyana's cheek, and Wila shouted upon her back.

"Five damn arrows in my shield!" she cried to Lyana. "Bastards."

Lyana could not spare the woman a glance, but she heard the whoosh of Wila's arrows flying by her ears. Two arrows pierced sailors upon ships below. The sails and masts blazed.

Lyana growled, flew along the water, and dived again. More ships burned, and more griffins and dragons fell pierced with arrows and spears.

Screeches sounded in the south.

Black shadows took flight.

"Here they come!" Lyana shouted over her shoulder to her warriors. "Griffins—into battle formations, go! We'll hold them back. Dragons, you keep burning those damn ships!"

She growled, beat her wings madly, and shot forward. A hundred nephilim rose from the trees alongside the riverbanks like giant diseased crows. They shrieked and drove toward her. Lyana roared and blew her flames. Griffins shrieked around her and reached out their claws. The nephilim crashed against them with thuds and exploding fire.

Blood splattered the trees and turned the rivers red. Dragons shot below, spraying fire. Ships burned and sank. Arrows filled the sky. Nephilim rose everywhere, and claws thrashed at Lyana, and she roared and bit into diseased flesh, then spat out maggots. Griffins shrieked and fell and clawed all around her.

Lyana shot between nephilim, soared higher, and gazed south. The river stretched into the horizon, thick with hundreds of ships. All along the riverbanks, more nephilim were taking flight. Southern Iysa still lay too far to see.

But we will reach the city, Lyana swore. *We will pave a path of fire toward it, and we will burn it down.*

"Dragons, keep burning the ships!" she shouted. "Griffins, battle flights of four—hold those nephilim back!"

The griffins and nephilim crashed and bit and clawed, and blood sprayed in mists. Below, dragons flew against the ships, and smoke rose in plumes.

Lyana cursed as she killed. It would be a long, bloody flight south.

ELETHOR

They streamed across the desert, thirty thousand strong, a swarm of dragons and griffins all bearing archers of Osanna upon their backs. The dunes raced beneath them and the mountains loomed ahead.

Elethor bared his fangs.

Thirty thousand. It was the number of souls who had lived in Requiem before the wyverns attacked. Thirty thousand. They would crush the Palace of Whispers and they would catch Solina and they would burn her.

"We will show you no mercy today, Solina," he hissed as he flew, flames in his mouth. "We will take no prisoners. You will stand no trial in our fallen halls. Today you die."

Scales clanked and fire blasted. Treale darted up to his side. The black dragon stared with narrowed eyes, teeth bared. A snarl left her maw, and a dragonhelm rose upon her head, crowned with blades.

"My king," she said and gave him a deep stare. "I fly by your side. I will kill for you. I will burn the enemy for you."

"Not for me, Treale," he said. "For Requiem. For the souls of our fallen. For the souls who still live."

All around them flew their warriors: dragons of Requiem with flames in their nostrils, true dragons of the east with fluttering beards, griffins with beating wings and yellow eyes, and upon every beast's back a warrior of Osanna bearing arrows and spears. They flew grimly, staring ahead in silence, rising and falling like waves upon the wind. Thirty thousand—a great northern host of light and fury.

The dunes rolled below, soon giving way to rocky fields, boulders, and hills. The noon sun pounded when the host flew over the mountains, and their shadows raced across rocky slopes. Nothing lived here; Elethor saw no plant or beast. There were only these rocky peaks, this white sky, and this glaring sun. The silence unnerved him and he growled.

Where are you, Solina?

They kept flying, a cloud of scale and steel. The mountaintops jutted beneath them like the fallen bones of ancient stone gods. Finally they saw it ahead, and Elethor hissed and his heart twisted.

The Palace of Whispers.

It still lay leagues away, but even from here, Elethor could barely believe its size; it looked larger than a city. He could not decide whether the Palace of Whispers was a mountain covered with towers, archways, bridges, and walls, or whether he flew toward a fortress so massive it had grown to mountain size. Hundreds of towers rose here, and hundreds of windows and archways led into shadows. All were built of the same tan, hard limestone of the mountains around them; Elethor could see no other color. The Ancients had built this place thousands of years ago, and time had done its work. The towers rose, craggy and twisting like stalagmites. The walls lay crumbling and bent like castles of sand after a wave. And yet, despite its age and dilapidation, this place still held power; Elethor felt it emanating like heat.

He kept flying toward the mountain. His host flew behind him. Elethor growled deep in his throat.

It's too silent, he thought. *Damn too silent.*

He could see no movement upon the towers or walls of the great fortress. No nephilim shrieked or flew. No banners fluttered. The ruins seemed dead, and that unnerved Elethor more than a cloud of demons.

"I fly with you, my king," Treale said, voice strained. Upon her back, her rider—a young man named Jadin—nocked an arrow.

They flew closer. The mountain grew ahead. Soon it loomed before them, a monolith large enough that nations could live within it. Still silence covered the land; Elethor heard nothing but the beating wings and snarls of his host. No Tiran soldiers. No nephilim or wyverns or phoenixes. Nothing but desert wind and those old stone battlements.

Only a league separated them from the palace now. The towers and walls dwarfed them. Thousands of windows and archways peppered the mountain like maggot-holes. And still—silence. Stillness. Nothing but rock and wind.

A creak sounded.

A twang followed.

Something moved upon a tower ahead.

Elethor growled.

A lone trebuchet had fired. The missile flew their way—a round ball of clay. It arced in the sky, dived down toward them, and slammed against a griffin.

An explosion tore the sky.

A boom rang out so loudly Elethor screamed. Light blasted. The impact tore the griffin apart; the beast scattered into gobbets of flesh. Flames burst out in rings. Ten more griffins—those who surrounded the one hit—tumbled down, lacerated and bloodied, wings and limbs torn off.

"Tiran fire!" Elethor shouted. "Keep flying—topple those towers!"

He had barely finished his sentence when a hundred twangs sounded ahead. A hundred clay balls flew toward his host.

"Dodge them!" Elethor howled. "Fly higher!"

He soared. Upon his back, his rider—a gruff, mute knight of Osanna—fired an arrow and hit a clay ball two hundred yards away. It burst with light that blinded Elethor, and the blast of air sent him spinning backward. He crashed into a griffin, beat his wings, and rose higher. His warriors were scattering. Explosions rocked the sky, one after another. One clay ball slammed into a dragon, light blazed, and blood and flesh flew. A single, severed arm tumbled down toward the mountains.

"Keep flying!" Elethor roared. His ears rang. He did not know if anyone could hear him. "To the towers! Burn those catapults. Treale—with me!"

The black dragon flew above, scales splashed with blood. She nodded, dived, and flew at his side. They drove toward the fort's towers. Hundreds rose ahead, and more catapults fired. More balls of clay arced through the sky.

Elethor darted left and right, dodging the missiles. Treale flew at his side, whisking around like a bee set to sting. The clay missiles missed them, and explosions blazed at their backs, blasting them with heat. The two dragons flew toward twin towers that rose ahead upon a peak; each held a catapult and Tiran soldiers in tan cloaks.

"Treale, burn the left one. I've got the right!"

He swooped toward the tower. The Tirans fired arrows. Elethor roared. One arrow snapped against his shoulder. Another thrust into his leg. He spewed a jet of fire.

The tower top blazed. Men fell burning and rolled. The catapult rose in flame. To his left, Treale blew fire against the other tower, and its men burned and fell like comets to thump against the mountainsides.

Elethor looked back at his army. Most were still flying toward the fortress. From a hundred other towers, more missiles flew. Every second, a blast blazed across the sky, and more dragons and griffins fell dead.

"Attack the catapults!" Elethor shouted. "Tear them down!"

A flight of griffins—four swooping birds—flew down toward one tower. A clay missile flew and slammed into one beast. The griffin burst into blood and gore. One other griffin shrieked and tumbled, burning. The remaining two swooped and their talons tore down the catapult. Arrows pierced them, they crashed upon the tower, and the Tirans leapt onto them with swords.

"Treale, there, the walls!" Elethor said. "Dive with me."

She snarled and flew toward him. They swooped together. Below upon a snaking wall Tirans were firing three more catapults. Behind them in a ditch, baskets lay stacked with balls of Tiran fire—a hundred or more.

The two dragons blew their fire, drenching the wall.

"Treale, soar!" Elethor shouted. "With me!"

They began to rise, flying straight up.

White light flooded them.

The sky burned.

Flames licked their feet and Elethor could hear nothing but the ringing, see nothing but white light. He thought that he had died, that he flew in the afterlife of starlight.

He could see the faces of his family—Orin, his father, and his mother. They awaited him, clad all in white, and smiled. They reached out to him.

"Elethor!" they cried. "Elethor!"

I'm flying to you... I can almost reach you... I...

"Elethor!"

A tail slapped against him. He looked and saw Treale flying by him. Ugly welts spread across her tail and back legs.

"Elethor!" she said. "The fortress—look."

He turned his head and looked down. He flew so high, he could cover the fortress with his feet. Dust rose in clouds. Elethor spun and began to dive, Treale at his side. When they grew closer, he saw it.

A great hole stretched across the fortress where the Tiran fire had burst. The opening loomed fifty feet wide, large enough for dragons to fly through. Inside, Elethor saw burrows and halls where men raced.

"We're going in, Treale," he said. "Can you fight? Is it bad?"

She snarled and howled in rage. "I can fight! I fight for you, my king."

For the first time, Elethor saw that the rider on her back was gone. Her saddle was singed black. When Elethor looked over his shoulder, his stomach plummeted and he wanted to gag. His own rider still sat upon his saddle—a charred corpse with a gaping skull.

Elethor cursed, tore off the saddle, and let the man fall; they would have to bury their dead later. He dived. Treale dived at his side. They pulled their wings close and curved their flight, racing toward the opening in the mountainside.

"Griffins and dragons!" Elethor roared as he flew. "Into the mountain! Into their halls. Rally here—we enter the darkness."

Thousands of dragons and griffins heard his cry and flew around him. Clay balls shot toward them. Blasts flared. Fire blazed. Griffins and dragons tore apart. Elethor roared, shot a stream of fire into the hole, and men inside burned.

He was first to enter. He dived into the opening and blasted fire in every direction. Upon staircases, bridges, and crumbling floors, men screamed and burned and fell. Arrows clattered against his scales. One slammed into his chest, and Elethor howled and snapped it off. He blew more fire.

He landed upon a rocky floor. Around him loomed a cave carved by the blast. Along the walls, halved hallways and chambers crumbled. It looked like a great ant hive that a giant had punched. Men scurried everywhere, firing arrows, and

Elethor blew more flames. Treale and other dragons flew into the cave behind him, and their fire turned the place into an oven.

When the flames died, they revealed a chamber full of charred Tiran corpses. Elethor flapped his wings, grabbed onto the opening of a corridor, and shifted into human form. He ran into the shadows to find more Tirans firing arrows. He raised his shield, and the arrows peppered it. Men shouted and raced toward him, swinging swords.

Treale leaped at his side, her own sword blazing. Elethor raised his blade and snarled. Behind them, more of their warriors—soldiers from both Requiem and Osanna—raised their swords.

They had entered the mountain. The search for Solina began.

MORI

The skies above Irys, ancient capital of Tiranor, swirled with blood, fire, and endless beasts of scale, feather, and rot.

Everywhere Mori looked she saw them. Salvanae streamed around her like banners in a storm, shooting lighting from their mouths. Griffins shrieked and swooped, talons outstretched, to tear down buildings. Dragons blew fire across streets and forts. Upon their backs, the soldiers of Osanna shot a rain of arrows that clattered against streets, rooftops, and the armor of Tiran soldiers.

The warriors of the enemy were not idle. Nephilim filled the sky like murders of undead crows. Phoenixes blazed and shrieked and crashed into dragons, burning them down. Wyverns beat their leathern wings and spewed their acid; the foul liquid tore into bodies and rained blood upon the city below.

Mori had seen the fall of Nova Vita, but she had never seen such slaughter, tens of thousands falling together, and a city of a million souls—twenty times the size of Nova Vita at its largest—burning and crumbling. As she flew between the beasts, her heart pounded, her eyes stung, and she could barely breathe.

"Bayrin!" she shouted. "Come with me. We're going to the palace. I know the way."

She winced, snarled, and pulled her wings close to her body. She dived, skirted around a soaring wyvern, and arced over a nephil. She dared not breathe fire—not yet. She needed to save her flames.

"Mori!" Bayrin shouted behind her. "Bloody stars, Mori, you know, we are part of a phalanx, and—damn it!

Daniel Arenson

The green dragon cursed, swerved around a phoenix, and barely dodged two swooping nephilim. Mori spared him only a glance. She kept flying, dodging the creatures, seeking the palace between the flames.

"Princess Mori!" cried the rider on her back, a young man of Osanna. "Mori, wyvern on your tail!"

"Shoot the rider!" Mori replied. "Keep your arrows flying!"

Crossbow bolts whizzed around her. Upon her back, she heard her rider respond with arrows. Mori kept flying, rising and falling between the combatants. Behind her, she heard Bayrin cry for their phalanx—a group of one hundred dragons and salvanae—to follow. Mori could not even spare them a glance. She had to find the place. She—

There! Among flames and smoke ahead spread a cobbled square, an expanse large enough for armies to muster upon. Mori knew this place. Here was the Square of the Sun, a sprawling disk of stone in the south of the city.

This is where she whipped me. Mori clenched her jaw and swallowed. Her eyes burned and she could barely breathe. *This is where she chained me for the crowds to see. This is where I screamed and bled.*

Pain pounded through Mori. She could feel those whips upon her back again, tearing her skin, tearing her mind; she had never imagined pain could blaze so powerfully, shake and claim and twist her insides until she could not bear it. She could feel the chains around her wrists again. She could see the cruel jailor and feel his rough fingers forcing her jaw open. Mori screamed. She dived down, blasted fire at two nephilim who rose toward her, and skimmed along a street. She roared her flames, and men and women fell dead before her. Mori screamed and flew through the stone canyon.

Queen's Archway rose ahead. Roaring, Mori flew under it, her claws grabbing soldiers like an eagle grabbing prey. Past the archway, she soared high above the Square of the Sun, soldiers still screaming in her claws. She tossed the men down, knocking them against their comrades below, and bathed the square with fire.

The Palace of Phoebus rose before her from flame. A great staircase led from the square below to the palace gates. The Faceless Guardians flanked the ivory doors, statues that rose taller than dragons.

That is the place. That is where she hurt me.

Mori roared and wept. She flew toward the palace. Arrows fired all around her. Two shot through her wings. Another pierced her shoulder. On her back, her rider screamed and fell silent. Mori kept flying, howling, rage and pain tearing through her.

She flew up the stairs, clawing men apart, and soared up the palace walls. She bathed those walls and towers with fire.

Roars sounded behind her. The dragons of her phalanx descended upon the palace, howling and blowing flames. Their tails lashed at towers. Their claws tore at walls. Nephilim flew to face them. Mori roared and shot flames at the beasts. One nephil grabbed her leg, and she clubbed it with her tail, tearing the beast off.

She flew higher, shooting up in a straight line. Before her rose the Tower of Akartum, the tallest spire in Tiranor, perhaps in the world; it scratched the sky, looming above the city like a great needle of stone and platinum. Archers lined its top, and arrows flew, and Mori roared her fire until the archers burned and fell. She circled the tower, tears in her eyes. The city spread burning below her.

I screamed. I hurt. I cried. I will always scream, Solina. Always. Every night I will scream in my dreams, and every night I will feel those whips again, and I will destroy this place. I will crush these stones that held me.

She slammed her tail against the tower, again and again. She screamed. Stones cracked. Mori howled and barreled into the tower, claws lashing, teeth biting, eyes weeping. Bricks rolled.

Always. Always, Solina. Always you will hurt me. But know this—know that I'm the one who crushed your glory.

The Tower of Akartum cracked. With one more swipe of her tail, Mori sent it crashing down.

The great pillar of stone slammed into the palace. The roofs below collapsed. Walls fell. The lesser towers crumbled. Dust rose in clouds, and the dragons howled and soared.

The Palace of Phoebus, Solina's ancestral home, fell below them into a ruin of flame and dust and blood.

Mori rose higher, tears in her eyes, until she flew so high the cold air spun her head and she could barely see the streets below. When she looked over her shoulder, she saw her rider dead, pierced with a dozen arrows. Below across the city, fires burned and thousands of warriors flew and killed and died.

ELETHOR

They charged down the hall, a thousand warriors swinging blades, trampling corpses beneath them. The soldiers of Requiem charged with longswords, clad in breastplates bearing the Draco stars. The soldiers of Osanna fought at their side, bull horns engraved upon their armor, their one-handed swords lighter but fast as striking asps.

"Get to the staircase!" Elethor cried, sword drenched in blood. He swung that blade with both hands, cleaving the armor of a Tiran warrior. "Take those stairs!"

This place had once been a banquet hall, Elethor thought; faded murals of feasts covered the walls, featuring the Ancients dining on roasted ducks, bowls of pomegranates, and peacocks still bright with feathers. This had been a place of life; today death filled the hall.

Dozens of Tiran soldiers stood between Elethor and the staircase leading deeper into the fortress. They wore armor so pale it was nearly white, the breastplates sporting the Golden Sun of Tiranor. Their sabres swung, spraying blood in arcs, the pommels shaped as sunbursts. Their visors swooped like beaks.

Columns rose every few feet, supporting a low ceiling. Torches crackled. Along the walls, archways led into deeper shadows; more soldiers fought there. There was no room here for dragons or nephilim; here was a war of blade and armor, of hacking forward every foot through blood and entrails and corpses.

"Elethor!" Treale shouted at his side, her sword clanging against Tiran sabres. "What's up those stairs?"

Elethor took a sword's blow to the breastplate and cursed. He swung Ferus down, severing the Tiran arm that had attacked him. With another swing, he slew the man.

"I don't know!" he shouted back. "But we've got to move deeper. Let us fill every corridor, chamber, and staircase in this place."

He had no map of the palace. He did not know where Solina hid. *We will fill this mountain like water spilled into an ant hive,* he thought. *Wherever you lurk, we will find you.*

Finally, with a sword swing that clove a man's helmet, Elethor reached the stairway across the banquet hall. He shouted orders, and his forces split into five phalanxes. Each phalanx—a hundred soldiers strong—dashed into another hallway or chamber, leaving the banquet hall littered with corpses. Elethor ran up the staircase, leading his own phalanx, a hundred warriors of both Requiem and Osanna.

You cannot hide, Solina, he thought as he raced upstairs. *We will bang down every door and overturn every brick until we find you.*

Tirans raced down toward him. Blades swung and men fell dead, and Elethor kept climbing. Treale fought at his side, eyes narrowed and lips tightened; the staircase was only wide enough for two to fight abreast. Their hundred warriors ran behind them, awaiting their turn to fight.

"Solina!" Elethor shouted. He slew a man and climbed another step. "Solina, come and face me! Emerge from hiding, or are you a coward?"

A Tiran ran down toward him, thrusting a spear. Elethor cursed and dodged the weapon; it thrust between him and Treale. Their swords both swung, tearing into the man. They kept climbing. Through the walls, Elethor heard the battle ring across the palace; thousands of his troops were racing through the darkness, filling the mountain.

They fought for every step. They slew a dozen men before they burst into a second chamber—a columned hall lined with archways and torches. Murals covered the ceiling, depicting birds with the heads of men, and a dusty mosaic sprawled across the floor, its stones forming dolphins in a green sea. Fifty Tirans filled this chamber, and with battle cries, they charged forward.

"For Requiem!" Treale screamed and ran toward them.

Elethor ran at her side, and blades swung, and behind them their comrades burst into the chamber. Steel rang and blood washed the floors. Sabres slammed into Elethor's armor, denting it; he could feel his flesh bruising beneath. One sabre cleaved his pauldron, cracking the steel but only nicking his flesh. He kept swinging Ferus, painting the room red.

"Solina!" Elethor shouted. "Damn it, Solina, come face me!"

He snarled as he fought. Sweat drenched him. His wounds blazed. Solina could be anywhere in this fortress; how could he find one woman in this labyrinth? Perhaps she wasn't even in the mountain; perhaps she had fled to fight at another front. He swung Ferus at her men, craving to swing the blade into the queen.

"Solina!"

He charged through the chamber, his warriors at his sides. They barged through a doorway, fought up another staircase, and ran down a corridor, cutting men down. All across the fortress, Elethor heard steel ringing and men shouting; his other phalanxes were spreading across the place, filling every hallway, staircase, and chamber like poison seeping through veins. When he passed by an arched window, Elethor saw griffins and salvanae still fighting outside; the onslaught of Tiran fire had ended, and now nephilim—too large to fight in these halls—were charging at the beasts.

They raced through an ancient library, its shelves rotted away, its scrolls disintegrating under their boots. By a stone door, Treale slew a man, letting the crumbling papyrus drink his blood. For a moment no Tirans charged at them, and Treale leaned against a wall, lowered her head, and breathed raggedly. Blood covered her armor, helmet, and sword. Elethor stumbled toward her, leaned against the same wall, and for a moment they panted together.

"El—" Treale said, coughed a few times, and tried again. "Elethor, I... I can smell them. Rot. Worms. Nephilim are here."

Elethor nodded and wiped blood and sweat off his brow. Northern men, both of Requiem and Osanna, trudged through the dust toward them, blades raised and armor dented.

"The bastards are fighting our griffins outside," Elethor said.

Treale shook her head. "No, Elethor, there are nephilim in here. Inside this mountain. The rot is rising from somewhere deep inside." She shuddered. "There's something festering in the heart of this mountain. It's the stench of nephilim, but somehow worse, more powerful."

Elethor sniffed. He could smell the blood, the crumbling scrolls, and their sweat—and overpowering it all, the stench of nephil rot. Treale was right. This stench wasn't coming from outside—at least, not all of it. A hive of these creatures lurked deeper. He raised his blade.

"Follow your nose, Treale. Wherever this smell is coming from, I wager that's where we'll find Solina."

They broke down a door, charged into a corridor, and slew three more men. Their warriors ran behind them.

They combed the palace for hours. They kicked down doors of corroded bronze. They swung their blades. Blood washed the palace and corpses piled up. A hundred warriors followed Elethor down a columned hallway; a dozen died when

Tirans charged from one chamber. A dozen more replaced them, rushing down a staircase from a room they had claimed. This palace was a great, dusty hive of ancient stones and smashed statues. They fought hallway by hallway, room by room, bridge by bridge. Elethor thought the labyrinth would never end, and yet the smell grew stronger, and he moved deeper into the mountain. He left all windows far behind. The only light here came from the torches men carried. These halls were old, older even than the ruins of Bar Luan. Dust rose to their ankles, and wind moaned like ghosts.

"Down here, Elethor!" Treale shouted at his side. Her eyes were wide, and her chest rose and fell as she panted. "I can smell them. Here!"

She ran down a spiraling staircase. Elethor ran at her side, and dozens of their men followed. The stairs corkscrewed around a towering statue of an Ancient, his face stoic and his sandstone robes cascading like silk. At the foot of the statue, the stench of rot flared so powerfully Elethor nearly gagged.

A rough hallway plunged downward, its walls lined with torches. At the tunnel's end rose doors of bronze, large as the gates of palaces. Firelight limned the doors; flames burned behind them. Grunts, snorts, and gurgles rose from the chamber beyond.

Nephilim.

Elethor paused and looked at Treale. She raised her blade and stared back with tightened lips. Their men crowded behind them, armor dented and bloody, eyes grim.

"Once we enter, Treale, shift into a dragon," he said. "If nephilim are back there, the place is large enough to shift."

She nodded. "We'll break down the doors and burn them all."

She took a step back, raised her shield, and made to charge down the corridor. Elethor placed a hand on her shoulder, holding her back.

"Wait, Treale," he said softly. "Before we go in there..."

She looked up at him with huge, dark eyes like pools of endless night, and Elethor swallowed, suddenly not sure how to proceed. They had survived this far, but now a fear gripped him like icy fingers around his spine. Treale's eyes seemed so large to him, so young, so loyal. Despite all the men she had slain, she seemed a mere youth to him now, an innocent young woman blinded by love for her king.

And he was afraid for her. He was afraid for all those who followed him, who obeyed his orders without question, who plunged into darkness to fight at his side. If too many nephilim lurked beyond these doors, there would be no sky to flee to.

It is victory now, Elethor thought, *or death—death for me, my men, and this young woman who only a few years ago placed a frog on my dinner plate, then fled squealing and laughing, a child with no care in the world.*

"El?" she whispered. "Are you all right?"

He held her shoulder. "Treale, if we don't make it out of here, I want you to know something."

Her lips parted, and Elethor knew she was remembering that night—that night upon the hill where she had kissed his cheek, where they had talked about their lives, where for one night Elethor had forgotten about Solina, forgotten about Lyana, and had almost loved her, almost left the world for her. He had thought about that night often, and today in her eyes, he saw that she had never forgotten—that she had relived her lips upon his cheek countless times.

"What is it, El?" she whispered.

"Treale, you fought bravely. You proved your honor. Whatever happens beyond those doors, you are Requiem's finest; never doubt that. Will you kneel before me?"

She gasped, swallowed, and nodded. She knelt, caked with blood and ash, and held out her sword in open palms.

"I, King Elethor Aeternum," he said, "knight you a bellator of Requiem, a warrior of starlight. Rise, Lady Treale Oldnale."

She rose, tears in her eyes.

"But I ran from battle," she whispered. "When the wyverns attacked, I—"

"You flew to find your family," Elethor said. "I will not fault you for that. And damn it, Treale. You saved my bloody sister, for stars' sake. That's got to count for something, no?"

She laughed, eyes damp. "A knight, Elethor! Bloody stars. Two years ago I thought I'd be a puppeteer." She wiped her eyes, clutched her sword, and nodded down the hall. "Now that I'm a knight and about a hundred times braver, are you ready to go kill the queen?"

He nodded. She clasped his shoulder and bared her teeth. He gripped her shoulder too. They shared one long, final stare, then turned and ran shouting down the hallway. Their men screamed and charged behind them. They smashed against the bronze doors.

These doors were ancient, forged thousands of years ago, and they crashed open, and Elethor and Treale burst into a great chamber.

Countless nephilim screeched, white eyes blazing like molten fire.

Elethor shifted into a dragon and spewed his flames. Treale shifted too and her fire screamed across the chamber. Nephilim shrieked. Fellow Vir Requis burst into the room behind them, and more dragons blew fire, and nephilim crashed against the ceiling and walls, and a column cracked.

The hall blazed, an inferno of flame and flesh and scale and tooth. A nephil burst through fire and thrust claws, and Elethor roared, blood upon his chest. Another nephil leaped onto Treale and knocked her down, and she rolled and wrestled it, her tail flailing. The beasts flew everywhere, a great living mass, and Elethor lashed his claws, bit maggoty flesh, and whipped his tail.

A flaming halo crackled, and a towering nephil rose ahead, wings spread out like the sails of a demon ship. Lord Legion shrieked, and the sound cracked the walls, and rubble fell from the ceiling. Men died in his jaws, and the Nephil King laughed, and all around him his minions spread, an endless sea of the fallen.

We cannot win this, Elethor realized, and fear clutched him, and for a moment he froze. *They are too many. I led my people to death.*

Legion chewed and swallowed men, licked his lips, and charged toward Elethor. Legion's great arms swung, and Elethor blew his fire, but the arms slammed into him. He flew and crashed against a wall, cracking it. More nephilim mobbed him. Three beasts dragged Treale down and bit into her back, and she screamed.

"Enough!"

The voice rang across the chamber, clear even over the shrieks and roars.

The nephilim froze.

Elethor fell, wheezing, and his wings draped at his sides. He looked up to see Solina sitting upon a throne of living flesh and scales. One of the nephilim formed her backrest, its head above her own, drooling upon her. Two more nephilim formed her armrests; she laid her hands upon their ridged spines. A crown like claws of gold rose upon her head. Nephil drool and pus covered her white gown, and the creatures of her throne licked her with long, white tongues.

"Elethor," she said with a crooked smile. "You cannot win this war. Look around you! A thousand nephilim fill this hall. You have brought...." She squinted. "Oh my, Elethor, but you have only one dragon left, a scrawny female one too."

Elethor growled and looked around him. A hundred men of Osanna and Requiem had charged into this chamber with him. They lay dead upon the floor, torn apart, limbs scattered and bodies crushed. Already nephilim feasted upon them, sucking up bodies like owls sucking up mice.

Only Treale still lived. The young black dragon lay on her belly, and Legion stood above her, his claws pressed down against her neck. Treale growled and tried to rise, but could not. Legion smiled above her, tongue darting, and his halo flamed blue.

Elethor looked back at Solina.

He roared and blew a jet of fire toward her.

She leaped back, and several nephilim slammed against Elethor. Claws swung. Fangs dug into him. He screamed. He burned them. His fire exploded and showered back upon him. Blows thudded against him, and a nephil clawed his cheek, and pain blazed, and more claws slashed his belly, and he roared. Claws drove into his back, and Elethor howled, and his magic left him.

He crashed to the floor in human form.

Legion lolloped toward him, grinning. The Nephil King reached down, wrapped his claws around Elethor, and lifted him like a demonic child lifting a discarded toy.

Elethor hung in the air, dazed, the claws nearly crushing him. Legion shook him wildly, and Elethor's head spun, and he could not see or breathe. All around him the nephilim leered and howled.

"Enough!" Solina shouted again.

The nephilim froze. Legion stood holding Elethor in one fist, pinning his arms down. Blood dripped into Elethor's eyes, and he could barely breathe. It felt like Legion's grip would snap his ribs.

He looked aside and saw that Legion was clutching Treale in his other hand. She too had resumed human form, and she hung in Legion's grip only feet away from Elethor. Blood dripped from her, and her face was pale. She whispered to him, but her voice was so weak Elethor could not hear.

"Treale!" he cried hoarsely.

She gave him a pleading look, eyes full of pain. Her lips uttered his name silently.

"Legion, hold them before me," Solina said. "Hold them still."

She rose upon her throne. The nephilim that formed her seat shifted, creating a ramp of spines and ribs. Solina descended and walked across the bloody floor, hands on the hilts of her sabres.

When she reached Legion, the nephil lowered Elethor and Treale in his claws, holding them a mere foot above the floor. Elethor struggled and kicked and screamed, but could not free himself.

Solina touched his cheek, and her eyes softened.

"Still you fight," she whispered. "Even when all your hope is lost. Still, here in my hall, you struggle."

He spat out a tooth. Blood filled his mouth.

"Fight me," he said. "You and me. No dragons. No nephilim. Just the two of us—sword to sword."

She raised her eyebrows. "Are you..." She laughed. "Are you challenging me to a duel? This is no epic poem of olden days, Elethor. This is no romantic farce." She caressed his hair. "I don't wish to fight you, El. I never did. All I ever wanted was peace."

He laughed mirthlessly, hanging in the claws. "Peace? You wanted peace when you slew my family? When your beasts crushed my city? When you slaughtered children in our tunnels?"

She placed her hands in his hair. She kissed his ear—her lips were soft and full—and whispered.

"I slew them, Elethor, so that we could have peace. So that all those who taunted us, who tried to stop us, who whispered against us—so all of them went away. I killed them, and I will kill everyone else, until all the world is just you... and me." She nodded up toward Legion, whose head drooled above them. "Show him, Legion. Kill the girl."

Elethor shouted.

Clutching Elethor in one hand, Legion tossed Treale down from his other hand. She slammed hard against the floor, and her blood splattered.

"Treale, shift!" Elethor cried.

She looked up at him. Legion's claws thrust. Treale rose to her feet and began to shift.

A claw crashed through her breastplate.

Treale gasped. Her magic vanished. She hung upon the claw, head and limbs tossed back, gasping. Her legs kicked in midair. Blood filled her mouth.

Legion shook his claw and flung her back down.

"Treale!" Elethor shouted. He howled. With strength he had not imagined in him, he tore at the claws that clutched him.

"Let him go, Legion!" Solina said and laughed. "Let him see her!"

Elethor crashed to the floor, banging his knees. He rose, rushed to Treale, and knelt over her.

His eyes stung. His breath caught. She lay on her back, a hole in her chest. She trembled and gasped, and her hands reached toward him. Blood poured from her chest.

"El," she whispered.

With shaking fingers, he tore off her armor. He rifled through his pack, pulled out a bandage, and placed it against her wound, knowing that it was too late; the blow had pierced through her. He held her, one hand under her head, the other against her cheek.

"I'm here, Treale," he whispered. "I'm here."

She convulsed, legs twitching, chest rising and falling. She could barely speak.

"El," she whispered. "El, do you... do you remember that night?" Her body shook like a fish on a boat's deck. "Do you... do you remember? Under the stars, how... how I kissed your cheek?"

He held her and caressed her hair. "I remember, Treale. I never forgot. Ever."

Her blood flowed, and her trembling eased, and she smiled with blue lips. "El, do you remember how we talked about puppets?"

He blinked tears from his eyes. "I remember," he whispered.

"I... I liked that night," she said. Her breath shook. "El, can I... Please, can I kiss your cheek one more time? Please. I want to... I want to pretend I'm there." Tears flowed down her cheeks. "I want to be back on that hill under the stars."

He lowered his head, and she kissed his cheek with trembling lips, smearing him with blood. He kissed her forehead and caressed her hair.

"Don't leave me," she whispered.

"Never," he said. "Never, Treale. I'm here. I'm right here. Tell me about your puppets. Tell me about all the shelves and piles of them, and all the puppet shows you performed."

She placed her arms around him. A soft light touched her eyes. She trembled against him.

"I had...." Her tears fell. "I sewed them, Elethor, so many... so many. Hundreds of puppets. Green ones. Yellow puppets. And..."

Elethor lowered his head and a silent sob shook his chest. He laid Treale down upon her back. She stared up, mouth open and eyes glassy. His tears wet her face, and with a bloodied hand, he closed her eyes.

Goodbye, Treale. Fly to your puppets. Fly to our starlit halls and wait for me there, and one day you will tell me all about them again.

He rose slowly to his feet.

He turned toward Solina.

He raised his sword, howled, and lunged at her.

She only stood, sighing, as nephilim swooped toward him, and claws grabbed him, and he screamed as wings and scales and rot covered his world.

LYANA

Ships burned along the Pallan, a line of fire blazing across the desert. Once this river had teemed with life. Merchants, soldiers, and fisherman had sailed upon their barges and cogs. Reeds, palm and fig trees, and rustling fields had lined the riverbanks. Ibises, falcons, jackals, and hundreds of other animals had drunk from these waters. Today under the cruel sun the river crossed the desert like a scar, her sails, trees, and farms burning, her animals fallen or scattered.

This place was the vein of Tiranor, Lyana thought, *pumping blood to her capital. Today we burned this vein and left Irys to choke and rot.*

The capital perhaps was choking now, but her sister city—Iysa, great southern jewel of the desert—still pulsed. Lyana kept flying south, her host around her: thousands of dragons and griffins all bearing riders. Before them in the desert, the Pallan widened into a sprawling oasis, and here rose the white walls and towers of Iysa.

Lyana had heard stories of this city. Here did Tiranor build her ships, forge her steel, and mine her jewels. She had imagined a place bustling with enemy forces: battalions of archers upon the walls, phalanxes of wyverns and phoenixes circling overhead, and swarms of nephilim festering and screeching for blood.

Instead, as she flew toward the white walls, she found a ghost city.

The walls of Iysa stood barren, their battlements like sun-dried jaws upon sand. The towers stood silent; no war horns blew upon them, and only a single, tattered banner flapped from one, hiding and showing the Golden Sun. Lyana frowned, flying closer. Behind her flew her warriors.

"It's too quiet," said Wila, her rider. "Nephilim guarded every cog along the river. Won't they guard a city?"

Lyana sniffed. She could smell the rot of nephilim, but could not decide if they lurked here in hiding, or had left their stench and fled. She flew higher and over the walls. Below her, the streets of Iysa spread like a barren labyrinth. Shops, temples, forts, homes—all lay silent and still. Lyana saw no movement but for a few flapping tunics upon lines and a dog that fled into an alley. Docks stretched into the river, naked of ships.

When Lyana looked south of the city, she saw many footprints in the sand heading toward distant hills. She squinted and gazed into the horizon; she could just make out fleeing beasts aflight, perhaps wyverns or nephilim.

"They fled the city," Lyana said. "They heard of our approach. They ran rather than fight."

Lyana heard the creak of Wila tugging her bowstring.

"I don't like this," the rider said. "Nephilim—the spawn of demons—fleeing from battle? Something is wrong here. This is a trap."

"Let's be careful," Lyana agreed. "As far as we know, Solina loaded up the city with Tiran fire, and some poor bastard down there is just waiting for us to land so he can blow the place up."

They circled above the city—dragons, griffins, riders. Their wings scattered dust and leaves and bent the trees below. By a domed temple, movement caught Lyana's eyes. She stared down, squinting, to see several men cowering in a courtyard. They wore rags, iron collars encircled their necks, and dust filled their white hair. Welts and blood covered them. Chains ran from their ankles to heavy iron balls the size of watermelons, too heavy to even drag.

"The city folk left their slaves," Lyana said. "Those too old, weak, or wounded to flee with them."

She circled above the temple. Rough bricks formed its dome, and several palm trees swayed alongside it. When her shadow fell upon the slaves, they wailed and covered their heads. They were thin, ribs showing between the tatters of their rags, and whip lashes covered their backs. Blood stained their lips.

They're dying of thirst and heat, Lyana thought. She looked around the city, cursing. *Damn it.* She could still smell rot here somewhere—did nephilim hide in these houses, or did their stench merely linger? Was this a trap and the slaves the bait?

She looked over her shoulder at her rider. Wila sat with an arrow nocked, her face stern and her golden hair billowing. Her breastplate bore the bull horns of Osanna in silver, and a golden pin—shaped like the walls of Confutatis, the White City—clasped her gray cloak.

"Wila," Lyana said, "keep that arrow nocked. We're going to help these men."

Wila frowned. "My lady, I don't like this. Nephilim waited for us on the beaches. They hid along every league of the river. This place is too quiet. I say we burn the damn city from the air."

A sigh clanked Lyana's scales. "I would, but... Wila, too many innocents have died. We have slain too many women and children. How many cowered in the hulls of the ships we burned—the wives, sons, and daughters of merchants shipping supplies to Irys? How many women and children now hide in that northern capital as dragons rain fire upon it?" She shook her head. "We do not crave the death of our enemy's innocents. We are not Solina; she slew our children with relish. I have killed my enemies, Wila, and perhaps while doing so, I have killed innocents too, bystanders whose only sin was standing too close to those who seek my own death. This will haunt me. This blood I cannot wash from my hands. This blood I had to shed. But here in this city, seeing abandoned slaves cowering below me, I cannot blow my fire. If I did, would I not be as Solina is? Fighting a monster, would we not become monsters ourselves? I will save them if I can. If I can save the innocents of the enemy, perhaps after all this blood and fire, I can save my own soul."

She dived toward the courtyard. Her claws clattered against the cobblestones, and the chained slaves whimpered.

Lyana whipped her head from side to side, sniffing the air. The drool and pus of nephilim seeped between the cobblestones and puddled in a corner; the stuff reeked. The creatures had been here not hours ago.

"Please," whispered a slave, an old man with a white beard. "Please don't hurt us, don't burn us, please..."

Still in dragon form, Lyana approached the chained men. In the sky, griffins and dragons circled over the city; some were descending to land upon roofs and streets. The chained slaves flinched whenever a shadow crossed them.

"I'm not going to hurt you," Lyana said. "Where are the nephilim? Where—"

Stars.

Lyana growled and took flight.

Stars damn it.

These slaves were not chained to balls of iron. They were chained to clay balls of Tiran fire.

She had not soared fifty feet when the temple ceiling crashed open, the doors shattered, and nephilim burst screeching outside.

The air cracked. The Tiran fire exploded below. Fire raged and white light flooded Lyana, and the slaves' blood splattered her. Her ears rang, and claws grabbed her leg, pulling her down. She roared.

As she plummeted, she glimpsed the rest of the city. From every temple, fort, and hall, nephilim burst into the sky. Tiran fire exploded. Flames and blood showered across Iysa.

Lyana crashed back onto the temple courtyard. One nephil grabbed her leg, and three others leaped onto her. The slaves were gone; nothing remained of them but blood and gobbets of flesh. The temple walls had shattered opened; archers stood there, and arrows flew at Lyana.

She roared and blew her fire. Upon her back, Wila screamed and fired her own arrows. Lyana's flames crashed into a nephil, slamming it against a wall. Another leaped onto her shoulder, and claws dug, and Lyana screamed and bit. Her teeth sank into the beast's flesh, and she tasted its rot and maggots.

"Take her alive!" shouted a Tiran soldier in the temple. "Her horns are gilded—this one is a noble. Take her alive!"

Lyana screamed and flapped her wings, struggling to rise. She kicked wildly, freed herself, and flew ten feet.

Three more nephilim swooped from above, crashed down onto her, and she slammed into the cobblestones again. They cracked beneath her. She roared and blew fire.

"Wila, run!" she screamed. She did not know if her rider even lived. Arrows peppered her, clattering against her scales. One pierced her chest, and Lyana roared in pain, and claws tore at her, and teeth bit, and pain flooded her.

Light and song and ringing flowed across her.

Her magic tore free like a bandage from a wound.

She lay in human form, the nephilim dwarfing her. She gripped her sword. She drew a foot of steel. She screamed and claws grabbed her, tightened around her like a girdle of bone, and lifted her.

She screamed and kicked and spat, tried to shift again, and shouted every curse she knew. She was still screaming when they shoved a sack over her head, and wings flapped, and her legs kicked in midair. Wind whipped her, her head spun, and terror pulsed in her chest.

ELETHOR

Legion's claws wrapped around Elethor's chest, pinning his arms down and nearly cracking his ribs. Elethor could barely breathe, barely make a sound. His wounds burned; so many cuts and bruises and welts covered him, he felt like a slab of beaten meat. He tried to shift but could hardly muster the power to stay conscious.

"Yesss," Legion hissed. The nephil was carrying him down a dark hall, his clawed feet clattering. "Yessss, struggle, weredragon. I like it when you struggle."

The demon's tongue dipped to lick Elethor's cheek. Elethor grunted and closed his eyes. The beast's head rose above his own—the creature stood thrice his height—and his jaws leaked drool and pus that stank of corpses.

"Soli—" Elethor began, but Legion squeezed his claws tighter, suffocating his voice.

The queen walked ahead, not turning back to regard him. She held a torch, lighting walls covered in faded murals depicting the Ancients battling serpents and raising fire in their palms. As they moved down the hall, Elethor shut his eyes and thought of Treale.

Fly to our starlit halls, daughter of Requiem, he thought. *Await me there among the souls or our fallen. You sing now among them.*

Solina led them through many halls, stairways, and doors, until finally she brought them to a towering archway whose keystone sported engravings of lions. Solina walked through the archway, and Legion—carrying Elethor in his grip—followed.

They entered a hall the size of a palace, easily the largest chamber Elethor had seen in this mountain. He thought that the fallen courts of Requiem could fit into this chamber with room to fly around them. Limestone columns rose from shadow to support a wide, domed ceiling like a stone sky. In the center of the chamber, a tower rose from a pit; a bridge led from the doorway to the tower top.

Solina took several steps onto the bridge, turned around, and smiled at Elethor.

"Welcome," she said, "to the Hall of Memory. Legion! Carry him onto the bridge. Let him see what lurks below."

She smiled crookedly, turned her back toward them, and continued walking across the bridge.

Elethor snarled and struggled against Legion's claws, but they squeezed further, and he was so tired, so hurt, his skull too tight, his chest aching. He wanted to scream, to break free, to lunge at Solina and kill her. And yet he could barely keep her in focus. He had lost too much blood, had fought too much, hurt too much.

Legion began to walk along the bridge, his claws clattering and scraping again the stone. Clanking, squealing, and screeches rose from the pit below, and a stench wafted so powerfully Elethor choked and gagged. Legion laughed—a sound like snapping bones—and held Elethor over the pit.

His breath left him.

Elethor closed his eyes.

He knew then: There was no hope. Not for him and not for his people fighting across the desert.

This flight south was folly. This was all in vain.

The spawn of nephilim filled the pit below the bridge, spreading all around the tower. Their eyes burned red. Their claws and teeth dug at one another's flesh, feeding and licking and sucking blood. They screeched to see Elethor hanging above them. They leaped and tried to claw at him, nearly reaching his feet. Countless filled this place, a writhing mass like a nest of maggots.

"Do you like them, Elethor?" Solina cried ahead, voice echoing. "My servant Legion spawned them himself. A million writhe below you, growing larger. The strong, you see—they feed upon the weak. They climb the mass. They will soon be large enough to fly and cover the world." She looked over her shoulder, and her eyes softened in mock concern. "I am quite afraid, my dear Elethor, that they will soon feed upon the rest of your weredragons."

Then she laughed, turned back toward the tower, and kept walking across the bridge.

Legion hissed and his drool sprayed. He followed, carrying Elethor farther along. As they walked, the nephil spawn leaped at the bridge, clawed at its edges, then fell back into the pit. Their veined wings beat uselessly, still too brittle for flight. They screeched and licked their maws.

"Weredragon blood!" they cried, voices shrill like possessed children. "Let us eat his organs!"

They walked for what seemed the length of cities before the bridge reached the tower. Upon the tower top lay the still, silvery surface of a pool.

It's some kind of well, Elethor realized. *A towering one rising from the demon pit.*

Solina stepped onto the pool's rim, placed one foot into the water, and looked over her shoulder. Her eyes again softened, but this time Elethor saw no mockery in them, only old sadness like a lone doll upon a shelf in an abandoned home.

"It's time, Elethor," she said. "It's time to go home."

She stepped into the well, moving deeper and deeper down hidden stairs until her head disappeared underwater.

Legion hissed and chuckled. With a screech and spray of rot, he tossed Elethor forward.

Elethor tumbled and crashed into the water.

Silver streams flowed across him. His blood seeped and rose through the water like red ghosts. He sank. He closed his eyes. He thought of Lyana's green eyes and hands in his, clung to her memory, and waited to die.

Warmth fell upon him.

Sunlight played against his closed eyelids.

His body felt...

Whole, he thought. *Healed. Young.*

His pains vanished like a nightmare fleeing the dawn. He could not remember feeling so nourished, healthy, and strong in years. Softness caressed him; he lay in a plush, warm bed.

He opened his eyes and inhaled softly.

My bed, he thought. His eyes watered. *My bed at home. In Requiem.*

Not the cold, hard bed in Requiem's palace, a great thing of dark oak the kings of Requiem slept in. No—this was *his* bed, the one he had built himself for his small home upon the hill.

He was in that home now. A tear streamed down his cheek. He had not seen this place in two years—not since the phoenixes had burned it. He sat up and looked around, eyes stinging and breath shaking.

Shelves lined the walls, brimming with leather-bound books, geodes, rolled-up maps, and wooden figurines he had whittled. Larger sculptures of marble stood upon the floor: Solina in her youth, nude and beautiful as sunlight over the forest. Outside the windows—stars, how could this be?—he saw Requiem. Not Requiem as he knew her now, burnt and fallen and crawling with beasts. This was the Requiem of his youth. It was spring, and the sky was blue, and dragons glided outside—not haggard survivors, but gleaming dragons of blue, gold, and green.

"I'm home," he whispered.

He left the bed and found that he wore a green tunic with a silver collar—stars, he remembered this tunic!—and that his body was younger, slimmer, not scarred from war. He looked at his shoulder where, a year ago, wyvern acid had burned him; the flesh was unblemished. He touched his cheeks and found them smooth, his beard gone.

Are these the halls of afterlife? he wondered. He had always imagined them like glittering columns and starlit halls. This felt more like a memory come alive—a memory of youth when everything was bright, fresh, and pure in the world.

He moved through his room, laughing softly, disbelieving. He ran his fingers over his cherrywood table. He lifted the statuette of a turtle, the one he had carved for Solina. He looked out the windows to see Nova Vita roll across the hills, bright in the spring sun, her birches rustling.

This is Nova Vita years ago, he realized. The potter shop below the hill was only being built now. The cypresses outside his window were still young.

It's ten years ago, he thought. *Maybe nine. And I'm only eighteen here, a mere youth and prince, not a haunted, scarred king.*

Under scrolls and books, he found his handheld mirror and looked upon his reflection. His cheeks were softer. His brown eyes had seen less pain. No scar rifted his face; that face was young, thoughtful, and pale.

"Solina always did say I was too pale," he mumbled.

"You always were," came her voice from behind him.

He turned to see her at the doorway, and his breath left him.

She stood barefoot, leaning against the doorframe, and gave him a crooked smile. She wore one of his old tunics. It was loose around her, and she was naked beneath it; he could see the golden smoothness of her legs and the tops of her breasts. Her hair cascaded over her shoulders, rivers of platinum like water under moonlight. She was young here in this memory, closer to twenty than thirty, and her face glowed with youth, and her blue eyes stared at him with all the temptation and coyness of forbidden young love.

She's beautiful, he thought. This was not Queen Solina, the cruel tyrant of Tiranor, the mad woman she had become. No. This was *his* Solina, the young Solina he had loved, the Solina he had pined for, the Solina she had been. This was the woman who had filled his bed for years, then his dreams for years after that. This was Solina of sunlight, of stolen kisses, of maddening love and sex and flame.

"Solina?" he whispered.

"I am here, Elethor," she said. She walked toward him, took his hands, and smiled. "It's me, El. It's me. Do you remember?"

Her hands were soft and warm. He held them and looked at her, and looked around, and his eyes dampened again.

"I remember. Solina, how—"

She placed a finger against his lips.

"Does it matter?" she whispered. Her smile left her, and her lips trembled, and she embraced him. She clung to him desperately, and her fingers pressed against his shoulders. "Hold me, Elethor. Hold me tight."

He held her. They stood like this for long moments, and her tears wet his shoulder. He caressed her hair, and suddenly he was no longer King Elethor of Requiem, a jaded warrior. That man faded away, and he was Prince Elethor again, eighteen years old and caught in her light, and this was *real.* This was him again. This was home, this was youth, and the world was bright and no darkness could fill it.

"How can this be, Solina?"

She looked at him. A tremulous smile found her lips, and she touched his cheek.

"I made this place for us," she said. "Do you remember this day? It's the day your father, brother, Lyana, and all the others flew east for some fair. You and I remained here in Nova Vita—no duties, no dinners, no obligations, just... us. Just a perfect day of sunlight and being lazy and..." She lowered her eyes shyly. "And making love." She looked back up at him, her eyes damp. "It was our day. A perfect day. It was the best day of my life, El—the best one ever. It *is* the best day. We can relive this day now! Again and again forever, and... and the others will never come back. There will never be war here, or pain, or exile, or any of those bad things. Just you and me, young forever, in love forever. Our perfect day."

He pulled away from her, walked to the window, and looked outside upon the hills of birches and cypresses. Above in the sky, the dragons glided. Solina came to stand beside him and placed a hand on his shoulder.

"Where are we?" he asked.

"In Requie—"

He turned toward her. "Solina, where are we?"

She looked aside, eyes pained. "Does it matter, El? Does it matter where this place is? It's real to me. It's real to you." She looked back at him, tears trembling in her eyes. "Don't you remember?"

He placed his hands upon the windowsill, lowered his head, and understood. He spoke softly.

"We're still in Tiranor. We're in the bowels of the mountain, and around us the nephilim spawn, and... this is some... some illusion of the water. Of the pool we entered." He grabbed her arm. "Isn't it, Solina?"

"So what if it is!" Her face flushed. "So what, Elethor? Who cares what lies out there?" She swept her arm around. "*This* is what matters. This place, not anything else. These books, and statues, and... and, Elethor, the turtle you carved me. You remember the turtle." She pressed herself against him and tried to kiss him. "I love you, Elethor, and that is what matters. That is all that matters. And you love me too. Here you do. Here you've always loved me."

He sighed and lowered his head. "It's not real, Solina."

"My memory is real. This day existed, El. It was real years ago; it's real again, real enough. It was my best day. Have you forgotten it?"

He looked around him, seeing his books, his sculptures, his bed. He looked at Solina—his love.

"I remember," he said softly. "It was my best day too."

Tears streamed down her cheeks and she embraced him. They stood together by the window, holding each other close.

"Then let us stay here," she said. "Your city that you loved still stands here. The people whom you loved still live. I will leave the Memory Pool sometimes—to govern my empire, to deal with the dirt, blood, and cruelty of the world. You can wait for me here, and read your books, and sculpt your statues. I will return to you every day. We will make love every night. Like this forever—young and happy. Out there, in the world, we are killers, Elethor. I killed so many; you did too. Our bodies are scarred there, our souls cold and drenched with blood. But not here. Here we are young, and good, and pure of heart." She touched his cheek. "It's finally over, El. All the pain. My exile. Our war. It's over now. The pain is gone, and nothing but joy and light remain."

He looked at her young, earnest face, unblemished by the scars of war. Her skin was smooth and supple, a soft golden hue, and freckles covered her nose. Her eyes were deep blue, her lips full and pink, her hair so soft in his hands.

Is this not all I ever wanted? he thought. *Is this not what I spent years yearning for? Is this not perfection, eternal bliss?*

He breathed deeply, and his chest ached. He had it here—all he had desired! He could spend the rest of his life in his home with the woman he loved, the woman who had claimed his soul and still clutched it, the woman who—

The woman who slaughtered children in our tunnels, a voice whispered inside him. *The woman who slew my father and brother. The woman who destroyed my kingdom and butchered my people.*

He thought of Lyana, his wife. Here, a decade ago, he hated Lyana—an imperious youth who would lecture him about this or that until he wanted to strangle her. And he thought of Lyana the woman, his wife, a warrior who had fought at his side, loved him, and flown through fire and death with him—a woman braver than any he had known, a woman of a heart pure and strong like steel forged in dragonfire, of soft light and goodness and eternal sadness, a woman who would always fly by his side.

I loved Solina in my foolish youth, he thought. *But I walked through the Abyss with Lyana, and I loved her as a man, and I fought with her for all that we believe in, for all that our people hoped and killed and died for.* Solina was a flame, a fire that had lit his youth, flickered bright, and spread into a wildfire that burned him. But Lyana was no flame—she was starlight, blinding in the darkness, guiding him home.

"And what of those who still live?" he said, voice suddenly hoarse. "What of Lyana, my sister, and the others?"

Something dark crossed Solina's eyes. Her jaw tightened. She looked aside and spoke tautly.

"They will live," she said. "I will not kill them. I will not hunt them. You have my word, Elethor. I vow to you." She looked back at him and again took his hands. "If you remain here with me—with your Solina, with your love—I won't harm any more of your people. Those who still live can leave this land, fly into exile, and find whatever life they still can."

He tore himself away from her. He walked to the back of the room where his statues stood. He faced them: likenesses of Solina carved in marble. A sigh ran through him, and he closed his eyes.

"No," he said softly. "No, Solina. You say we are young here and pure. Are we pure, Solina? What defines our evil—our actions or our hearts? You slew my family. You butchered my people. You—"

"Not me, Elethor! Not this me. Not this Solina here." She walked toward him and grabbed his arm. "Not this Solina who stands unscarred before you."

She breathed heavily, chest rising and falling, and she was beautiful, and young, and temptation itself barefoot in dawn's light.

"That evil is inside you," he said. "It always was; I was blind to it. I saw your beauty. I felt your kisses. I ignored the cruelty of your heart. Your hands slew my family years from now. Your heart drove those hands; it has always beaten inside you. I will not stay with you here. I will not be part of this mockery, this fake dream, this—"

She slapped him—a slap so hard he sucked in breath and saw stars.

"You will!" she hissed between clenched teeth. Her eyes blazed. "You will stay with me here, or she will die, Elethor. She will die in pain. I will kill her." She spun toward the doorway and screamed. "Legion! Bring the whore!"

The door to Elethor's chamber creaked open.

The nephil's head thrust inside, nearly as tall as a man.

Elethor growled and instinctively reached for his sword, only to find it missing. The sight of this rotted, bloody creature here, in perfect old Requiem, spun his head. Legion grinned, and

Daniel Arenson

his fangs shone, and his drool pooled on the floor. Dried blood encrusted the spikes and horns across his head, his halo crackled, and worms crawled inside his left eye.

Like a scuttling insect, Legion crawled into the chamber—even crouched, he barely fit through the door. Rot dripped from him to seep across the floor, and his stench swirled, thick as moldy stew in the air.

Then Elethor saw what Legion clutched to his belly, and he let out a hoarse cry.

Holding her close against him, Legion carried a bloodied, bruised Lyana.

"Lyana!" Elethor shouted and made to grab her, but Solina held him back.

"Don't move, El!" she warned, her breath against his ear. "If you move, he will crush her. See how frail she is! See how sharp his claws are around her little ribs."

Elethor froze, head spinning and breath panting. Lyana moaned, her eyelids fluttered, and she looked up at him. Her one eye was swollen and bruised. Her lips bled. When she saw him, she gave a soft gasp and whispered his name. This was not the Lyana of ten years ago, the imperious girl with the upturned nose and bouncing red curls. This was the Lyana he had married, her hair shorter, her eyes deeper and wiser.

"Lyana," he whispered.

He looked into her eyes and saw fear, anger, and pain, but above all love for him and Requiem, a brittle strength like an old sword drawn for one last battle.

"Look at her," Solina whispered. She stood behind Elethor, her hand on his shoulder, her lips against his ear. "Look at her there, bloodied and nearly crushed in the claws of my servant. Look at her, the great knight, the proud queen, the loving wife—look at her. Broken. Weak. Almost dead."

Elethor would not remove his eyes from Lyana, but he spoke to Solina.

"She is stronger than you will ever know, Solina," he said. "She is stronger than you will ever be."

Solina took a step forward, touched his cheek, and whispered.

"We will see, Elethor. We will see." She turned toward the nephil and his prey. "Legion! Kill the girl. Kill her like you did the last one."

Legion grinned and raised Lyana toward the ceiling, and his jaws opened, and Lyana cried out.

"Wait!" Elethor shouted.

Legion froze, holding Lyana a mere foot above his jaws.

"Wait!" Elethor repeated. "Solina, wait."

The Queen of Tiranor smiled softly. She nodded at Legion, and the nephil lowered Lyana to his breast and held her close, a spider clutching a fly.

Elethor lowered his head, pain pulsing through his chest like demons inside him, scratching at his heart and ribs. Again he saw all the dead: his father, his brother, Treale, and countless others, all dead for this war between him and Solina. He could bear no more—not Lyana. Not her. He clenched his fists at his sides, turned toward Solina, and stared at her.

"Let Lyana go," he said, "and I will stay with you here." He exhaled slowly and lowered his eyes. "You win, Solina."

"El," Lyana whispered. "El, I—"

The claws tightened around her, constricting her breath and voice. Blood trickled from her lips.

Elethor stepped toward his wife, heart wrenching. He wanted to touch her, comfort her, hold her and whisper to her, but Legion's foot thrust out and kicked him back, and Elethor fell several paces. Solina caught him, wrapped her arms around him, and stared into his eyes.

"You made the right choice, Elethor," she said. "You grieve for her now; I know. You will forget her in time. You will forget her and you will love me again." She turned to her demon. "Legion! Take the girl back to the bridge. Let her go! She is free."

The nephil bowed his dripping, spiked head, and his tongue lapped up drool from the floor. Clutching Lyana to his belly, the creature retreated back out the door, leaving a trail of slime.

Elethor gave a wordless cry, wrenched himself free from Solina, and ran after them. He passed through the doorway, and stench hit his face, and shrieks filled his ears, and he found himself standing outside the pool again. Around him rose the columns of the Hall of Memory. Below in the pit, the million nephil spawn rotted and shrieked and fed upon one another. Legion was already retreating along the stone bridge, moving from the Memory Pool toward the archway that exited the chamber.

"Elethor!" Solina cried behind him.

He ignored her and raced along the bridge.

"Wait!" he shouted. "Solina, let me speak to her! Let me say goodbye. Then you may have me."

"Put her down, Legion!" Solina shouted. "Let him speak to his whore!" She laughed. "Let them cry together one last time; it will amuse me."

The vermin in the pit screamed and leaped and clawed at the rims of the bridge. Their father, the towering Lord Legion, cackled and tossed Lyana down. She thudded against the bridge, and the vermin all around clattered and screeched and clawed, grabbing at the bridge and trying to reach her, then falling back into the pit.

Elethor ran. He reached Lyana, knelt above her, and held her, and for a moment he could not speak from pain. She was hurt. They had removed her armor and torn her clothes, leaving her ragged and bloodied. Dirt and ash matted her hair and caked her face.

"Lyana," he whispered. "I'm here. I'm here."

She struggled to her feet and stood on trembling legs. Elethor held her waist, and she placed her hands on his shoulders. They stood in the center of the bridge. Solina stood behind at the pool; Legion retreated to stand at the archway. All around in the pit, the wretchedness and darkness of the world screamed and bled and fed, their cries echoing in the chamber.

"Elethor," Lyana whispered and tears filled her eyes. "Elethor, no."

He touched her hair. "It's the only way, Lyana. Leave this place. Fly to the others. Find Mori and Bayrin and whoever still lives and flee this desert. Promise me, Lyana."

She stared at him, and her eyes hardened, but then she trembled and pulled him into a crushing embrace. They held each other as the creatures screamed all around.

"I love you, Elethor," she whispered, her head against his shoulder. "I love you always, my husband, my king. They will sing your name in the halls of Requiem. Always."

He touched her cheek and looked into her eyes—those eyes that would once taunt him, madden him, infuriate him... and which now spoke of Requiem's halls, of warm embraces on cold nights, of her steel and fire and love that had taken him through this war, that would remain inside him even in the very pit of darkness.

"I love you too, Lyana," he said. "More than the fallen halls of our fathers, and more than memories of spring. You must lead Requiem now. Our people will follow your fire, and it will lead them home. Two winters ago, I told you this in the Abyss: Whatever strength I have is yours. I will keep you safe, then and now, even in the heart of darkness. Leave this underground. Find our sky. Lead our people to light." He took her hand and placed it against his chest. "I cannot fly with you now. But I will think of you upon the wind, and I will smile, and I will wait... I will wait until we fly together in starlight."

She tightened her arms around him, and they kissed—a deep kiss that tasted of blood, tears, and memories of home, a kiss of fire such as they had never shared, a last flame of stars.

Claws grabbed Lyana's shoulders.

Legion pulled her back, wrenching her from Elethor's arms, tearing their kiss apart.

"Elethor!" she cried, eyes wide.

Legion began dragging her back along the bridge. She reached out to him. Their fingertips touched, shooting warmth through him. Then the beast pulled her into shadow, and she cried his name and disappeared under the archway into darkness.

Elethor stood alone upon the bridge, cold and empty, and stared at the archway.

Goodbye, Lyana. May your wings find our sky.

He turned back to face the Memory Pool. Solina stood there upon the bridge, her eyes soft. She stepped toward him and held his hands.

"You did the right thing, El," she said softly. "I know how much I hurt you. I see the pain in your eyes. But I only hurt you for us, Elethor. For our life. For our memories. Lyana was never yours, El; you know that. She tempted you. She stole you from me, and she hurt you too, and you weep for her now. But you've chosen me. I always knew that you would." She kissed his lips. "You've returned to me at last—to your Solina." She wept and held him. "It's over, Elethor. It's finally over, and we are together again. Come, Elethor. Come with me into the pool. It's time to go home."

Her kiss stung against his lips. Her hands touched his cheeks. Her eyes were huge, drowning in her pain and madness. He touched her hair, and she smiled at him tremulously.

"Goodbye, Solina," he whispered. "I loved you once. I loved you for years. You held me for so long. But that boy in the pool, a boy caught in your light... he is only a memory too." He kissed her cheek. "Goodbye, Solina—fire of my youth, flame and curse of my life."

Standing before her, he shifted into a dragon.

Solina gasped and fell back.

Elethor beat his wings. The vermin below screeched. He soared in the chamber and blew his fire, and roared, and his cries echoed. As Solina lay upon her back and the spawn howled, Elethor shot forward and slammed into a column.

"Elethor!" Solina screamed. She rose to her feet. The firelight painted her face red. "Elethor!"

He slammed into the column, again and again, howling his rage and blowing his fire.

"Legion!" Solina screamed. "Legion, kill the weredragon!"

The nephil screeched outside. Claws clattered. Elethor blew a stream of flame at the archway, and Legion screeched. He kept slamming against the column. Cracks raced along it.

Fly from this place, Lyana. Fly far. Lead our people home.

He slammed into the column once more, and it cracked.

Elethor pulled back, wings beating, and watched the column fall.

It crashed into the pit, crushing spawn beneath it. Legion leaped into the chamber, and Elethor blew his fire again, and the nephil screeched and blazed. Solina screamed upon the bridge. Cracks raced along the ceiling, and chunks of rock fell.

Elethor flew and slammed into another column.

Rocks rained from the ceiling. The second column collapsed, and the spawn below wailed, and Elethor slammed into a third column until it too cracked. The pillar crashed down onto the bridge, crushing it. Solina screamed and leaped back. The bridge crumbled, and the ceiling rained stones, and Solina fell back into the pool. She vanished underwater as all around, columns fell, boulders rained, and vermin screamed and died.

Bricks buffeted Elethor. A chunk of the ceiling crashed down against Legion, and the blazing nephil tumbled into the pit. At once his spawn covered him and began to feast, ripping at their father's flesh, tearing gobbets loose from bones. The prophet howled, voice rising into a storm, so loud and shrill the sound cracked another column. Then the vermin grabbed Legion's jaw, ripped it free, and burrowed into his head. Soon they were feasting upon his eyes and maggoty brain. Legion's flaming halo gave a last crackle and guttered away.

Fly, Lyana, Elethor thought. *Fly far and never return.*

Rocks slammed against him. A column crashed and hit his tail. The walls crumbled, falling and burying the vermin beneath them. A blast shook the chamber and fire blazed outside. Another blast shook the palace, and Elethor realized: The hoards of Tiran fire were bursting.

A final crack raced along the ceiling, and the chamber collapsed.

Rocks slammed into Elethor and he fell. Bricks pummeled him. Dust blinded him. Only the Memory Pool remained standing now; the palace crumbled around it. Blinded and roaring with pain, Elethor crashed into the pool.

He slammed against the floor of his old home in Requiem.

Silence rang in his ears.

The fire, the screeches, the crumbling of columns—all was gone.

Here, he heard nothing but a breeze in the birches outside, the song of birds, and the flap of distant dragon wings.

A moan sounded behind him.

Elethor pushed himself onto his elbows and turned to see Solina on the floor. A great chunk of column pinned her down. Her blood seeped from beneath it.

"El," she whispered. Blood stained her lips. "El... will you hold my hand? For the end?"

She reached out a trembling, bloodied hand.

A boulder crashed through the ceiling and landed beside Elethor. It cracked the floor, shattered his bed, and knocked him down.

He lay beside Solina, and bricks rained onto him, falling through the ceiling of his home. Fire blazed above.

"El," she whispered. "Hold my hand. Please."

She reached out, grasped his hand, and held it tight.

"I love you, Elethor," she said. "I'm sorry. I'm sorry for how much I hurt you. All I wanted was to be with you here. I'm sorry."

Rocks rained. His home trembled. A column tore through a wall, and his shelf of books and statuettes crashed down. His marble statues fell and cracked. The wooden turtle shattered.

He tore his hand free from Solina's.

He crawled toward the fallen wall. A brick slammed onto his back. He dragged himself over the debris and outside onto the hill.

He crawled a few more feet until he lay in spring grass. Birches rustled at his sides, and the city of Nova Vita rolled below him, towers and roofs emerging from a verdant forest. White clouds glided above, and the dragons flew, shimmering bright under the blue sky.

It is a beautiful place, Elethor thought and smiled softly. *It is home. It is the best memory of my life. It is a good place to die.*

Chunks of column, wall, and ceiling fell from the sky and crashed into the forest. Elethor lay back in the sunlight, took slow breaths, and let his hands play with the grass. Above him in the spring morning, the sky fell.

LYANA

She hovered outside above the desert, watching the Palace of Whispers crumble.

Blasts of Tiran fire sounded across it. Lights flared. The towers upon the mountaintop crumbled first, raining dust and bricks upon the walls below, and then those walls too fell, and soon all the bridges, archways, and pathways of this ancient edifice collapsed. Dust rose in a cloud and rolled across the desert. Some nephilim tried to escape. They burst from the ruins, only to have boulders, fire, and crumbling towers crash against them and bury them upon the mountainsides. Griffins fled shrieking.

Nothing will escape, Lyana thought. *All that lives there dies.*

She watched, eyes damp, wings flapping as she hovered before the ruin.

"Elethor," she whispered.

Love of my heart. Light of my life. My husband. My king. Goodbye, Elethor. You fly now to your brother and parents. You will dine at their side among the glittering columns.

She let out a sob.

"And watch over me, El. Watch over me from the stars, for I'm afraid and alone."

Wings thudded behind her. Snorts rang through the air. Lyana turned to see Bayrin and Mori flying over the mountains from the east. They were ragged, scales stained with ash and blood, and they panted as they flew. When they reached Lyana, they hovered at her sides. They gaped at the crumbling palace, tongues lolling.

"Bloody stars!" Bayrin said and spat flame. "We heard you were captured and chased you for three days, Lyana. What the Abyss is that?" He gave her a sidelong glance. "Did you blow up that mountain?"

Lyana lowered her head. Below her, dust and debris rolled across the desert.

"It was the Palace of Whispers," she said softly. "The lair of Solina and all her devilry. Elethor destroyed it."

Mori gasped. "Elethor!" the princess said. "Lyana, is... And Treale..."

Bayrin snorted smoke. "Stars, Lyana, where are they?" He looked around from side to side, as if seeking them. He sucked in his breath and looked back at the clouds of dust. "Lyana, are..."

Lyana looked at her brother. He appeared blurred to her, and she blinked, and her throat burned.

"We have to leave, Bayrin," she whispered. "We have to fly north. Back to Requiem. Please, Bayrin. Take me home."

She could speak no more. Her eyes stung too much. She turned and flew over the desert, fleeing this place, fleeing the pain inside her. Bayrin and Mori flew at her side, wailing and roaring flame, and their tears fell upon the desert. They understood, and they sounded their cry, a great song of mourning and pain for their fallen, for their king, for their guiding star. Lyana roared with them, a keen of starlight.

For Treale. For Elethor.

They flew for a long time.

They flew over dunes. They flew over the ruins of southern cities, their palm trees charred, their rivers littered with burnt ships, their towers fallen. They flew north over the sea, ragged survivors behind them, a thousand Vir Requis haunted and wounded and crying for their fallen. They flew over the ruins of Requiem: her blackened forests, her hills littered with dead, and finally her fallen courts among the ash of King's Forest.

His words echoed in her mind. *You must lead Requiem now. Our people will follow your fire, and it will lead them home.*

Once Nova Vita had stood here, a city of new life, a revival for Requiem among the holy birches. Once towers had risen here, white and pure against the sky. Once harpists had played music here in white halls, and dragons had flown overhead, singing the songs of their people. This had been a city, a hope, a living dream, the heartbeat of a nation.

This is where my parents raised me, Lyana thought. *This is where I loved Orin, and where I loved Elethor, where I was knighted and where I fought, where I watched columns fall and dead rain.*

She landed in the ruins of the palace. A single pillar rose from the debris, three hundred feet tall, its capital shaped as dragons: King's Column, raised by the first King Aeternum millennia ago. Even the cruelty of Queen Solina could not topple it, and all the claws of her beasts could not scratch its marble. Lyana shifted into human form, held her sword before her, and knelt before this column. It led from ruin into starlight, from death into hope, from memory into dream.

"This is where I fought, this is where I killed, this is where so many died," Lyana whispered. "And this is where I will lead. I swear to you, stars of Requiem. I swear to you, Father and Mother. I swear to you, my Elethor. I will lead Requiem in your path, and I will rebuild her halls, and starlight will forever shine upon us."

She turned from the column and looked over the ruins.

Her people stood there, a thousand Vir Requis dressed in white, Requiem's color of mourning. Many here were wounded. Many were scarred, limbless, broken—but strong.

Yes, they are still strong, Lyana thought, looking from face to face. Their eyes were grim and haunted, but determined. *We will rekindle our fire.*

She climbed onto a fallen column and stood before the crowd. Bayrin and Mori stood before her, hand in hand. The others sprawled around them over the strewn bricks, toppled columns, and smashed statues. All looked upon her. They had flown south in winter, and snow had covered these lands. Today spring warmed Requiem, and among the ruins, Lyana saw birch saplings sprouting.

This forest will live again.

Upon the column, Queen Lyana Aeternum spoke to her people, voice ringing clear above the ruins.

"We gather in desolation," she said. "We gather in grief. We stand here in spring to mourn our long winter." She looked from person to person—elders with white hair, children with solemn eyes, and warriors with scarred faces and scarred souls. "Today we all mourn a loss. Everyone who stands here grieves for family, for friends, for loved ones. We grieve for those who died. We grieve for our fallen kings. Let us look to our sky, and let us pray for them."

They raised their heads and stared into the sky of Requiem. It was a clear spring sky, cold and bright and empty of clouds, yet Lyana thought that even in the light of day, she could see the Draco constellation, the stars of her fathers.

You are there now, Father and Mother, she thought, and a soft smile touched her lips. *You are there, Orin and Elethor. You watch over me. You are with me now. I can feel your light upon me, and I am afraid, but I know that I am never alone.*

She returned her eyes to the crowd.

"We are the survivors of Requiem," she said. "And we are her hope. We are Vir Requis, and we have known pain, and we have known tears, and we have known too much blood, too much death. But we are strong, and we are eternal; forever our starlight will glow. It has glowed here for three thousand years since King Aeternum raised this column and carved our stars into its stone.

Queen Gloriae found this column standing in ruin after the great
wars three hundred years ago; she rebuilt these halls and let
starlight fall upon them. King Elethor led us to victory and to
hope, and now this torch of starlight passes to me. And I vow to
you, children of Requiem, I will rebuild these halls, and we will
watch this forest bloom again." She raised her voice and cried to
the stars, knowing that Elethor could hear her. "Requiem! May
our wings forever find your sky."

All across the ruins, the survivors of Requiem repeated
her prayer.

Standing upon a smashed mosaic, Mori smiled at Lyana,
her eyes soft and warm. She knelt upon the broken stones before
her queen.

"Queen Lyana," she said softly. She held her sword
before her upon open palms. "I serve you, my queen."

Bayrin knelt too, blade held before him. Behind them,
more people knelt, and soon a wave flowed across the survivors.
They all knelt before Lyana upon the ruins, eyes gleaming, lips
whispering.

Lyana stood before them, and her eyes stung, and she
tasted a tear on her lips.

"I will lead them well, Elethor," she whispered and looked
to the sky. "I will lead Requiem down a path of starlight, and I
will not stray from it to the left or right, and I will honor your
memory. I swear this to you, my husband. I swear this to you,
stars of my fathers."

Those stars now did shine in the sky; Lyana could see
them, and she laughed through her tears.

The birch saplings rustled.

Spring turned to autumn. The leaves turned red and
scuttled across the ruins of Requiem.

All around the city, masons and carpenters toiled, and
smithies rang, and people bustled. The first homes stood upon

hills, and new columns rose in the ruins of the palace. The farms gave their crops, and baking breads, foamy ale, and hot apple pies filled Nova Vita with their scents, and for the first time in years, Lyana heard laughter ring through the city. Life and light shone.

On a cool autumn morning, Lyana lay upon her fur rug in the small, hillside temple they had built. She dug her hands into the fur and closed her eyes, but she did not scream. Mori clutched her one hand, and Bayrin held the other, and with a gasp and joyous pain, they had another in their family.

Lyana held her son to her breast, smoothed his hair, and smiled.

"Our son, Elethor," she whispered and looked to the ceiling. "He looks like you."

Mori laughed and gasped at the babe.

"Look at his hair!" the princess said. "It's brown like mine. And his eyes, Lyana—they're green like yours." She gingerly touched the babe's head. "What will you name him?"

Bayrin cleared his throat. "She's going to name him Bayrin, of course. After me. What do you think?"

The babe mewled and fell asleep against her, and Lyana stroked his hair, feeling warm and safe.

"I will name him Elarath," she said softly. "And I will raise him to know of his father, and his grandfather, and the great kings who came before him. He will be a great king too someday."

Bayrin patted the child and smiled down upon him.

"Your father was a good king, little one," he said. "You better follow in his footsteps, or Uncle Bayrin will make you regret this day."

Mori punched him, and Bayrin gasped and feigned indignation, and Lyana smiled and held her son close.

"Sweet El," she whispered to the child. "The birches whisper, dawn gilds our mountains, and light shines upon the forest. You are home, El. You are home."

MORI

Mori stood upon the fortress walls, watching winter's first snow fall.

The flakes swirled, glided, and coated the forest below. The trees spread into the distance: young pines, birches, and maples rising from memories of war. Icicles hung from their branches, and the snow soon covered the forest floor, a glittering carpet like fields of stars in a white sky. All around Castellum Luna, this small southern outpost, the snow and light of winter rolled into the horizons.

Mori took a deep breath of the cold air. The wind kissed her cheeks, billowed her hair, and sneaked into her cloak. She looked down at her hands and caressed her luck finger, the sixth finger on her left hand.

You've always brought me luck, she thought. *You've always helped me.*

She placed her hands upon the battlements and looked back into the southern horizon, watching the snow glide down and coat the trees. It was four years to the day since she had stood here, a frightened young girl, and watched the first phoenix rise from the south.

I was so afraid then, Mori remembered. *Everything scared me: the creak of armor, the rustle of leaves, and the wilderness that rolls on forever like a sea.*

And now... who was she now? No longer a youth. No longer so afraid, perhaps. Four years ago, she had come to Castellum Luna as a frightened girl, and here her world had burned around her. Now she stood here as a woman, older, stronger, a lady of this fort. She ruled Castellum Luna now.

"And I will not let these walls fall again," she whispered. "I will be the eyes of Requiem and her long arm in the wilderness."

She held her luck finger and thought of Orin. He had stood here upon these walls four years ago and fallen.

I will stand here every winter, Mori thought, *and I will remember you.*

Footfalls sounded behind her, and Mori turned to see Bayrin climbing the stairs from the courtyard. She smiled down at him, and he joined her upon the walls. In his arms he carried their little bundle wrapped in furs. Mori felt her heart melt like butter over hot bread. She took her daughter from her husband's arms, held the child close, and kissed her forehead.

"Good morning, Treale," she whispered.

The babe reached out and touched her cheek and smiled. She was a child of pale skin, red hair, and large gray eyes. Mori thought her the most beautiful child in the world.

"I swear," Bayrin said, "I've never seen a babe go through so many swaddling clothes. We're going to need a whole castle's worth of them delivered down here. Does Lyana's baby soil himself this much too?"

Mori cooed at the child. "Don't listen to him, Treale." She kissed the babe. "If he complains some more, bite him."

Silently, she added words she would not speak aloud.

May you never know loss, my child, she thought, holding Treale close. *May you never know war. May you grow in a world of peace, knowledge, and light. May your soul never be broken like mine.*

She looked toward the southern horizon. Four years ago the flame of Tiranor had risen here. They had tortured and killed her brother within these walls. They had raped her by his corpse as she screamed. They had flown north from this fortress until they reached her city, and they toppled it.

Mori closed her burning eyes.

How do I go on? she thought. *How can I be a mother to Treale when still the nightmares fill my every night, when still the pain clutches me and does not let go, when still the loss pounds through me?*

She blinked and looked south through her tears. She knew the answer. She knew that this pain would never leave her: the pain of those she had lost, of her shattered innocence, of her captivity in Tiranor. Those memories would always haunt her. Those scars would forever clutch her soul, and many years from now, she would still wake up in darkness, afraid and trembling and back underground in chains.

Some scars do not heal, Mori knew. *Some memories do not leave us. Some hurts are too great; they will forever be within me.*

She looked at her child, an innocent babe. Treale reached out toward her, fingers grasping, lips smiling. And Mori smiled back.

But I have Treale, she thought. *And I have my husband, Bayrin.* Her tears fell. *And I have some light in my life. Stars of Requiem—let whatever light still shines upon me, and whatever joy still fills me, be a beacon for my daughter. I will raise her in your light, and may she never know the pain I feel.*

Bayrin placed an arm around her and held her close. Mori hugged her daughter to her breast, and they stood together on the wall, watching the snow fall.

THE END

NOVELS BY DANIEL ARENSON

Standalones:

Firefly Island (2007)
The Gods of Dream (2010)
Flaming Dove (2010)

Misfit Heroes:

Eye of the Wizard (2011)
Wand of the Witch (2012)

Song of Dragons:

Blood of Requiem (2011)
Tears of Requiem (2011)
Light of Requiem (2011)

Dragonlore:

A Dawn of Dragonfire (2012)
A Day of Dragon Blood (2012)
A Night of Dragon Wings (2013)

KEEP IN TOUCH

www.DanielArenson.com
Daniel@DanielArenson.com
Facebook.com/DanielArenson
Twitter.com/DanielArenson

3070280R00186

Printed in Great Britain
by Amazon.co.uk, Ltd.,
Marston Gate.